To C

Beyond Instinct

Don't read this one late at night !

By
Lynn Ames

Lynn Ames

BEYOND INSTINCT
© 2011 BY LYNN AMES

ISBN: 978-1-936429-02-8

OTHER AVAILABLE FORMATS

eBOOK EDITION
ISBN: 978-1-936429-03-5

PUBLISHED BY
PHOENIX RISING PRESS
PHOENIX, ARIZONA
www.phoenixrisingpress.com

CREDITS
EXECUTIVE EDITOR: LINDA LORENZO
COVER PHOTOS: PAM LAMBROS
AUTHOR PHOTO: JUDY FRANCESCONI
COVER DESIGN: PAM LAMBROS, WWW.HANDSONGRAPHICDESIGN.COM

Dedication

To Mom, who taught me that all things are possible.
Even after all these years, I still miss you every day.

Acknowledgments

No author is an island, to mangle a phrase. *Beyond Instinct* is a product of my fertile imagination, but the underpinnings for the story were born twenty-five years ago. In 1983, I made an extraordinary journey to Burkina Faso, West Africa (then Upper Volta), to visit my college roommate, who had become a Peace Corps volunteer.

I spent three weeks traveling around the country, meeting the people and observing their culture; it was a life-changing experience. Lo these many years later, I still carry the lessons of humility and happiness that I learned from the Burkinabe.

My deepest thanks to Dana J. Francis for thirty years of friendship and for introducing me to such incredibly rich cultural experiences. Your expertise in all matters West African was invaluable in the creation of this story.

As with any thriller, there are so many details that must be factually correct or at least plausible. To Dr. Hellen Carter, who always ensures that my bullets fly straight; to Clair Bee, who taught me everything I know about pyrotechnics; to Dr. Stephen Colodny, who kept my characters alive—barely; to Ann Marie Clinkscales, whose knowledge of Andrews Air Force Base was crucial; to Jac Hills for timely information regarding the Tuareg; and to my source at the FBI, for verifying facts and protocols—you all give my books the credibility that makes possible the suspension of disbelief.

I am blessed to have what I think is the finest team in the history of novel-writing. To my beta readers who read through my manuscripts chapter by chapter during the creation-phase and give me critical feedback—you have my eternal gratitude.

To my primary editor, Linda Lorenzo, who looks forward with such relish to sinking her teeth into my manuscripts—may I never disappoint you.

To the readers who continue to clamor for the next book—you make it all worthwhile.

Happy reading!

PROLOGUE

The early morning mist rolled in over the Potomac, matching Vaughn Elliott's mood. She'd been back in the States less than forty-eight hours and wasn't looking forward to spending her first "free" afternoon briefing the section chief on the ins and outs of extricating a questionable asset from a jail in San Salvador.

The phone on her hip vibrated, eliciting a groan. "Elliott," she barked.

"I heard a rumor you were back."

"Hey." Vaughn's voice softened immediately. "Where are you?"

"I'm in town."

"Really?"

"Really." Sara McFarland's voice held its usual mirth, bringing a smile to Vaughn's lips as it had since the first time they'd met in college twenty-two years ago.

"Can we get together?" Vaughn asked.

"That was my plan. Meet you at the usual place?"

"Sure." Vaughn checked her watch. "I've only got a couple of hours though."

"They've already got you hopping? Good thing you never suffer from jet lag."

"Tell me about it. See you in fifteen."

"Bye, V."

Vaughn closed the phone and tapped it thoughtfully against her chin. She tried to remember the last time she and Sara had seen each other. It had been too long.

Sara was her first lover. When the CIA recruited them both before graduation, they hadn't realized their assignments would take them to different parts of the globe. Distance and time separated them over the years, but their deep affection for one another never waned.

Vaughn shoved off from the railing and headed toward the Metro. It would be great to catch up.

❖❖

Sara stared appraisingly at the tall, handsome woman who shouldered her way past the crowd at the counter on the way to her table. Apart from a smattering of gray hair mixed in with the chestnut, Vaughn looked much the same as she had that first day in Art History 101 when Sara accidentally dropped a heavy text book on her foot.

"What are you looking at?" Vaughn's eyes narrowed.

"Just ogling," Sara said lightly. "After all these years, you still have that effect on me." She watched with pleasure as a blush crept up Vaughn's neck and spread to her cheeks.

"Stop it."

Sara smirked. "Why would I? Making you blush is one of my favorite pastimes."

"I've noticed." Vaughn walked around the table and scooped Sara up into a hug. "How are you?" she whispered against Sara's ear. "You look a little tired."

Sara disengaged herself and sat back down. "Yeah, well, not all of us get the cushy assignments."

"Uh-huh. What was it this time? Muscovites smuggling love notes in vodka bottles?"

"Hardly." Sara swallowed hard and leaned forward. "I was in Kabul, and I've discovered some real nastiness."

"It's a war zone, hon, not a playground."

Sara glanced up at the face of the only human being on earth she truly trusted with her life. She smiled grimly. "Do you remember what they said about 'Nam? About the drug-smuggling ops?"

Vaughn pursed her lips. "Yeah. There was talk of some of our guys hiding the stuff in the corpses of American soldiers and getting it back here that way, knowing no one would desecrate the bodies by searching them."

"Exactly."

"What are you getting at?"

Sara fidgeted with her napkin. "You know how much of the world's heroin is produced in Afghanistan?"

"Far more than I want to think about."

"Right."

"You're saying the same thing's going on now?"

"I always knew you were a sharp cookie." Sara patted Vaughn's cheek. "I'm finally going to be able to prove it too."

"Wai—wait a second here. You're talking about putting the screws to our people?"

"These are really bad apples, V. They've got to be stopped. Imagine what the mothers of those poor soldiers would think if they knew."

"Sara." Vaughn reached across the table and covered Sara's hand. For all intents and purposes, the two looked like long-time lovers out for a Sunday coffee. "You know how much I love your strong notions of right and wrong. It's one of the reasons I fell for you so hard, but—"

Sara broke in, "It's also one of the things that appealed so much to the Company, remember?"

"Yes, I remember. They loved your zealous patriotism and heightened sense of justice. But this is different."

"No, it's not." Sara lifted her chin and set her jaw defiantly.

"You're talking about going against people who've been trained in the same deadly warfare and dirty tricks that you and I have."

"I realize that," Sara snapped. "I'm a big girl now. I've got as much blood on my hands as you do, Vaughn."

The pained look on Vaughn's face stopped Sara cold.

"I know you do, Sara. That's my fault. I never should've let you say yes to them."

"You couldn't have stopped me. I wanted to go."

"Only because I did."

Sara nodded grudgingly. "I would've followed you to the end of the earth and back again. And I admit that I was an idealistic kid back then who thought I could save the world."

"You still are."

"Maybe a little." Sara balled her hands into fists. "I'm so close, V. I've got them. There's a delivery coming in late this afternoon. A flight from Kabul with fourteen bodies is due to arrive at Andrews. All I need is to get my hands on the proof."

"Andrews? That's not the usual protocol. Why isn't it Dover?"

"I don't know. It doesn't matter. It's going down at Andrews, and I'm going to be there when it does."

"You're not seriously thinking of going in by yourself," Vaughn said, her voice rising an octave.

"I can't trust anybody. I don't know how deep this goes."

"No." Vaughn's lips formed a thin line. "No, you're not going."

"They have to be stopped."

"Find another way."

Sara crossed her arms over her chest. "There is no other way. I have to catch them in the act, and this is my only shot."

"If you don't know how deep it goes, you'll probably just end up with a flunky."

"No. I've been watching them for months. I finally decoded the messages on the shipping end when I was in Kabul last week. The big fish is supposed to be here today."

"So you say," Vaughn said with a healthy dose of skepticism. She leaned forward. "How, exactly, do you plan to pull this off?"

"Don't worry, V. I'm not some rookie. I've got a plan." Sara knew her irritation was showing.

"This is crazy," Vaughn said, running her hands through her hair. The gesture was one familiar to Sara. Vaughn did that whenever she was truly upset.

Sara softened her tone. "Please don't worry about me. I'll be fine. I tell you what, I'll meet you for dinner tonight to prove it."

"The hell you will." Vaughn worried her lower lip with her teeth. "If you're going, then I'm in too."

"Over my dead body," Sara said, her anger returning.

"Good one."

"I'm serious."

"If it's too dangerous for me, then it's too dangerous for you too, doll."

"You're not being fair."

"All's fair in love and war, remember? What time and where? What's the plan?"

Sara frowned. She hated that Vaughn had always been able to talk her into a corner. Grudgingly, she offered, "The caskets of the John and Jane Does are on a plane that arrives at 1715. The protocol is that the plane is led into a hangar at the far end of the tarmac and the caskets are unloaded in the privacy of the hangar, while all eyes will be on another bird. That one is carrying the IDed corpses for the public ceremony. I've got a mechanic's uniform and a badge that will get me close to my plane. I just need to get access to one of the caskets."

"What do you plan to do then?"

"Get the evidence, bag it, and get a copy of the manifest to see who signed for delivery of the goods. Oh, and see who shows up to collect the bounty."

"You know the big guys will keep their hands clean."

"They've gotten greedy and sloppy in the past few months. The message I got was that they would all be here today. This is the biggest shipment yet, and they want to supervise personally."

"Are you sure your source is good?"

"Positive."

Vaughn was staring hard at her, and Sara stared back. It took great self-control for her not to squirm under the scrutiny. She knew Vaughn was testing her resolve.

"Okay, then we go together."

"No." Sara slapped her palms on table. She lamented, yet again, that Vaughn never seemed to have faith in her ability to do the job. "I can do this, V."

"I know you can, hon, but there's no way I'm going to let you go in without backup. And there's only one person I trust to watch your shapely backside—that's me."

"I appreciate the compliment, I think, but I've got it under control."

"It isn't a matter of control, damn it! This isn't an exercise, Sara. If this is as big an operation as you say, it's got to be sophisticated. That means high-level involvement and high stakes. They're not going to let you just waltz in and collar them."

"I know that."

"What are you going to do once you have the proof?"

"I've got someone inside the FBI who's got a clear channel to the top."

"This is nuts."

"I'm going, Vaughn. You can't stop me."

"Maybe not. But you can't stop me from joining you, either."

"You'll create too much suspicion. I've been planning this for months."

"Find a way to get me in."

Their faces were close together, nostrils flaring, eyes glittering.

Finally, Sara conceded. "There's a locker inside the terminal, number 342. There'll be a uniform in there for you. I'll meet you there at 1600 hours." Sara shoved her chair back and stalked away.

๛๛

Vaughn's meeting ran late. By the time she reached Andrews Air Force Base, it was past the appointed hour. She swore under her breath as she skidded to a halt in front of locker 342. There was no sign of Sara.

"Damn it, Sara. You'd better not be doing anything stupid," Vaughn muttered as she quickly shrugged into a set of greasy coveralls, zipped them, and pulled on the battered sneakers Sara left for her. She secured the fake ID and sprinted toward the tarmac.

She was inside the hangar and had nearly reached her destination; in fact, she could just make out Sara's silhouetted form approaching the open cargo bay and the line of caskets on a mechanized conveyor belt. Out of the corner of her eye she noticed movement. It was little more than a suggestion of a shadow, but it was enough.

Vaughn veered off behind a nearby pallet and cautiously inched her way around it, her Glock-40 held out of sight down by her side. She caught a glint of steel—the barrel of a gun, and it was pointed in Sara's direction. She swung her arm up, tucked, rolled underneath the shadow, and kicked the legs out from under a compact man whose face resembled a pug.

The man's head hit the concrete with a hard thud and his gun skittered across the floor. One look at him told Vaughn he was unconscious, and would be for a while. The same look told

Vaughn he was Company through and through. She took the time to retrieve several items from his pockets and dragged him behind the pallet.

"Shit. Shit." Vaughn took off again at a dead sprint toward Sara. When she was about ten feet away, she yelled, "It's a set-up. Get down!"

Even as she screamed, she watched helplessly as Sara bent over and lifted the lid of the nearest casket. The world narrowed down to just the two of them as a huge sonic boom knocked Vaughn off her feet. The last thing she saw was Sara's head exploding and her lifeless, but completely intact, lower body crumple to the ground.

Vaughn scrambled to her feet, only to have her legs give way. She blinked her eyes furiously in an attempt to focus. *Sara. Oh, God, not my Sara.* Vaughn crawled forward. She was vaguely aware of people running everywhere, and the fact that her right arm felt like it was on fire. Something was sticking to her side. She looked down. Blood soaked through the left side of the coveralls. Breathing was agony, and the ringing in her ears would not abate.

None of it mattered.

Vaughn reached Sara and gathered her close with her right arm. She doubled over as a sharp stab of pain ripped through her. She sucked in a breath and hissed it out through clenched teeth. When she finally straightened and looked down, pieces of bone and tissue were stuck to her bloody coveralls.

The flesh from Sara's face was gone, and only tiny fragments of bone remained where her jaw had been.

With her left hand, Vaughn felt around on the ground, mindlessly gathering small bits of skin and bone, and pushing them into the wide crevices where Sara's face had been.

Vaughn rocked Sara. "It's okay, beautiful girl. You're okay. I'm here. I'll never let you go again." Tears streamed down her face.

Vaughn lashed out viciously when hands tried to pry her fingers from Sara, and a shockwave of pain shot through her. A shadow appeared and Vaughn became aware of someone in a military uniform standing over her. His mouth was moving, but she heard no distinct sound. She felt herself being lifted. Although she tried to hold on, Sara slipped from her grasp. Vaughn cried out.

She struggled against the hands that were forcing her to lie down flat. Several faces loomed over her. They were blurry and she was unable to make out distinct features. Vaughn blinked, but her vision wouldn't clear. Again, she could see mouths moving but could not make out any words. An oxygen mask was placed over her nose and mouth and she felt hands strapping her down. Vaughn wanted to scream. *I have to stay with Sara...to protect her.*

The world began to spin. Seconds later, everything went black.

CHAPTER ONE

One year later

A blast of hot air assaulted Vaughn as she disembarked from the plane. She squinted in the bright sunlight, quickly donned her shades, and headed in the direction of baggage claim. *Welcome to West Africa.*

"Vaughn Elliott?"

"Who wants to know?" Vaughn barely glanced sideways to acknowledge the presence at her shoulder. Her eyebrows shot up into her hairline when her gruffness was greeted with lilting laughter.

"I'm Sage McNally, political officer at the U.S. Embassy and your control officer here in Mali. Welcome to Bamako."

Vaughn tipped her sunglasses down and faced the owner of the laugh. Her heart stuck in her throat, and she shoved the shades back up. *Sara. The smile, the eyes alight with amusement, the petite build and Irish complexion.* Vaughn swallowed hard and struggled to regain her equilibrium.

"I-I'm sorry. I didn't mean to laugh." Sage, having clearly mistaken Vaughn's reaction for anger, shifted uncomfortably from foot to foot. "It was just…"

"S'okay." Vaughn looked down at Sage's outstretched hand and grasped it in a firm handshake. "I'm Vaughn Elliott, Diplomatic Security."

"Nice to meet you." Sage paused, seemingly unsure how to proceed. "Um, I thought we would get your bags, then I could take you to the hotel and we could talk over lunch. Is that okay with you?"

"Fine." Vaughn turned her attention to the young Malian standing at rigid attention just behind and to the right of Sage.

Sage followed her line of sight. "Henri is our driver. He'll get your luggage."

Vaughn pointed to a small duffle just appearing on the luggage carousel and looked at Henri. "Le voilà."

The young man plucked the bag up and slung it over his shoulder.

"You travel pretty light," Sage said. "Usually poor Henri gets stuck hauling multiple suitcases."

"Yeah, well, I'm not most people." Sage flinched at the brusqueness of her tone, and Vaughn instantly regretted it. *It's not her fault she reminds you of Sara.* Marginally more softly, Vaughn said, "I've traveled extensively and often, so I've gotten the packing thing down to a science."

"Oh."

Sage was silent the rest of the way to the car.

Damn it, Vaughn. Give the girl a chance. "So, have you been in Mali long?"

"A year-and-a-half. My tour here is almost up."

"Where were you posted before this?" Vaughn studied Sage's profile as they sat in the back seat of the Toyota 4x4. From this angle, she bore less resemblance to Sara.

"I was in Brussels."

"Wow. Mali must have been quite a come-down from that."

"You'd think so, wouldn't you? But I wanted to come here. My specialty is French-speaking African countries, so this is where the action is for me." Her good humor apparently restored, Sage laughed easily.

To her surprise, Vaughn found that she was relieved. "Hmm, chocolate, culture, all of Europe at your feet...or dust, heat, inedible food, and rudimentary accommodations. I can see your point."

Sage blushed. "Well, when you put it that way, it does sound pretty ridiculous."

"Nah, you followed your passion. Good for you. More people should do that."

"Here we go," Sage said as they pulled into the parking lot of a Hilton. "There's a pretty good restaurant in here. The food is definitely edible. How about if I meet you at the bar after you've checked in?"

"Sure. Give me fifteen minutes."

Sage noted that Vaughn was back in exactly fifteen minutes, despite a change in wardrobe. She was unsurprised. Punctuality seemed in keeping with the woman's no-nonsense demeanor. She studied Vaughn as she made her way to the bar. Without her reflective sunglasses, she still cut an imposing figure.

"Shall we get a table?"

"Sure."

At her signal, the host appeared at Sage's elbow. "Oui, Mademoiselle Sage?"

"Un table pour deux, s'il vous plaît, Maxim."

"Bien sûr, Mademoiselle." To Vaughn, he said, "Right this way."

"Merci, Monsieur." Vaughn answered in impeccable French.

Once they were seated, Sage said, "Your accent is better than mine."

"I would hardly think that could be judged by a few simple phrases."

Sage waved her hand dismissively. "Perhaps, but I can always tell someone who's comfortable with the language from someone who isn't. Where did you study?"

"Paris, in my youth."

Sage pursed her lips. Vaughn's tone implied that further illumination would not be forthcoming.

It was Sage's avocation, as well as her vocation, to read people. It was clear that Vaughn cultivated her aloofness. This, of course, aroused Sage's curiosity all the more.

She had not been able to glean anything from the information she'd received about Vaughn from Washington several days ago. That was not unusual, but what was odd was that the information had not come via the normal route.

While Vaughn had hardly shown herself to be chatty, Sage decided to forge ahead. "Well, it's nice that at least they managed to send someone who speaks the language." She paused for effect and adopted what she hoped was a casual tone. "Maybe that's because your assignment didn't come through the usual channels?"

When Vaughn neither responded nor reacted, Sage tried again. "I mean, normally I would've gotten news of your arrival and background information from some mid-level bureaucrat at State. You were different."

Still Vaughn remained maddeningly silent.

Sage sighed. The direct approach seemed the only way. "So, why did your assignment come directly from the secretary of state? I'm assuming that's where the assignment came from, since that's who sent me your details."

Vaughn shrugged, her eyes fixed on a spot somewhere over Sage's shoulder. "I don't know. Why don't you ask the secretary?"

"Very funny." Sage decided to try a different line of questioning. "Where were you before? You must have been somewhere exciting, right?" She knew that Vaughn's classification was 01—meaning she was an experienced officer.

"This is my first assignment."

"Wow." Sage couldn't hide her surprise. "The secretary of state himself sends you to protect a high-level congressional delegation your first time out of the gate? No offense, but that seems pretty strange."

"Not really. I've been in law enforcement for twenty-one years. I'm no rookie. I'm fully capable of coordinating security for this visit. Feel better now?"

Sage blushed as Vaughn fixed her with a pointed stare. "Oh, I wasn't questioning your ability. Honest." Sage bit her lower lip. *In for a penny, in for a pound.* "Which agency were you with? Do you have any good stories to tell?"

"Another branch of government. And no, I don't have any good stories to share. I've been behind a desk for the past year."

Vaughn's voice was flat, but there was something in her eyes that told Sage there was much more to the story.

"You don't strike me as the kind of person who would enjoy pushing papers. What'd you do to end up in the doghouse?"

"Can we please talk about the assignment?" It was more a command than a request.

"Of course. I'm sorry. I didn't mean to upset you." Sage cleared her throat and adopted her best business-like tone. "As you know, a congressional delegation led by the senate majority leader will be here three weeks from now. It's part of a larger visit that will include Ghana, Senegal, Cameroon..."

"And, naturellement, gay Paris on the way home," Vaughn interjected.

"Of course," Sage conceded. It was a well-established practice that "fact-finding" or goodwill trips to third-world countries by VIPs would include a high-value bonus location like France.

"Mali is the last stop before Paris, so by the time they get here they'll probably have had their fill of hospitals and schools."

"Normally, I'd agree with you, but Mali is strategically important to the U.S. It's a model for democracy we can only hope other West African nations would adopt." Sage warmed to the topic. "Mali has had four democratic, multi-party presidential elections since 1990. That's remarkable."

"Is that so?"

Vaughn smiled at her indulgently and Sage got the distinct sense that she was being patronized. "Are you playing me?"

Vaughn barked a laugh. "What makes you think so?"

Sage frowned in answer.

"I have done some homework, but I'd rather get your perspective. I really wasn't jerking your chain, Sage."

It was more of a concession than Sage expected. "Okay. So, what is it you want to know?"

A waiter appeared with their food, and conversation was temporarily suspended.

When he'd gone, Vaughn said, "Tell me about the scheduled stops, personal observations about the politics, situations our group might encounter..."

"Right. Well, the new president is a bit eccentric and fancies himself a ladies' man, so that might present an interesting dynamic with Majority Leader Stowe."

Vaughn raised an eyebrow. Madeline Stowe, the first female leader of the Senate, was a shrewd politician with a well-deserved reputation for eviscerating anybody, of either sex, who treated her with anything other than complete respect and professional courtesy.

"Maybe we should sell tickets. Could be quite a show," Vaughn said. "By the way, I'm impressed." She held up a forkful of coq au vin. "Real French food."

"Mmm, don't expect that outside of the hotel."

"Good to know."

Sage continued around a mouthful of food, "The audience with the National Assembly will be less fascinating—just a mutual rah-rah session. Then there's the obligatory party thrown by the ambassador..."

"What about the stops outside Bamako?"

"There are two visits scheduled to schools in the countryside. These are more like photo opportunities and made-for-television events."

"Anything I should know about the areas around the schools? What are the people like?" Vaughn asked, taking a last bite and pushing the plate away.

"The schools border on Tuareg territory—up near Timbuktu. Generally speaking, the Tuareg keep to themselves. Every now and again they get riled up about something, but mostly they stay true to their nomadic roots, riding around on their camels in the desert, trading goods, and looking imposing in their flowing dark indigo robes with only their eyes visible."

"Only their eyes, eh?"

Sage nodded. "Beginning at age twenty-five, every Tuareg male wears a head veil—it's a turban that also wraps around their neck and lower face. They're never seen without the veil, even by family."

"Are the Tuareg worked up about anything at the moment?"

"Nothing in particular, but it's good to remember that they have no allegiances except to themselves."

"Noted." Vaughn pushed back from the table. "So what's on tap for the rest of the day?"

Sage regarded her with something akin to awe. "You're not jet-lagged?"

"Nope."

"I didn't schedule any meetings for today because I didn't think you'd be up to it, but I could show you around town and give you a sense of the place."

"Sounds good, unless you have other things you need to be doing. I don't want to take you away from your work." Vaughn pushed away from the table and stood up.

Sage signaled the waiter. "Not a problem. I'm at your disposal for as long as you need me. It's my job to schmooze, get intelligence, and be visible. Since I've set up meetings for us with Malian officials, I can kill two birds with one stone."

"I've got it," Vaughn said, placing a restraining hand on Sage's wrist as she looked at the check and reached for her wallet.

Sage shook her head and smiled. "Embassy business. The government's picking up the tab."

"Better yet."

∽⟡∼

The heat created the illusion of steam rising off the pavement as they rode toward the outskirts of town. Abruptly, the quality of the pavement changed.

"I take it we're leaving the city limits," Vaughn said drolly.

"You really do have great powers of observation."

Vaughn chuckled. "Told you I was good at what I do."

They'd spent several hours touring the capital city, and Vaughn was finding it increasingly difficult to maintain an air of remote detachment. Sage's enthusiasm and genuine curiosity were hard to resist. Vaughn glanced out the window, noting the periodic appearance of small earthen huts. It was a far cry from the bustle of Bamako.

Over the course of her career, she had been in many third-world countries, although she had never been to Mali. The barren landscape reminded her of neighboring Burkina Faso. The entire country looked like a red-clay tennis court, the natives lived in extreme poverty, the climate was arid, and yet the people seemed happy.

"Have you ever been to West Africa before?"

"Mmm. Once or twice. I was just thinking this place reminds me of Burkina Faso."

"I can see that," Sage said, "but politically, the two nations are worlds apart. Burkina Faso traditionally has been very unstable. I can't count the number of coups they've had in the last twenty-five years."

Vaughn flashed back to the last time she'd been there. It was a coup that she'd been ordered to help engineer in the summer of 1983. She wondered what Sage would think if she knew. "In that case, better to be here than there."

"That's very true."

"How did a nice girl like you get to be in the diplomatic corps?"

Sage shrugged. "It's not a very interesting story, really. I always wanted to go into the Peace Corps. So I signed up right after college. Since I was fluent in French, they sent me to West Africa."

"There are a lot of French-speaking countries," Vaughn said. "Why West Africa?"

"I thought it would be exotic and fascinating. My purpose in going into the Peace Corps was to help save the world. I didn't really think Paris, Switzerland, Belgium or Canada needed rescuing."

"True." Vaughn looked over at Sage. "How did you find the experience? Was it everything you expected?"

"Yes and no." Sage shifted her attention from the road to make brief eye contact with Vaughn. "It was certainly a part of the world that seemed like it could benefit greatly from Western ideals and technologies."

"Sounds like there's a 'but' in there somewhere."

"Mmm. The longer I was there and the more time I spent with the people, the more I began to question why our ways were supposed to be better than theirs. Was it simply our arrogance? Who were we to tell them the way they'd been doing things for centuries wasn't the 'right' way? Or could we really improve their lives? Should we, just because we could?"

Vaughn smiled. Sage's face was alive with the passion of conviction. For the first time in a year, Vaughn was enjoying the company of another human being. *Welcome back to the world, Elliott.* "What did you decide in the end?"

"I never really reached a firm conclusion. I mean, the area was rife with famine, people were starving, and disease was rampant. Still, the people were generally happy. Go back to the States and watch folks in a grocery store. They have everything they could ever want, all in nice, neat little rows with more choices than they know what to do with, and they're miserable. They complain about the checkout lines, the fact that the bananas aren't ripe enough, their brand of toothpaste isn't on sale…you get the idea."

"Mmm. The people who have nothing, who lead simple lives that revolve around survival, seem to be more content than the society that has every advantage."

"In a nutshell, yes."

"But it still doesn't eradicate their very real suffering."

"Exactly. So what's the answer? Get them healthy and let them be as unhappy as we are?"

"Is it fair to assume that they would be? That seems a bit of a leap. Maybe they've sufficiently internalized the things that make them happy and external factors won't affect that." Vaughn was enjoying the intellectual conversation. It seemed like forever since the last time she'd gotten outside of herself. *Since the last weekend you spent with Sara.* She closed her eyes against a stab of pain.

"Are you okay?"

Vaughn opened her eyes to see Sage staring at her, her brow furrowed with concern. She became aware for the first time that the car had stopped.

"Fine," Vaughn answered, more curtly than she intended.

"Right," Sage said, and turned her head away. Her jaw muscles were tense, and Vaughn cursed herself.

Sage continued, "I thought you might like to see the Marché— the market. It only happens once a week out here. Vendors come from all over to ply their wares—goat meat, fabrics, tools, wood carvings. If you're not up to it…"

"No. I'd love to see it. Lead on," Vaughn said, unbuckling her seatbelt.

Sage got out of the car without saying another word.

Way to go, Elliott.

CHAPTER TWO

Vaughn paced the length of the suite and back again. Sage had dropped her off without saying more than a handful of words during the three-hour drive back to Bamako. Vaughn offered to buy her dinner, but Sage had politely declined, pleading exhaustion. When Vaughn inquired about seeing her in the morning, Sage simply shook her head and mumbled something about having paperwork to do in the office.

"Damn it, why should I care?" Vaughn punched the air and dropped onto the sofa in the living room area. "She's a big girl. If she's got her knickers in a knot, it's not my concern."

Even as she said it, Vaughn knew it was a lie. She did care. In fact, she cared a lot more than she wanted to, and that was what had her so agitated.

When her satellite cell phone vibrated itself off the coffee table, she lunged to catch it. It had to be Sage. She hadn't given the number to another soul since her arrival, and she had no expectation of hearing from anybody else.

"Vaughn?"

"Justine?" Vaughn sat up ramrod straight, her body instantly tense, Sage temporarily forgotten.

"The one and only."

"Do you have anything new?" Vaughn tried to clamp down on a surge of adrenaline.

"Now there's a warm and fuzzy greeting. Long time no talk to, Vaughn."

"Yeah, like eleven months." Vaughn didn't want to think about her stay at the Company clinic where she was taken after the explosion. "Please tell me you've got something."

25

"I'm fine, thanks. How are you? How are the ribs? And the arm? Has the scar healed?"

Vaughn sighed. It was clear she wasn't going to rush Justine. "I'm fit as a fiddle, thank you."

"How are you doing otherwise?"

Justine's voice was full of genuine concern, but this was not a discussion Vaughn was willing to have. "As I said, I'm fine."

"So you did." After an awkward pause, Justine continued, "I still miss her too."

Vaughn clenched her jaw shut on a sob. The pain of losing Sara was as fresh as it was the day it happened. She squeezed her eyes closed. After several beats, she said, "Do you have a lead? I'm assuming that's why you called."

"Very well. Are you still nursing a grudge against Edgar Fairhaven?"

The name set Vaughn's teeth on edge. She replayed in her mind the day Fairhaven walked into the college dorm room she and Sara shared and filled their heads with notions of patriotic service to their country. *Bastard.* If it hadn't been for him, they might have had normal lives, and Sara would still be alive.

"If I could strangle Fairhaven myself, I would."

"I'm not sure you'd get away with it."

"Probably not, but I'd enjoy it."

"You're in Mali?"

The abrupt change of topic was jarring, and although Vaughn didn't see the relevance, she was intrigued. "How'd you find that out?"

"I have ways." Justine laughed evilly. "We know everything."

"So you'd have people believe. You forget, I know better."

"Okay, point taken. But we do know most of everything. And I've made it my business to keep a discreet eye out for you."

"I don't know whether I should say 'thank you' or 'butt out.'"

"A simple 'thank you' will do. Seriously, Vaughn, I'm glad to see you out in the field again. It's where you belong. Your talents were wasted behind a desk."

"It's only Diplomatic Security."

"DS serves an important function. Don't sell yourself short. Not only that, but this is a big assignment—the esteemed majority leader's first big trip abroad since her elevation."

"Don't patronize me."

"Hey, I'm not. Don't get surly on me."

"Sorry. I've had an unsettling day." It was an admission Vaughn wouldn't have made under normal circumstances, but she was tired and the interaction with Sage was too fresh in her mind.

"Let me ask you a question. Whose idea was it that you shift from the Company to DS?"

"It was a mutually agreed upon outcome for an untenable situation," Vaughn said. Her words were devoid of any emotion.

"Meaning?"

"Meaning, I was told in no uncertain terms that moving to DS was the only way I was ever going to get out from behind a desk and finish out my career with the federal government. Otherwise, I would've been buried under mountains of paperwork for the rest of my working days."

"Who told you that?"

"Conroy." Vaughn spat the name. She made no secret of her disdain for her new section chief.

"Hmm. Do you have any idea who recommended you for this assignment?"

"Didn't care enough to ask. The instruction came in the form of a secure letter from the secretary of state himself."

"You didn't find that odd?"

"It gave me a moment's pause, but I honestly didn't have any idea what the protocol was for doling out assignments. I figured it was a form letter created by some flunky and signed by the big guy." Vaughn thought back to her earlier discussion with Sage. "My contact here questioned the deviation from form, but before that I had no inkling that it was anything unusual."

"Who is this contact? Do you trust this person?"

"She's a mid-level career diplomat."

"Do you have any reason to doubt anything she's told you?"

Vaughn considered. "No. She's the genuine article." Vaughn decided not to mention how much Sage reminded her of Sara. She didn't see the point. "Why the twenty questions, and when the hell are you going to tell me what you've got?"

"Bear with me. It's all related."

"How so?"

"Fairhaven's the one who pushed you for this particular assignment."

"Fairhaven? Why?" Vaughn furrowed her brow.

"That's what I can't figure out."

"I didn't think he'd concern himself with a peon like me, now that he's number two in the Company."

"And *I* didn't think he was all that cozy with State," Justine said. "Obviously, he's still got his eye on you."

"I haven't so much as put a paperclip out of order on my desk."

"That he knows of, anyway."

"True," Vaughn conceded. She hadn't done anything overt to follow up on Sara's death. She'd left that to Justine and her contacts. But Fairhaven knew her well enough to know that she wouldn't let Sara's death go without finding out who was responsible and bringing them to justice.

"Anyway, my point is that Fairhaven's fingerprints are on your marching orders, and that can't be good. You need to be careful."

"I appreciate your concern, but I'll be fine." Vaughn's tone was dismissive.

"Still could care less what happens to you, I see."

"You're wrong. I do care." *At least until we find Sara's killers.*

"Why don't I believe you?"

"Suit yourself." Vaughn shrugged. "What else do you have?"

"What, that isn't enough?"

"No."

"You're right, but it's all I have at the moment."

"Okay. Let me know if you get anything else."

"Of course. Take good care of yourself, Vaughn."

"I'll do my best. Justine?"

"Yeah?"

"Thanks."

"Don't mention it."

Vaughn shut the phone and threw it on the sofa. So, Fairhaven was still pulling her strings. She drummed her fingers on the coffee table. Maybe he just wanted her as far away from D.C. as possible. She shook her head. It smelled, and she knew it.

Five strides took her to the room safe in the closet. She punched in the number sequence and the door swung open. Inside was an accordion-style file folder. Vaughn removed it, kicked the door shut, and retreated to the sofa.

She spread several documents and news clippings on the coffee table. The headlines screamed at her from the yellowed newspapers: *Al Qaeda Strikes at Andrews, One Dead. President Promises Action; President Declares Terrorist Attack Won't Demoralize the American People.*

Vaughn fingered the article. *"The President labeled the death of Andrews Air Force Base mechanic Sara McFarland a tragic loss. He vows to go to Congress for additional funding for the war on terror."*

Angrily, Vaughn shoved the article aside. It fluttered to the floor. She picked up a sheaf of papers. On top was a document marked "Confidential" and titled *"Transcript of Interview with Field Agent Vaughn Elliott, conducted by Section Chief Edgar Fairhaven."*

Vaughn's eyes skimmed over the page. She noted that Fairhaven had edited out the beginning of their conversation. She had no trouble recalling the exchange, though.

"Elliott, I've seen you do a lot of stupid things over the years, but this one tops them all."

"What do you want, sir?"

"I want to know what the hell you and McFarland were playing at."

"I don't know what you're talking about," Vaughn said.

"Bullshit, Elliott. You've put me in a hell of a position, you know that? Do you have any idea how many strings I had to pull and how many favors I had to call in to make this go away?"

"I need some rest."

"You'll have plenty of time for that, believe me. You're going to be on desk duty for the rest of your life. But right now, I want answers."

"I have none to give."

"God damn it, Elliott!"

The interrogation—"interview" was too genteel a word for what Vaughn had been put through—lasted hours. Vaughn ran her finger over the top page and flicked to the next. There were twenty pages in all. Twenty pages of nothingness.

She'd told Fairhaven nothing beyond what he could have verified on his own. Sara had phoned her. They met at a coffee shop. Sara claimed to be on assignment. Vaughn was worried that she lacked backup and showed up to provide same. No, she had no idea what Sara was working on. A friend needed her assistance, and she answered the call. Period.

No matter how many ways he asked the question, no matter how deep he dug, he could come up with nothing more specific than that. Vaughn wasn't sure why she didn't trust Fairhaven enough to tell him the whole truth, but she learned over the years to listen to her gut. Her gut screamed at her to tell him nothing.

Toward the end of the grilling, she felt her strength and will slipping. It had only been one day since the explosion, and her grief and the seriousness of her injuries were overwhelming.

That's when Justine Coulter came to her rescue. Dressed as a trauma nurse, she kicked Fairhaven out of Vaughn's room. The patient, she insisted, had reached her limits. At the time, Vaughn was too grateful for the reprieve to wonder just who this angel was who brought her salvation.

It was only later she discovered that Justine had been planted at the clinic at Sara's request in case anything went wrong with the operation.

Vaughn shuffled the transcript aside and picked up a second document. It was a very unofficial lab report prepared by one of Justine's contacts.

> The residue from the explosive is orange in color, which, upon initial inspection, would indicate Semtex.
>
> However, further testing indicates that the orange color is dye. The explosive was C-4 disguised to look like Semtex.
>
> Conclusion: While the explosive presents as Semtex, the plastic explosive of choice for terrorist cells like Al Qaeda, the substance is, in reality, C-4, commonly used by intelligence organizations and the military. In addition, items taken from the person of one Anthony Sturges have been positively identified as military-grade blasting caps.

Vaughn smiled wolfishly. "Gotcha." She had taken the blasting caps out of the pocket of the agent she knocked unconscious in the hangar. She turned the page again to reveal a document titled, *"Report of Unusual Death: CIA Agent Anthony Sturges."* This was an internal Company document.

Vaughn took in the details. Sturges had been with the Company for thirty-one years, since the Vietnam era. His body was found by a jogger along a path near the Potomac less than a week after the incident at Andrews. He had eaten a bullet through the roof of his mouth. His death was ruled a suicide, and the case was closed.

"Suicide my ass," Vaughn hissed. She dropped the pile of papers on the coffee table with a thud and balled her fists in frustration. The Fairhaven development was interesting and added grist for the mill but got them no closer to finding the scum responsible for Sara's death. Vaughn couldn't even be sure they were connected.

The sense of hopelessness that was Vaughn's constant companion for the past year settled in the pit of her stomach. She went to the minibar and pulled out a bottle of scotch. It was what she always did when the memories became too much to bear.

Sage sliced through the water, her body a guided missile on a mission. The churned-up wake she left behind matched her mood perfectly. *Damn you, Vaughn Elliott. Why should I care if you're a jerk?*

She executed a perfect flip turn and headed in the opposite direction. *I mean, it's not as if we need to like each other to work together.*

Sage took two more strokes and a breath. *Arrogant daughter-of-a-warthog.* One more stroke and Sage's head hit the wall with a thud. "Ouch! Damn it all to hell." The oath came out as one word. She stood up in the shallow end, rubbed her head where a knot was already forming, and whipped off her swim goggles. "That's just great. Perfect end to a perfect day."

She rolled her shoulders and experimentally turned her head from left to right. The movement jarred her head and she uttered another oath. With a sigh, she looked up at the stars twinkling overhead. "What're you looking at?" She pushed herself out of the pool, grabbed her towel, and headed into the house to find some Ibuprofen. At least she wouldn't have to deal with Vaughn in the morning.

CHAPTER THREE

S age stared at the dispatch in her hands, trying to make sense of the words on the page. She read aloud: "The camels are in place and ready to spit. Your job is to give the shrew an education at recess on the 23rd. She'll need some fresh air between classes. Confirm receipt and destroy immediately."

Sage shook her head. "What the hell does that mean?" She shifted papers around on the desk until she unearthed the envelope that went with the message. "No wonder."

With a pen she scribbled on the back of the envelope, "Re-deliver to Ambassador Dumont." Sage initialed the note and placed it in her outbox.

She shuffled more papers, but her mind kept wandering. She hadn't heard a word from Vaughn all morning. Although she'd tried to convince herself that she didn't care if she ever heard from Vaughn again, she checked her voicemail one more time. "Damn you."

Since she wasn't getting any work done, Sage decided to walk down to the mailroom. It was housed in the basement of the embassy building, two floors below her office. She snatched up the wrongly-delivered communiqué and headed for the stairs.

The clerks with clearance to handle classified communications were housed in a separate area of the basement, around the corner from the main mailroom.

Sage stopped in front of the desk of the harried head clerk. "Excuse me…"

"I see you. I see you. Just give me a minute."

Sage looked around for a visitor's chair but found none. Instead, she wandered over to a bulletin board.

"What part of 'classified' don't you understand, young lady?"

Sage whirled around. The clerk hadn't even looked up. "I-I'm sorry. I was just…"

"Never mind. What do you want?"

Sage didn't appreciate being taken to task by a level-three clerk, but more than that, she objected to being treated like some errant schoolgirl. She stormed back to his desk. "One of your clerks made a mistake. I thought I would help you out by giving you a chance to correct the error, as it was rather egregious, but if you'd rather deal directly with the ambassador, I'll just take it to him."

"That won't be necessary." The clerk was out of his chair in an instant. "Let me see…" He took the envelope from Sage and examined it carefully. Finally, he looked up. "You opened this?"

"It was delivered to me," Sage said drolly.

"Yes, yes. Didn't you read the envelope first?"

"Obviously not, or I wouldn't have opened it, now would I?" Sage was beginning to regret the decision to leave her desk.

"This is not good. Not good at all." The clerk was shaking his head. He flipped the envelope over again, then consulted a clipboard hanging on the wall behind his desk. "Richard!"

Sage took a step back, wondering if her hearing would ever recover.

"Get over here!"

A young man with glasses and an owlish face appeared at the head clerk's elbow. "Yes?" He pushed the glasses up on his face.

"You handled this message?"

Richard examined the envelope. "Yes, sir. It came in this morning's pouch from Washington."

"Can you read, Richard?"

Sage almost felt sorry for the hapless clerk.

"Of course, sir."

"What does it say on the bottom of the envelope?"

Richard squinted at the small printing. "The printing's smeared."

"Can you read the words or not?" the head clerk snapped.

34

Richard furrowed his brow and refocused on the words. His Adam's apple bobbed as he swallowed hard. "Ambassador's eyes only," he mumbled.

"I'm sorry, I couldn't hear you. Come again?"

"Ambassador's eyes only," Richard repeated, marginally louder this time.

"What part of that instruction didn't you understand?"

"I—"

"Do you realize that I'm going to have to personally explain this to the ambassador?"

"Um, I guess, sir."

"Do you have any idea how displeased he's going to be?"

"I can imagine, sir."

"Would you like to tell me how you made a mistake this big?"

"The envelope was in the pouch marked 'Congressional Visit,' sir. I knew that Sage was handling the event, and I just thought..."

"That was your first mistake. You thought," the head clerk spat. "Congratulations, Richard. You just got yourself busted back to non-classified. Get out of my sight."

"But, sir..."

"I wouldn't push it. You're lucky I don't fire you outright."

"He made an honest mistake," Sage said, stepping forward.

"There's no room for mistakes, honest or otherwise, in the classified section. You're not off the hook, either." The head clerk pointed a bony finger in Sage's direction. "You read a privileged communiqué."

"First of all, I have top-secret clearance." Sage was having difficulty reining in her temper. "Second, don't try to deflect the responsibility for this screw-up. It's yours, and yours alone." Sage didn't bother mentioning that the contents made no sense to her anyway.

"We'll see about that."

Sage pivoted on her heel and stalked away. "Miserable son-of-a-gun."

When she hit the street level, she shoved open the front door to the building and stepped outside. She needed fresh air. The idea surprised a laugh out of her as the first wave of heat struck her like a fist. "Just perfect."

⊰⊱

Vaughn pressed her lips together and prayed for patience. "Tell me again what the conditions are along the route from school to school."

"I'm telling you, it's Timbuktu. Lots of sand, historic sites, museums, a few camels…"

"And I'm telling you," Vaughn said, uncrossing her legs and leaning forward, "I want a full schematic of the area, including the hole each of those camels pisses in, by tomorrow."

"Whoa, there's no call to get nasty."

Vaughn glared at the man she'd come to think of as "Malian incompetent number one." She stood and stretched. This was going nowhere. Idly, she wondered if Sage was having a better morning than she was. She shoved the thought aside.

"Look. The congressional visit is less than three weeks away. You are my core team. My go-to guys." Vaughn made eye contact first with the regional security officer, a beefy American who looked like he'd enjoyed far too much French cooking, then with the assistant RSO, and finally, with the two Malians who acted as investigators and liaisons with Malian authorities.

She sighed. *There's a reason why I always work alone.* "All right. Show me the ballroom where the ambassador's party will be."

As they walked to the ballroom, Vaughn found herself looking around for Sage. She didn't know exactly where Sage's office was, but she'd been given a blueprint of the building. The political section was housed on the second floor. The ballroom was on the first floor, but maybe Sage would be coming or going from the building.

Vaughn thrust her hands in her pockets. The last thing she needed was the distraction of a cute woman. Especially when that woman reminded her of Sara.

They passed the front door and Vaughn could've sworn she caught a glimpse of Sage standing outside. *Keep your eye on the ball, Elliott. You do the assignment, complete it successfully, and then pack for some other exciting hot spot.*

"Here we are."

"Okay." Vaughn tried to remember the RSO's name—Sidney or Stan...Stephen. That was it. "Stephen, take me through an event like this. What type of food are we talking about? Is it stand-up or sit-down? Appetizers or a seven-course meal? Dancing? What?" She knew she could've asked Sage, but...*The less contact with her, the better.*

"No dancing. Lots of glad-handing, pomposity, introductions, speeches, drinking, and appetizers. Black tie. Doubtless someone more familiar with these things will be happy to give you all the particulars."

Vaughn frowned. She was pretty sure she knew who that someone was. "I'll need a copy of the guest list."

"You'll have to get that from the political section."

Vaughn sighed. It seemed all roads led to Sage, after all. "Can you give me a rough idea?"

"The president, the prime minister, members of the prime minister's cabinet, members of the National Assembly, local politicians, and a few noted citizens."

Vaughn pulled out a small notebook and began taking notes. "I'm assuming the president has his own security. How many, and will they be in attendance as well?"

"His bodyguards go everywhere with him. There are six of them. I'd be surprised if he took a leak without them." Realizing what he'd said, Stephen reddened. "Sorry, ma'am."

"Forget it," Vaughn waved away the apology. "Nothing I haven't heard or said before. I'll need names and background checks on every member of the president's team. And the same for the prime minister, assuming he has his own team."

She moved toward a door at the far side of the room. "Where does this go?"

"Kitchen. It's convenient for the caterers."

"We'll need security stationed both inside the kitchen and on this side of the door." Vaughn measured the room with her eyes. "Two Americans checking IDs and invitations as folks enter the building, and two Americans and two Malians doing the same thing just outside the ballroom doors. I'm sure the Malians can help verify that the partygoers are who they claim to be."

"Is that really necessary?"

"Yes." Vaughn cut him off. "And I want four Malian gendarmes on each wall inside the reception."

"Ma'am, we've never had any trouble—"

"Have you ever had a visit led by such a high-ranking American official?"

"No, ma'am."

"Didn't think so. And stop calling me ma'am."

"Yes, ma'am—err, Agent Elliott."

Vaughn rolled her eyes. "Just call me Vaughn. It'll be a lot easier on both of us." She walked toward the exit, the group following in tow. "I'm sure you have your own way of doing things, Stephen, but I've been sent here at the behest of the secretary of state himself to ensure that nothing happens to the majority leader and her party. Rest assured that's exactly what I'm going to do."

"Yes, ma—Vaughn."

"I want to personally interview every security officer you bring in, including the gendarmes. I want full dossiers on all of them, and I do mean full. Is there any chance of meeting with the head of the president's security team?"

"I don't know. I'll look into it for you."

"Make it happen, Stephen." Vaughn swung through the ballroom door and plowed into someone passing in the corridor outside. She reached out instinctively and grabbed the person around the waist to keep her from falling. "I'm sor—" She froze when she realized the woman was Sage.

"Don't worry about…"

"Hi," Vaughn said, staring a little too long into those dazzling blue eyes. "Fancy meeting you here."

Sage took a step back, forcing Vaughn to release her grip. "Not really. I work here."

"Having a good day?" Vaughn smiled at Sage's irritated tone.

"Spiffy. You?"

"About the same." Vaughn looked over her shoulder. "You guys can go for now. Call me as soon as you have the information I've requested." To Sage, she said, "Are you busy? Can I buy you lunch?"

Vaughn watched as a series of emotions flitted across Sage's face. *Your eyes are so expressive. I can see every feeling reflected there.* She resisted the urge to reach out and brush a wisp of hair away from Sage's eyes. *You're fighting with yourself because you want to say yes, but you wish you could make yourself say no.*

"I suppose that would be all right. But I've only got time for the cafeteria."

"Lead on."

After they'd walked a little way, Vaughn said, "I thought you told me you were at my disposal for the length of my stay? If that's the case, your idea of availability and mine seem to be different."

"I've got responsibilities too." Anger flared in Sage's eyes and her chin jutted out, seemingly defying Vaughn to disagree with her. Vaughn found the look nearly irresistible.

"I certainly didn't mean to imply that you didn't. Sorry if you took offense. I was only tweaking you." She hoped her tone sounded sufficiently conciliatory.

"I'm sorry," Sage said. "I've had a crappy morning, including an argument with the biggest ass ever created, and I shouldn't take it out on you."

"Who's the ass? Want me to take care of him?"

"He's the head clerk in the classified section of the mailroom and I—" Sage shook her head. "Never mind. I don't want to think about it anymore. Let's have a peaceful lunch."

"As you wish. But if you change your mind and want me to clobber him or just rough him up a bit, let me know."

Sage laughed, finally, and Vaughn found herself feeling much relieved. She wasn't entirely sure she liked just how important it had been to her to restore Sage's good humor.

Once they were seated, Sage asked, "How's it going so far?"

"Slowly. Malian time and sensibilities are a little more laid back than I'm accustomed to."

"Yeah, I should have warned you about that. It's tough to get them worked up about much."

"I'm going to need a few things I hope you can help me with."

"Such as?" Sage took a bite of her chef salad.

"A full list of attendees for the ball, a formal itinerary for the event, a briefing on the president's…proclivities…anything you think I might need to know to avoid any embarrassing security concerns or situations."

"You don't ask for much, do you?"

"Nope." Vaughn took a bite of a surprisingly good hamburger. "I thought you said we wouldn't find any good food outside the hotel."

"This is the American Embassy. In here, you get American food. Trust me, when you eat in any of the restaurants in the city or in an outside village, you'll see what I mean."

"I do trust you." Vaughn pressed her lips into a thin line. There was more truth in the statement than she wanted to admit. She was not someone who trusted easily, so the revelation, so close on the heels of the other thoughts swirling in her head, was unsettling. Impulsively, she said, "We could start over dinner tonight. I still owe you a dinner from last night."

Sage seemed on the verge of declining, so Vaughn pushed ahead. "After all, the visit is only three weeks away, and there's so much I'm going to need to know. There's no time to waste. Not to mention the fact that I don't know anyone else here and you'd be leaving me to fend for myself."

"Oh, sure. Lay it on thick, why don't you." Sage tapped her fingers on the table as if considering the notion. "Okay. But we're not eating out. I'll cook."

"You'll cook?"

"Something wrong with that?"

"Not at all. Tell me what I can bring, what time, and where."

Once they had settled the details, Sage rose. "I've got to get back to work. I'll see you later."

When she'd gone, Vaughn murmured, "Indeed you will."

Ambassador Raymond Dumont ran two fingers nervously under his collar. He scanned the communiqué for the second time, nodding as he read. Then he read the note from the head mail clerk. Most unfortunate. The situation would have to be dealt with. He pressed the intercom button.

"Yes, sir?"

"Please send Nathan Trindle to my office."

"Trindle, sir? From the mail room?"

"Yes." Although his executive assistant was clearly perplexed, she had served seven ambassadors over the course of her career. In addition to an excellent institutional memory, discretion was her strong suit, a trait for which she was well rewarded.

"Right away, sir."

Dumont got up and went to the window. For several moments, he watched the traffic on the street below. People went about their business—for them it was just another ordinary day in the Malian capital. He envied them. He wished, not for the first time, that he could return to the simple days of being just another State Department flunky.

There was a light rap on the door, and he turned. "Come."

"Nathan Trindle is here, sir."

"Thank you, Doris. Send him in."

Trindle stood uncertainly in the center of the room. "You wanted to see me, sir?"

"Yes, Trindle. Sit down." The ambassador pointed to a pair of well-appointed visitor chairs in front of his desk. He continued to stand. He wanted Trindle to be as intimidated as possible, and while he knew being summoned to the ambassador's office should have been enough, he wasn't taking any chances.

The clerk was sitting on the edge of his seat, nervously bouncing his legs up and down. Dumont picked up the envelope from his desk.

"Does this look familiar to you, Mr. Trindle?" He held the envelope up so that Trindle could see it but did not let him touch it.

"Y-yes, sir. I brought it up here myself, sir."

"I see. Your note indicates that a very serious breach in protocol occurred with this item. Why is that?" Dumont kept his voice deadly calm.

"I-I'm not sure, sir. It seems the classified clerk who originally handled the piece made a faulty assumption."

"Is that so?"

"Y-yes, sir. The envelope was in the grouping to do with the upcoming congressional visit, so the clerk mistakenly forwarded it to the political officer."

Dumont stroked his beard, then took a deliberate step forward so that he was looming over Trindle. "Who was this…unfortunate clerk?"

"Richard Ashton, sir. I've already dealt with him. He'll never handle another classified document, I promise you."

"I should hope not. Did Mr. Ashton happen to read the contents of the envelope, Mr. Trindle?"

"No, sir. He did not. I questioned him within an inch of his life, and I am willing to swear that he only looked at the outside of the envelope before delivering it to the political officer. She read it."

"We'll get to that in a moment. And you, Mr. Trindle? Did you open the envelope and read?"

"Absolutely not. I swear to you on all that I hold dear, all I did was re-seal it and bring it straight here."

Dumont could smell the man's fear, but there was no evasiveness in his eyes. The ambassador held eye contact for a few seconds longer just to be sure. No, he hadn't looked.

"You spoke with Dr. McNally yourself?"

"Yes, sir." Trindle sat up a little straighter. "She read the letter, sir. She told me so."

At that moment, Trindle reminded Dumont of a weasel. He looked a little like one, and he most certainly acted like one. "Did she say anything else?"

"No, sir, just that she read it because it was delivered to her."

Dumont stared at Trindle a moment longer. "Very well, Mr. Trindle. You may go. I expect that nothing this egregious will ever happen under your watch again. Do you understand?"

"Yes, sir."

"If it does, it will be your last mistake. Are we clear?"

"Crystal, sir."

Dumont waited until the door shut and he was alone again. He pushed the intercom button.

"Yes, sir?"

"I don't want to be disturbed for any reason, Doris."

"Yes, sir."

Ambassador Dumont loosened his tie and undid the top button of his shirt. He knew what he had to do. It was a shame, but it was out of his hands. He picked up his secure phone and dialed a phone number from memory.

CHAPTER FOUR

Your home isn't what I expected." Vaughn was studying a Georgia O'Keefe print on the wall in Sage's well-appointed living room.

"Feel free to look around. I'd give you a tour, but my hands are full," Sage called from the kitchen.

"What are you making?" Vaughn laughed when Sage jumped.

"How did you do that?" Sage grabbed a paper towel to clean up the mess she just made.

"Do what?"

"Sneak up on me without me hearing you."

"Tricks of the trade."

"You need that in the security business?"

"Sometimes." Vaughn sniffed appreciatively over Sage's shoulder. Sage bumped her with her backside to create some space between them. "Mmm, chicken cordon bleu. Fabulous. Obviously, you like to cook."

"When you live in some of the places I've lived, you learn all kinds of handy skills."

"Like where to get the ingredients for fancy French dishes when they aren't readily available to the populace?"

"It pays to have connections. Jacques runs the kitchen at your hotel and does their ordering. He occasionally is nice enough to order a little extra in exchange for a few American dollars."

"An industrious woman. I like that." Vaughn noted the blush as it crept up Sage's neck. She found it most endearing.

"I get by." Sage moved to the oven. "It'll be a little while before dinner. Sorry about that. I got caught up at work."

"It's not a problem. I'm in no hurry."

Sage straightened up and closed the oven door. "Now, then. Why don't we sit by the pool?"

"Sure." Vaughn picked up the glass of wine Sage poured for her earlier, then followed her through the living room and out onto a spacious patio.

Candle-lit lanterns at even intervals created a pleasant glow and just enough light to see. There were two chaise lounges, several straight-backed chairs, and a table.

Vaughn put her glass on the table and walked to the edge of a regulation-sized pool. "Nice. Nobody could say you were living in squalor."

"No, that's true. But it's sometimes hard to reconcile the way I get to live with the conditions of the people, you know?"

Vaughn turned her head to gaze into Sage's eyes. There was such integrity and earnestness in them. It aroused a protectiveness in her that rang alarm bells, but Vaughn chose to ignore them.

"Yeah, I can understand that." Because she wanted to reach out and touch Sage, Vaughn shoved her hands in her pockets. She stepped back and dropped into one of the upright chairs. "So, we got sidetracked yesterday. You were about to tell me why you joined the diplomatic corps."

Sage selected the seat opposite her. "Do you want the long version or the short one?"

"Are we in a rush?" Vaughn posed the question casually, although she knew what she wanted the answer to be.

"No. I take it that means you'd like me to bore you with the extended version?"

"I seriously doubt you could bore me, Sage." Because she still wanted to, Vaughn touched Sage fleetingly on the back of the hand. *Soft.*

"Right. Umm...right. Well, as I told you, I went into the Peace Corps straight out of college. When I came back, I was at loose ends. I knew I wanted to do more with what I had learned and experienced, but I had no idea where to start."

"Hmm," Vaughn said. "I imagine coming back to the States must have been a bit of a culture shock for you."

Sage laughed. "No kidding. Between the time I left and the time I came back there were so many new technological advances

I felt like I'd fallen into the Twilight Zone. It was major sensory overload."

"How long did that last?"

"Longer than I want to admit." Sage got up and walked a few steps toward the pool. She stared into the water and spoke with her back to Vaughn. "I was sort of a lost soul for about a year. Then I decided to go to grad school. I did an extended program and got my masters and PhD. Worked my way through by teaching French at night to continuing-education students."

"Sounds like a full load."

Sage returned to the table and rested her arms on the back of her chair. "I didn't have much time to think about it then, nor did I want to. I think if I'd analyzed how much I was taking on, it would have paralyzed me. My parents never put all that much value on my education, nor did they understand my passion for third-world countries. So I was on my own."

"Without any support system." Vaughn noted the lines of tension that had formed around Sage's mouth. She wished she could make them go away.

"Pretty much." Sage pushed off the chair and turned away. "I'd better go check on dinner."

"Don't—" Vaughn jumped up and intercepted her. "Don't run away." She put her hands on Sage's shoulders. "I didn't mean to bring up painful memories. I'm sorry."

"It's okay."

Vaughn felt Sage relax under her touch. The contact had quite a different effect on Vaughn. She swallowed hard. It was simply that she hadn't been with a woman since... That had to be it. *Get a grip, Elliott.* She dropped her hands to her sides. "What was your degree in?"

"International Studies. American University's School of International Service."

"So I guess I should call you 'doctor' then, eh?"

"That would be overkill. Thanks for the thought, though."

Vaughn noted that she was still within Sage's personal space, and that neither one of them had made any effort to move. "And then?" She held Sage's gaze.

"A professor of mine recommended the diplomatic corps. I took the appropriate tests." Sage shrugged. "The rest, as they say, is history." She stood there a moment longer. "I really do have to check on dinner."

"Shall I go with you?"

"That won't be necessary. I'll only be a minute."

❧❧

When she was alone in the kitchen, Sage braced her arms against the counter. "For the love of Pete." Her cheeks were flushed and her heart was fluttering in her chest. There was something so magnetic about Vaughn. "This is ridiculous. She's moody...she can be rude and abrasive...I don't want to be attracted to her."

Sage went to the sink and splashed cold water on her face. "I'm just going to keep my distance, that's all."

"Keep your distance from what?"

Sage gasped and her pulse hammered in her ears. "Don't do that!"

"Let me guess. I startled you again."

Sage's cheeks were on fire. How much had Vaughn heard? "Keep my distance from hot ovens on hot nights." *Lame.* "Dinner will be ready in about five minutes."

"Great. I'm starving."

Sage didn't want to look at Vaughn, so she busied herself getting dishes from the cupboard.

"Can I help?"

Sage could hear the amusement in Vaughn's voice as she struggled on her tip toes to reach the top shelf. "No. You can sit down at the table. I can handle this."

"I'm sure you can."

Sage got her fingertips on the plates and eased them toward her. She would rather have had bamboo shoots shoved under her fingernails than admit she needed help.

When she turned her head around, Vaughn was—what? Staring at her backside? Sage narrowed her eyes and brought the dishes to the table, setting them down a little harder than was required. Should she address the growing sexual tension between them or ignore it? After the day she'd had, Sage didn't feel like playing games. "Nice view?"

"Actually, it was."

"Glad I could provide some entertainment for you." Although she knew she was blushing again, Sage didn't look away.

"I'm sorry. I'm sure that was rude, but I did offer to help."

"Yes, you did. So, what're you saying, it's my own fault you were forced to stare?"

"Did I truly offend you or are you just in a feisty mood?"

Sage relented. "Feisty, I guess. Remnants of the day. I apologize." She rolled her shoulders to loosen the tight muscles.

"I could do that, if you like."

Sage went rigid. Was Vaughn playing with her or was it more than that? "No, thanks." Unconsciously, Sage wiped her palms on her jeans. The timer sounded, and she gratefully busied herself taking the food out of the oven.

"My mouth is watering."

So is mine. She wasn't thinking about the food. "Maybe you'd better taste it before you make up your mind."

"I'm sure I'll love it," Vaughn said suggestively.

I can't take much more of this. Time to get on safe ground. "You know all about me now, and I know nothing about you. Tell me something about yourself."

"There's not much to tell."

"I don't believe that for a second." Sage placed the chicken on their plates, then turned her attention to dressing the salad. "You're obviously a highly intelligent woman. Why law enforcement?"

Vaughn looked thoughtful for a moment, and Sage wondered if perhaps she was deciding how much she wanted to share.

"I guess I was a lot like you—I wanted to save the world. You chose diplomacy, and I chose justice."

There was a wistful quality to Vaughn's voice that Sage hadn't heard before. "Why justice?"

"Actually, it sort of chose me."

"That's an enigmatic thing to say."

"Is it?"

Sage watched as Vaughn took a forkful of food, moaned in delight, and threw her head back. Sage swallowed hard and licked her lips. She would've given anything at that moment to have been the cause of that reaction.

"It's…" Sage cleared her suddenly dry throat. "It's okay?"

"It's marvelous. You can cook for me anytime."

"Thank you. I figured since you had the coq au vin at lunch yesterday, it was a safe bet that you liked chicken."

"Very observant of you. Yes, I'd eat chicken every night of the week if I could get away with it."

"You can't? Get away with it, I mean?" Was there someone at home who cooked for Vaughn? Sage felt an unwelcome surge of jealousy.

"More like I don't often bother cooking for one."

Sage let out the breath she was holding. "Oh." She wondered if her relief was obvious. "You said you learned French studying in Paris. How did that come about?"

"My father traveled a lot. He was stationed in France for several years, so I was enrolled in a French school. When I got there, I didn't speak a word of the language."

"That must have been awful for you."

"Nah, I picked it up pretty quickly."

"Did your mother come with you?"

"She died when I was only a few months old. I never knew her."

"Oh, Vaughn." Sage couldn't help herself. She reached across the table and covered Vaughn's hand with her own. "I'm so sorry."

Vaughn shrugged. "I didn't miss what I never had, although sometimes I missed the idea of her."

There was the wistfulness again, and a vulnerability Sage doubted Vaughn showed often. "Your dad never remarried?"

"As far as I know, he never even considered it. He was a lone wolf who was very fond of rules and routine. I don't think there was any room in his life for anyone else."

"But surely he had room for you."

"As long as I didn't get in his way."

Sage noted the edge of sadness in Vaughn's eyes. She could imagine the small child, in a foreign land, struggling with an unfamiliar language, with no friends and no affection. It made her want to weep. "Sounds lonely."

Vaughn finally removed her hand from underneath Sage's. Sage immediately missed her touch.

"It was all I knew."

"That doesn't make it any better."

"I did all right."

Sage sensed that Vaughn wasn't someone who would accept pity. Time to change the subject again. "Du café?"

"Bien sûr. This is a top-flight restaurant. I'll have to remember to leave a generous tip."

Impulsively, Sage said, "Well, we want to be sure you'll eat here often."

Sage went back to the cupboard, this time acutely aware of the view she was affording Vaughn as she stood on her tip toes to reach the cups and saucers.

A pair of hands reached above hers at the same moment she felt the weight of Vaughn's body pressing against hers. A frisson of excitement coursed through her, and she shivered involuntarily.

"I hate to see a girl struggle."

Vaughn's voice was a seductive purr in her ear, and Sage's legs wobbled.

"Let me," Vaughn said, taking the china from Sage's unsteady hands and placing it on the counter.

Sage turned in the circle of Vaughn's arms. She looked up slowly to see those intense eyes staring hungrily at her. Without thinking, she framed Vaughn's face with her hands and ran her thumbs over generous lips. When she followed the thumbs with her tongue, Vaughn grabbed her arms.

"Sage." Vaughn's voice was full of needs, wants, and regrets.

"Don't talk," Sage urged. She tugged on Vaughn's lower lip with her teeth. She was rewarded with a gasp and a tightening of the hands on her biceps.

"Sage." Vaughn pulled her head back. "I want you—God knows I do…"

"Then stop talking." Sage licked the spot she'd nipped.

"You're too good for this."

"Too good to make love with you? Surely you have a higher opinion of yourself than that." Sage shifted subtly so that her thigh was nestled in between Vaughn's legs. "Or is that a nice way of saying I'm not good enough for you?" Insecurity dampened the fire burning in Sage.

Vaughn must have seen the flicker of hurt, because she leaned down and captured Sage's mouth in a heart-stopping kiss. "No, it's definitely not that," she said against Sage's lips long moments later.

Sage's eyes fluttered open. Idly, she noted that Vaughn's eyes were heavy-lidded with desire. *No, definitely not that.* "Then we don't have a problem." She leaned in for another kiss. Again, Vaughn stopped her.

"You need to understand. I haven't done this in a very long time. I…I don't want to hurt you."

"You won't, Vaughn." There was a genuine gentleness in Vaughn's kiss that told Sage she had nothing to worry about on that front.

"That's not what I'm talking about. I mean I can't—I won't—get involved. I have nothing to give emotionally."

Sage opened her mouth to say something and then closed it again. There was a finality in Vaughn's voice that she imagined masked a devastating hurt. It made her want Vaughn that much more.

"I'm not asking you to marry me. I'm a big girl, Vaughn. I know what I want, and right now what I want is to make love with you." Sage punctuated the point by removing her shirt. She watched Vaughn's eyes widen first in surprise and then in lust. She was glad she'd chosen the black lace bra.

Slowly, she unbuttoned and unzipped her jeans to reveal a hint of the matching panties. She watched Vaughn's gaze follow her movements. It made her feel reckless in a way she never had before. One-night stands were something Sage McNally read about in romance novels, not something she did. "See anything you like?"

Vaughn growled low in her throat. Her fingers reached out and gently stroked the tops of Sage's breasts. With equal care, she reached behind and unfastened the bra, slipped the straps off sensuous bare shoulders, and let it fall to the floor. For several heartbeats, she simply stood there looking.

"As a matter of fact, I do see something I like."

Before Sage had a chance to react, Vaughn's mouth was hot on her breast, her tongue teasing Sage's erect nipple.

"Oh, God, yes." Sage fisted her hands in Vaughn's hair and pulled her closer. Vaughn's hands slid under her panties, a finger gliding fleetingly through her wetness before both hands settled on her buttocks.

"Ngh." Sage was incoherent with need. "Please." She clawed at Vaughn's shirt, ripping it from her pants. Her fingers kneaded the soft skin and firm muscles of Vaughn's back.

Vaughn picked her up by the hips and deposited her on the counter, shoving aside the dishes. Her lips were hot against Sage's abdomen, and Sage shoved at her own jeans to get them out of the way.

In seconds, the jeans were on the floor, and Vaughn's mouth was against the satin of her panties. Sage spread her legs wider, begging Vaughn to take her. When Vaughn ran her index fingers under the material and stroked her lower belly, Sage couldn't stand it any more.

"God, Vaughn. Take me. Now."

The words seemed to unleash something primal in Vaughn. She tore the panties from Sage's body and pulled her forward toward the edge of the counter. A finger flicked again through Sage's wetness before Vaughn lowered her head to feast.

Sage's whole body jolted at the sensation of Vaughn's mouth devouring her. Her heartbeat thudded in her ears as the first orgasm ripped through her. Before she had a chance to catch her breath, Vaughn entered her with two fingers, then three, filling her, bringing her rapidly to another peak, and then another. Sage sunk her fingers into Vaughn's shoulders, needing the contact to tether her to the earth. Her body shuddered one last time and her breathing began to settle.

As she was about to open her mouth to speak, Vaughn picked her up from the counter. Reflexively she wrapped her legs around Vaughn's waist. The sensation of her hot, slick center against Vaughn's bare abdomen set off new shockwaves of pleasure.

Vaguely, she wondered how Vaughn's shirt had lost its buttons, but she ceased to think when Vaughn deposited her on her back on the bed. Hot, ravenous kisses rained down on her breasts, her belly, and her inner thighs.

"Vaughn—" Sage's voice strangled on a sob when Vaughn's tongue lapped at her center, then stroked the length of her clit.

Vaughn's mouth continued its quest as her fingers matched the rhythm of her tongue, buried deep inside Sage.

Sage felt herself cleave in two as the climax ripped through her. She clung to Vaughn, her breath still coming in pants, her mind a complete blank. Slowly, she eased her grip. She brushed the hair from Vaughn's face.

"Are you okay?" Vaughn asked the question softly, as if she was afraid of her own power.

"I'll let you know when I can think again." Sage laughed. When she saw the shadows cross Vaughn's face, she sat up. "I'm fine, Vaughn."

To Sage's shock, Vaughn began to cry.

"No, no, no. Stop." Sage pulled Vaughn to her and rocked her.

"I-I'm sorry. I didn't mean to—"

"Vaughn, look at me." Sage put two fingers under Vaughn's chin and lifted her head so that they were eye-to-eye. "You were fantastic. Amazing. You didn't hurt me, and you didn't do anything I didn't want you to. I'm the one who seduced you, remember?"

Vaughn swiped angrily at the moisture on her face. "I should've been stronger."

"Please don't ruin the most incredible sexual experience of my life. No one has ever made me come like that. No one." She ran her fingers through Vaughn's tangled mane and kissed her forehead. "Please stop beating yourself up. I don't want to feel badly about tonight. I want to savor it."

Vaughn gave an embarrassed laugh. "Are you for real?"

"Of course I am." Sage teased Vaughn's lips apart with her tongue and kissed her sweetly. "Doesn't that feel real to you?"

"I'm not sure." Vaughn smiled, and Sage thought it might be the most beautiful sight she'd ever seen.

"Well, I'd better do something to make you sure." Sage ran her tongue along Vaughn's jaw and down her throat. She felt the pulse pick up under her ministrations.

"Sage."

"Hmm?"

Vaughn pushed her away with difficulty. "I can't."

"Of course you can." Sage resumed her exploration. Her fingers trailed down Vaughn's side, and stopped abruptly when they encountered a jagged ridge. "What's—"

"No." Vaughn pushed her away more forcefully. "Don't."

For the first time, Sage noticed a wild edge of fear in Vaughn's eyes. She looked like she was about to bolt.

"Okay." Sage stroked her face. "Okay, Vaughn. I'm sorry."

"It's not you."

"It's okay."

"I just—"

"Shh. You don't need to explain it to me." Sage pulled Vaughn to her and rocked her again until she felt both of their heartbeats settle.

Vaughn started to get up.

"No," Sage said. "Please don't go."

"Sage—"

"Please, Vaughn. Stay the night. Hold me." She could see Vaughn weighing her decision. "I promise not to misinterpret anything or to touch you anywhere you don't want to be touched. I just want to lie with you."

Without a word, Vaughn slipped out of her jeans and unhooked her bra. She stretched out and opened her arms.

Sage fell into them gratefully and closed her eyes. "You smell good."

"Mmm-hmm."

Within seconds, Sage drifted off.

CHAPTER FIVE

Vaughn woke with a start, dazed and vaguely confused. *Sage's house. Shit.* She reached beside her. The bed was warm but empty. *Shit.* She cracked an eye open. Through the blinds she could see that the sun had barely cleared the horizon.

The smell of coffee brewing caught her attention. She gave an appreciative sniff and followed her nose. There was a note under a coffee mug on the counter.

"As I recall, I owed you a cup. Gone for a quick run, back in a flash. I peg you for an early riser. It's 5:15 a.m. now. I'll be back no later than 6 a.m. Surely you don't have anywhere you have to be before that. Please stay for breakfast. I make a mean omelet. No strings attached, I assure you. Sage."

Vaughn poured herself a cup of coffee and took a long sip. *Mmm. You can cook and you make a great cup of coffee. Points for you, Sage.*

Vaughn shook her head and bit her lower lip. She never should have let this happen. Sage got past her defenses, and that was something Vaughn had hoped to prevent. As if to reinforce the extent to which she lost control, Vaughn looked down and found her shirt, minus the buttons, tangled on the kitchen floor.

A vision of Sage, her eyes unfocused, her head thrown back in passion, sent a bolt of lightning directly to Vaughn's groin and stopped her dead mid-sip. She groaned out loud. A shower. What she needed was a cold shower. She checked her watch. There was enough time to take a quick shower and be gone before Sage got back. Besides, Vaughn mused, she shouldn't walk into the hotel lobby smelling like sex.

The water was tepid. It didn't matter how she adjusted the knobs. It wasn't hot, and it wasn't cold. It was just tepid. *Figures.* Vaughn ran her head under the spray. She soaped her shoulders, under her arms, and lathered her breasts. *Jesus.* They were so sensitive.

She pinched her nipple and gasped as she felt herself grow instantly wet. With her forehead pressed against the shower wall, she slid her fingers inside. As her excitement mounted, a vision of Sara loomed over her, a playful smile on her lips. The scene morphed into Sage's face, enraptured, as Vaughn made her come that last time. Vaughn came with a strangled cry.

Her chest heaved with the effort of breathing, and her tears mingled with the shower spray. *What have I done?*

Quickly, she shut off the water and toweled herself dry. Her watch was on the shelf above the sink—5:55. If she tried to escape now, she might run into Sage on the street. No, it would be better to stay and set boundaries before things got any further out of hand.

⋘⋙

Sage turned the last corner. Her mind was churning, and her center was still throbbing, aching for more of Vaughn. She closed her eyes momentarily. *Forget about that. She made it perfectly clear it was a one-time thing. She wouldn't even let you touch her.* Yet, Sage had clearly seen the need in her eyes. It was obvious that she was restraining herself. *Why?* What was that scar on her side, and what of the emotional wound that clearly went with it? Real pain had shown in Vaughn's expression, and Sage found herself wanting desperately to help her forget.

Sage smirked. If she were going to be honest with herself, she wanted a great many things where Vaughn was concerned. Her own behavior had been so far out of character, it was as if some sexual animal took over her body. In the past, Sage had never been bold or sexually aggressive. *Well, it was certainly worth it.* She smiled. Given the opportunity, she wouldn't mind unleashing that beast again.

She was so caught up in the idea that she never noticed the vehicle pulling up alongside her. Two figures jumped out.

"Hey!" A black hood was thrown over Sage's head as a second pair of hands pulled her arms roughly behind her back. Her nostrils flared as she began to hyperventilate. She tossed her head left and right, trying to see, trying to lose the hood. She felt the cold steel of handcuffs snapping around her wrists and screamed.

Panic and adrenaline propelled her into action and she kicked out as hard as she could. Nothing but air. *Where are you?* A yank on the handcuffs pulled her backward. She dug her heels into the ground. One of her shoes came off. Still, she held her ground.

A blow rocked her head back and she tasted blood. *Good. One in front.* Sage lowered her shoulder and threw herself forward. *Gotcha!* She stumbled forward and landed on one of her attackers. He uttered an oath in a tongue she didn't understand and shoved her roughly off him. The ground was hard, unforgiving. *Go!* Heart pounding, she gathered her legs under her, ready to make a run for it.

A knee crashed into her back, pinning her down, a hand thrust her head into the dirt, and someone had hold of her ankles. It was as if they were everywhere and she didn't stand a chance.

No! Sage kicked out again—a wild animal cornered—but the grip held firm. Before she could do anything more, her feet were bound with some sort of rope. She rolled to one side. Hands shoved her onto her back. A beefy forearm pressed roughly against her throat and constricted her windpipe.

Fear clawed at her. *They're going to kill me.* Sage struggled to breathe. She arched her back and threw her shoulder forward, trying desperately to dislodge the forearm. As she started to black out, the pressure disappeared. Relief washed through her. She took in a huge gulp of air, which was abruptly cut short when a fist punched her in the stomach. She rolled over, coughing and gagging.

Hands jerked her wrists. She was dragged backward by the handcuffs, her cheek, hip, and shoulder bouncing along the bone-dry earth. Pinpricks of pain sliced through her. It felt as if her shoulders were being ripped from their sockets *Help me! God, please, someone help me.* Hands lifted her off the ground and tossed her. She landed awkwardly on what she assumed was a car seat. Her ears were ringing from the combination of the blow to the head and the repeated bouncing on the unforgiving dirt.

She opened her mouth to yell that she was an American diplomat, then thought better of it. She wasn't sure if that would count in her favor or against her. *Think. There has to be a way out.*

Car doors slammed, and she pitched backward as the vehicle lurched into motion. She smelled sweat and unwashed bodies. Angry voices argued. Then only the sound of raspy breaths, followed by the metallic squawk of what sounded to Sage like a walkie-talkie. Calm words, spoken in the unfamiliar language. Inside the hood, Sage's eyes widened in fear.

❦

"Yes?" Ambassador Dumont's voice was thick with sleep as he answered the phone and clicked on the light on the bedside table in his residence several blocks from the embassy.

"It is done." The voice was heavily accented, but the words, spoken in French, were crystal clear.

"No casualties?" Dumont sat up, wide awake now.

"Not of the kind you mean."

"Good."

The line went dead. The ambassador continued to hold the receiver in his trembling hand, closing his eyes in relief. He understood the necessity of the action—after all, there could be no chances taken at this point—but he didn't want a death on his conscience.

After several seconds, he depressed the plunger and dialed a number by heart.

"Report."

Dumont swallowed hard. The voice on the other end of the line was all business. "Mission accomplished."

"Excellent."

"How am I supposed to explain the absence? Questions will be asked."

"Use your imagination, Ambassador. I'm sure you have one of those." The voice was oily.

"Y-yes. Of course. When will the replacement be here? After all, we have an important visit coming up. We need a control officer."

"We are well aware of your needs. Someone will report to your office tomorrow morning."

"Will this person be aware of the situation?"

"You are not to discuss anything with anyone."

"I wasn't planning on it. I just want to know—"

"You know everything you need to know."

Again, the line went dead. Dumont mopped his brow. This was not what he'd had in mind when he told the president he'd be honored to serve his country as ambassador.

Sage tried to gauge her position in relation to her captors. She believed she was alone in the back seat of the vehicle. She counted four distinct voices in front of her, two immediately in front of her, and two more farther up front. *Lousy odds.* Still, with every passing second, she knew her chances of getting away were diminishing. *You can do it. Think of something.* She wiggled her toes and brushed against what felt like an old-fashioned window crank. Her feet were close to the door. If she could just get enough leverage and the right angle, maybe she could find the door handle, work it open, and throw herself out. It was a long shot, but better than whatever these goons had planned for her.

Carefully, Sage rolled from her side onto her back and felt around with her shoeless toes. Hard plastic. She bent her knees and wiggled her toes until they hooked under what she thought must be the door handle. The voices continued to trip over each other in front of her. *You're only going to get one shot at this. Make it count. Oh, God. If this doesn't work...* She took a deep breath and yanked her toes upward. Hot, dusty air rushed in as the door flew open.

Voices shouted and Sage rolled to her stomach again and thrust herself onto her knees. She rocked forward off the seat, and something came down hard against her temple. The last thing she thought of before darkness overtook her was Vaughn.

Vaughn pulled on a T-shirt she found in one of Sage's drawers. It was a size too small, but it would do for now. She zipped her jeans, paced, and checked her watch again—6:25 a.m. Sage had left at 5:15. She should've been back by now. Vaughn peeked out the front door. There was no activity on the street. She knew she should just leave, but the idea didn't sit well with her.

Vaughn had spent too many years trusting her gut. And right now, her gut was telling her something was wrong. Maybe Sage had turned an ankle or wrenched a knee and was stranded or limping home. It wouldn't hurt to look.

After a brief search, Vaughn found a spare key hanging on a nail in the pantry. She locked the front door and checked the sun. Instinctively, she knew that Sage would head in the direction of the rising sun. *Bet she'd want to enjoy the view.* But did she run a loop, or did she go out and back?

A quick survey of the neighborhood told Vaughn that it was possible to make a circuit. She believed that's what Sage would've done, so she headed west on foot, assuming that would've been Sage's return route.

When she'd gone about half a mile, Vaughn halted dead in her tracks, bile rising in her throat. A single sneaker was sitting on its side some five feet off the pavement. Vaughn picked it up. It was still tied, and roughly the size of Sage's feet.

As her heart thumped uncomfortably against her ribcage, Vaughn took a deep breath and scanned the area. Some of the brush had been flattened. She squatted down and ran her fingers over a darker patch of ground, brought her fingers up, rubbed them together, and sniffed. Blood. *Oh, God.* Her eyes closed involuntarily. Was Sage hit by a car?

Vaughn followed the path of the blood and the irregular patterns of what appeared to be drag marks. She counted at least four pairs of footprints, including a pattern that matched the bottom of the sneaker she now cradled against her chest. No, Sage hadn't been hit—not by a car, anyway. She'd been taken—against her will if the blood spatters were any indication.

Vaughn's heart sank. Visions of Sara's mangled body flooded her mind. She squeezed her eyes shut tightly. *Not this time.* It wasn't over yet. She would get to Sage in time.

I swear to you by everything I am, I will find you and bring you back. And if they killed Sage? Vaughn wouldn't allow it. Not again. She set off at a run back to Sage's house. She had work to do.

❦

The sun was hot on her back and the ride was bumpy. She was on her stomach. Her thighs and pelvis chafed against the fabric separating her skin from something stiff that might be leather. The observations seeped into Sage's awareness even as her head and shoulder throbbed painfully. She extended her senses. A pungent odor assaulted her nose, and the sound of hooves clip-clopping on the arid earth greeted her ears. She knew horses. This wasn't a horse.

A camel? She listened more closely. *Correction—several camels. The desert. Where no one will find me for years.* Sage whipped her head back and forth, ignoring the spikes of pain and peering in vain through the darkness of the hood. The muscles in her back and neck seized and Sage arched reflexively to relieve the cramping. As she did so she felt herself sliding. And sliding. And falling. She let out a strangled cry as her side hit the ground. Hard.

Shouts rent the air all around her. Loud male voices. Sage tried to catch her breath. She rolled as the voices got closer. Her overriding instinct was to run. But even as Sage struggled to get her feet under her, she realized the futility of the effort. With her feet bound and her hands still handcuffed behind her back, she stood no chance. Her eyes filled with tears. *I'm going to die and no one will know what happened.* She bit her trembling lower lip. *No, Vaughn will figure it out. Vaughn will save me.*

Sage tensed as rough hands hauled her to her feet. Her whole body ached. An argument raged around her, and the tone of it scared her senseless. The sudden silence that followed disconcerted her even more. Finally, she felt a hard tug on the rope around her ankles. The pressure of the rope disappeared. In its place were vice-like hands. She supposed they didn't want to endure another one of her kicks. An arm came around her neck. Two others grabbed her arms as the handcuffs were undone.

Sweat born of fear dripped between Sage's breasts. There was no point in struggling—there were too many of them. The darkness became more pronounced as a piece of cloth was pulled over her head. The material was yanked down, covering her body. A long robe. *Tuareg.* She was sure these men were uncomfortable with the amount of skin her running outfit showed. In addition, putting her in a robe would make her less conspicuous. *Although the hood might be a dead giveaway.* The thought would've made her laugh, except the absence of outside noise told her they were not just in the desert but also far from any civilization. Knights in shining armor were likely in short supply out here. The knowledge settled heavily in the pit of Sage's stomach.

As she tried to puzzle through what the Tuareg could possibly want with her, she was lifted and set atop a camel. Calloused hands tied her to what she assumed was a saddle. At least this time, her hands were in front of her. She tested the bonds around her wrists. Hemp. Tightly tied hemp. Escape would be impossible. *For now.* Sage fought against the wave of hopelessness that washed over her.

Vaughn. Again it was the one name that calmed her in the face of despair. Vaughn would know something had happened to her. Vaughn would come for her. She was sure of it.

The papers on Sage's desk revealed nothing of consequence. Routine documents—reports for her superiors in Washington that spoke of crops, drought, and the nutritional needs of the people. Legal pads held doodles of scenes Vaughn assumed reminded Sage of home. Vaughn's gut contracted painfully. She wondered if Sage would ever get to see that home again. *She will. You can't think like that. There's no room for doubt.*

Every minute that went by was an opportunity lost. Finding a kidnap victim in the first hours was crucial. After that, the odds of finding her alive diminished significantly.

Vaughn yanked opened the file drawer in the desk. She rifled through the contents, checking the titles on the folder tabs. *Thank you, Sage, for being anally organized.* Again, Vaughn found nothing that would give her any clues. The mail was next, then the closet, Sage's pocketbook, and finally her computer.

Vaughn hunted through the list of folders on Sage's hard drive. She found the one marked "Congressional Visit," and opened it. The file titled "Vaughn Elliott" contained a copy of her assignment and the cover letter from the secretary of state. It said a hard copy of these documents would be sent separately under official seal. Standard operating procedure, Vaughn was sure.

She tapped her finger thoughtfully against the keyboard. She revisited her conversation with Sage about the method of her assignment and the break in protocol. She remembered, too, her exchange with Justine about it. Was it possible that Sage's disappearance had anything to do with Vaughn's assignment? Vaughn raised a questioning eyebrow. It was one possibility among many she would consider.

Vaughn opened the next file—a detailed preliminary schedule for the delegation while they were in Mali. She printed out a copy. Another file held the profiles of every member of the delegation. Again, Vaughn hit print. The last document in the folder was a schedule of meetings Sage had set up for the two of them with various politicos. One of them was scheduled for that day. With a heavy heart, Vaughn printed that document too. She checked her watch. 7:43 a.m. Time was slipping through her fingers, and there was nothing in the house to help.

Maybe she should stay in case anybody showed up. *Pathetic. She's not going to come walking through the door, Elliott.* Reluctantly, Vaughn grabbed the car keys from Sage's pocketbook, let herself out, locked up, and folded herself into the driver's seat of Sage's car. She smiled sadly as her knees hit the dashboard and she had to move the seat back.

At the hotel, Vaughn checked her room. It was undisturbed. *One point against Sage's disappearance having anything to do with me.* She changed into a fresh pair of dress pants and a cotton dress shirt, slipped her Glock-40 from under the false bottom of her leather briefcase, inserted a fresh clip and returned the gun to its hiding place. The documents she had taken from Sage's house fit into the main compartment of the briefcase.

Vaughn tore a page off the scratch pad the hotel had conveniently left by the bedside phone and shredded it.

Methodically she moved around the suite, placing tiny pieces of paper in the runners of the drawers. If anyone opened a drawer, the paper would fall into the next drawer. It wouldn't be noticed by the intruder, but Vaughn would know.

Such precautions were second nature to her. Any agent worth her salt would use such techniques to ascertain whether anyone had searched her room. *But you're not an agent anymore, Elliott, are you?* Vaughn closed her eyes tightly. This was no time for a crisis of confidence. No, she hadn't been able to save Sara, and maybe the Company had no use for her anymore, but Sage needed her.

Vaughn bit her lip and surveyed the room, spying what she wanted. *That'll do it.* She picked up her previously discarded shirt and broke off one of the threads where a button had gone missing. It wouldn't do to get wistful about how that button had popped off. There was no time for such sentimentality.

Vaughn picked up the briefcase, walked to the door, hung the "Do Not Disturb" sign and carefully placed the miniscule thread in the door-locking mechanism. A piece of paper would've been too obvious in this location. She didn't want to tip off anyone breaking into the room that she was suspicious. Maybe this wasn't about her, but she couldn't discount the idea completely. Still, why else would anybody want to take Sage? On the face of it, it made no sense.

Vaughn was going to have to do a lot more digging to get to the bottom of this. And fast.

When she stepped outside the hotel, Henri was waiting for her. There was a good place to start.

The thirst was nearly unbearable, and the heat was stifling. Sage fought to stay upright. Sweat poured down her face and she was having difficulty breathing. She wasn't sure how much longer she could go on.

With a shout, the caravan came to a stop. The camel knelt. Sage's pulse raged in her temples as strong hands grabbed her jaw under the hood from behind. Foul breath made her gag. A voice spoke harshly in her ear, but she understood none of the words.

She could guess at the meaning, however, when he tightened his grip as the hood was removed. She was unable to turn her head in any direction—unable to see the faces or even the bodies of her captors. She squinted her eyes in the bright sunlight. There was nothing in front of her but desert. *This is it. They're going to leave me here to die.*

Within seconds, the hood was replaced with a blindfold. Sage rolled her eyes skyward and gave thanks. *Well, at least I can breathe now.* The hands released her jaw. She moved it from side to side and grimaced. *That'll leave a mark.* Nearby, she could hear activity. It sounded like the party had dismounted.

Her head began to spin. If she didn't get water soon, they might, indeed, have a dead captive on their hands. It was time to take a chance. She licked her lips. "Please, can I have some water? D'eau, s'il vous plaît?"

The talking around her ceased momentarily, then several voices began to argue. On the chance that they were trying to puzzle out what she had said, she mimed needing a drink by tipping her head back and opening her mouth.

More discussion followed before Sage felt something pushed against her lips. The foul breath was back. She tipped her head back as water was poured first over her face and then down her throat. She lowered her head, sputtering and choking as the overflow spilled out of her mouth. The motion sent a shockwave of pain through her skull.

The canteen was pushed against her mouth again, and she tipped her head back, more slowly this time. After several more sips, the water was replaced by something solid against her lips. Sage recoiled reflexively and sniffed. Dried goat strips and something else unidentifiable. Despite her repulsion, Sage knew she needed to eat something. She hadn't had anything since dinner with Vaughn the night before. With a sigh, she opened her mouth and accepted what was offered. *On the bright side, if they wanted you dead, they wouldn't bother feeding you.* It was small consolation.

CHAPTER SIX

Good morning, Henri." Looking for all the world as though she'd just awakened from a restful night's sleep, Vaughn greeted the driver in the French of her youth.

"Good morning." He held the car door for her.

As he pulled out into traffic, Vaughn started up a casual conversation. "I've been getting to see a little of your country."

"Are you enjoying yourself so far?"

"I am, but my head is spinning. It seems like there's so much to know." Vaughn tried her best to appear overwhelmed.

"I'm sure Mademoiselle Sage can help you with that." He peered at her in the rearview mirror.

Pay dirt. Vaughn noted that he said her name with great affection and not a hint of nervousness. Whatever happened to Sage, it was clear that Henri had no knowledge of it.

As if the answer didn't matter to her in the slightest, Vaughn asked, "You like her? Mademoiselle Sage?"

"Oh, yes. She is very nice."

"She's been here a long time. I imagine there must be someone who doesn't think as kindly of her as you do." Vaughn raised an eyebrow as if to say, "C'mon, you can tell me the truth."

"No, ma'am. Everybody adores her." He seemed to search for words. "She has a special light about her. It is impossible not to like her."

"She gets along well with the staff?"

"Oh, yes. And the authorities too."

"Is that so? How do you know that?" Vaughn kept her voice light.

"My cousin is the driver for Jean Baldour."

"Jean…?"

"He is the head of the National Assembly. My cousin tells me Baldour always looks forward to meeting with Mademoiselle Sage because 'she understands the issues.'"

"He said that?"

Henri nodded his head solemnly. Then his face split into a wide grin. "He also says that she is nice to look at."

The comment surprised a laugh out of Vaughn. "Does he now?"

"He is a man," Henri said, and shrugged, as if no other explanation was necessary.

They pulled into the embassy compound.

"Will you be needing me later?" Henri asked.

Vaughn narrowed her eyes in thought. "Yes. I believe I will, Henri."

"Here is my card. Just call this number."

"Thanks," Vaughn said and slid out of the back seat.

Ambassador Dumont shrugged out of his suit jacket. "Who is Vaughn Elliott?" He stood looking down at the daily schedule in the middle of his immaculate desk. His executive assistant sat across from him.

"The DS sent from Washington to oversee security for the upcoming congressional visit."

"Ah, right." Dumont rubbed his suddenly damp palms unconsciously on his pants. He hadn't recognized the name.

"You're meeting with her and Sage at 10:30 a.m."

Dumont coughed at the mention of Sage's name.

"Are you okay, sir?"

"Fine," he choked out.

"Shall I get you some water?"

"No. I'm fine. Um, I've sent Sage on an assignment. A temporary replacement will be here tomorrow. In the meantime, please have all her mail and phone calls forwarded to me."

"Sir?" The executive assistant's brow creased in confusion. "I don't remember seeing any paperwork on a new hire."

"No, no. I'm sorry. My mistake. It was a last minute thing—came directly from Washington. I'm sure the paperwork will be here later today."

"Of course. I'll keep a sharp eye out for it."

Dumont waved her off. His mind was still on the prospect of the morning's meeting. He bit his lip. The last thing he wanted was to meet with this Elliott character. Maybe he could cancel.

"Is there anything else, sir?" The executive assistant's voice sounded hesitant.

Elliott would probably be looking for McNally. He would have to see her and allay any suspicions. "Huh? Oh. No, no. That's all." He ran two fingers under his collar. *God, I hate this.*

"Hi. I'm wondering if you could help me?" Vaughn stood over the desk of some bureaucrat on the second floor. "I'm looking for Sage McNally's office."

"Oh, Sage is down that way," the man said, pointing to the right. "Third door from the end of the hallway."

"Thanks." Vaughn wandered down the hall, making sure to appear as though there was no hurry. She checked out offices to the left and right for inhabitants. The offices on either side of Sage's were mercifully empty. She ducked into Sage's office and closed the door behind her. A broad-daylight search wasn't what she normally would've executed, but there was no time to waste. She would have to take her chances.

The desktop was well-organized, much as it had been in Sage's home. Vaughn searched the in- and out-boxes; everything seemed routine. She checked the drawers and found nothing out of the ordinary. Ditto the filing cabinets. *C'mon, Sage. Help me out here.*

She turned in a circle, trying to figure out what she might have missed. That's when she noticed the desk blotter. It contained all of Sage's appointments for the month, along with assorted doodles. *Bingo.*

Vaughn cocked her head to the side. She could hear footsteps echoing some distance down the hallway. Quickly, she tore off the top sheet, folded it, and put it in her briefcase. By the time the door opened, she was sitting nonchalantly in a visitor's chair.

"Oh. Hi." A tall, gangly man of about thirty stood with one hand on the door knob. In the other hand, he held a tray with two cups of what smelled to Vaughn like coffee. "Um, is Sage here?"

"Sorry." Vaughn shook her head. "I was sort of wondering where she was myself."

"You are..."

"Oh, I'm sorry. Here." Vaughn stood and took the tray from the man, setting it on the blotter. If he was unobservant, he wouldn't notice that a page was missing. "I'm Vaughn Elliott. Diplomatic security from D.C."

"Ah. Sage mentioned you'd be coming. I'm Donald Easton. Public affairs officer." He held out his hand and Vaughn shook it. "Hmm. Odd that Sage wouldn't be here. We start every day with coffee and share intelligence. It's not like her to be late."

"Every day, huh?" Vaughn's mind was calculating. *Could be a good source.*

"Yep. Like clockwork. I bring the coffee. She usually brings something homemade to eat."

"Sounds like a good arrangement to me." Vaughn paused for effect. "So Sage didn't mention to you that she wouldn't be here today?"

"Heck, no. With the congressional visit coming up, we had a lot to talk about."

Donald Easton seemed genuine enough. A nice guy, if a bit geeky. "Please, go ahead and drink your coffee. It'll get cold."

"Do you need some? I could go get more."

"Thank you, no. I'm fine." Vaughn crossed her legs, indicating that she was settling in for the long haul; she hoped he would take the hint. He might be able to give her a good lead, albeit inadvertently. She didn't want to waste the opportunity. "What does a public affairs officer do?"

"Public relations, the media. That sort of thing."

"You and Sage work closely together then?"

"You bet. The two positions go hand-in-hand."

"Is that right? So you and Sage are tight?"

"We've worked together for a year-and-a-half. I'd like to think we're good friends."

"That's nice, since you have to spend so much time together."

"You're telling me. It could've been a nightmare. I've had postings like that. But Sage is great. I love her."

I just bet you do. Vaughn kept her face blank. Time to change the line of questioning. "You're familiar with all of the political factions and the politics of the region?"

"Naturally."

"Maybe you can fill me in a little bit while we wait for Sage."

"Sure. Happy to help." Easton sat down in the other visitor's chair and unbuttoned his suit jacket.

Thank you, Lord. "Are there any volatile factions that might have a grudge against Americans?"

When Easton seemed to hesitate at divulging too much information, Vaughn pushed forward. "If I'm going to keep the congressional delegation safe, I'll need to know if there's any group in particular I should pay attention to." *And I need to know where to start looking for Sage—fast.* It was all Vaughn could do to sit still, but she had no choice. Without knowing who was involved, the fastest way to find Sage was to gather as much information as she could.

"At the moment, everything seems pretty calm. Nobody's feathers are especially ruffled. It should be a pretty uneventful visit, if you're worried about protests and the like."

"Well." Vaughn gave him what she hoped was a relieved smile. "That ought to make my job a little bit easier."

"Yep. It should be a walk in the park."

"It's never that easy, but it sure would be nice if you were right..." *If he's right and there are no obvious enemies, your chances of finding Sage quickly just went down the drain.* Although she didn't hold out much hope, Vaughn had to try one more time.

"For real, Donald? Nobody hates us this week? This must be the only place in the world where that's true." *Give me something to work with, please.*

"For real, and you can call me Don."

"Okay, Don." Vaughn checked her watch. According to the schedule she'd printed out at Sage's house, she and Sage were due to meet with the ambassador in fifteen minutes. She made a show of frowning. "Damn. We're supposed to meet with the big guy now."

"Dumont?"

"Yeah. What's he like?"

Don shrugged his shoulders. "He's a nice enough guy. Career public servant who rose through the ranks. Now that he's been elevated, he likes to think he's a big fish, if you get my drift."

"I do." *In other words, he's a pompous ass.* "Thanks for the assessment. I hate to go in cold."

"I can't believe Sage isn't here yet. I wonder if she had a flat tire or something? Even if she did, knowing her, she would've run the rest of the way."

"Well, I wouldn't worry. I'm sure she'll turn up." Vaughn stood. *As soon as I find her.* She held out her hand. As Don shook it, she said, "Where can I find you if I need anything else?"

"Next door." He jerked his thumb to the left.

"That's handy. Thanks."

"Good luck."

Vaughn picked up her briefcase and stepped into the corridor. "Which way?"

"Up," Don said. "Stairs are over there." He pointed across the way. "Go to the top and make a left."

"Got it. Thanks, again. Send Sage up if you see her." Vaughn waved and set off for the third floor.

"Ah, Ms. Elliott, good to meet you." Ambassador Dumont rose and came around the desk to shake Vaughn's hand.

His hands were clammy, his eyes were beady, and he had facial hair. Vaughn took an immediate dislike to him. "A pleasure to meet you, sir." She made a show of looking around. "I thought your political officer, Sage, would be joining us. I stopped by her office on my way up here but was unable to locate her. I was hoping she was already with you."

"With m-me? Ah, good heavens, no."

Vaughn studied the ambassador. Her gut was screaming. *He's definitely nervous.* "No?" She raised her eyebrows innocently.

"Sage is on assignment." Dumont turned away from Vaughn and walked back behind his desk.

Vaughn's jaw clicked shut just before the ambassador turned around. *On assignment?* It was all she could do not to come across the desk and shake him. Instead she said, "I was under the impression that Sage's assignment for the next three weeks was to be the control officer for the upcoming congressional visit."

"Exactly right," Dumont agreed. He looked everywhere but at Vaughn.

"She was supposed to liaise with me." *Look at me, you scumbag.*

"True, Ms. Elliott, but there are other aspects of the congressional visit that fall within Sage's purview as well."

"Do you mind telling me what assignment you gave Sage and when I might expect her back?" Vaughn kept her tone inquisitive, an effort that took all her self-control.

"Not at all." Dumont bit his lip and shuffled some papers on his desk. "There are two school visits planned during the course of the delegation's stay in Mali. I sent Sage to meet with officials from both schools."

On the face of it, the story would've seemed plausible enough, except that Sage had spent the night with Vaughn and hadn't said a word about going out of town. More than that, Vaughn had seen the sneaker, the blood, and the drag marks with her own eyes.

"When did she leave?" Vaughn knew she needed to be careful. She didn't want to tip her hand, and it wouldn't do to be impertinent to the ambassador. Still, she needed to play this out.

"I-I'm not sure. I gave her the assignment yesterday. I assume she either left last night or this morning." Dumont sat up straighter, seemingly taking umbrage at being questioned by Vaughn. "I realize Sage's absence may leave you feeling adrift, Ms. Elliott. But there are many details that need to be attended to in the coming weeks."

The ambassador clearly intended to take some measure of control over the meeting. "Please don't be concerned—I've taken your needs into consideration. While Sage is gone, I've sent for another expert to assist you."

This time Vaughn couldn't keep the surprise off her face. "You—" *You didn't waste any time, did you?* "Is there a way to get in touch with Sage while she's...away?"

"I'm sorry. No. Cell phones are useless outside of the city. Please don't worry, Ms. Elliott. I've taken care to make sure you have everything you need and our full cooperation. Obviously, the security of the delegation is our first concern, but there are others, as well. As a result, it was my opinion that one control officer would not be sufficient to cover all of the many bases that need to be covered in such a short period of time."

Don't be concerned; don't worry; I've got every detail covered. Vaughn mocked him in her mind. She balled her hands into fists and stuck them in her pockets. It wouldn't do to throttle the ambassador on her first assignment. Washington might frown on that.

"You're right, I'm sure, Mr. Ambassador. Who is my new contact and when will I get to meet him or her?"

"Tomorrow morning. I can't recall the name at the moment, but I'll have my executive assistant set up a meeting for the two of you."

"That's most kind of you." Vaughn got the feeling she was about to be dismissed. Before that happened, she wanted a little more information. "I'm scheduled to meet with some of the local and national political leaders in the coming week. Is there anything you think I should know? Do you have any concerns?"

Dumont seemed to consider. "No. Relations between our two countries are good, and our personnel have been well accepted in the community."

"Do you have any advice for me? Anything in particular I should focus on? Any of the activities or events which you think might be more problematic than any of the others?"

"I expect the visit to go off without a hitch." The ambassador met Vaughn's eyes for the first time. "It's your job to make it so, is it not?"

"Yes, sir, from a security standpoint, that is certainly true. And I assure you, it will." Vaughn hoped he could not see the anger snapping behind her eyes. "Are there any questions I can answer for you, sir?"

"Not at this point, Ms. Elliott. I'm sure you know your business quite well. If you need anything further from me, just let my executive assistant know."

"Thank you, sir, I'll do that." Vaughn picked up her briefcase, pivoted, and strode out of the office. She didn't stop walking until she was two blocks away from the embassy.

"You miserable son-of-a-bitch. You sanctimonious, lying sack of shit!" Vaughn turned left, then right. Finally, she growled deep in her throat and thrust her free hand in her pocket.

The sun was high in the sky. At least five hours had passed since Sage disappeared. Vaughn closed her eyes. She could be almost anywhere by now. *I need help.* Purposefully, Vaughn headed for the hotel. It was time to call in reinforcements.

≼ঠ৯≽

"Oui, Mademoiselle?" The clerk at the registration desk in the Hilton was all polite attention.

"I don't want to trouble you," Vaughn said, "but I wonder if you might have a different room available for me?"

"Is something wrong? Can I do something? Is your room not satisfactory?"

"No, no." *Just a precaution.* "I wonder if you might have something available on the top floor, though? I'd love to enjoy the view."

"Bien sûr." The clerk's fingers flew over the keys. "Ah, I have just the thing." He looked up at her. "Your room is registered to the U.S. State Department. Will that stay the same?"

"Yes. It's direct billed to their account, correct?"

"Oui, c'est ça."

"That's perfect."

The State Department probably had fifteen or more rooms booked in the hotel on their account. It would be harder for anyone to target Vaughn's room if they weren't sure which one was hers. If that had been her only concern, though, she could've stayed in the same suite.

The room switch was in case anyone already had found Vaughn and planted a listening device in her suite or set up surveillance. She hadn't brought equipment to detect such things—hadn't, in truth, figured on needing it.

Since the ambassador appeared to be involved, or at least complicit, Vaughn had to assume the kidnappers were a sophisticated bunch with advanced tools. She made a mental shopping list of supplies and technology she should acquire.

"Shall I have someone move your things, Mademoiselle?" The clerk was holding out the new room key to her.

"No. That won't be necessary. I'll take care of it. Thank you so much for accommodating me."

The hallway was empty when Vaughn emerged from the stairwell. The thread still was intact in the door lock. A quick check of the drawers showed that they hadn't been tampered with. *That doesn't mean someone isn't listening or watching.*

Vaughn didn't want to take any chances. She packed up her few belongings, made a last sweep of the room, and headed for the top floor. Once she had settled in, she pulled out her cell phone. First, she called Henri to tell him she wouldn't need him after all. Then she dialed an international exchange.

"Oui." The voice on the other end of the phone was a deep rumble.

"Jackson, my man, is that any way to greet an old friend?"

"Vaughn Elliott? Is that really you?"

Vaughn laughed. "In the flesh."

"I'll be dipped in chocolate."

She laughed at the use of such an American expression in heavily accented French. "How's tricks?"

"You reappear in my life after twenty years, and you act as though I saw you yesterday. You are something, Vaughn Elliott."

"I've missed you, Jackson. But I've kept tabs on you. There's been less wanton police brutality in Burkina Faso since you became the head gendarme. I'm proud of you."

"You knew of my promotion?" His voice swelled with pride at the compliment.

"You bet. You were always one of my favorites."

"You taught me well."

"You were easy to teach. But enough of that. I don't want you to get too much of a swelled head."

Jackson laughed—the full, rich sound of a man who enjoyed life. "So, the truth is you didn't call to reminisce, yes? What is it you need, Vaughn Elliott?"

"Perceptive, as always, Jackson. I need your help. I've run into a bit of trouble next door in Mali."

"You're in Mali?"

"Yes, and I'm feeling like a fish out of water."

"Crossing borders and interfering in another country's politics is risky business."

"I know. I wouldn't ask if it wasn't desperately important, my friend. And I don't want anything official. In fact, the less official, the better, if you get my drift."

"Hmm. I do. I do, indeed. Tell me all about it, and I will see what I can do for you."

Vaughn smiled for the first time in hours. *Hold tight, Sage. The cavalry is coming.* After explaining the situation to Jackson, she hung up and dialed another number.

"Hi, I need help..."

CHAPTER SEVEN

S age had no concept of how much time had passed, except that the heat of the sun seemed less intense. She estimated that they'd been traveling for hours. Her body ached, the blindfold itched and, despite the paucity of water she'd been given, her bladder was making itself known.

Other than the noise of the camels' hooves and her captors' continual bickering, there wasn't a sound to be heard. Although Sage hadn't given up on escaping, she knew her chances of surviving on her own this far from civilization were slim. She clung to the hope that if they had wanted her dead, they would've killed her already.

It took several seconds for Sage to realize that the camels had come to a halt. She pitched forward as the camel went to its knees. Rough hands pulled her from the camel's back, even as others untied her from the saddle horn. A sharp object prodded her in the back, propelling her forward. She heard what sounded like a shovel digging, and her heart leapt into her throat.

She whipped her head right and left. *They're going to bury me alive.* Sage had seen documentaries on ancient customs where offenders were buried up to their necks in the sand and left to die. Her knees buckled. Strong fingers gripped her elbows and held her upright.

Voices next to her ear made her jump. She was lifted off her feet and set down in a narrow hole. It was deep enough for her to stand in. *Oh, God.* A sob rose in her parched throat. Desperately, she twisted her wrists, trying to free herself. Strong hands gripped hers, stopping her motion. Words were spoken that she didn't understand—a command. When she didn't respond, the voice said, in halting, mangled French, "pee."

Enthusiastically, she nodded. The hands released her and she heard footsteps recede a short distance away. She squatted. When she'd finished, she was lifted back out of the hole. *Thank you, God, for not leaving me to die.* She wanted to weep.

Pressure on her shoulder forced her to sit. A water bottle was thrust between her hands and she drank greedily. Around her, she heard the creak of leather and the pounding of wood. They were erecting tents, stopping for the night. She closed her eyes in thanks behind the blindfold. She'd lived through the day.

Vaughn hunched over the desk and smoothed out the page she had taken from Sage's blotter. She compared the appointments listed with a roster of embassy employees she'd pulled from her briefcase. "Sometimes being a pain in the ass is a good thing," Vaughn muttered to herself. She'd insisted, over his vehement objections, that Stephen conduct thorough background checks on everyone connected in any way with the embassy. As a first step, he'd provided her with the roster during their initial meeting.

Sage didn't have anything on her calendar for the previous day. The appointment with the ambassador was marked for that morning. Vaughn noted that she and Sage were scheduled to meet with Jean Baldour the next day and tour the hall where the National Assembly held session. Senate Majority Leader Stowe would address the assembly on the second day of the delegation's visit.

Sage had made a notation next to the entry—*make sure Agent Elliott has a chance to look at the layout for security purposes.* Vaughn smiled, pleased that Sage understood her needs.

Similar appointments were scheduled for the remainder of the week. Vaughn drummed her fingers on the table. *Certainly not the behavior of someone who thinks she's going out of town.*

The ambassador had said he'd only ordered Sage to make the site visit the previous day. Although she knew in her gut that he was lying, training and experience forced Vaughn to consider every possibility, including the slim chance that the assignment was real. Perhaps Sage hadn't had time to mark it on the calendar or adjust the schedule. "Ridiculous. She would've told me during dinner."

Vaughn frowned. Maybe Sage had planned to break the news when she got back from her run. Telling Vaughn she was being passed off to another control officer in the middle of their interlude might have been a real mood killer. She might well have decided to table the discussion until morning. "If that's true, then we're back to square one and the ambassador's off the hook."

The phone on the table vibrated and Vaughn snatched it up quickly. "Yes?"

"As of fifteen minutes ago, I'm officially on vacation."

"Justine..."

"Don't, Vaughn. You called. I answered. I want to do this."

Vaughn balled her free hand into a fist. She didn't want to involve Justine. If the Company found out, it could jeopardize her career. Vaughn had only asked her for some intel and a few pieces of equipment.

As if reading her mind, Justine said, "You can't give your full attention to Sage and focus on the congressional visit at the same time, and you know it. If you try, you'll be endangering all of them. It's your first assignment for State, and it involves the safety of the highest ranking elected female in U.S. history. You don't have a choice, Vaughn. The visit has to be your priority."

The truth of Justine's remark hit Vaughn like a sledge hammer in the middle of the chest. "Okay. I won't tell you I'm not grateful as hell for the extra eyes and ears."

"Good. I've been working on the intel. Not much there. Dumont is a career civil servant. Did his undergrad at University of Pennsylvania, then went directly on to grad school—Fletcher, which is part of Tufts."

"Childhood?" Vaughn asked, pulling out a note pad.

"His parents were well-off. Father a hot-shot lawyer with a big firm in New York. Mother was a career socialite. Little Raymond went to a private high school and, by all accounts, led a pretty sheltered life as a boy."

"Poor little rich kid. Did he join the diplomatic corps right out of Fletcher?"

"Yep. His first assignment was in..."

Vaughn could hear the clicking of keys on a keyboard.

"The Ivory Coast. After that he did stints in Niger, Mali, Brussels, Switzerland—"

"Wait! "He was in Mali before?"

"Yes. From 1992 to 1994."

"Hmm. That's interesting, don't you think?"

"It makes sense that they would appoint him to an ambassadorship in a place he was already familiar with, Vaughn."

"True. Still…it's worth exploring, anyway."

"I've already got someone doing a little digging."

"Do you now?"

"What? You didn't think I'd know enough to follow up on something with obvious potential significance?"

"Mea culpa. I should've trusted that you'd have it covered." Vaughn did her best to sound contrite. "When did Dumont get appointed ambassador?"

"Last year. Confirmed by the Senate in October."

"When was he nominated?"

"Two years ago. The Senate was holding some of the nominations hostage in a disagreement with the White House over the nominee for ambassador to the United Nations."

"Ain't politics grand?" Vaughn tapped her pen on the pad. "It might be worth looking into how much money our illustrious ambassador contributed to the president's election campaign. How much do ambassadorships go for these days?"

"Vaughn Elliott. You are so cynical." Justine chuckled knowingly, and Vaughn realized that she had already investigated this angle.

"Well, how much was it?"

"A cool quarter of a million dollars."

Vaughn whistled. "That's a lot of dough for a career civil servant."

"Mmm-hmm. Sure is."

"I suppose you're already following the money trail."

"Naturally. Looks like he inherited a bundle from his daddy."

"So he bought himself an office in a third world country. Wonder what Paris goes for?"

"More than I've got in my bank account, that's for sure."

"You and me both." Vaughn walked to the window and looked out at the lights winking in the city. "Not to rush you, but when do you think we'll have answers on Dumont's previous stay in this lovely backwater?"

"Tomorrow or the next day."

Vaughn thought about Sage, out there somewhere, bleeding and alone. She pressed her forehead to the glass. "See if you can't expedite that, okay?"

"We'll find her, Vaughn. I promise you we will. Keep the faith."

"Thanks." Vaughn idly wondered if she even remembered what faith was and when she'd lost it in herself.

"By the way, I'll be there tomorrow. Late afternoon."

"You'll—" The announcement jarred Vaughn back to the moment. In order for Justine to get there so quickly, she would already have to be in Paris.

"I heard Bamako was a great vacation spot."

Justine's tone was light, but Vaughn could imagine what it had taken for her to arrange everything in less than four hours. "Where were you when I called earlier?" She hadn't thought to ask at the time.

"Finishing up an assignment in Brussels."

Vaughn swallowed around the lump in her throat. "I can't tell you what this means to me." Maybe faith wasn't such a bad thing to have. With Justine on the ground with her, the odds of locating Sage improved significantly.

"Don't mention it. Besides, I like having you owe me."

"Seems to me there are already debts outstanding on my tab."

"I'm stockpiling. Where should I meet you?"

For the first time since she'd seen the sneaker and the blood, Vaughn felt energized. "I don't know where I'll be at that point. It depends on what happens tonight and how my meeting goes with Sage's replacement in the morning." Then there was the matter of the appointment with Baldour. She strode back to the table and stared at the schedule on the blotter.

"A little bit too convenient, that."

"What, the replacement? Yeah, I thought the same thing. I'm telling you, Dumont couldn't look me in the eye. He knew it sounded bad. The prick." Vaughn gripped the sides of the table to keep from punching something. If only she could've shaken the truth out of him, Sage might be safe now.

"We'll get to the bottom of it, Vaughn."

"Time's not on our side."

"We'll move heaven and earth. You're doing everything you can."

Unspoken between them was the memory of Sara and the explosion. How many times had Justine said the exact same words back then?

"Everything I can isn't good enough." Vaughn's anguish was still close to the surface.

"Don't do this to yourself. You have to believe, Vaughn. If you don't, Sage doesn't stand a chance."

"We don't even know if she's alive."

"We don't know that she's not," Justine countered.

The muscles in Vaughn's jaw clenched. She couldn't argue with that. Shame washed through her veins along with doubts and self-recrimination.

"Who're you meeting with tonight?"

Vaughn recognized the deliberate change in topic and accepted it. "An old buddy of mine from a lifetime ago. A wild man from my time in Burkina Faso. I saw potential in him, rescued him from a jail cell, and molded him into a fine soldier for freedom. Now he's in charge of the country's police force."

"It's nice to have good friends nearby."

"Indeed, it is. He's a little jumpy. Wouldn't do for Burkina Faso to get tangled up in Mali's affairs."

"I'm sure you've assured him of the confidential nature of the operation."

"I have. I told him I wanted this as unofficial and untraceable as possible. I gave him my word I'd protect him if he helped me."

"Obviously he said yes."

Vaughn shrugged. "He owes me and he knows it. We'll be square after this."

"How much help will he be?"

"He knows the terrain, he's got some contacts, and he's sitting on a nice cache of firepower he got from us several years ago."

"That's handy. I couldn't begin to fathom how to explain that a tourist needed several semi-automatics, scopes, and night vision glasses."

Vaughn checked her watch. "I've got to get going. Give me a call when you touch down."

"Will do. Make sure you get some sleep tonight, Vaughn. You won't be any help to Sage if you're dead on your feet."

"These are the golden hours—if we don't find her within the first forty-eight hours..." Vaughn let the thought trail off. Some things didn't bear thinking about.

"Keep the faith. I'll be there soon."

"Thanks, Justine. Travel safely."

The street was dark, but Vaughn's eyes had long since adapted to the lack of light. Having arrived a half hour before, she stood in the shadows at the side of Sage's house. She'd watched as people arrived home, presumably from work. There was no unusual activity on the street that she could discern. If anyone was paying particular attention to Sage's house, it wasn't obvious.

"Nice to see you too," she said quietly to the man who had snuck up behind her.

"Damn, Vaughn Elliott. You're still good."

"Hello, Jackson. You're lucky I knew it was you. If I hadn't, you'd be dead by now."

"Then I'll consider myself fortunate. I assume there is a reason why we're meeting here."

"You always were a bright man. I want to show you a few things. Come with me." Vaughn moved to the back of the house and used the key to get in. Night lights burned dimly in the kitchen and hallway. It was all the illumination they needed, and all that she would allow within sight of a window. There was no sense taking chances on being spotted.

Vaughn moved down the hall to Sage's office. Since there were no windows in here, she clicked on the lamp. A quick survey of the area convinced her that no one had been there since she'd left that morning.

From the desk, she picked up a picture. Sage smiled up at her in a graduation cap and gown. Vaughn took a deep breath to settle the sharp, sudden ache in her heart. She held the photo out for Jackson.

"This is who we're looking for. Her name is Sage McNally."

Jackson, perhaps sensing something more than professional interest, put a beefy hand on Vaughn's shoulder. "She seems like a lovely girl. We'll get her back, mark my words."

Rather than trust her voice, Vaughn simply nodded and moved to a map on the wall. She cleared her throat. "Okay, based on the pins she's placed on the map, I'm assuming these are either places she's visited, or they're places with some sort of political significance." Vaughn glanced at Jackson. "What's your guess?"

Jackson studied the map. "Djenne, Mopti, Timbuktu. These are all major centers. I would not be surprised to know that she had visited all those regions. At the very least, she would have to be familiar with the politics in those parts of the country, and the politicians."

"Are any of these areas politically volatile? I'll be meeting with some Americans tomorrow to get their perspective, but I want to know what you hear on the ground."

Jackson pursed his lips in thought. "I would say not. Truthfully, Mali has been very quiet lately. We patrol the border and keep an eye on things, but I have not heard any reports to alarm me."

"What about splinter groups? Any of those?"

"There are, of course, factions. But there is no violent unrest or anti-American sentiment."

Vaughn blew out an explosive breath and ran her fingers through her hair. *Nothing. There's nothing to go on here.* "Let's go." Shutting off the light, she pulled Jackson along with her.

When they'd exited the house, he asked, "Where are we going?"

"First, we're going down the street. I want to show you where she was taken."

"You realize it is dark, Vaughn Elliott, right?"

"Mmm-hmm. Get in," she said, gesturing to the passenger seat of Sage's car.

They drove to the site of Sage's abduction in silence. After driving around the block to ensure that they were alone, Vaughn parked the car at an angle so that the headlights would provide illumination.

"Take a look and tell me your impressions. Then I've got a question for you."

"All right." Jackson made a wide sweep of the area, then focused in on the drag marks and the blood. Several times he knelt down and put his face practically in the dirt. Finally, he stood up.

"What do you think?"

"Four, maybe five of them and her. All men, judging from the size of the feet."

"I agree. And the feet are exactly what I want to talk about." Vaughn knelt down and motioned for Jackson to join her. "Look here. This is a pretty distinctive footprint."

"Agreed."

"I want to know what kind of shoe or boot makes that. I can tell you right now, it's no American military boot, and I've never seen a shoe that makes a mark like that."

Jackson squinted closely at the print. "I'll want to come back and have a look in the daylight to be sure, but my opinion would be that it's consistent with what a Tuareg rebel would wear."

"A Tuareg—I thought the Tuareg were nomads who rode around on camels up in Timbuktu?"

Jackson laughed. "It's a little more complicated than that. As I said, I'd like to have a look in daylight."

"All right." Vaughn relented because she had no other choice. "Did you bring me what I asked?"

"And then some. I have a brother who lives on the outskirts of town. That's where I'll be staying for the next few days. I've got everything stashed there."

"You won't be missed?"

"Even I am entitled to visit family once in a while." He clapped Vaughn on the shoulder. "It is very late. You should get some sleep. We will not find this woman tonight, but we will find her soon."

"I hope you're right, my friend." Vaughn thought once again of Sage, scared, bleeding, and alone. "You have to be right."

CHAPTER EIGHT

Ray Dumont stood on a balcony overlooking the city. His silk robe whispered in the breeze as the fabric brushed against the railing. It was late—very late—but his thoughts were churning and sleep would not come.

This posting was the pinnacle of his career. An ambassadorship. What would his father have said? He would've said the end justifies the means. If it took a little cash to tip the scales in his favor, what was the harm?

Ray had devoted his life to the diplomatic corps. It was only right that he should get something back in return. This nasty business would all be over soon, and he would be rewarded handsomely. The ambassadorship was only the beginning. He was going places in politics. Before long, his career would outshine his father's reputation and he would move out from under that long shadow. Ray Dumont would be remembered for himself, not for his heritage.

Would his father have worried about the petty details? No. "Don't sweat the small stuff, Ray." That's what he would've said. "Every person has to take care of himself. If mistakes are made, consequences must be paid."

Ashton, Trindle, McNally. They made mistakes. The consequences weren't on his conscience. Each of them was responsible for their own incompetence. Ashton and Trindle were lucky—their mistakes would be little more than black marks on their records. Dumont frowned. McNally was troubling. She had potential. It was a shame, really. But it couldn't be helped. Tomorrow her place would be taken by someone hand-picked for the job by Washington.

Dumont ran his fingers over the smooth surface of the railing. Aaron Torgensen. According to his dossier, he spoke impeccable French, was a professor of International Studies at Johns Hopkins, and was an advisor to the president on African affairs. He was not, technically, in the diplomatic corps, but Washington was making an exception in this case. Torgensen's presence was only temporary. When the delegation left the country, his work would be done.

It was important, in the face of the upcoming congressional visit, that the politics be handled by someone with extensive knowledge of the region, the political factions, and the history of the republic. The president wanted to ensure that the mission had every chance of success. This was important to the country.

When it was over, Dumont could get out of this God-forsaken place and continue his ascension. Yes, he was on his way to big things. With a smile, he turned and walked back into his sumptuous bedroom. Sweet dreams, indeed.

Sage heard muffled sounds outside the tent. She bit the side of her cheek to keep from screaming as she tried unsuccessfully to stretch her cramped back muscles. She was curled on her side on the hard ground in the fetal position, her hands cuffed around a wooden pole and bound to her ankles with a short chain.

With the blindfold still in place, Sage had little concept of day or night, but the absolute blackness led her to believe that dawn had yet to break. Physical discomfort, a blinding headache caused by the blow to the head, and dehydration had made it impossible for her to sleep for more than a few minutes at a time.

Despite her best efforts to identify sounds, she failed to pinpoint their location beyond knowing with certainty that they were not near any city or town. If there was water nearby, like the Niger River, she could neither hear it or smell it.

Footsteps came closer, and Sage gritted her teeth. At least to that point she'd been alone in the tent—or so she believed. Her heart rate spiked and she could not stifle a scream as something sharp was jabbed into her back. *My God!* Although she had no frame of reference for it, Sage could've sworn it felt like the point of a sword.

Harsh words rolled over her as her ankles were unshackled and she was yanked to her feet.

The pulse pounded in Sage's ears. *Relax, if they'd wanted you dead, they wouldn't have let you sleep first.* The point of the sword dug into the small of her back. Her legs felt like Jell-O.

Careful not to move too quickly, she took advantage of being upright and flexed her shoulders, then arched her back. She could hear the nervous shuffle of feet behind her, and so decided not to push her luck any further.

Other footsteps and voices approached. She heard the unmistakable metallic click of a gun being cocked. Sweat popped out on her forehead. Instinctively she thrashed against the handcuffs that tethered her to the pole. *No, I'm not ready to die. Not here. Not like this.* She whipped her head first right, then left, but the blindfold held.

A voice shouted, and Sage froze as the barrel of the gun touched her temple. She squeezed her eyes shut tightly and cringed. A hand clamped down on her shoulder. Her breath came in short rasps, sounding loud in her ears. Then the pressure of the handcuffs was gone. An arm wrapped around her neck and dragged her backward. Behind the blindfold, her eyes popped open wide.

The change in the air told her she was outside the tent. Before she could register any other impressions, the ground disappeared out from underneath her feet, and she gasped. The gun barrel stayed against her ear as the arm around her neck tightened. She fought for breath, choking. The pressure eased when her feet touched the ground, and she realized with a rush of relief that she'd been dropped into the "bathroom" again. When she was done, hands under her elbows lifted her back out.

She didn't struggle as she was marched forward, nor when she was hoisted atop the camel and her hands were fastened once again to the saddle. All that mattered was that she was still alive. She said a prayer of thanks.

❦❧

Nothing made any sense. Vaughn slapped her note pad hard on the table. If Jackson was right and the abductors were Tuareg and not American, then why was the ambassador so jumpy? What was the connection? Was there one?

"Damn it." Vaughn got up so quickly the chair toppled over backward and landed with a thud on the carpeted floor. She kicked it for good measure, paused, then kicked it again. The clock on the wall read 5:42 a.m. Sage had been gone for twenty-four hours. *Where are you, Sage? Are you okay?*

"Stupid question, Elliott. She's bleeding and frightened out of her mind. No, she's not okay."

Vaughn replayed, yet again, her meeting with Dumont. There was no question that he'd been nervous and deceptive. She hadn't imagined that. After interrogating hundreds of individuals over the years, she'd developed a keen sense for knowing when someone wasn't on the up and up. Dumont was definitely one of those. But what was he hiding? And, maybe more importantly, why?

More information. That was what she needed. Without it, she was just spinning her wheels. Sage had shared some of her background, but Vaughn needed to know more. Was there something in Sage's past that made her a target? Although it didn't feel to Vaughn as if the abduction was the result of an old grudge, she couldn't rule it out. Maybe Sage and the ambassador had a history of some kind.

Vaughn frowned. It could just as easily be that Sage had made a faux pas that had enraged some Malian political leader. Or that the kidnapping was purely political and not at all personal. As an American and the political officer, Sage was a symbol. Taking her would send a message to the American government.

Perhaps the ambassador had received a note from the kidnappers and feared for his own safety. That would've shaken him up. If they'd told him he would be next if he didn't cooperate, or that if he told anyone about Sage's abduction they'd kill her or him, it would account for his odd behavior.

But it didn't account for the ambassador being able to secure a replacement for Sage so quickly. It would remain to be seen who that replacement was. If it was someone from within the embassy or from a neighboring country, it would follow that he or she could've arrived within twenty-four hours. If not…well, that would certainly raise more questions in Vaughn's mind.

In any case, she was no closer to understanding why Sage had been taken, or where she was, than she had been when all this started.

Vaughn shook her head. What she needed was a half-hour power nap and a shower. It was going to be a long day.

≪≫

"Vaughn Elliott?"

"Good morning, Jackson." Vaughn dodged an old man riding a bike on the sidewalk and switched the cell phone to her other ear. "What do you have for me?"

"Ah, direct and to the point as always."

"When there's no time to waste, yes."

"I went back to the scene at daybreak. The footprints are definitely Tuareg, or at the very least, consistent with the Tuareg. I still believe there were four or five of them. That's a lot for one small woman, in my opinion. Don't you agree?"

"I do agree. What I can't figure out is, why was that necessary? To involve that many people would seem to indicate that they needed to be sure of success and that she was a high-value target."

"True," Jackson said.

"Why? What could be so important about a mid-level, seemingly well-liked, career diplomat who's never held a position more important than political officer?"

"You would know better than I. While you are working on that, I will map all of the known Tuareg enclaves anywhere within a one hundred mile radius of Bamako. My local contacts can make some very discreet inquiries. If anyone saw the woman or knows anything about what happened to her, I will find out."

"Thank you, my friend." While Jackson's approach was the only logical and practical way to proceed, they both knew it would take days, not hours, of detective work.

As if reading her thoughts, Jackson said, "I promise you, we will work as fast as we can."

"I know. Be careful. I'd rather not tip off anyone that we're searching."

"Understood. I will call you as soon as I know anything."

"Actually, I've got another member of the team flying in later today. I'd like us all to get together tonight, but not at my hotel."

"My brother's house is available."

"It's out of the way?"

"It's safe."

"Then we'll make it our headquarters. We'll meet where we did last night...1930 hours. You can drive us to your brother's." Vaughn closed the phone. She rubbed the sore spot over her heart. Slow, deliberate progress leading to Sage's eventual return wasn't good enough—not by a long shot. Every fiber of Vaughn's being demanded that she go out in the field immediately and turn over every grain of sand until she found her.

Running off blindly with no clear idea of where she is and no clue as to the motivations or capabilities of the kidnappers. Brilliant, Elliott. Stop thinking with your heart and use your head. Your heart won't save Sage now.

Vaughn shoved her hands in her pockets. Intellectually, she knew that finding Sage without gathering more information would be next to impossible. The embassy building loomed before her. Her gut told her the answers she needed were inside. Besides, Justine was right—the congressional visit had to be her priority—except that in her heart, it wasn't.

Aaron Torgensen was a tall, slim man. His dress pants were sharply creased and there were no wrinkles in his silk shirt. Vaughn noted the Gucci loafers and the expensive belt. Not exactly the attire of a government employee.

When he shook her hand, his grip was fish-like. But there was something else. *Calluses. He's got calluses on the inside and outside edge of his palms.* Vaughn tucked the impression away for later examination. Something else about him was bothering her. She couldn't shake a nagging feeling that she'd met him before.

"It's a pleasure to meet you, Vaughn. You don't mind if I call you Vaughn, do you?"

"Not at all, Aaron. You don't mind if I call you Aaron?"

"Of course not. I'd prefer it, in fact."

Even apart from her suspicions, something about the man irritated her. She chalked it up to the fact that he wasn't Sage. *Get over it, Elliott.*

"Did you have a pleasant flight?" Vaughn helped herself to a seat at the small conference table. They were tucked away in a corner room on the second floor that Vaughn imagined doubled as a break room for embassy employees.

"As pleasant as flights ever get." He joined her at the table. Although he smiled, his eyes remained cool.

"Where did they pluck you from?"

"Baltimore."

"Wow. That's rough. You couldn't have had much notice."

"No. But then, I didn't need much."

"I didn't realize political officers moved around so quickly." Vaughn would have a thorough background check completed on Aaron Torgensen before the day was out, but she was interested to hear what he would volunteer.

"I wouldn't know." At Vaughn's raised eyebrow, he said, "I'm not a political officer."

Fascinating. Vaughn tried for her best "perplexed" expression. "You're not?"

"No. I'm an academic. I teach in the International Studies department at Johns Hopkins."

"Wow. So how did you end up here?"

"Mali has been my life's passion. I'm considered somewhat of an expert on the country and its politics. Occasionally, I advise the president and the State Department. Based on the historic nature of the upcoming congressional visit, they asked me to come here and assist in assuring that everything went smoothly."

"That's impressive. It wasn't a problem to take off mid-semester?"

"The president has asked me to serve my country. Do you really think the university board members would say they couldn't spare me?"

"No, I suppose not. I imagine the prestige of having one of their instructors hand-picked for such an important assignment would outweigh any other concerns."

"Indeed. Now, shall we get down to business?"

Vaughn nodded. She had what she wanted from him, and she'd know soon enough if his story checked out.

~~⚬~~

Three hours later, Vaughn and Torgensen agreed to take a break—Torgensen to settle into the hotel before their early afternoon meeting with Jean Baldour, and Vaughn to check in with her security team.

Torgensen stood at the window in his hotel room at the Hilton. He pulled out his cell phone and pushed redial.

"Report."

"I'm in place."

"Good. Any difficulties?"

"I don't know yet. I met with Elliott this morning for several hours. We're scheduled to see the head of the National Assembly in an hour."

"Is she going to be a problem?"

"She asked a lot of questions, but I think she accepted the explanation."

"Did she ask anything about the girl?"

"No."

"Interesting. Keep an eye on her just the same."

"Right."

"And the good Ambassador Dumont?"

"I saw him briefly when I arrived. He's a nervous fellow, but I don't foresee any trouble with him."

"Excellent."

"If that's all, I've got homework to do before our meeting and not much time to get ready."

"Very well. Check in at least once a day, more if there are any significant developments."

"Yes, sir."

The line went dead. Torgensen looked at his watch. He had fifty minutes to become an expert on the National Assembly and Jean Baldour.

~~⚬~~

Vaughn did meet with Stephen and his team—just long enough to get from them the background files on all of the security officers who would play any role before and during the congressional visit. Then she dialed a number in Paris.

"Oui?"

"Bonjour, Sabastien."

"Elliott?"

"C'est moi." Vaughn heard the whir and click of machinery and keyboards in the background.

"What can I do for you today? Track down some hapless drug smuggler, ruin some foreign government's economy?"

"Nothing quite that exciting, I'm afraid."

"Are you slowing down in your old age? Is that it?"

"Watch it, pipsqueak. Do you have enough facial hair to shave yet?" Vaughn smiled indulgently. Sabastien Vaupaul was little more than a pimple-faced kid when she'd met him—a computer hacker who had unwittingly disrupted a large undercover case she was working. She saw in him tremendous promise as an ally and recruited him to join the CIA. He'd been her friend ever since.

"Touché," Sabastien said. "What absolutely vital piece of information do you need today, oh exalted one?"

"Cut the crap, Sabastien. I need some background checks."

"That's too easy."

"I also want a detailed topographical map with every known location of the Tuareg in Mali and neighboring countries. If there are more than two Tuareg living in an area, I want to know about it."

"How do you expect me to find that out?"

"You're the genius, remember? How about world census data, political parties, religious groups, places of worship, trade routes, that sort of thing? Use your imagination."

Vaughn heard Sabastien groan. "I suppose you want all this yesterday, right?"

"See, you are a genius."

"Give me the names for the background checks. I assume you want the works?"

"Yes. If they've gotten a parking ticket in the last forty years, I want to know it. Give me personal data, professional details, cross check any prior relationships—everything and anything you can find. Oh, and I want pictures too."

"Okay."

"Raymond Dumont—he's the U.S. ambassador to Mali—Sage McNally, who works for State, and Aaron Torgensen." Vaughn was certain that Justine had done a thorough job on her background check of Dumont, but it never hurt to have a second source.

"Got it."

Vaughn chewed her lower lip as she worked through what else she wanted. "Can you get me a phone log from any carrier, anywhere in the world?"

"Can birds fly?"

"Some, smart boy, but not all."

Sabastien laughed. "Point taken. Yes, most likely I can find a way."

"I want a listing of any incoming or outgoing call Dumont has made or received, both at the residence and in his office, in the past two weeks."

"Hmm…the ambassador probably has a tie line for long distance calls, so that might present a bit of a challenge. Still, I should have it in your inbox before the day is over."

"A tie line?"

"Umm-hmm." Vaughn heard the clicking of computer keys and she knew that Sabastien already was working on the case.

"What's a tie line?"

"It means all of his long distance calls are routed through an 800 number in the U.S."

"Is that a problem?"

"Nothing I can't overcome."

"Also, any internal or external calls Sage McNally made in the last week."

"Okay. She works in the embassy?"

"Yes. I figure what I'm looking for are calls made during work hours."

"Well, that narrows it down," Sabastien said. "Okay, I'm on it."

"Thanks. How long will it take for the rest?"

"That depends on the firewalls I have to bust through. I should be able to get everything to you by later tonight."

"Okay. Sabastien?"

"Oui?"

"This one's personal—so please keep it quiet."

"You always know you can count on me, Elliott."

"That's why I called you." Vaughn shut the phone and tapped it against the palm of her hand. Something was off.

Sabastien was the best in the information business, and he was a friend. Yet, he never mentioned Vaughn's transfer from the Company and he never questioned why, if she was no longer working, she would need this kind of intel. If he'd known that she was no longer on the payroll, he should've hesitated to do the work, or at least he should've indicated that Vaughn was putting him in a tough spot.

Was it possible that he didn't know she'd been dumped? She hadn't spoken to him in a year. He was a hidden asset, and as such, was isolated by definition. Still...

It was just one more piece of the puzzle that made no sense.

CHAPTER NINE

Y ou look great," Vaughn said, hugging Justine briefly.
"Thanks for the lie. I'm sure I look like crap. That flight always does me in."

"Better recover quickly, we've got work to do."

"I'm ready." Justine squeezed Vaughn's arm as they walked toward the parking lot. "We'll find Sage. I promise you, we will."

Vaughn took a longer stride, pulling away from the warm, comforting touch. She was afraid for Sage, but she had no intention of letting Justine see that in her eyes. "You know as well as I do that time isn't on our side at this point."

"Your friend Jackson is working the streets?"

"Yes. We're going to meet with him now. He's made a little progress." Vaughn told Justine about the Tuareg footprints and Jackson's canvass of the city.

"It's a good start," Justine said. "Solid work."

Vaughn unlocked the car doors and threw Justine's suitcase in the trunk. "Slow and steady isn't going to win this race, and I've got more questions than answers."

"Such as?" Justine slid into the passenger seat.

"The ambassador is too nervous not to be guilty of something, but I'm not sure what that is."

"Yet."

Vaughn nodded. "Right." She pulled out into traffic. "Here's another troubling item." She related her discussion with Sabastien and her concerns about his lack of curiosity regarding her change in status.

"Hmm. That is interesting. Do you think he's secure?"

Vaughn made a right-hand turn. "If you're asking me if I think he's a true friend, the answer is yes. I can't believe he'd knowingly betray me. I saved his ass from serious jail time and gave him a dream job doing what he loves to do."

"He could've been compromised without his knowledge."

"I've thought of that, and I'd say it's possible. Except that he's the best there is. I can't believe he could be monitored without knowing it."

"If he wasn't expecting it..."

"I suppose anything is possible." Vaughn waved her hand dismissively. "So here's the third troubling item. His name is Aaron Torgensen."

"Okay."

"He claims to be a professor of International Studies at Hopkins. Just happened to be available in the middle of the semester to fly here with perhaps two hours notice to take Sage's place."

"Sounds like Torgensen is certainly worth a closer look."

"I've got Sabastien doing a check. It's more than that, though."

"Oh?"

"I can't place him, but he looks familiar to me. Not only that, he's spent a lot of time shooting."

"And you know that because?"

"When I shook hands with him, his palm was callused in all the right places."

"Interesting."

"He and I met with the head of the National Assembly this afternoon. On the surface, Torgensen seemed knowledgeable enough, but he wasn't as comfortable with the discussion as he should've been if he was who he claimed to be."

"We should know soon enough, right?"

"Presumably."

"So," Justine said, "what do we have? We have two possible players in the ambassador and Torgensen, and a question mark in Sabastien."

"And the much larger question of why Sage was taken. Is it an independent event or somehow related to the congressional visit? Is there something going on here in Mali and the timing is coincidental to my arrival and the visit? Or is it about the majority leader and her party, and Sage is somehow tied into that?"

"All good questions," Justine said. "Why would it be about you?"

Vaughn blushed involuntarily, but if Justine were really going to help, she would have to know all the facts. "I spent the night with Sage just before she disappeared. She'd gone out for an early morning run at dawn and was coming back to make me breakfast." Vaughn sucked in a breath and held it, waiting to be judged.

"Oh. Well, that explains how you knew she was gone so quickly." There was no reproach in Justine's tone, for which Vaughn was grateful.

When a hand softly grasped hers on the steering wheel, Vaughn jumped.

"It's okay to move on, Vaughn. Sara would've wanted you to."

"I—" Vaughn swallowed around the sudden lump in her throat. "That wasn't what this was."

"Stop." Justine's voice was as soft as her touch. "Whatever it was, it's obvious you're worried about Sage. She's important to you, and that's nice. If you chose to spend time with her, she must be special."

"She's a nice kid."

"So let's get to the bottom of this. What you're telling me is Sage may have been targeted because she was tied to you."

"I can't rule it out, except that Dumont clearly didn't know that Sage and I had been together. So if getting to me was the objective, the ambassador wasn't in on it."

Justine didn't answer. After several seconds, Vaughn glanced her way. She looked lost in thought, as though she was trying to work through some problem in her head.

"What is it?"

"I'm not sure. Remember I told you Fairhaven's fingerprints were all over your assignment here?"

"Yes."

"I found out something else. It appears Fairhaven may be cozier with State than we thought. He has a history with the illustrious secretary of state."

"Is that so?"

"There's more. They were boyhood chums. Even went to the same college. It wasn't until they were in their mid-twenties that they went separate ways," Justine said.

"What pulled them apart?"

"Drugs."

"I'm sorry?" Vaughn stepped on the brakes harder than she had intended.

"The secretary got caught dealing. Apparently, Fairhaven used some of his new-found CIA capital to make the charges disappear."

"So the secretary owes him, and all these years later Fairhaven is collecting?"

"That's certainly one possibility."

"I still can't see why Fairhaven is so interested in me."

"Neither can I. But he is."

They were both quiet as Vaughn parked the car. She was mulling over the new revelation.

"Where are we?"

Before Vaughn could answer, Jackson hailed them.

"Please tell me you've got good news for me," Vaughn said, without preamble.

Jackson ignored her. "Sometimes Vaughn Elliott lacks manners. I am Jackson."

"Hi, Jackson." Justine shook his hand. "I'm Justine."

"Yeah, yeah," Vaughn said grumpily. "What's happening?"

"Let's get in the car, first." Jackson led the way to a beat-up old Renault.

As soon as they were inside, Vaughn asked, "Well?"

"If she's being held locally, nobody knows it. There are some Tuareg within and just outside the city limits, but not many. My contacts tell me it's more likely that, if the Tuareg have her, they've taken her to their home turf—meaning the northern desert. They'd be in their own element up there and much less conspicuous."

"The roads aren't paved heading north, right?" Vaughn was thinking fast.

"True, but once they got far enough outside the city, they wouldn't rely on a car."

"What?"

"They'd be on camelback."

"And that wouldn't look a little odd?" Justine asked.

"Out there, nobody asks questions if they value their lives," Jackson explained.

"Fantastic." Vaughn pounded the dashboard. "What you're telling me is that by now they're long gone."

"Looks like it." Jackson stopped the car. "We're here."

The house was unassuming—like all the other houses on the block. A lone figure waited in the darkness on the front porch.

"Jacques, this is Vaughn Elliott and her friend Justine." Jackson made the introductions.

"Pleased to meet you." Jacques was a short, stocky man who was the diametric opposite of his brother. "Come in."

Inside, the home was the picture of a bachelor pad. The furniture was mismatched and dirty dishes were everywhere. Jacques hurriedly cleared some space at a rickety old card table.

A detailed map of Mali hung on the wall. On it were a series of marks.

Jackson walked to the map. "These here," he pointed to several black dots, "represent the Tuareg strongholds to the north. We figure one of these is where your friend is being held. These here," Jackson shifted a little and pointed to a series of blue dots, "represent smaller concentrations of Tuareg. Most of these are settlements where livestock are raised. It's unlikely these Tuareg would be involved in something of the scope we're talking about."

Vaughn stood with her arms crossed. Conjecture wasn't certainty; she wanted certainty. Now more than ever, she needed what Sabastien could give her. "I've got someone mapping these electronically, using specific criteria. I'm hopeful that will help us narrow down the possibilities further."

She looked over at Justine. Exhaustion was etched in every line of her face. Jackson looked fatigued as well. Although she wanted to push on, Vaughn decided letting them sleep would be more productive. "Let's call it a night. We'll meet back here at 0600 hours. I should have more answers then." Vaughn closed her own eyes momentarily. They felt gritty. *I will not rest yet, Sage. Stay strong. I'm coming for you.*

She would have Jackson drop them back at the car, then she'd take Justine to the hotel with her and let her sleep in the suite's other bedroom. Vaughn would spend the next few hours reviewing the data from Sabastien. If there was a solid lead, she would follow it before morning while the others slept, and let them join her when they awakened.

∾∾

Sage's eyes drooped behind the blindfold. Fatigue enveloped her like a blanket, temporarily overpowering her fear. They had been traveling non-stop for hours. The extreme heat finally had stopped beating down on her scalp, so she judged it to be after nightfall. She slipped sideways in the saddle as her body surrendered to sleep, even as her mind struggled to remain vigilant.

A scream rose in her throat as hands jerked her out of the saddle and she fought to clear the fog from her brain. Sage was alarmed to realize that her hands had been unbound and she hadn't even stirred. She was handcuffed as soon as her feet hit the ground. This time the cuffs were attached to a belt around her waist so that she could not raise her hands or arms. She was marched forward.

After several steps, Sage's mind engaged and she extended her senses. The noises in this place were different. She could hear dozens of voices—some female—and the sound of a child crying in the distance. This might be her last chance to escape.

She tensed the muscles in her arms and gave a hard yank. The unexpected move separated her from her guard. With all of the energy she could muster, Sage ran in the direction of the voices, screaming in French as she did. "Help me. Please, help me!"

She stumbled over something and fell hard, landing awkwardly on her shoulders, chest, and cheek. She shoved herself off the ground with the heels of her hands, and propelled herself forward again. Although she tried, she could not raise her hands high enough to remove the blindfold.

Voices screamed and a shot rang out. Sage kept moving. *Please let them miss.* More angry voices joined the chorus. Her legs strained against the robe and she stepped on the hem several times. Still, she persevered.

After several more steps, Sage actually began to believe she might get away. Then something solid and hard careened into her from the side, sending her flying. Her left shoulder slammed into the ground, and she screamed in agony. Before she could move again, a breeze ruffled her hair. *Someone raising an arm.* As soon as the blow struck, everything went black.

⊰ ⊱

Vaughn showed Justine to her bedroom and then headed straight for her laptop. As she had hoped, there were several e-mails from Sabastien. The first was a detailed map outlining the positioning of some fifty Tuareg communities in Mali and neighboring Niger and Burkina Faso. Vaughn connected a tiny portable printer to one of the laptop's USB ports and printed the file.

The second e-mail contained the three background dossiers Vaughn had requested. She printed them, as well.

"What're you doing?" Justine peered over Vaughn's shoulder.

"I got the files from Sabastien." Vaughn tilted the screen so that Justine could read. "I figured you'd just conk out."

Justine squeezed Vaughn's shoulder. "I told you I'm here to help. I know you won't rest for the night until you've examined every available piece of information, so I thought another pair of eyes would make it go quicker."

"You should sleep."

"I will if you will."

Vaughn sighed and patted the spot on the sofa next to her, conceding that this was a battle she was destined to lose. Without further comment, she handed Justine the printout report on Raymond Dumont.

"Your information on him was pretty thorough. I just wanted to see if there were any inconsistencies or additions."

"Good thinking," Justine said, accepting the sheaf of papers.

Half an hour later, Vaughn stiffened and sat up straighter.

"What is it?"

"Look at this." She slid two pictures of Aaron Torgensen toward Justine. One was a current headshot and the other was a casual shot of a much younger Torgensen taken at a campus function. That was the one that caught Vaughn's attention.

"Okay." Justine focused on first one, and then the second image.

"Does that man look familiar to you?"

"Should he?"

"If you worked a case with him, he would. He was backup on a job I worked like fifteen years ago. I was never supposed to see him, but something went wrong and he had to break cover." Vaughn flung open her cell phone and waited for the call to be answered on the other end.

"Oui?"

"Good work, Sabastien. Now I need one more thing."

"Elliott, can't a guy get some rest here?"

"Yes. Later. Right now, I want you to get into the Johns Hopkins human resources files. I want you to find Torgensen's employment application, including fingerprints. Compare them to the Company employee classified files. Also, run a side-by-side comparison of the pictures of Torgensen you sent me and any facial match you find in the Company's files."

Sabastien whistled. "You don't ask for much, do you?"

"I thought you were the best. The best could get this done in a heartbeat."

"That's low, Elliott. You know how many firewalls the CIA has on its classified site?"

"No, but I'm sure you do. I'll be waiting." Vaughn terminated the call.

"I thought you were certain of Torgensen being CIA? Breaking into the Company's classified docs is a risk. Why take it?" Justine asked, when Vaughn got off the phone.

"Because I want documentation. IDing Torgensen gives us a big piece of the puzzle."

"Are you sure of that?"

Vaughn got up and went to the wet bar. "You want something?"

"No, thanks."

Vaughn poured herself a drink. "If Torgensen is with the Company and I can prove it with documentation, it means Sage was kidnapped by our own people."

"Maybe. But maybe not." Justine turned to face Vaughn over the back of the sofa. "What if Torgensen was sent undercover to get her back?"

Vaughn walked around the sofa and sat at the end opposite Justine. "Implausible. If Sage was taken by hostiles, the fastest way to get her back would've been to use someone already on the ground."

"In other words, you."

"Right."

"You're not an insider anymore, Vaughn. Not only that, but you've got a pretty important assignment already."

Vaughn took a sip and let the liquor burn her throat. "Okay. Let's say you're right. Then why the song and dance? Surely, there would be no reason to go through this elaborate Johns Hopkins cover story with me?"

"True."

"Not only that," Vaughn set the drink on the coffee table, "but if Sage was taken by hostiles, surely it would have huge implications for the upcoming congressional visit. I would have to be brought into the case and briefed, since the safety of the delegation is my responsibility."

Justine seemed to consider that. "Fair enough."

"Unless the Company didn't trust me to get the job done myself and sent Torgensen to back me up." Vaughn let the quick stab of pain in the center of her chest pass. "After all these years, could they really think so little of me?"

Justine touched her fleetingly on the knee. "No. I don't believe that. Besides, it doesn't add up. Security's not their thing, and why wouldn't their agent be out looking for Sage as a top priority instead of sticking with you?"

"Because Sage is dispensable to them." Vaughn picked up the drink and took a healthy slug to take the edge off that truth.

"They can't be sure of that unless they know for certain who took Sage and why. Otherwise, they can't accurately assess the threat to the delegation."

"Who's to say they don't know who took her?" Vaughn finished the last of the drink.

"If we haven't got solid proof yet, neither do they. You started working on the kidnapping before they even could have known about it." Justine stood up and stretched. "Let's move on to something you brought up on the phone with me yesterday. Say Torgensen is CIA. Does the ambassador know? If not, what's the Company's game? If he does know, again, what's the end game? And what does your mid-level career diplomat, whose life, by the way, looks remarkably unremarkable on paper, have to do with anything?"

"I don't know," Vaughn said in a frustrated whisper, burying her free hand in her hair. "I've been over it a thousand times in my mind. Sage didn't say anything to me that indicated that she thought she was in any danger. There was no political unrest, all of her papers look routine to me, and I don't know her well enough to tell you if her behavior during the time I was with her was anything out of the ordinary."

"Maybe you're the target. That could be where Fairhaven fits in. What if he knows you're still looking into Sara's death?"

"I've been thinking about that since you told me about the Fairhaven connection. If the Company wanted me dead, why wait until now? I've been a sitting duck behind a desk for a year. Not only that, but they had a week in the clinic when I was recovering from my injuries."

"If you got killed right after Sara, it would've been too suspicious. They needed to let the heat die down."

"Even so, as you said, what does Sage have to do with it? Why take her?"

"It was their excuse to bring in someone to replace her, to get Torgensen, or whoever he is, close to you."

Vaughn tapped the empty glass against her chin. "Maybe, but I don't think they'd risk the safety of the majority leader just to take me out of the picture. That would be incredibly irresponsible, even for the Company. They'd wait until it was over. And, let's face it, they wouldn't need to get that close to me—not as close as Torgensen is. Anyway, why not just take me instead of Sage? Why bother with the extra step? It would've been easier to replace me than to replace Sage this close to the visit. Seems too far-fetched to me."

Vaughn's cell vibrated on the coffee table and she snatched it up. "Yes?"

"Elliott?"

"You've got the fingerprint match?"

"Never mind that. We've got bigger problems."

"Spill it, Sabastien."

"They had a blind monitor on the Sage McNally file I sent you."

"Slow down and speak English."

"They put a trap on it. They know the file's been pulled and they know it's been sent to you."

"How?"

"I haven't figured it all out yet. I just know they're wise to you. You're on their team, why should they be watching your e-mail?"

"You didn't know I left the Company?"

"You—what the hell, Elliott. When were you going to tell me?"

Vaughn ignored the question. "This changes the ballgame. If you were deliberately kept in the dark about my status, it means you were a pawn to keep an eye on me. You've been compromised, my friend. We need to get you out of there."

"They can't trace the McNally file to me. I used a loop."

"It doesn't matter. They'll know you did it because I'm the one who ended up with the goods. Sabastien, you need to go to a secure location. Now. I'll call you later."

"But—"

"There's no time. I'm sorry. I wouldn't have involved you if I'd known."

"That's okay. This gig was getting kind of boring anyway."

"Be safe. I'll call you as soon as I can. Take your equipment with you, if you can. I'll see if I can keep your life a little more interesting than the Company did."

"Sure thing, Elliott."

"Hey, Sabastien?"

"Yeah?"

"Can you tell how long ago they made the trace to me?"

"I had set up an alarm. Just in case, you know? So I called you as soon as they tripped the alarm."

"Good. That ought to give me a few minutes head start." Vaughn thought for a moment. "Would they know they tripped an alarm?"

"What kind of amateur do you take me for? Of course not."

"Thanks."

Vaughn looked at Justine as she closed the phone. "Glad you didn't unpack. We've been made. We've got to get out of here. Get your stuff."

"Well, that confirms that Torgensen is CIA, anyway."

"Yes, and he's probably scouring the hotel for me right now. Let's move. We'll talk through it in the car."

Within five minutes, they were packed and headed down a back stairwell. Once they'd reached the safety of Sage's car, Vaughn called Jackson.

"How quickly can you get us out of the country?"

"We can leave right away."

"Good. Get ready to move. We'll be at Jacque's house in ten minutes. He'll have to hide my car."

"It is not a problem. I will be waiting for you."

CHAPTER TEN

W e have a problem that requires an immediate solution. This will complicate things significantly. Where are you right now?"

"I'm in the hotel." Torgensen hadn't thought he would hear from Washington again so soon. He pulled on a pair of jeans as he cradled the cell phone between his cheek and his shoulder.

"Good. Elliott has accessed Dr. McNally's background information. Most likely that means she knows that the girl has been taken—she's trying to find clues that might aid in a search."

"If Elliott is looking for McNally, it means nothing of value has been compromised yet. She was a top agent. If she had the information, she'd be acting on it, not looking for the girl." Torgensen checked the magazine clip in his Sig Sauer.

"You don't know Elliott. She has a soft spot for damsels in distress."

There was a pause on the line. Torgensen waited patiently.

"Still, I believe you are correct to assume that Elliott doesn't know anything...yet. We need to keep it that way."

"You want a permanent solution?"

"Yes. But it has to appear to be self-inflicted. Perhaps a booze-fueled moment of self-pity over her reassignment to something unworthy of her years of experience."

"I'll take care of it."

"I want to know as soon as it's done. Torgensen?"

"Yes?"

"Don't underestimate Elliott. That would be very foolish. She is extremely sharp and capable."

Torgensen smiled wolfishly. "I hope so. I'm looking forward to the challenge." He hung up the phone, finished dressing, and checked his weapon and ammunition one more time.

When he was satisfied, Torgensen picked up the room phone and dialed the front desk. "Hello? Yes, I wonder if you could help me. I met this really nice woman and I was supposed to meet her in her room for drinks, but I lost the piece of paper she gave me with her room number on it. I was hoping you could tell me where to find her."

✥✥

Jackson navigated the streets of Bamako in a Toyota 4x4. Justine sat in the front passenger seat, and Vaughn half sat half knelt out of sight behind the seats. She would stay like that until they got out of town.

Their escape from the hotel had been a close thing. Although it wasn't truly necessary, Vaughn wanted confirmation that Torgensen was, indeed, coming for her. She watched through a pair of binoculars from the driver's seat of Sage's car, parked a safe distance away, as Torgensen flew down the outdoor stairwell of the hotel. The butt of his pistol was visible in the waistband of his jeans.

She waited for him to give up the search and re-enter the hotel before she started the car and drove away. She and Justine had been silent on the drive to Jacques' house.

Now, as they bounced along the quiet streets in the middle of the night, it was time to determine a course of action. "How many hours will it take us to cross into Burkina Faso?" she asked Jackson.

"The rest of the night, at least." After a beat, he asked, "Are you sure that is where you want to go? I can offer you some protection once you are in my jurisdiction, to be sure, but I wonder why you would want to go there, rather than someplace where you would be less…conspicuous."

"Because I can continue to search for Sage from your side of the border in relative safety. These people don't know about you, my man, and they would never expect me to go across the border.

They'd assume either I would stay somewhere in Mali or I would go back to the States."

"Vaughn," Justine said, "Jackson and I can continue to search for Sage. You should disappear."

"No."

"Vaughn—"

"No, Justine. I won't sit on the sidelines while Sage is in danger."

"You're in just as much danger."

"I can take care of myself. I'm a trained professional. She's just..." Vaughn's voice trailed off. She cleared her throat. "Sabastien clearly said that it was Sage's files that were tagged."

When neither Jackson nor Justine said anything, Vaughn said, "Don't you see? They weren't worried about me. Sage was the target. They wanted to know if anyone was looking for her."

Justine nodded. "And now they're hunting you."

"Because they know I'm looking for Sage." Vaughn closed her eyes and prayed for patience. "They wouldn't care about me except for the fact that I'm poking my nose where it doesn't belong."

"Then what was Torgensen's role? They already had Sage."

"Maybe they were hedging their bets, in case I got too curious."

"Possibly," Justine conceded, "but something still feels off."

"It doesn't matter. The bottom line is that Sage was the primary target."

"What I can't figure out," Jackson interjected, "is why?"

It was a question Vaughn had been asking herself for hours. "I don't know, and as far as I can tell, there's only one way to find out."

"Rescue Sage," Justine said.

"Yes. Rescue Sage," Vaughn agreed.

Sage cracked first one eye open, and then the other. The pressure from the blindfold was gone, and yet she was still in complete darkness. Her head throbbed painfully; her brain felt as though it were rattling around in her skull. As her eyes adjusted to the surroundings, she could see that her hands were cuffed via a short chain to an iron ring built into a concrete wall. Her left shoulder was on fire. Although she couldn't be sure, she thought it might be dislocated. She'd seen in a movie once where someone had popped a shoulder back in by bashing it into a wall. The idea made her sick to her stomach.

She struggled into a sitting position, shocked to discover that the floor appeared to be made of concrete, as well. *Concrete in the desert? You're dreaming.*

Since Sage had no concept of time, it was impossible to know how far they might have traveled from the place where she had tried to escape. Maybe they weren't in the desert anymore.

Another look around told Sage that she was in a room roughly the size of a large shed. In fact, there were empty storage shelves on the opposite wall. *Where the heck am I?* She closed her eyes. The iron ring in the wall, the removal of the blindfold...wherever she was, it appeared that she was going to be staying for a while. She wasn't sure whether that was good news or not.

Sage angled herself around until her back was against the wall. Her new position provided a minor bit of relief from the pain in her shoulder. She leaned her head back against the wall. Without any imminent threat hanging over her head, and with the comfort of sight, she was able to relax for the first time since she'd been taken.

Her mind drifted for several minutes, until it settled on the one question that had been lurking just behind the fear. What in the world did the Tuareg want with her? The organized nature of the assault made it seem unlikely that hers was a random abduction. No, she was definitely the one they wanted. Yet, no one had given her any indication what this was all about—at least not in a language that Sage understood.

She wracked her brain. The Tuareg hadn't been antagonistic toward any American that she knew of. There'd been no reports of unrest among the tribes. The Americans hadn't done anything to provoke the wrath of the Tuareg. So why take a chance on creating an international incident? It didn't make sense. Surely, by now people were searching for her. Vaughn would've alerted the ambassador. Don would've called the regional security officer. Washington would've been notified.

Taking her was too much of a risk. So why do it? The stakes had to be incredibly high, as would the rewards. Who was in a position to make promises to the Tuareg? Was it about money? Were they looking for ransom? That didn't fit with anything she knew about them. They were traders, nomads. "Descended from a long line of warriors," she reminded herself. Even so, the last Tuareg uprising had been settled more than a decade ago.

Sage sighed. *What a mess.* She did her best to stretch out her legs and find a relatively comfortable position. She would think more about it all later, after she'd had a chance to rest. Within seconds, she was fast asleep.

∽☜☞∾

"What do you mean, Elliott's gone?" The voice was ominously low and full of danger.

"She must've known we were coming for her. The room is completely empty, and she's nowhere to be found." Torgensen was out of breath.

"Unacceptable."

"I'll find her. I'm tracking her."

"You'd better be."

"Yes, sir," Torgensen said, although the line already had gone dead.

∽☜☞∾

"Yes?" A sleepy Ray Dumont answered the phone on the fifth ring. Why did people insist on calling him in the middle of the night?

"Plans have changed."

At the sound of the voice, Dumont immediately came wide awake. "Yes, sir."

"I need you to contact your man. The detention order is now a termination."

"I-I'm sorry?" Dumont couldn't believe his ears.

"Do you have a hearing problem? I said kill her."

"It-it will take time."

"You don't know how to find your man?"

"No, sir. I mean, yes, sir, I do." Dumont was beginning to sweat. "But it will take time, once I get in touch with him, for him to travel to the...detention center. There is no regular cell reception inside. They don't have satellite phones. He'll have to go there personally."

The silence on the other end of the phone was more uncomfortable for Dumont than any words could've been.

Finally, the voice said, "How long will it take?"

"At least twelve hours."

"You're lucky I'm in a generous mood. I'll give you fourteen. God help you if the assignment is not complete by then. Oh, and Dumont?"

"Yes, sir?"

"There will be a new DS assigned to the congressional visit in the next couple of days."

"But I thought that Vaughn Elliott—"

"Elliott is no longer your concern."

"Yes, sir."

"However, tell your man that if she shows up, I want her killed on sight."

"Um, right. Got it."

The line went dead.

Dumont mopped his brow. He depressed the button for an outside line and dialed a number from memory. As he did so, he saw his dreams and aspirations vanishing before his eyes.

⤚⤙

"Sabastien? Where are you?" Vaughn held the phone tightly to her ear and plugged the other ear with a finger to block out the noise of the road and the truck.

"Never mind that. I think I have something for you."

"What are you talking about? And why do you sound like you're out of breath?"

"You told me to move, remember? So I'm moving. Listen to me, Elliott. You asked me for a log of all of the ambassador's calls."

"Yes."

"You know me. I can never do things halfway."

"So?"

"So you're going to want to kiss me. I didn't just stop at a log. I bugged his phone."

"How did you—never mind. I'm sure I don't want to know."

"Communications are computer based, aren't they? I simply tapped into the source. Anyway, I've got two calls for you. The first was inbound to the ambassador's residence ten minutes ago. It was from an untraceable number in D.C."

"How do you know it was from D.C. if it was untraceable?"

"Are you going to ask questions or are you going to listen to what I have to tell you?"

"I'm listening."

"Whoever it was has some juice, I can tell you that much. The ambassador was practically wetting himself."

"What did they say?"

"That's the problem."

"What is it, Sabastien?" Vaughn thought she might go through the phone line and strangle him.

"It was an order to have your friend killed."

Vaughn doubled over as the air rushed out of her lungs. *Oh, God. Sage. I'm so sorry.* She thought she might be sick and struggled for control.

"Vaughn?" Justine's voice was full of concern. It was enough to galvanize Vaughn into action.

Vaughn straightened up with difficulty and swallowed the bile. "The order was given to the ambassador? You're sure?"

"Positive. But the ambassador told him it might take up to twelve hours to get it done because 'his man,' as he called him, needs to get up there and it would take that long. Seems there's no regular cell phone service wherever they are."

Vaughn shoved the fear for Sage's safety to the far recesses of her mind. Sage needed her to be clear-headed now. "Did they name the man?"

"No."

"Well, one thing we know is it isn't Torgensen. If it was, the ambassador wouldn't have been the one giving him the order. It would've come directly from D.C. with no intermediary. The man they're referring to must be Tuareg or at least working with them. Jackson was right." Vaughn was thinking out loud. She looked at

Justine. "Remember when you told me that Dumont had served in Mali before?"

"Yes."

"I wonder if Dumont's connections with the Tuareg kidnappers date from that time."

"Elliott, it doesn't matter," Sabastien broke in. "I told you there was a second call tonight. The ambassador called his man. I was able to put a trace on that number. We've got him."

"We do?" Vaughn's heart rate accelerated.

"We do. First, I think you're right about the man being Tuareg. His French was halting and crude. Second, his number is Bamako-based, even though it's a cell. So, if you're already heading north, you'll have a head start on him."

Vaughn addressed Jackson. "We're heading north, right?"

"We are heading east at the moment."

"Head north. Now." Vaughn put the phone back to her ear. "Sabastien, do you know where he's going, exactly?"

"No, they never said. But they said it would take him twelve to thirteen hours by car."

"That narrows it down."

"I've already done the calculations. My best estimate says they are somewhere in the region around either Timbuktu or Gao."

"Timbuktu or Gao. Jackson? How long would it take to drive from Bamako to Timbuktu?"

"Somewhere in the neighborhood of twelve to thirteen hours, give or take," Jackson said.

"If they were going to Timbuktu, why wouldn't the man just fly?" Vaughn directed the question to Jackson. "There's an airport in Timbuktu."

"The Tuareg are a poor people. They would not have the money to fly. If someone were to give him the money to fly, he would stick out, how would you say it, like a sore finger."

"Sore thumb, Jackson. Sore thumb, but I get the idea."

"He wouldn't disguise himself to get there quicker?" Justine asked.

"The Tuareg are a very proud people. They would not hide themselves."

"Okay, so he's driving. What are the chances that he's going to Timbuktu and not Gao?"

"Gao is more like a fourteen or fifteen hour drive," Jackson answered, "and it would be more difficult to hide someone there. Fewer people and lots of police activity because it's near the border with Algeria."

"Okay, Jackson. Take us to Timbuktu." Vaughn addressed Sabastien. "Wouldn't a major city like Timbuktu have cell signal?"

"In some spots, perhaps, but likely not in most, and not if they were inside a fairly secure structure."

"What makes you think they're in a secure structure?"

"The ambassador used the expression 'detention center.' I've been investigating the area, looking for anything that fits the description."

"I think I love you."

"All the women say that, Elliott. So far, I don't have anything. But I'm also working on the theory that they'd want to be somewhere outside of town so as to draw less attention to themselves."

"Makes sense," Vaughn said. "And?"

"I'm still working on that. I'll call you back as soon as I have anything or if I pick up any other calls."

"You're my hero."

"I know. There's one more thing."

"Let's hear it."

"Wherever this is, they've got orders to shoot and kill you on sight."

"Is that all? Call me when you have something else."

"Goodbye, Elliott. Be careful out there."

"You too."

When she'd hung up the phone, Vaughn told Justine and Jackson, "There's good news and there's bad news."

"Give me the good news, first," Justine said.

"Okay. We know that, at the moment, Sage is alive." *That's something, anyway.* "Not only that, but we have a much stronger idea of her general location and a head start, I hope."

"What's the bad news?"

"The bad news is that they're going to kill her when the guy with the orders gets there. That would be twelve hours from now, and he knows exactly where he's going."

"Great."

Vaughn stared out the window at the inky darkness. "There's more, and I think it's only fair to share it."

"What is it?" Jackson asked.

Vaughn met Jackson's eyes in the rearview mirror. "The man will also bring with him orders to kill me on sight. When they see that I'm not alone, you'll become targets too. I can't ask you to take that kind of risk."

"Vaughn Elliott, I am with you all the way in this."

"Me too," Justine added. "They may be expecting you, but the two of us will be a surprise. That's a real advantage."

"Please do not forget the supplies I took the liberty of packing for us," Jackson said.

"I can't tell you how much I appreciate that, my friend." Vaughn was impressed at the amount and variety of firepower Jackson had loaded in a hidden compartment under the bed liner of the truck. It would come in handy now.

"You should both get some sleep while I am driving. It has been a long few days, and you will need to be at your best. There is nothing to do now but watch the desert go by. Use your time wisely."

Although Vaughn knew Jackson was right, she was reluctant to close her eyes.

Jackson met her gaze again in the mirror. "I am fine. Wide awake. I promise you will not miss anything. If you do, I will wake you."

"Vaughn," Justine said softly, "if we don't get some shuteye, we won't be clearheaded. If we're not, this could end very badly. Don't we owe it to Sage to be at our best?"

Vaughn didn't answer. She simply nodded around the lump in her throat.

CHAPTER ELEVEN

He had turned the city upside down looking for her. If Vaughn Elliott was anywhere in Bamako, she was well hidden. Torgensen was a man who trusted his instincts; they'd kept him alive for many years. His instincts told him she was long gone. What he didn't know, and couldn't seem to figure out, was where.

It was possible that she'd fled the country to save her own ass, but Torgensen didn't think so. Everything in her service record and psychological profile indicated that she was more likely to stay and fight than run. That left two possibilities. Either she was biding her time and would turn him into the hunted instead of the hunter, or she was going after the McNally woman.

Washington was convinced that Elliott would try to save the hostage for altruistic reasons. Torgensen had it figured differently. McNally had been an unfortunate complication. If she hadn't stumbled across that message, she would still be at the embassy doing her job. Elliott couldn't know that. Most likely, she was exhausting resources trying to figure out the motive behind taking an unremarkable political officer. It would've stunk to high heaven to someone with Elliott's experience.

She'd go after McNally all right, but because she would deduce that McNally had a piece of information she needed, not because Vaughn Elliott was softhearted. People in their line of work couldn't afford to be softhearted.

He picked up the vibrating phone.

"Report."

"I need to know where McNally is being held. I believe Elliott is on her way there."

"So she slipped past you."

"No, sir. She was gone before I was given the order to take her out."

"And she has managed to elude you since."

"I will complete the assignment as soon as you give me the information I need." His voice was clipped.

"I have other people on that end looking for her. Why do I need you?"

Torgensen clamped down on his temper. "Because I am the best at what I do. Are they trained assassins?"

The silence on the other end of the line grated on Torgensen's nerves.

"Very well. An extra bit of insurance wouldn't hurt. But Torgensen, I want you to fly under the radar. We can't have you interfering with anything else. I want you to do it from a distance, and only, I repeat, only if others fail."

"Elliott is my assignment. You brought me in—"

"Enough."

Torgensen wrote the location on a scrap of paper as it was related to him.

"If I find out you haven't followed my instructions, there's no place you'll be able to hide that I won't find you."

The call terminated in his ear. Torgensen hated that. He packed up his few belongings. He would go to the airport, fly north, finish the job, and be done with it.

◈◈

Sage closed and opened her eyes. Experimentally, she turned her head. The pain was still there, but the sharpness had turned into a dull thudding behind her eyes. She supposed the sleep had helped. *Yeah, that and being stationary.*

A door opened and she blinked hard as a beam of light shined directly in her eyes. She tried to raise her hands to block the brightness, but the chain was too short.

"I am sorry," a soft male voice said in broken French, "but you cannot see what we look like. I thought this would be better than the blindfold."

"Yes. Thank you," Sage said. Her voice was harsh from disuse.

"I have brought you some food and water."

"Thank you."

"And a bucket, in case you need it. I regret that the lodgings are not what you are used to. It is nothing personal."

"I understand." Sage considered asking questions but feared that doing so would stop the meager flow of conversation altogether.

"Well, here you are."

A tray was pushed in front of her from a different angle and Sage realized for the first time that two men, not one, had entered the room. She supposed that was for security purposes. As if she could be a threat to them given her current position.

As the men backed out of the room, Sage said, "Wait! Can you tell me what time it is?"

The man who had spoken to her hesitated but didn't answer. In another couple of seconds, the door closed and Sage was plunged once again into the dark.

She waited for her eyes to readjust and then examined the items on the tray. Vegetables, some kind of flatbread, some unidentifiable food product, and water. Suddenly, she was famished. The short length of chain attached to the ring at the base of the wall required that she bend in half to shovel the food into her mouth. She tried to pick up the bread in her left hand and dropped it as a lance of pain started at her shoulder and seared a path down her arm to her fingers.

Sage sucked in a quick breath and held it until the throbbing eased. She picked up the bread in her right hand and scooped up a paste-like substance with it. The food wasn't particularly tasty, but to Sage it was manna from heaven.

When she'd eaten everything on the plate and drunk half the water, she sat back. She would save the rest of the water and ration it. Who knew when her captors next would feed her.

As she shifted to make herself more comfortable, she went over the brief bit of conversation she'd had with the soft-spoken man. Something stuck in her mind. "It's nothing personal," he'd said. Sage mulled that over. Nothing personal.

"You're losing it. That only confirms what you already know—it wasn't specifically about you." And yet, she'd been the target. What if he'd used the word "personal" to indicate that it was professional? Sage reviewed everything she had been working on in the past month. There was nothing remotely controversial. She went back to one of her core questions. Was it just that she was an American? Again, that made no sense.

Maybe if she reviewed the meetings she'd had, the reports she'd written, the appointments she'd planned. It wasn't the most exciting way to pass the time, but at least it would be productive. Perhaps if she could determine why she'd been taken, she could talk her way out.

⊰⊱

"Yes?" Vaughn scrubbed a hand over her eyes and blinked. The vibration of the cell phone against her hip had awakened her from a fitful sleep.

"Elliott, you're going to owe me forever." Sabastien sounded impossibly smug.

"I'm sure. What do you have?"

"A likely location. At least, I think it is."

"Okay." Vaughn sat up and searched for a pen.

"There's a U.S. AID food distribution warehouse about ten miles northwest of Timbuktu. It hasn't been used in several years."

"What's around it?"

"Nothing. The nearest neighbors appear to be at least three miles away. The facility was used during the last big drought to supply the Malians with food and water."

"In use recently enough to be in good repair, but vacant long enough to be forgotten by most," Vaughn said. "It's perfect. Give me the coordinates."

Sabastien did.

"I assume you're using Google Earth?"

"Among other sources, yes."

"Can you zoom in close enough to tell me what's around it? Is it desert? Are there other buildings? Are they going to be able to spot me from a mile away?"

Vaughn heard the clicking of keys.

"Looks like the best approach might be from the north. The main door faces east. Hmm...not much in the way of shelter, although there are a few small outbuildings where I assume the AID workers stayed while they were there."

"I don't suppose you could find a blueprint of the facility, could you?"

"Elliott, Elliott. Don't be ridiculous. Of course I can. The bigger question is how I'm going to get it to you."

Damn. He's right. Vaughn cracked her knuckles as she considered the problem. "Jackson, how far are we from Timbuktu?"

"Perhaps two-and-a-half hours. Maybe a little less. I will stop soon to put more petrol in the tank."

Vaughn looked out the window. They were surrounded by desert on every side, without a sign of other civilization. It was unlikely that she could get an Internet connection anywhere out here, and she didn't want to take a detour that would add time to the trip. "You're going to have to talk me through it, Sabastien."

"Damn, Elliott. Okay. Give me half an hour. I'll call you back."

In the front passenger seat, Justine stirred. She stretched and looked around. "What's going on?"

"Sabastien pinpointed a likely spot where they could be keeping Sage."

"Excellent. Where is it?"

"A U.S. AID distribution center ten miles northwest of Timbuktu. It's been standing vacant for a few years, and it's isolated with the exception of a few outbuildings that he thinks look like temporary living quarters."

"Bingo," Justine said. "Where are we now, Jackson?"

"On the way from nowhere to somewhere."

"Very funny."

"Sadly, it is true. I will stop here and let you stretch your legs for a minute while I refill the tank. Out here, only a fool doesn't travel with his own supply of petrol."

"I'm very glad to know you're not a fool," Justine said fondly.

"You are safe out here, Vaughn Elliott. We would see anyone coming long before they would see us."

"Good to know. Justine, help me organize the things we're going to need." Vaughn waited for her to get out, then unfolded herself from the small jump seat. She jogged in place, trying to restore the circulation in her legs.

"Sorry about the cramped accommodations," Jackson said over his shoulder as he filled the tank.

"I'll live," Vaughn said.

"That's the plan, champ." Justine playfully punched her shoulder.

Together they walked to the back of the truck and lifted the bed liner. Underneath was a cache of weapons and accessories—rifles, shotguns, pistols, revolvers, night vision goggles, long-range scopes, silencers, Kevlar vests, and enough ammunition of various kinds to supply an entire army.

Vaughn picked up the parts of a rifle and expertly assembled them into a whole. "A Steyr. The assassin's ultimate tool. Very nice. Jackson, you're scaring me a little, my man."

"You never know what you might need in any given situation. Some wise person once taught me that."

"Wise, indeed," Vaughn said and smiled. She remembered exactly when, and under what circumstances, she had given Jackson that advice. "I'm pleased that you took the recommendation to heart."

Justine removed three vests, two more rifles, a hunting knife, fifteen ammunition clips, a Glock, a Sig Sauer, and a .38 Special. "Jackson, were you preparing for war?"

"I hoped not. Certainly four or five Tuareg will be no match for us."

"Assuming there are only four or five of them, with no local backup and no Company presence," Vaughn said. "I find that hard to believe, especially if they know I'm coming. At the very least, I would expect that Torgensen will be pissed as hell that he missed me and eager to finish the job."

"How do you know he's not still chasing his tail in Bamako?"

"He's too smart and too experienced for that. I think we have to assume the worst possible scenario and prepare for that. If we're wrong, I'd rather be wrong on the overkill side, pardon the pun."

"Agreed," Justine said, loading the selected hardware behind the driver's seat.

"How about if I drive for a while so you can get some sleep?" Vaughn asked Jackson. "You've got to be exhausted."

Jackson handed her the key. "I would not mind a short nap. All you have to do is follow the road."

"Such as it is," Vaughn mumbled. In truth, the road was nothing more than hard-packed dirt, barely distinguishable from the surrounding desert.

"Wake me up before we get to Timbuktu. I know a way around the city."

"Okay." Vaughn slid into the driver's seat and adjusted it for her height, while Justine squeezed herself into the jump seat.

"Grab my briefcase, will you?" Vaughn pointed to the floor underneath Justine's feet. See if you can find anything on Sage's blotter page that I missed. There's a file folder with the names of every embassy employee if you want to try to cross-reference some of them.

"Got you."

Vaughn started the engine and drove off. With any luck, they would have Sage, safe and sound, before the day was over.

Torgensen paced in the waiting area for his flight. Malians seemed to have no regard for schedules. The flight was scheduled to take off two hours ago. No one at the airline seemed the least bit concerned about the delay. Valuable time was slipping away. He had no idea how far behind Elliott he was, but he fully intended to arrive before her. Assuming she didn't fly.

Washington had checked the manifest of the only other flight to Timbuktu that day. Unless she was using an alias, Elliott wasn't on it. Torgensen himself questioned the ticket agent at the counter. No one matching Elliott's description boarded any domestic flight that day.

Unless the intel was faulty, even with the flight delay, he should still be able to beat her to Timbuktu. Not only that, but he had the added advantage of knowing exactly where he was going.

Presumably, she was on her own. The Company had raided the apartment of the scrawny little geek who sent Elliott the McNally file. It was empty and looked as if someone had left in a hurry. He was on the run, Torgensen was sure. Like all geeks, he most likely was terrified. There was no question he would be more interested in saving his own scalp than in helping Elliott.

"Sir?"

"What?"

"We are ready to board the plane now."

"Good." Torgensen collected his bag and slung it over his shoulder. In a few hours his job would be done, and he could get out of this God-forsaken country.

⨳

Sage took a sip of water. She estimated that several hours had passed since the food delivery. In the intervening time, she hadn't heard so much as a footfall outside the door.

Although she knew it was useless, she braced her feet against the wall and yanked one more time with all her might on the chain. Neither the iron ring nor the chain budged. Renewed shockwaves of pain radiated from her shoulder, even though she had used only her right arm in the effort. She hissed and panted, trying to catch her breath and simultaneously clamp down on the cry rising in her throat. As she slumped back against the wall, tears streamed down her face. "Vaughn will be here any minute. She knows what happened and she's coming for you." Wanting with all her heart to believe it, Sage repeated the mantra several times.

⨳

Nassir Bahim was tired and irritable. He hated being ordered to do things. He was Tuareg, proud descendant of generations of warriors who ruled the desert. Nassir spit on the ground as he thought about his dealings with Ambassador Dumont. There was a time, many years ago, when they were both young and idealistic. Nassir had respected Dumont. He believed that Dumont cared about his people. Not any more. Dumont changed—he'd become hard and ambitious.

Nassir's father was the leader of his people. Dumont was the political officer at the U.S. Embassy. His father encouraged Nassir to sit in on their meetings, which he did. It appeared to him then that Dumont had a genuine interest in the venerable history of the Tuareg and a respect for their heritage.

When Nassir's father became gravely ill, Nassir turned to Dumont, appealing to him to help get prescriptions that were unavailable in the desert. Dumont came through, supplying needed medicine and even bringing a doctor out to examine the patient, despite the fact that Nassir wasn't able to pay for either the doctor or the medicine. In the end, Nassir's father died anyway.

Still, Nassir was grateful to Dumont for his extraordinary efforts on his father's behalf, and pledged to him to return the favor if ever Dumont needed anything. So when Dumont called him to seek his help several weeks ago, Nassir felt he had no choice but to say yes. Honor demanded it. He was, after all, bound to Dumont for past good deeds.

What he was about to do—what he already had done—would have disappointed his father, he knew. But his father wasn't here, and Nassir's word was his bond. He would complete the jobs, erase the debt, and be done with it.

⬥⬥

When they were on the outskirts of Timbuktu, Vaughn shook Jackson. "I need you to take over the driving."

Jackson rubbed his eyes and sat up, yawning. "Right." He got out and went around to the driver's side, switching places with Vaughn. As he put the truck in gear, he asked, "Any word from your man?"

"Yeah, he called while you were sleeping. Sabastien says we want to approach from the north—there's a side entrance that opens into a hallway. The nearest office is around the corner, so the area may be unguarded."

"That makes sense."

"Once we get inside, there are several storage rooms, some larger than others. I figure they're holding Sage in one of the smaller rooms on the west side of the building."

"I hate to be the one to mention this, but what if we're wrong? What if this isn't the right place?" Jackson asked.

Vaughn's pulse jumped as doubts she'd been holding at bay made themselves known. She opened her mouth to speak, closed it again, and cleared her throat.

Justine cut in. "Sabastien has checked out every likely hiding place in Tuareg territory. None of them offers the kind of privacy and security that this one does. Vaughn is right—this is where Sage is. I'm sure of it."

"We will know soon enough," Jackson said. "It is only a few miles from here. You realize, if we take the truck in, we will be spotted long before we ever arrive."

"I know." Vaughn chewed her lip. "The best scenario, of course, would be to go in after dark."

"Darkness is several hours away," Jackson said, pointing out the obvious.

"No kidding." Vaughn said. "Chances are whoever is coming will be here long before then."

"Perhaps we can do something about that," Justine offered.

"What do you have in mind?"

"What if the man never gets there? Or is at least delayed?"

"I'm listening," Vaughn said.

"Jackson, I know you routed us around the city. But I assume we've joined up with the main road now, right?"

"Yes."

"Is this the only road out of town?"

"No, but to get where we are going, it is the most direct, most accessible route."

"I noticed a tool box in the back. I don't suppose you have any nails or screws in there, do you?"

"I believe I just might."

"A flat tire would be most inconvenient, wouldn't it? It might take an hour or more to repair."

"It might at that."

"It's not a guarantee," Vaughn said. "And what if he has already arrived? Or if Torgensen has? Tuareg man may not have flown, but I'm betting if Torgensen is coming, he did."

"He would've been carrying weapons," Justine reminded Vaughn.

"I recognize that, but it's a domestic flight. This isn't the States. He probably wouldn't have any trouble carrying a cache on board. Would he, Jackson?"

"Possibly not."

"Okay, say you're right and one of them beats us there," Justine said. "It still wouldn't hurt for us to lay down some nails."

"If he isn't ahead of us, which I think is unlikely, he would be a sitting duck, as you Americans say. We could wait and take him out."

"We can't kill just anyone who happens onto this road. I imagine he's not the only Tuareg with a car," Vaughn said.

"We would lay down the nails and keep going," Justine said. "By the way, even if Torgensen flew, he would have to drive from Timbuktu. He'd pass through this way too."

"Okay. Let's do it."

Jackson stopped the car, and Vaughn and Justine jumped out. Within minutes the road behind them was littered with nails and screws and they were on their way once again. They would find a place to park the truck out of sight a mile or so before reaching the facility and go the rest of the way on foot.

Vaughn closed her eyes and leaned her head back as they bounced along the last few miles. Her heart was hammering in her chest. They had made so many assumptions to get here. What if they were wrong and it cost Sage her life? *No. You can't think like that. This is no time for second-guessing.* She tried hard to set her emotions aside and listen to her gut. Her gut told her that Sage was here, and that she was still alive. She prayed that she was right.

The plane had barely come to a full stop before Torgensen was out of his seat. He would pay a local to borrow a car outside the airport. All that remained was for him to find someone interested in American cash and then to drive the last short distance. The end was in sight.

CHAPTER TWELVE

Nassir got out of the car and brushed out the sleeves of his robe. He had stopped only twice during the drive, and his body felt stiff. A brisk walk around the exterior of the facility got his blood flowing again. The warehouse really was ideal. It was isolated, with excellent sight lines. As a result, it required a minimal number of guards, which suited Nassir just fine. The fewer people involved, the better.

As he reached for the front door, the barrel of a rifle poked out at him.

"Identify yourself."

"It is I, you fool. Nassir. And why are you guarding the front door from inside? I told you I wanted at least one man outside at all times. In fact, I would like a perimeter set up. We may be having an unwanted guest."

"Yes, sir." The man opened the door wider to admit his leader. "I will get the perimeter set up immediately."

Nassir fell into step alongside him. "No, I want to meet with everyone first. Gather them in the conference room and let me know when you are ready." Nassir peeled off and disappeared through a door along the corridor. He was intimately familiar with the layout of the building, having selected it himself for the detention center.

The room was spare—concrete walls and floor, bare walls except for a detailed map of Mali, and no windows. The furniture consisted of two metal folding chairs, a metal desk, and a more comfortable chair. Nassir settled behind the desk and folded his hands on the smooth surface. During the long drive, he had managed to avoid thinking about the precise details of his mission. Now that he was here, there were decisions to be made.

He saw no need to make the girl suffer. She was nothing more than a pawn in this American's personal jihad. The question was, what method of death would be the most humane? A bullet to the head? A knife to the heart?

"Sir? We are ready."

Nassir waved the man away on a sigh and rose from the chair. Dumont might have been in a hurry to be rid of the girl, but Nassir did not feel the same urgency. After all, she was not going anywhere.

In the conference room, Nassir stared at the faces of the eight men sitting around the table. He had hand-picked them for this assignment. Like him, they were all descendants of warriors. Unlike him, they were not born to lead, only to follow. Their participation had been neither coerced nor required, and yet Nassir felt a strong sense of responsibility for their involvement. *Damn you, Dumont.*

"We have had a change in plans." He met each of their eager gazes in turn from a standing position at the head of the table. "There are complications I could not have foreseen. What must be done must be, but I will not compel you to be a party to it. If, after you hear what I have to say, you choose to leave, no one will blame you. I will not blame you." Nassir paused for effect. He could see the unease in their body language.

"I am with you."

"You have not yet heard what I have to say. I think you would be wise to wait." Nassir smiled indulgently at his younger cousin. The young man had been following him around like a puppy dog since he was a little boy.

"It does not matter—"

Nassir cut him off with a gesture of his hand. "As you know, originally we were asked only to detain the woman and hold onto her for a specified amount of time. Since then, there have been new developments. Our assignment has changed. Now, the woman must die." Again, Nassir looked at each face. For emphasis, he added, "At our hands."

The room went completely still. The air was heavy with the weight of Nassir's words.

"Surely this woman has not committed a crime so heinous—"

Nassir cut his cousin off. "It is not ours to judge her or to question. We are charged only with carrying out an assignment." Despite his own doubts and regrets, Nassir managed to say the words with conviction. "As I said, you are free to leave without prejudice. I will think no less of you."

"The question is, will we think less of ourselves if we stay?" Nassir heard the mumbled comment from Faquir, a serious, quiet young herder from a neighboring village. He had been the last recruit and was brought in only as an extra body.

"I will need your answers before we leave this room. I want a perimeter set up, and I need to know how many men I have to work with. Also, there is a woman who may try to liberate the prisoner."

"A woman?"

At the derisive tone, Nassir snapped. "I would not underestimate her. I am told she is very capable with a gun and should be considered dangerous."

"What does she look like?"

"I do not know. I only know we have orders to shoot to kill if we see her."

The men shifted uneasily. Finally, Faquir spoke up. "You are asking us to execute not one but two women?"

"Potentially, yes."

"This is not what we agreed to do."

"It is what will be done," Nassir said. "Now, who among you wishes to leave?" None of the men responded, which only served to increase his irritation. "Do I have to ask each of you individually? I've already told you, there is no shame in walking away. Now, I ask one more time, are you with me?"

This time, Nassir's question was greeted with eight hesitant yeses.

"Good. Set up the perimeter. I want every possible approach covered and a man on both entrances." Nassir walked out without further comment. He closed the door behind him and returned to the office down the hall. If it was possible, his mood was even fouler than it had been when he arrived. In the end, he knew he could not ask these men to do what he would not. He would have to pull the trigger himself.

కిసీ

The first thing Vaughn spotted from their vantage point behind the back corner of one of the out buildings was the car parked directly outside the front entrance. Her heart dropped in counterpoint to the uptick in her pulse. *Shit. Oh, shit. No, no, no.*

Justine's hand squeezed her shoulder and Vaughn twisted away. She hadn't meant for her emotions to be that transparent. Justine persisted, gripping her harder this time. She was pointing to a spot in the distance.

"Sentry," Justine whispered. "They wouldn't need a sentry if Sage wasn't still inside."

It took a moment for the logic of Justine's statement to sink in. Vaughn looked through the binoculars. She took in as much of the perimeter as she was able to from her hiding place. *Three guards visible, and probably the corresponding number on the other side of the building. She's right. If Sage were already dead, they wouldn't bother. They'd have cleared out by now.* Her pulse slowed minutely. She backed away and gestured for Justine to follow. They joined Jackson, who was leaning against the back of the hut.

"Okay," Vaughn said. "Three armed Tuareg are visible from here. Sabastien said the building was symmetrical. I'm guessing there are another three on the other side."

"Don't forget that there are probably at least a couple more men inside," Justine said.

"Right. So we're most likely looking at eight or more. The six out here, plus a couple guarding Sage."

"I like the odds," Jackson said, loading a clip of bullets into one of the silenced Steyrs. Even the bullet cartridges were specially designed to muffle sound. "But how do we know your friend is still alive?"

"Sage must be alive, otherwise they'd be gone," Vaughn said, ignoring her own lingering doubts. "Apart from that, the only other thing we know for certain is that Tuareg man was far enough ahead of us that we never saw him."

"Or we lost sight of him when we were walking. Remember, the road wasn't in our sightline the whole time," Justine said.

"Since I don't think we're going to get close enough to check the hood of his car for heat, let's assume he's been here a while and there's no time to spare," Vaughn said. "We need to pick off all six outside men in quick succession, before they have a chance to raise an alarm."

"We're using .300 Whisper cartridges in silenced barrels. They will not even know what hit them, and neither will anyone else until it is too late," Jackson said, affixing a long range scope to the rifle.

"Right," Vaughn agreed. "Aim for the head. Get a side angle and hit them in the ear if you can. I doubt they have vests on under their robes, but I don't want to take any chances. We've got no room for mistakes. I'll take the one to the left of the door. Justine, you get the one on the right. Jackson, you take out the perimeter man. Let's do it on a count of three. Then we run like hell to the back of that outbuilding," Vaughn pointed to a structure some forty feet away, "and quickly assess the positioning of the other three men."

Vaughn was anxious to get going. Sage was in there, and if she died before they reached her, she would never forgive herself.

"You know we haven't accounted for Torgensen," Justine said.

"If that is not his car then he is behind us. Hopefully he will be busy fixing a flat tire right now," Jackson said.

"If not..." Vaughn said, "if Torgensen is here, we'll know soon enough and we'll adjust accordingly."

"Agreed," Justine said, loading the third Steyr and checking the scope.

Vaughn sighted the target as she waited for Justine to finish her preparations. The front door was some one hundred yards from where they crouched, well within range of their weapons. "Inside, we use the silenced Sig Sauers. Chances are any noise will echo in there."

The three of them removed the Sigs from the waistband of their pants and loaded clips for them as well. Vaughn shifted her shoulders to adjust the Kevlar vest so that its weight was distributed evenly across her back. She noted that Jackson and Justine were doing the same thing.

"Okay." Vaughn looked into Justine's eyes, then Jackson's. "Ready?"

"Yes."

"Yes."

Hang on Sage. We're almost there. Although she wasn't one to pray, Vaughn mumbled, "Please, God, let her be okay."

"She will be," Justine said in a voice loud enough for only Vaughn to hear.

Vaughn nodded and swallowed the lump in her throat. There was no room for emotion in the middle of a mission. She shoved her fears to a remote compartment in her brain. It was time to go to work.

She moved into position and waited for Justine and Jackson to do the same. Both acknowledged Vaughn's nod when they had their weapons aimed and ready. "One, two, three."

The door opened and Sage blinked. This time there was only one man, and he did not shine the flashlight in her eyes. Backlit as he was by the naked bulb in the hallway, she could see that he was tall, thin, and carried a gun with a long barrel.

Sage's hands began to tremble. The man held no food and, apart from the traditional head veil, made no effort to hide his face. Despite the oppressive heat, her teeth began to chatter.

He stared at her for what seemed like a very long time.

"Dr. McNally."

"Y-you know my name?"

"Yes, although I do not know much about you beyond that." His French was passable.

"Why was I taken? Why am I here?" Sage's voice broke from nerves. There was something about this man, something about the way he held the gun with such ease. But there also was something akin to sympathy in his eyes, which glinted in the light when he turned slightly to look behind him as he did now. He said something over his shoulder in dialect to someone Sage couldn't see.

When he turned back to face her, he was silent for several seconds, and Sage wondered if he would answer her.

"In all honesty, I do not know the whys. You might look inside yourself for the answer."

"In-inside myself?"

"I came to see you personally…" The man's voice trailed off, as he seemed to reconsider what he wanted to say. For a second, Sage thought he looked indecisive. "I came in here because I will ask no other to do what I must do," he said in a rush. "And because I want to apologize to you directly. When I was ordered to detain you, I was told only to hold you until further notice. I was not ever told that the assignment would change, although perhaps I should have anticipated that eventuality."

Sage nodded dumbly, trying to comprehend what he was telling her. His eyes were focused on the wall behind her, as if he had forgotten she was sitting there.

"My men covered your eyes because it was important that you not be able to identify them after you were released."

The import of his words sank in, and Sage's breathing began to quicken. *You're not hiding yourself now.* Her gaze dropped to the gun in his hand. *It doesn't matter if I know what you look like. I won't be able to tell anyone if I'm dead.* The trembling in her hands extended to the rest of her body. *Oh, God. No!*

He moved toward her and spoke more softly. "My name is Nassir. I think you should know the name of the person who unjustly takes your life. I want you to know this was not my choice, and I am truly sorry for what I must do."

Sage tried to raise her arms, and the pain in her shoulder wrenched an involuntary scream from her. "Wait!"

Torgensen noted the three dead bodies around the front of the building. "Well, that answers one question. Elliott is definitely here, or at least she was."

The positions of the bodies indicated all three had been hit in the head and each of them before he'd had time to open his mouth or raise a weapon. Torgensen's respect for Elliott grew. He would have to handle this one with care. His smile was predatory. *This could be fun.*

Of course, it would have been more fun to watch Elliott in action, which would have happened if he hadn't taken a wrong turn out of Timbuktu and ended up four-wheeling off-road through the desert instead of staying on the road.

Torgensen used his binoculars to check the tire tracks leading up to the building—there was only one set, and it led in, not out. There were no footprints heading away from the facility, either. "No, she's still here."

Torgensen recalled with disdain his strict instructions not to interfere with anything else that might be happening. Fine then, he would watch from a distance and wait for the others to fail.

He used his hands to dig himself a pit in the sand with a direct sightline to the front door. Once Elliott had dispatched all of the guards, there would be no reason for her to be cautious; therefore, it seemed most likely she would come out the front. Even if she did not, it would not matter. Eventually, she would have to come that way. She and McNally would each walk directly into a bullet from his M-16.

Vaughn, Justine, and Jackson stepped over the guard lying directly in front of the north entrance. So far, everything had gone exactly to plan. Six men down, each taken out with a single shot, and not a sound beyond the thud of bodies hitting sand.

They paused in front of the back door. Vaughn shifted the strap for the assault rifle until the gun rested across her back. She pulled the Sig Sauer from her waistband and waited until the others followed suit.

"Okay," she whispered. "I open the door, Jackson, you get whoever's behind it. Then you two flank me as we go in. No words once we're inside. Keep your eyes sharp—hand gestures only."

Justine and Jackson nodded their assent as they checked silencers and ammunition clips. Vaughn mouthed the count to three and, with one fluid motion, shot out the lock to the door while shoving it open hard with her foot. Her foot met some resistance, as though the door had hit something solid, and she indicated with her head that someone had likely gone down behind it.

Jackson flew past Vaughn, gun raised. He leaned over and put a bullet between the eyes of the man who was attempting to regain his balance.

That was when Vaughn heard it—a blood-curdling scream that felt like a shot of adrenaline in her heart. *Sage.* Frantically, she motioned Justine and Jackson to watch for others as she sprinted down the hall, following the direction of Sage's voice. *Too far. She's too far away.*

Then Vaughn heard a shouted, "Wait!"

The single word from Sage propelled her forward at lightning speed. As she spied the open doorway less than five feet in front of her on the right side of the hall, she felt a bullet whiz past her ear. She barely looked up in time to see a man in front and to the left of her go down, a neat hole blossoming in his forehead. Without breaking stride, she motioned to Justine for her to take Jackson and check the rest of the building.

Vaughn reached the opening two steps later. She dropped to one knee in the doorway even as a man whirled toward her, gun in hand. She had less than a second to register the sight of Sage, cowering on the floor behind him, her eyes wide with terror.

Vaughn's first shot sent the man's weapon flying across the room. The second hit him in the kneecap and had him howling in pain and writhing on the floor. She barely heard Justine behind her.

"All clear, Vaughn."

She nodded her head and said softly, "Take him to another room. Find out what he knows. Then kill him." She never took her eyes off Sage.

As soon as Justine moved into the room and secured the man, Vaughn put her Sig Sauer away, dropped the rifle off her shoulder, and closed the last steps between her and Sage. She dropped to the floor and gathered Sage gently in her arms.

"I've got you. No one can hurt you now. No one will ever hurt you again." Sage trembled against her.

After several moments, Vaughn pulled back far enough to take Sage's face in her hands. Her trained eyes took in the bruising around Sage's eyes and temple. She stroked Sage's face and hair, her fingers feeling for contusions at the same time.

"Hi. Boy, am I g-glad to see you." Sage's voice was thick and unsteady when she finally spoke.

"Not as glad as I am to see you." Vaughn leaned forward and kissed her forehead and nose.

"He— He was g-going to k-kill me."

"I know, honey. It's over. He's gone now."

"T-there are more of them."

"Not any more." The child-like tone of Sage's voice broke Vaughn's heart. "No one can hurt you now. I'm here. I won't let anything happen. I promise."

She reached into a pocket of her vest and found a handcuff key. Vaughn hoped a bit of levity would take the edge off Sage's fear. "Let's get these off you, okay?" She pointed to the cuffs on Sage's wrists. "I'm not into kinky."

"No? Color me shocked." Sage smiled weakly.

Good girl, Sage, you haven't lost your sense of humor. You're going to be okay. I'll make sure of it. "That's it, keep making fun of me." Vaughn used the key to remove the cuffs.

"Thank you," Sage said. "Thank you for rescuing me. I knew you'd come." She launched herself into Vaughn's arms. "Argh!" Immediately, she crumpled against Vaughn.

"What, what is it?" Vaughn heard the hissed breath that followed the scream. She pulled back far enough to see the grimace on Sage's face and the pallor of her skin, visible even in the semi-darkness. Tears leaked from the corners of Sage's eyes. Vaughn's attention moved from Sage's face to her body. She saw immediately the odd angle of Sage's arm. "Your shoulder's dislocated."

"I know," Sage said through clenched teeth. "I j-just wasn't brave enough to b-bang myself into the wall to f-fix it."

"That doesn't really work, just so you know."

"Oh."

"But I have someone with me who can fix it for you. Come on, let's get you out of here. Can you walk?"

"I t-think so."

"I'll help you." Vaughn gently put her arms around Sage's waist and pulled them both to their feet.

They stood for several minutes, Vaughn holding Sage, and Sage burrowing against the safety of Vaughn's solid presence.

Vaughn could feel their hearts beating against each other. She closed her eyes and said a prayer of thanks that with Sage, at least, she'd been in time. Sage whimpered against her.

"Shh. It's okay, baby. You're going to be okay." Softly, she stroked Sage's back until the trembling subsided.

Vaughn didn't know yet who it was, but whoever was responsible for this would pay—with their lives. She wouldn't rest until it was done.

CHAPTER THIRTEEN

His leg was on fire, his hand throbbed where the bullet had nicked it, and he was fading in and out of consciousness. *I will not have to endure much more. Soon my time will be over, and I can rest.*

"I'll ask you again. Who do you work for?"

Nassir closed his mouth on a scream as the big man poked his finger into the wound.

"She is asking you nicely. I suggest you answer her. We can keep you alive and in a great deal more pain than you are in now. Or we can put you out of your misery."

Nassir clenched his teeth. It wasn't that he felt any particular allegiance to Dumont. It was that he was a warrior, and he would die with honor. He would not sell out like a common rat.

Again, the finger poked at the place where his kneecap once had been. He squeezed his eyes shut tightly as tears streamed down his face. "I," he ground out, "am impervious to pain."

"Is that so?" The big man asked, squeezing his injured hand.

Nassir panted to control the agony. "Yes."

"Whoever you're protecting, do you honestly believe they would do the same for you?" The woman asked the question softly.

"That does not matter to me. I am a warrior, descendant of a long line of warriors, and I will finish out my time with honor."

"Like you were going to let that woman finish out her life?"

"That was regrettable. I…" Nassir stopped talking. He had already said more than he intended.

"You what?" the woman asked.

"You may torture me forever. I have said all I will say."

As the man raised his hand again, the woman reached out and stopped him. She motioned him to the side. Although they moved several steps away and Nassir was fighting to stay conscious, he thought he heard her instruct him to stop, that they would not get any more useful information, and that they were not barbarians.

It was the last thing Nassir heard before oblivion took him.

⚜

Vaughn supported Sage with an arm around the waist as they exited her prison. She watched as Sage blinked hard in the brightness of the corridor.

"Close your eyes for a second and open them slowly. Give yourself time to adjust." Vaughn stopped their progress and waited for Sage to follow her instruction.

"That's a little better. Thanks."

"You're welcome." Vaughn noticed that as they moved forward, Sage clung to her more tightly.

Vaughn turned toward her and gave her a reassuring smile. "You're safe. I promised...remember?"

"I—" Sage gasped, stopped short, and ducked behind Vaughn.

Vaughn looked around to see what had caused such a violent reaction. Jackson was walking toward them, gun out, blood spattered liberally on his Kevlar vest and pants.

"Put it away," Vaughn commanded, gesturing at the weapon. She pulled Sage gently into her arms, careful not to jostle her shoulder. Sage was shaking and crying.

"It's okay. He's with me. Shh. It's okay. This is Jackson. He's an old friend." She motioned for Jackson to stay where he was, and continued to soothe Sage until she quieted and the shaking stopped.

"I'm sorry. I—"

"Don't apologize." Vaughn's heart bled for this innocent woman who would carry the scars of this episode for the rest of her life. "It's to be expected." She tipped Sage's chin up to meet her eyes. "I meant what I said, Sage. Anyone who wants to do you harm will have to go through me first."

"And me," Jackson said.

"And him," Vaughn said, smiling into Sage's frightened eyes. She faced forward once again, turning Sage with her. "Dr. Sage McNally, this is my good friend Jackson. Jackson is chief of security services for Burkina Faso."

"It is a pleasure to meet you, Dr. Sage McNally. Any friend of Vaughn Elliott's is a friend of mine."

"I-it's nice to meet you, sir."

"I taught Jackson everything he knows." Vaughn winked at Sage.

"It is true. I trust her with my life, and you can also."

"That's good to know," Sage said.

"What's the news?" Vaughn asked Jackson.

"We could not get anything out of him. I am sorry."

Vaughn shrugged. "I didn't really think you would, but it was worth a try. He's gone?"

"Yes. I have seen to it personally."

"W-what do you mean, gone?" Sage asked Vaughn.

"That man will never hurt you, or anyone else, again."

"Y-you killed him?" Sage directed the question to Jackson.

He looked at Vaughn before answering, his expression conveying a question of its own. Vaughn nodded.

"Yes, ma'am."

"Oh." Sage said, her voice hollow and small. She shivered against Vaughn's side. "Was that really necessary?" She looked up at Vaughn. "I mean, he was very apologetic about what he had to do. I got the feeling that he truly regretted—"

"Sage, that man was about to kill you."

Sage trembled again. "I know, but it wasn't his idea, and he seemed honorable…" She paused. "I guess that sounds stupid. It's just…"

"I know. I'm sorry," Vaughn said, marveling at the ability of this woman to see the best in a person who had been about to end her life. "We had to."

Sage said nothing more as they continued down the corridor. When they turned the corner, Justine was coming toward them. This time, although there was a hitch in her step, Sage continued bravely forward.

"You must be Sage," Justine said. Vaughn watched Justine eye Sage appraisingly.

"Yes."

"Hi. I'm Justine. I'm a friend of Vaughn's."

"Boy, Vaughn, you sure seem to have a lot of friends for someone not very likeable."

The comment surprised a laugh out of all of them.

"That, my dear, is the understatement of the year," Justine said. She finished closing the distance between them and squinted into Sage's eyes. To Vaughn, she said, "Concussion for starters."

Vaughn nodded. "A dislocated shoulder too. Can you do anything for her here?"

"I think so."

"Among her many talents, Justine is a trauma nurse," Vaughn explained to Sage. "She's a handy person to have on your side."

"There's a room around the next corner. I've already set it up as an examination room." Justine winked at Sage. "I always like to be prepared."

"Wow. I guess so."

"Bring her this way," Justine said to Vaughn.

"I do not want to intrude, Vaughn Elliott," Jackson said, "but I do not think it wise to stay here too long with Mr. Torgensen still in the picture."

"Who is Mr. Torgensen?" Sage asked.

"Nobody you need to be concerned with," Vaughn answered, before anyone else could. She looked at Jackson. "You're right. I just want to get Sage stabilized and make sure she's okay before we travel."

"I will check the perimeter while you and Miss Justine help Dr. McNally."

"The hell you will," Vaughn said sharply. "Nobody steps outside this building alone."

"I meant only that I would try to assess the situation from inside. Also, I will find something to secure the back door again."

"Okay." Vaughn relented. "But I don't want you taking any risks, do you understand? If you find anything odd or out of place, you're to come get me. No heroics."

"I understand."

"I mean it, my friend." Vaughn shook her finger at him.

"Right."

Vaughn turned to Justine. "Lead the way."

❦

Justine had done well setting up a trauma area, Vaughn thought. A long table was positioned in the middle of the room. A smaller table to the side held some instruments, gauze, and strips of cloth of varying sizes.

"Help her onto the table," Justine said to Vaughn.

"I can—"

Before Sage could finish the sentence, Vaughn lifted her up and deposited her gently on the table. When she looked down, she realized she was between Sage's knees, in almost exactly the same position they'd shared in Sage's kitchen. It seemed like a lifetime ago.

Sage's eyes met and held hers for a second, and Vaughn wondered if she was thinking the same thing.

"Okay," Justine said, breaking the spell. "Let's have a look." If Justine had any idea what had just transpired, she didn't show it. She picked up a flashlight from the side table. "I'm going to shine this in your eyes. I'm pretty sure you suffered a concussion, but I'd like to see your pupil responses just the same."

"I think I might have suffered more than one, if that's possible. They hit me several times with something hard. I tried to escape more than once." Sage said it matter-of-factly, and Vaughn's admiration for her courage grew.

"I wish I had a pen light, but this will have to do," Justine said, holding up a regular flashlight.

"That's okay."

Vaughn moved to the side and watched Justine check Sage's pupils, then do several visual acuity tests with her fingers to see if Sage was suffering from any double or blurred vision.

When she was done, Justine replaced the flashlight on the instrument table. "Yep. I think it's safe to say you had a couple of good knocks on the noggin. I don't think there's any permanent damage, but if we were in the States, I'd insist on you having a CT scan to be sure."

"I'll make sure we get her one when we get her home," Vaughn said.

"Home?" Sage asked, looking from one of them to the other.

"Can you check her shoulder?" Vaughn ignored Sage's question. *Oh, yes. When I get us out of here, you're going back to the States until I can be sure you're out of danger.*

"I'd say you're right," Justine said, looking at the odd angle at which Sage held her arm. "It's definitely out."

"I got banged around on the ground a few times," Sage said meekly.

Justine smiled at her. "You were very brave to fight back, you know."

"Not really," Sage said.

"Oh yes, you were," Vaughn said, stepping closer. She understood that Justine was trying to distract Sage from what she was about to do.

"Help me get this off her, Vaughn." Justine gestured to the robe.

"Right."

"Lift your hips for us?"

Sage did as commanded, and Vaughn and Justine pulled the robe up to Sage's abdomen.

"Now stay still. Let Vaughn and I do the rest of the work, okay?"

"Okay."

Together, Vaughn and Justine worked the garment over Sage's head, and finished by sliding it off her bad arm. Vaughn sucked in a quick breath as anger flooded her. Sage's body was a mass of dried blood and bruises. She clenched her fists. It was lucky for her captors that they were already dead. What she wanted to do to them at this moment was far worse than a quick bullet to the head.

Her eyes met Justine's and, for the briefest second, she saw her own rage reflected there. Just as quickly, it was gone, replaced by calm professionalism.

"I'm going to put your shoulder back in place first, and then we'll get you cleaned up so we can see what else we need to do, okay?" Justine addressed Sage as she put together a makeshift sling.

"Sounds like a plan." Sage smiled bravely. "Will it hurt much?"

"It will hurt a lot less than it did when it was dislocated. When you get home, you'll need to see an orthopedist. There could be something torn in there, and you might need surgery to repair it."

As Justine judged the angle she would need to take in order to put Sage's shoulder back in place, Vaughn moved forward. "If you want, you can squeeze my hand. Grip it as hard as you want, you won't hurt me."

"Thanks." Sage slid her good hand into Vaughn's and entwined their fingers. "I'll try not to be too much of a baby."

"Nobody would accuse you of that," Vaughn said. With her free hand, she reached out tentatively and stroked Sage's cheek. She was keenly aware of Justine observing her out of the corner of her eye, but she didn't care.

"Ready?" Justine looked at Vaughn over Sage's head. "Brace her on that side, will you?"

"Of course." Vaughn spread her feet slightly to improve her balance. She pulled Sage toward her until her head was burrowed against Vaughn's shoulder.

Vaughn watched as Justine moved directly in front of Sage and applied pressure to the front of her shoulder. She felt Sage's breathing quicken in anticipation of pain.

"Let your arm go lax. I'm going to move it for you, okay?" Justine asked Sage.

"Okay." Sage's eyes were tightly shut.

Justine manipulated Sage's arm until the elbow was bent at a ninety degree angle, palm facing out. Then she rotated the forearm downward toward the floor while continuing to push on the ball of the shoulder with her other hand.

Vaughn felt Sage go stiff against her, then slump forward. Sweat dotted her forehead. "You okay?" she whispered into Sage's ear.

"Uh-huh," Sage said tightly. "Dandy."

"Feel better?" Justine asked, watching Sage.

Sage straightened up and shrugged her shoulder experimentally, never letting go of Vaughn's hand. "Much. Thanks."

"You're welcome." Justine moved Sage's arm until her hand was over her heart. "Keep it in this position. After we get you cleaned up I'll put the arm in a sling."

"Is there running water?" Vaughn asked.

"Surprisingly, yes. Walk this way." Justine led them down the hall.

"I'll check on Jackson while you work on Sage," Vaughn said. She felt Sage go rigid against her side and the hand holding hers tightened its grip.

"Hey, you're all right. Justine will take good care of you."

"Please, don't leave me. Don't go."

Vaughn was helpless against the plea in Sage's voice. When she turned to look at her, there was real fear in her eyes. "I'm right here. I won't go anywhere. I promise."

"Thanks." Suddenly, Sage's eyes were filled with tears.

"Hey, hey. It's okay. You're safe, honey. You're safe."

Sage stopped walking and threw herself into Vaughn's arms. Vaughn staggered back a step at the unexpected onslaught.

Justine caught Vaughn's attention and mouthed that she would check on Jackson. Vaughn nodded. She wrapped her arms around Sage and rocked her, resting her cheek on the top of Sage's head.

After several minutes, Sage sniffed and lifted swollen eyes to Vaughn's. "I-I'm s-so s-sorry. I don't know what's the matter with me."

"I do. Sage, you've been through an incredibly traumatic time. It's natural for you to be afraid. For a while, you're probably not going to want to be alone. Don't beat yourself up about it. You're a very, very brave woman."

"You're just being nice to me."

Vaughn caressed Sage's cheek and shifted a lock of hair out of her face. "No, I'm not. You did great. You fought and you used your head to stay alive. Most people would've panicked or given up."

Sage wiped her eyes with her good hand. "I knew you would come for me. That's what kept me going."

"You..." Vaughn's heart skipped a beat.

Sage smiled and nodded. "I kept telling myself that you would know what happened, and that you would find me."

"That's a serious amount of faith."

"I knew it was well-placed." Sage rested her forehead against Vaughn's chin. "I just needed to stay alive until you got here."

Vaughn didn't know what to say to that, so she said nothing.

Justine reappeared a moment later. "Everything appears to be secure. It's getting dark out there."

"That's a comforting thought. I'd rather deal with Torgensen in the dark than in daylight. Where's Jackson?"

"I've got him preparing Sage a little something to eat."

"Good idea." Vaughn pulled back so that she could look at Sage. "When's the last time you had anything to eat?"

"I don't remember. One of the men brought me something earlier in the day. I think it must've been breakfast. Who is Torgensen?"

"Torgensen is my problem," Vaughn said. The last thing she wanted was to tell Sage that the ambassador had replaced her with a trained assassin.

"Vaughn—"

"Let's get you cleaned up. We can't stay here too much longer." She walked forward, propelling Sage along with her.

Twenty minutes later, she and Justine escorted Sage into the kitchen. Her arm was restrained in the makeshift sling; she had stitches in her head and in her thigh where dirt and grime had hidden a long gash. They eased Sage into a chair by the small table.

"Everything okay?" Vaughn asked Jackson.

"Yes. I was able to contact some friends using Justine's phone. They will meet us and get you out of the country. If something happens to me, they will still be expecting you."

"What could happen to him?" Sage looked at Vaughn, confusion in her eyes.

"Nothing's going to happen to anybody. You should eat." Vaughn picked up the plate Jackson had prepared and slid it in front of Sage.

"All appears to be quiet," Jackson said. "Perhaps too quiet."

"If Torgensen is here, why hasn't he made a move?" Justine asked.

"Why would he?" Vaughn countered. "Remember, he thinks I'm alone. Assuming he's out there, he will have seen the dead guards." Vaughn saw Sage flinch and paused. "Maybe we should discuss this outside."

"No!" Sage cried. She looked around wildly. Vaughn moved to her and took her hand.

"We'll be right outside in the hallway."

Sage shook her head vigorously.

Vaughn tried one more time. "This isn't going to be pleasant conversation."

"I don't care. I can hear it."

"Vaughn—" Justine's voice held a warning.

"Okay. We'll talk about it here." She ignored Justine's glare. "If Torgensen saw the dead guards, he's got to assume either I've taken out the rest of them, or I'm already dead. Either way, there's no reason for him to come charging in. He can wait me out and have the advantage of not giving away his position."

"I agree," Jackson said. "Which means we might want to split up when we leave. At least one of us should go out the back door."

Vaughn frowned. She didn't like the idea of leaving someone uncovered. It was clear to her that Sage would not go with anyone but her. That made their exit more difficult. Whatever else happened, Sage had to be protected.

"Can I talk to you over here for a minute?" Justine asked Vaughn. "We won't leave the room," she said to Sage.

Vaughn moved to the far corner where Justine joined her. "What?"

"Have you asked Sage if she knows why she was taken?" They were both whispering.

"No. You see her. She's in no condition emotionally to be subjected to questioning."

"Agreed. But it's obvious that she has information that someone thought was worth killing her for. If anything happens to her…" Justine let the thought hang in the air.

"Nothing's going to happen to her. Hasn't she been through enough for one day? Can't you see that she's hurting and exhausted?" Vaughn knew she was being unreasonable.

"Vaughn—"

"What do you want me to do, browbeat her?"

"No. I just want you to ask the question."

Vaughn folded her arms across her chest. The last thing she wanted to do was traumatize Sage further. It was bad enough that she would see the dead bodies either way they exited the building.

"If it was anyone else, you wouldn't be hesitating."

Vaughn's head shot up, her eyes daring Justine to say more. The two women stood toe-to-toe and glared at each other. Finally, Vaughn relented. "Okay. I will ask the question. But I will not push her, and neither will anyone else. Got it?"

"Agreed," Justine said. They returned to the table.

"Sage," Vaughn began. "I know you're tired and hurting, but we need your help."

"What do you need?"

"These men who took you…do you have any idea why? What did they want?"

Tears sprang immediately to Sage's eyes. "I d-don't know. I've been asking myself the same question. I can't figure it out. I don't know what I d-did to deserve this…" Her body began to shake.

Vaughn shot Justine a dirty look. She gathered Sage in her arms. "You didn't do anything, honey. Don't worry about it. We'll talk about it again later. It's not important right now."

"We should go," Jackson said. "We have a distance to travel, and it would be better to arrive under cover of darkness."

"Yes," Vaughn agreed. "Let's get ready."

"What's the plan?" Justine asked.

"Jackson, I hate to say this, my friend, but I disagree with your strategy. We should all go out the front, at staggered intervals. As soon as the door opens, Torgensen will give away his position. He is only expecting to face a single opponent. It will give us our best shot at taking him out."

Silence enveloped the room momentarily as the others considered the logic of Vaughn's plan.

"The last person will take Sage," Justine said.

"Yes," Vaughn conceded grudgingly. Since Sage would not leave her side, Vaughn would have to be last out. The first two people through the door would be the most vulnerable. That meant that Jackson and Justine would be exposed to a much bigger risk than Vaughn would. Ideally, she would have insisted on being the first person out.

She frowned. Could she get Sage out first, draw Torgensen's fire, and protect Sage at the same time? No. Justine was right—the object was to keep Sage safe. Taking her out last would ensure that she had minimal exposure.

There was no way around it. "I'm not happy exposing you two this way," Vaughn said as they readied their weapons and walked to the front entrance.

"It is necessary, Vaughn Elliott, and I would not have it any other way."

"Jackson's right, and you know it," Justine added.

"Maybe, but I don't have to be happy about it."

"I will go first," Jackson said, his head held high. "The meeting place is at a checkpoint just inside the border with Mauritania. It is the closest border. Getting to my country would take too long. Take the road west."

"You can show us, yourself, my friend, when we get there," Vaughn said. "Everybody ready? Jackson will go, then Justine after a three second wait, then me and Sage." She looked at Sage, whose eyes were glassy with fear. She squeezed her hand. "You just stay behind me. If anything happens to me, go with Justine and Jackson. They will protect you."

"Vaughn?" Sage's voice was tight with panic.

"It's going to be fine. Just stay low and follow my instructions or theirs, okay? Can you do that?"

"I think so."

"You're okay to run?"

"Yes," Sage said.

"Good." Vaughn took off her Kevlar vest.

"What are you doing?" Sage asked.

"You're going to wear this." Vaughn threaded Sage's good arm through the armhole, even as Sage resisted, and zipped her injured arm inside.

"You're going to need that."

"No. I'll be fine. I have a gun." Vaughn smiled reassuringly. She took a deep breath. "Everybody good to go?"

Jackson and Justine checked their weapons one last time.

"Yes."

"Yes."

"I guess," Sage said. Vaughn squeezed her hand. She motioned for Justine to flatten herself and Sage against the wall.

"Okay. Jackson, on the count of three…"

CHAPTER FOURTEEN

V aughn checked to be sure that Justine had Sage well out of danger. As Jackson prepared to push open the door, Vaughn unbalanced him, knocking him back a step. "I can't let you do it, my friend. Justine, take care of Sage."

Before any of them had a chance to react, Vaughn shoved past Jackson and through the door, tucking and rolling as she went. She saw the muzzle flash a split second before a bullet ripped into her exposed torso. Time slowed. Behind her, she heard Sage scream and Jackson swear. In her peripheral vision, she caught a glimpse of Justine struggling to restrain Sage, a look of shock on her face. "I'm sorry," she said silently to Justine. "This is not your fight, and you are the only one medically qualified to help Sage. Keep her safe."

Vaughn continued to roll with the momentum, landing on her stomach, the rifle still in her hands. Unbearable heat radiated throughout her body. She tried to draw in a deep breath, but her lungs were on fire.

Focus. The flash was to the left, behind that dune. She eyed the landscape through her night vision scope and squeezed the trigger three times in rapid succession.

Someone was scrambling close to her. *Jackson? Justine?* She saw another muzzle flash in the distance. A fraction of a second later, there was a strangled moan, and the nearby figure fell to the ground hard, twisting at an impossible angle.

Vaughn could hear her own labored breaths. *Drowning. It feels like I'm drowning.* Even in her diminished capacity, she recognized that her time was running out. Before long, she wouldn't be able to protect any of them.

She adjusted her sights and fired five more rounds. Through the scope, she watched as Torgensen's body contorted. Sweat poured into her eyes and she blinked to clear her vision. *Have to end it now.* With one last effort, Vaughn squeezed off two more shots—the first hit Torgensen in the middle of the chest, as evidenced by the dark circle that blossomed over his heart; the second snapped his head back. It was over.

The rifle slipped from Vaughn's shaking hands as she began to cough. A trickle of blood coated her lower lip. She turned on her side, desperate to see who had fallen next to her, but her vision was badly blurred. She thought she saw a figure looming over her. With a last gasp, she choked out, "Torgensen's dead. Get Sage out." Then she slipped away.

⋙⋘

Justine saw Vaughn's body jerk as the bullet hit her. "Vaughn!"

"No! No! Vaughn!" Sage surged forward, pushing off the wall.

Justine reacted instinctively, years of training and experience kicking in. She threw her body in front of Sage and pinned her to the wall, a forearm under her chin. She took one quick look over her shoulder at the scene outside. In the time it had taken her to secure Sage, Jackson had regained his balance and bolted out the door. In the space of a heartbeat, he was gone, a bullet through the ear. The dead weight of his body held the door open.

"Shit!" They were out of the direct line of fire, but Justine would've preferred more cover.

"Vaughn!" Sage pummeled Justine with her one available fist, trying desperately to break free.

Remarkably, Vaughn continued to shoot off rounds. Justine put a finger to Sage's lips. "Shh. You can't help her now. Stay against the wall. Sage, stop struggling, do you hear me? Sage!"

Sage's face held all the anguish Justine felt.

"Vaughn," Sage said more softly. "We have to help…"

"We will. We will. But we can't help her by getting ourselves shot."

Justine felt some of the fight leach out of Sage as her eyes glazed over in shock. "Promise me you'll stay right where you are.

I need to give Vaughn some backup. I can't do that if I have to worry about you."

Sage didn't answer. Justine shook her lightly. "Promise me. And if something happens to me, I want you to go out the back door. Here's a gun." Justine pulled the Sig from her waistband and tried to put it into Sage's lax hand. "It's loaded. Use it if you have to. There's an outbuilding about twenty yards away. Hide inside until morning. There's a car out front. Here is the key." She pulled the ignition key she had removed from the Tuareg's robe out of a pocket of the Kevlar vest. "Head west to Mauritania. Jackson's people will meet you there."

Sage simply stood staring over Justine's shoulder, her jaw slack and her hand hanging loosely at her side.

Justine shook her head. *It's no good. I can't leave you.* She chanced another look back, realizing that everything had gone very still. The only sound she could hear was...a strangled cough? "Wait right here. Don't move."

Justine wasn't sure Sage would follow her instruction, but she had to chance it. She turned and watched as Vaughn rolled onto her side. Justine dropped to her belly and commando-crawled through the opening. She scanned the horizon through her night scope. *There.* To the left, some one hundred yards away, she saw a figure slumped face-first in the sand.

Vaughn coughed again, a horrible, gurgling sound. Justine scrambled the last few feet until she was kneeling over her. Vaughn tried to speak. Justine put her ear next to Vaughn's lips to hear.

"Torgensen's dead. Get Sage out."

"I'm going to get us all out, champ. Stay with me." Tears formed in Justine's eyes and she blinked them away. *You're a trained professional. She needs you. Get your shit together.* She lifted Vaughn's wrist. There was a weak pulse.

"Vaughn!" Sage screamed.

When Justine looked up, Sage was standing over them.

"Is she..."

"She's alive," Justine said. "We've got to get her back inside. Can you carry her feet with your good arm? I'll take her upper body."

"She's bleeding," Sage said in that shock-induced monotone.

"Sage, Vaughn needs our help now. Can you do it?"

Sage nodded and picked up Vaughn's ankles as Justine linked her arms under Vaughn's armpits.

Justine directed them back to the temporary triage room, where they lifted Vaughn onto the table. The front of her shirt was smeared with blood and her face was white as a sheet except for her mouth, where drops of blood stained her lips.

Justine ripped Vaughn's shirt off near the site of the wound. Fortunately, the wound wasn't bleeding profusely. She reached for Vaughn's carotid pulse and noticed that her Adam's apple had shifted several centimeters to the left from its normal center position. *Tension pneumothorax.* Vaughn's lung had collapsed and the chest cavity was filling with air. If she didn't relieve the pressure soon, Vaughn would die. Justine looked over to Sage, who stood stock still, staring at Vaughn's inert body.

What Justine needed was a hollow needle, but she didn't have one. She would have to improvise.

"I need your help, Sage. There's an office around the corner with an old Bic pen on the desk. I need you to get it for me."

Sage didn't budge.

"Sage? Did you hear me?"

"What?"

"Vaughn needs you. There's an office around the corner to the left with an old Bic pen on the desk. I need you to run and get it for me."

"Uh-huh. Pen. Got it." Sage turned to go, hesitated, then looked back at Justine.

"It's completely safe now, Sage. There's nobody here but you, me, and Vaughn." *Come on, kiddo. I need your help.*

Sage nodded. This time she made it out of the room.

"Poor kid," Justine mumbled. She went to the sink and washed her hands. Then she located some gauze. With the heel of her hand, she applied direct pressure to the wound. She would have to stop the bleeding until they could get Vaughn somewhere sterile to take out the bullet, but the bigger issue was relieving the pressure in her chest cavity so that the lung could re-inflate.

"I know you can't hear me, Vaughn, but Sage and I need you to fight. I'm going to do what I can, but the rest is up to you." Justine tried not to think about the fact that they were hours away from proper medical help—hours that Vaughn might not have.

It was impossible to tell the full extent of damage the bullet might have done without operating. The entry wound was in her right upper chest. There was no exit wound and the trickle of blood from the mouth meant that internal bleeding was a possibility. Even once they arrived in Mauritania, they would have to hope that Jackson's friends were resourceful and could get them to a doctor.

"I've got it." Sage was back, and Justine was grateful to see that her eyes looked far less glassy.

"Good girl. Bring it here. Then I need you to take my place."

Sage handed Justine the pen. "What do you need me to do?"

"Put the heel of your hand in the wound and push hard. We have to stop the bleeding."

"What are you going to do?"

Justine was taking the ink out of the pen, leaving a hollow plastic tube. "Her lung has collapsed. I have to get the air out of the chest cavity so it has room to re-inflate."

"How?"

Justine peered at the wound over Sage's shoulder. "I have to insert a tube in Vaughn's chest." She pulled the knife from its sheath, found a candle and lit it.

Sage stared at her. "What're you doing?"

"Sterilizing the knife."

"You're going to stick a knife in Vaughn's chest?"

Justine felt for the intercostal space between the second and third ribs and held a finger between the two ribs to mark her place. "Sage, this is the only way we can save her. You hear those gurgling sounds? She's drowning. We have to make it easier for her to breathe. Will you help me?"

"Yes," Sage said softly. Her whole body was shaking.

"Hold her steady."

"Will she feel you cutting her? Even though she's unconscious?"

"She might feel pain. That's why I need you to hold tight, okay?" Justine knew that it was critical that she make the cut and insert the plastic tube in just the right spot; if she hit the intercostal artery, Vaughn would bleed to death. She held the knife poised over the spot she had marked with her finger until her hand steadied. Sweat dripped into her eyes, and she shook her head to clear her vision.

Sage looked away as the knife pierced Vaughn's skin. Vaughn flinched, although she didn't regain consciousness.

Justine fashioned the hole to match the size of the tube and made the insertion. There was a whoosh of air, and the trachea came back to the mid-line. Justine stood up straight and wiped the sweat from her eyes with her arm. *That's half the battle.*

"Sage, this is very important. We have to maintain suction, and we don't have any equipment."

"What do you need me to do?"

"When she takes a breath in, put your finger over the tube opening. When she breathes out, take your finger away."

"Okay. For how long?"

"I don't know, yet. We need her to stabilize, and I don't know how long that will take. I'll tell you when to stop." Justine didn't want to tell Sage the whole truth; the lung was re-inflated for the moment, but Vaughn surely would die if they couldn't get her to a surgeon soon.

⤞⤝

"Yes?" Dumont answered the phone on the fourth ring. He glanced at the clock—4:20 a.m. These idiots had to stop waking him in the middle of the night.

"Report."

"I haven't heard anything, sir."

"Nothing?"

"No. But that isn't surprising. Nassir wouldn't have a way to report until he arrived back here. It's a thirteen-hour drive. I wouldn't expect to hear from him for hours, yet."

"I don't like it."

"I'm sure Nassir and his men can handle one or two women, don't you think?" Dumont asked. He was trying to keep the aggravation out of his voice, but he was tired. All he wanted was for this to be over with so he could get on with his life.

"Vaughn Elliott is not just any woman, you idiot, and at least some of Nassir's men are dead."

"D-dead? How do you know that?" Dumont sat up, suddenly fully awake.

"That is not your concern."

"Right, sir. Shall I call you as soon as I hear anything from Nassir?"

"*If* you hear anything from Nassir," the voice hissed. Then the line went dead.

⤔⤝

Justine drove the car while Sage sat in the back with Vaughn's head in her lap. Vaughn was still unconscious, and her breathing was shallow but steady. Although the tube remained in her chest, it was no longer necessary for Sage to cover and uncover the opening.

In the end, Justine knew there were no good options. Vaughn wouldn't live if they drove all the way to Mauritania. They needed a Plan B.

"Sage, can you see if Vaughn's cell phone is in her pants pocket?"

After several seconds of fumbling, Sage said, "Got it."

"Give it to me." Justine took the phone and scrolled through the incoming calls. When she found the number she wanted, she pressed "send."

"Elliott?"

"Sabastien? This is Justine. I'm with Vaughn. She's been shot. I need you to help me."

"What can I do?"

Justine bit her lower lip in concentration. The Tuareg captors were all dead. Torgensen was dead. Whoever was pulling the strings might be getting nervous that no one had checked in, but they should still have a small window to get out before the net closed.

To Sabastien, she said, "We're supposed to meet some allies in Mauritania, but Vaughn can't make it that far by car. I need air transportation out of Timbuktu—someone who can fly low. Either that or a private clinic with a surgeon who won't ask any questions."

"It's before dawn there, right?"

165

"Afraid so," Justine said.

"It's not a problem. It may work to our advantage—less people around and fewer questions. I can probably get you a small airplane with a private pilot. I doubt I can find you the kind of medical expertise you'd need inside Mali."

"If you can get me someone who can take off right away and get me to..." Where did she want to go? Where could they get Vaughn treatment? Torgensen's involvement meant that she couldn't trust any CIA safe houses or clinics. "Sabastien? Can you hold on a minute?"

"Sure."

Justine put Vaughn's phone on the passenger seat. She dug in her own pocket and pulled out her cell phone. Barely glancing down, she hit redial.

"Oui."

"Hi. I'm Justine, a friend of Jackson's. I know we were supposed to meet you across the border, but we've got a situation, and we can't make the rendezvous point."

"Where is Jackson? Is he hurt?"

"Dead, I'm afraid."

"Ah, merde." Justine heard the anguish in the voice.

"I've got a gravely injured woman here. I think I can get us a small plane out of Timbuktu. Where can we fly to so that I can get a surgeon to treat a bullet wound to the chest?"

The man cleared his throat, and Justine gave him a moment to compose himself. "Fly to Nouakchott. It is the capital of Mauritania. I will have someone meet you there with an ambulance on the tarmac. You will be taken care of. I will join you at the clinic and make arrangements to get you out of Africa as soon as the patient is stabilized."

"Thank you."

"Mademoiselle Justine?"

"Yes?"

"You can buy silence in Timbuktu with cash."

"Good to know. Thanks. See you soon." Justine closed her phone and retrieved Vaughn's cell off the passenger seat. "Sabastien? You still there?"

"Right here. I've been working on your problem. I've got you a pilot. He wants $1,000 American cash. He'll fly as low as you want and he doesn't care where you want to go. Payment up front."

Justine shook her head. "I don't suppose you had time to check him out?"

"Actually, I did a preliminary check, that's how I picked him. He's a French expatriate—a former decorated soldier who knows how to keep his mouth shut. I thought he might prove useful beyond the flight."

"You work fast. See if you can dig a little deeper. If you find anything of concern, leave me a voicemail. I'll pick it up when we land. Tell him we're going to Nouakchott." Justine pulled off the road. They had arrived back at Jackson's truck. "We should be at the airport in twenty minutes."

"I will relay the message. Justine?"

"Hmm?"

"Will Elliott be all right?"

"I don't know, Sabastien." Her voice sounded husky with emotion, even to her own ears. "I'll call you."

By the time Justine and Sage had transferred everything to the truck, ditched the car, and settled Vaughn, another five minutes had passed.

It took them another twenty minutes to find the airport. Vaughn's breathing was becoming more labored.

"Is she going to be okay?" Sage asked, as they pulled into a parking space.

"I hope so," Justine answered. She lifted Vaughn's eyelids, took her pulse, and re-checked the tube. She looked up at Sage, noting that her face was very pale. "I need you to stay put for a minute while I go negotiate," Justine told her. "Keep talking to Vaughn. You're doing great."

When Justine returned ten minutes later, Sage was kissing Vaughn's forehead and whispering to her as tears flowed down her cheeks.

Justine bit her own lip. *Keep it together.* "We're all set. I'm just going to pack a few things."

Justine went to the back of the truck and pulled out a duffle. In it she placed two of the Sigs, ammunition, a knife, some first aid supplies, Vaughn's briefcase, several changes of clothes for her and Vaughn, and an extra one of Vaughn's T-shirts for Sage.

⋖⋗

The flight was choppy because of the low altitude at which they were flying, and although Justine used the plane's emergency system to increase the percentage of oxygen in Vaughn's blood, her condition continued to worsen. Her skin was clammy, her breathing even more shallow than it had been. Her pulse was thready. The altitude was increasing the pressure on her lungs, but it was a chance Justine knew they had to take. A six-hour car ride would've meant sure death. A one-hour flight offered a better chance of survival.

"Justine?"

Justine heard the panic in Sage's voice. It mirrored the panic rising in her own chest. Vaughn was slipping away and there was nothing more she could do for her without proper facilities and a surgeon. "How much longer?" she asked the pilot.

"We are descending now. Ten minutes."

"Thank God," Sage said.

Justine said a prayer that Jackson's friend had arranged everything as promised, and that it would not be too late for Vaughn.

⋖⋗

Ray Dumont paced in front of his office window. He looked at his watch for the fourth time in as many minutes. The sun was peeking over the horizon. Surely, Nassir should have been back by now. He could see no way out of what he had to do.

He returned to his desk and picked up the phone.

"Report."

"There has been no word, sir. Nassir should have been back by now. I'm afraid…"

"As you should be."

The line went dead.

❦

As the plane approached the runway, Justine could see the ambulance waiting. *Thank God.* She hoped the clinic wasn't too far away.

Before the wheels even touched down, the ambulance sped forward.

"Sage," Justine whispered, "I need you to help the men in the ambulance with Vaughn. These are friends of Jackson's—they're our friends. Vaughn needs you to be strong. Are you going to be okay?"

"I'm fine," Sage answered, sitting up a little straighter. "I'm sorry. I know I haven't been at the top of my game. You must think—"

Justine put a hand on her arm. "I think you've been through a horrific ordeal, and it's not over yet. You've done incredibly well. Vaughn would be very proud of you."

"I will just need to secure the propellers," the pilot said, once the plane had come to a full stop. He lowered the steps and went outside.

Justine took the Sig out of the duffle and tucked it inside her overshirt while Sage's attention was fixed outside. It always paid to be prepared, although she hoped she wouldn't have to use it. She checked her phone and Vaughn's as well. There were no messages.

"You may exit now," the pilot said.

"Wait here one second, Sage." Justine descended the steps to meet a wiry man with weathered skin the color of fine dark chocolate. "Justine."

"Abrim."

"We are all set?"

"Yes."

"The patient is very critical."

"I understand."

"I need you to help load her into the ambulance, then I need to talk with the pilot."

"I understand." Abrim turned back to the ambulance. "Salam, come help."

Justine watched as a huge behemoth of a man lowered a stretcher out of the back of the ambulance.

Justine led Salam onto the plane. She made eye contact with Sage and winked. "You go first. Salam and I will transfer Vaughn."

Sage nodded, reluctantly letting go of Vaughn's hand.

Once Salam and Abrim had put Vaughn in the ambulance and Sage was safely inside, Justine re-boarded the plane. "I just have to grab my bag," she said to the pilot.

"Mmm-hmm," the pilot said without looking up. He was engrossed in writing in his log book.

When she returned to the front of the plane, Justine said, "I want to thank you for helping us."

The pilot shrugged. "You paid me."

"That's true. How would you like to make a lot more money?"

The man shrugged again. "I like money."

"In a few days, as soon as my friend is able, we will need to travel again, except this time we'll be going farther, and we'll need a jet. Are you interested and can you arrange that?"

The pilot regarded her shrewdly. "For the right price."

"And that would be?"

"Twenty thousand, American cash, up front."

"Done, but you get half when we get on the plane, and half when we reach our destination. Also, I'll need you to accompany us to the hospital now."

"Why?" The pilot's eyes narrowed.

"That's part of the deal," Justine said. "Take it or leave it. I'll give you five seconds to decide. We're running out of time."

She didn't want to kill him, but they couldn't afford to leave any loose ends. If she couldn't keep him secure, she would have no choice.

"Deal. Let's go."

"Bring the log book with you," Justine said, as she deplaned.

"Everything okay?" Abrim asked as she joined him at the back of the ambulance.

"Yes, thanks. We're going to have an extra passenger." She motioned in the direction of the pilot, who was waiting at the front of the ambulance. "How long before we get to the clinic?"

"Ten minutes. Nate, Jackson's friend, is already there making the arrangements."

"I'm glad Jackson has such good friends."

"He was a good man." Justine noted the wistful expression on Abrim's face.

"Yes, he was." She climbed into the back of the ambulance with Vaughn and Sage—it was better that they stay out of sight. Abrim shut them in, directed the pilot to a seat, then slid behind the wheel for the short drive.

CHAPTER FIFTEEN

Justine was surprised to find the ambulance equipped with oxygen, intravenous fluids, IV needles, a blood pressure cuff, a stethoscope, and bandages. She fixed the oxygen mask over Vaughn's nose and mouth and put in an IV to run three liters of ringer's lactate that she found in a compartment next to her elbow. Then she wrapped the blood pressure cuff around Vaughn's arm, and took her blood pressure.

"How bad is it?" Sage asked.

"She's tough."

"You're not answering me."

In truth, Vaughn's blood pressure was dangerously low, and her pulse was barely discernable. "I—" Justine stopped short. "Shit. Sage, I need you to bang on the glass. Tell Abrim to hurry."

"What—"

"We're losing her. Vaughn. Damn you, Vaughn, stay with me. You've gotten this far, don't you dare die on me now."

For the next five minutes, the only sounds were of Justine murmuring to Vaughn, tires squealing, and Sage weeping.

Two men in overcoats stood on a pedestrian bridge overlooking the Potomac River.

"Torgensen has been compromised. I don't know whether Elliott is dead or alive. I'm sending someone in to mop up."

"What of McNally?"

"I can't know that until my man gets inside."

"I don't like it, Ed. This has become very messy."

Edgar Fairhaven's jaw muscles jumped. It *was* messy, and that irked him almost as much as having it pointed out.

"You promised me this would go away."

"It will."

"When?"

"Soon."

⊰⊱

The ambulance doors were thrown open and Sage jumped in fright. Salam and Abrim appeared.

Salam moved around Justine to grab the top end of the stretcher. Within seconds, they were gone, moving through double doors at the back of a blind alley and into a non-descript building. Sage followed behind, hurrying to catch up to the stretcher. She barely registered the presence of the pilot, who followed behind at a slower pace.

Inside, a man in surgical scrubs was shouting instructions to several other people nearby. He asked Justine several questions Sage couldn't hear.

They were rushing down a hallway toward what Sage presumed was an operating room at the end. The doors swung shut just as Sage reached them. She watched through a tiny window as strangers surrounded Vaughn. Finally, Sage spotted Justine slumped against the wall; she thought she saw her crying.

"Excuse me?"

Sage jumped at the touch and whirled around.

"I'm sorry. I didn't mean to startle you. I'm Jackson's friend, Nate."

"Hi. I'm Sage. It's okay. I'm a little on edge."

"You are the one they went to rescue, yes?"

"Yes." Tears sprang into Sage's eyes. "It's all my fault. If it wasn't for me, Jackson would be alive and Vaughn—"

"You mustn't blame yourself. People like Jackson and Vaughn, they are trained professionals. They knew the risks."

"But—"

"Come with me."

"I can't. Vaughn is in there."

"Yes, and she will be for a while. Meanwhile, you look like you could use something to eat and a place to lie down."

"I'm fine. I—"

"Sage, please. Someone will inform us as soon as they know anything about your friend." Nate tugged gently on her good hand, and Sage reluctantly moved away from the operating-room door.

"Who is that?" Nate asked, pointing to a man standing off to the side.

"He was the pilot. Justine brought him here with us." Sage shrugged. "I'm not sure why."

"I see. Wait here. I will be right back." Sage watched as Nate walked into the operating room. She could see him having a brief conversation with Justine. When he came back out, he spoke to Salam, who escorted the pilot out of sight.

When Nate rejoined her in the corridor, Sage asked, "How do you know Jackson?" She and Nate walked to a small kitchen down the hall from the operating room.

"We are, how do you say, peers?"

"You mean you work together?"

"I have the same position here in Mauritania that Jackson holds—held—in Burkina Faso. Over the years we became great friends. We have done each other many favors. I owe him my life, so I was happy to repay him."

"I'm so sorry for your loss," Sage said, touching the back of Nate's hand.

"Thank you. Jackson was a fine man, and he held your Vaughn in great regard. From the way he told it, she turned his life around, gave him skills and confidence as a young man, and helped him get his current job."

Sage smiled. Vaughn liked people to think she was cold and unapproachable, but the more she saw and heard about her, the more Sage understood that the front Vaughn presented had little to do with the woman inside.

"You have affection for this woman, yes?"

Sage blushed. "What?"

"You care about her."

"Oh. Yes. Vaughn is a special person."

"She will be all right. You will see."

"Sage?"

Sage got up so quickly she toppled the chair. Justine was standing in the doorway. Her hair was disheveled and her face looked haggard. "Is she…"

"She's resting comfortably right now."

"Can I see her?"

"Sure. Don't expect much, though. She's on a ventilator."

"Excuse me, Nate." Sage hurried down the hallway with Justine. "Is she conscious?"

"No. It could be a few days for that."

"Did they get the bullet out?"

"No. They just put in a proper chest tube. Sometimes that's a better option than opening up someone's chest."

"So the bullet will just stay in there?"

"Yes."

"Wow."

They arrived at a room just to the right of the operating room. A large bed dominated the space. Two folding chairs sat off to the side. Vaughn lay in the center of the bed hooked up to a ventilator, a tube running out of the right side of her chest, and a nasogastric tube in her nose. To Sage, she looked impossibly pale and still.

She hesitated just inside the door.

"It's okay," Justine said gently. "You can sit with her, hold her hand, talk to her. Actually, it would probably be good for her." *And you.*

"Can she hear me?"

"I'd like to think she can."

Sage took several halting steps until she was standing next to the bed. "Hi. You look like hell." Her hand shook as she reached out to touch Vaughn's fingers. They were so cold. "Oh, God. I'm so sorry." Once again, tears slid down Sage's cheeks. "This is all my fault. Jackson's dead, you're…" Sage slumped forward until her forehead touched the back of Vaughn's hand. "And I don't even know why. Why did all of this happen? What did I do to deserve this? I don't understand."

"Sage." Justine laid a hand on Sage's shoulder.

Sage turned toward her and fell into her open arms. "Why? Can you tell me why?"

"No, I can't. Not yet, anyway. Vaughn and I think it's something you know or something you saw."

"I've tried and tried to think what it could be, but I just don't know." Justine's hand rubbed her back, and Sage absorbed the comfort.

"We'll figure it out. Don't worry."

"What a mess." Sage straightened up, stepped back, and wiped her eyes. "Sorry to fall apart...again."

"Don't worry about it. You're doing great."

"Justine?" Sage frowned. "Will they try again? Are they going to keep coming for me? Will I ever be safe?"

"We'll keep you safe. I promise you."

"Vaughn promised me the same thing, and look what it cost her." Sage swallowed hard and looked at Vaughn, who was lying there fighting for her life because of her.

"Sage, look at me."

Reluctantly, Sage dragged her eyes away from Vaughn and focused on the compassion in Justine's gaze.

"Vaughn made her choice willingly, and I guarantee you she'd make the same choice again in a similar situation."

"She shouldn't have to, and neither should you."

"That's what people like me and Vaughn do. It's our job. It's what we know."

"Vaughn was pretty mysterious about her background. Maybe if I knew more about her, I'd understand."

"I suspect you know everything you need to know in your heart."

Sage nodded, acknowledging the truth of that. In her heart, she knew Vaughn was fiercely protective, loyal, strong, honorable, passionate, tender when she let her guard down, deeply wounded, and unquestionably brave. She trusted Vaughn with her life and, she realized with a jolt, she trusted her with her heart.

"Yes, I guess I do," she said aloud with wonder.

"I need to go talk to Nate. Why don't you sit with Vaughn for a while?" Justine pulled one of the chairs over to the side of the bed.

"Okay." Sage waited until Justine left the room before she took Vaughn's hand in both of hers. "I need you to live, Vaughn, so I can tell you how I feel. Please, don't leave me. You have so much to live for."

～❦～

"We need to talk," Justine said when she found Nate sitting alone in the kitchen.

"Yes, we do. I imagine you want to know who I am."

"That would help, yes."

"I am Jackson's friend. I am also in charge of the police force here in Mauritania. That is why Jackson knew I could help."

"I'm sorry for your loss. I didn't know Jackson very well, but I could tell that he was an honorable man."

"That he was. I shall miss him." Nate paused to compose himself. "In our last conversation, he told me of the girl's kidnapping, and he asked me to keep all of you safe. It is a charge I take very seriously."

"Thank you." *And thank you, Jackson.* "Where is the pilot?"

"He is enjoying our hospitality at the moment. I will have his plane moved someplace more discreet."

"Thank you."

"What else can I do?" Nate asked.

"I regret to say that I was unable to bring Jackson's body with us. He should have a proper burial in his own country. Also, if his involvement was known it might create an international incident."

"That is to be avoided. I will see to the recovery of his body right away."

"Yes, time is of the essence. I imagine someone will come looking for those who are missing soon. They will want to confirm identities."

"I understand. I assure you, my people will get there first," Nate said. He pulled a cell phone from his pocket, dialed a number, and spoke rapidly in a language Justine didn't understand.

When he had hung up, Justine said, "I don't want to create any problems for you. As soon as Vaughn is able to travel, we should go."

"I can arrange passage for you, and I can get your pilot a plane. Until then, he will be...supervised."

"I appreciate that."

"Where do you want to go?"

"I don't know yet. Somewhere in Europe. I know Paris would be easiest, but that would be too obvious. Plus, I don't think our pilot would want to go back home. Perhaps Switzerland or London."

"It can be arranged."

"It will be at least a few days yet. Is that going to be a problem?"

"No, you will be safe here. To any outside observer, this is just another house on a busy downtown street."

"Where are we, anyway?" Justine asked. She had yet to see a window.

"This is a secret clinic I maintain for circumstances that require more…discretion."

"I noticed your equipment is rather advanced for this part of the world, if you don't mind my saying so."

Nate shrugged. "I have interesting connections and the means to trade for things that occasionally require a degree of sophistication not readily available in a third world country."

"Your…entrepreneurship…is admirable."

"Thank you."

"And the doctor?"

"He was trained in France. I compensate him well. His family is protected and he wants for nothing. In exchange, he is always available to me."

"I must say, I'm both impressed and grateful. I don't suppose he has any skill as an orthopedist?"

"He is trained in many disciplines."

"Sage's shoulder—I think something may be torn in there, but I'm not a doctor. Also, she took several hard blows to the head."

"He can examine her. I'll have him do it right now."

"Justine!"

Justine heard the urgency in Sage's scream and went running. "What is it?" She felt Nate on her heels.

Sage pointed at Vaughn's chest tube. Blood was pouring into the tube.

"I will summon the doctor," Nate said.

"Tell him we're going to have to get her back into surgery right away." Justine shoved the chair out of the way and put her fingers on Vaughn's carotid artery to feel for her pulse.

"Wh—what's happening?" Sage looked terrified.

The doctor came into the room at a run. "What's going on?"

"Blood in the tube," Justine said.

"We will have to operate right away. Abrim! Get her into the operating room."

"Justine?" Panic pitched Sage's voice higher.

"Not now, Sage." Justine ran alongside the stretcher. They would have to crack Vaughn's chest open to stop the bleeding and tie off whichever artery had ruptured. If they didn't hurry, Vaughn would bleed to death before their eyes.

⊷⊷

"Report," Edgar Fairhaven barked into the phone.

"Ten dead—one white male whom I assume is Torgensen, and nine Tuareg. Six were shot from long range, the other three in close quarters. One, the leader, I'd guess, appears to have been tortured."

"How was Torgensen killed?"

"I'd say a long distance firefight. He was shot three times— once in the throat, once in the heart, and once in the forehead. Somebody had pretty good aim."

"Elliott," Fairhaven mumbled. "The girl?"

"No sign of her. There's a set of open handcuffs on the floor of the room where they must've been holding her. There's blood on the concrete, enough to have been caused by a gunshot wound, and a trail that leads to another room down the hall."

Fairhaven pinched the bridge of his nose where a tension headache was rolling in like a storm cloud. "I suppose it would be too much to expect that Elliott is lying dead around there somewhere?"

"Elliott's not here, but there's a bucket-load of blood on the ground right outside the front entrance, several sets of footprints, and drag marks. Somebody's badly injured."

"Hmm. Could be the girl, could be Elliott."

"There's more. I found a car abandoned and partially hidden about a mile from here. Blood in the backseat, but none in the driver's seat and none on the steering wheel."

Fairhaven pursed his lips together. "That's interesting. So, either they had help getting away, or the car belonged to the Tuareg leader and Elliott used it to get back to where she had stashed another car. It would make sense that she went in on foot—she'd want the element of surprise."

"Does she have any medical training?"

"Why?"

"It looks like somebody set up a makeshift triage room. There's a tray with rudimentary instruments, bloody gauze, needle and thread, and strips of cloth."

Fairhaven frowned. "I suppose it's possible that she would be able to handle herself in a medical emergency." He didn't like it. More and more he was wondering if Elliott hadn't had some outside help. That was another complication he couldn't afford.

Presumably, she had the girl. By now she would've questioned her, if she was able to talk. They were going to have to consider whether or not the plan was still viable. And, more than anything else, they needed to capture Elliott and the girl alive, and keep them that way long enough to figure out exactly what they knew and whom they had told.

"I need you to keep on the trail. I want to know exactly who was in that car, where they went, and I want to know it yesterday." Fairhaven slammed down the phone.

CHAPTER SIXTEEN

Justine leaned against the wall. Sweat stained her shirt and pooled on her upper lip. The surgery had taken four hours, and they'd come close to losing Vaughn more than once. As Nate had promised, the surgeon was quite skilled. Once inside the chest cavity, he had managed not just to tie off the intercostal artery but also to tease out the bullet and remove a rib fragment that was pressing against the lung.

As Vaughn was wheeled next door into the recovery room, Justine washed off some of the blood and sweat. She was dead on her feet, but there was one more thing she had to do before she would rest.

"Sage?" Justine found her pacing the hallway.

"How is she?"

"She's in recovery now."

"Is she all right?"

"The doctor was able to stop the bleeding, and remove the bullet and a rib fragment."

"Oh-kay. That's good, right?"

"Yes, that's very good."

"Is she out of danger?"

"Her chances are much improved."

"Why won't you answer the question directly?" There were tears in Sage's eyes. "What aren't you telling me?"

"I'm not hiding anything from you, Sage. I believe Vaughn is out of danger, but time will tell. She's still going to be on a ventilator for several days, and she's got a long road in front of her."

"Can I see her?"

"In a little while. For now, we both need to get some rest."

At that moment, Nate came around the corner. "Everything okay?"

"As good as it can be at the moment," Justine said. "Is there somewhere Sage can go to rest?"

"I know the way," Sage said. "You'll come get me as soon as I can see Vaughn?"

"Yes. I promise." Justine waited for Sage to walk away before addressing Nate. "How are we doing?"

"Jackson's body was recovered successfully, Salam is keeping your pilot company, his plane has been moved, and I have secured a small jet for your trip."

"That's great news. I can't thank you enough."

"It is nothing. Are you hungry?"

"Actually, more exhausted than hungry."

"There is a room next to Vaughn's. It has a bed. It may not be the most comfortable, but…"

"I'm sure it will feel like heaven."

"The doctor will remain on the premises until your friend is out of danger."

Justine nodded.

"You also mentioned having him examine Sage. He will do that once you are all rested."

"Thank you. I need to check on Vaughn."

Nate touched her shoulder as she turned. "You are very tired. There will be a nurse with Vaughn full-time. You do not need to worry about anything. She will come and get you if there is any change."

"Very well."

"Rest. You will need your strength."

Justine was too tired to argue. Instead, she simply headed down the hall to her room.

⸙⸕

Edgar Fairhaven sat across the table from his boyhood friend, Brian Pordras.

"I don't like it, Ed. It's too messy."

"So you've said before. I'm not crazy about it myself. But we're making progress."

"What progress? We don't have containment. Without containment, we can't move forward. If we don't move forward, we're both finished."

"You worry too much. My man has identified the occupants of the vehicle. They didn't cross any border by car. A plane took off from the airport in Timbuktu before dawn with three passengers. The pilot told one of his buddies he was headed for the capital of Mauritania. My man is on his way there now."

Secretary of State Pordras bit his fingernail. "Three passengers?"

"Yes. McNally, Elliott, and a CIA operative named Justine Coulter. Her prints were lifted from the steering wheel."

"A CIA—"

"Yes," Fairhaven said with distaste. "This is not the first time Coulter's name has come up. I'm afraid she's picked the wrong side. A pity. She'll have to pay the price, of course."

"Ed, I don't like it. This just keeps getting bigger and bigger."

"Like I said, you worry too much. My man is tracking them down even as we speak. He'll tie up all the loose ends and we can go ahead as planned. It'll all be over in forty-eight hours."

"It had better be. If not..."

"You worry too much. Pick up the check, will you?" Fairhaven rose, put on his overcoat, and left the restaurant.

Vaughn blinked. Her eyelids felt so heavy. As she came more fully awake, she heard sobbing and felt the pressure of a hand in hers. She squeezed.

"Vaughn? You're awake?"

Vaughn tried to focus on the face leaning over her. *Sage.* She tried to speak but choked on something in her throat. Her eyes opened wide.

"Shh. Don't try to talk. You're okay—you were shot. You're in a hospital on a ventilator."

Vaughn blinked to indicate that she understood. She tried to reach up and wipe away the tear that tracked down Sage's face, but couldn't.

Sage kissed her hand. "Let me get Justine. I'll be right back."

Vaughn closed her eyes. When next she opened them, Justine was standing over her.

"Welcome back. Nice of you to join us."

Vaughn tried once again to answer, her attempt coming out as a strangled gurgle.

"You're on a ventilator, champ, so no talking for now. I'll get the doctor and we'll discuss whether it's safe to start weaning you off it. Don't go away."

Although she could think of several smart retorts, Vaughn had to satisfy herself with a glare.

After a lengthy consultation, the doctor and Justine agreed that they could begin to reduce Vaughn's dependence on the ventilator.

"Vaughn," the doctor said, leaning over her, "slowly your lungs will begin to do more of the work, as they are able. Still, it will take a day or more before we can take you off the ventilator completely. I'm going to need you to be patient. Your friend Justine, here, tells me that's not your strong suit."

Vaughn mimed the symbol for pen and paper. Sage, having anticipated this request, stepped forward with a legal pad from Vaughn's briefcase and a pen.

Vaughn motioned to Justine to come closer. *Are we safe?*

"Yes, for now."

Where are we?

"Mauritania, at a private clinic."

Jackson?

Justine shook her head. "I'm sorry, Vaughn."

Vaughn closed her eyes. Jackson had been a great friend. He had died for a cause that wasn't his own, and for that Vaughn was sorry. Her eyelids grew heavy again, and she closed her eyes.

෯෯

"Report," Fairhaven said.

"I'm in Nouakchott. If the plane and pilot are here, they're well hidden."

"Keep looking. What else?"

"I've checked every hospital in the city and surrounding environs."

"And?"

"Nothing. If they're still here, they've gone underground. Otherwise, if whoever the bleeder was has died, that means there's nothing holding them back and they're probably gone by now."

"They can't be gone." Fairhaven clenched his fist and dug his nails into his palm. "Find them!" He disconnected the call.

The sound of the door bursting open awakened Vaughn from a light doze.

"Someone's been making inquiries," Nate said to Justine, who sat in one of the folding chairs at Vaughn's bedside.

What kind? Vaughn scribbled furiously.

"Casing the airport looking for the plane and the pilot, and asking around at every hospital in a fifty-mile radius."

Hospitals?

"Yes."

That means they've been to the site and they know one of us is wounded.

"So it would seem."

Any description of who's on our tail?

"One male, roughly thirty-five to forty years of age, six feet four inches tall, African American, athletic build, brown hair, brown eyes."

What has he found?

"Nothing. But he's not done looking."

What will he find?

"Nothing. The bigger problem comes when we try to get you out of here."

Vaughn pulled on the hem of Justine's shirt and tapped her pen on the pad. *How soon can I be moved?*

Justine shook her head. "Once we get you completely off the ventilator, the chest tube will have to be in for two to three days longer. In other words, at least three or four more days."

Vaughn squeezed her eyes shut in frustration. She considered their options. Finally, she opened her eyes and wrote: *I want to talk to Justine alone.*

When it was just the two of them, Vaughn wrote: *Have you talked to Sage about what she knows?*

"Yes. She can't figure it out. I thought we would go over it with her together as soon as you're off the ventilator."

Vaughn tried to think. It was hard to concentrate through the haze of pain medication. *The two of you should leave the country. Even when it's safe to move me, I'll slow you down. Get Sage someplace safe.*

"Not so fast, champ. We're not going anywhere without you. First of all, you need medical supervision—that means me. Second, Sage will never agree to leave you."

Damn it. I'll catch up with you later. If we can't keep Sage safe and find out what she knows, all of this will have been in vain.

"Nate assures me we are as safe here as we could be anywhere in the world. As for figuring out what Sage knows, we stand a better chance of getting to the bottom of that together. You've met the players and done the homework."

You're not thinking clearly.

"I'm not the one on pain meds and hooked to a ventilator. I'm thinking just fine, thank you. Has it occurred to you that whoever is looking for us would never expect us to stay here for any period of time? When he can't find us, he'll assume he's lost our trail and we've moved on."

They won't give up that easily. They'll keep coming—sending more agents if necessary.

"That would be true no matter where we went. This is a safe place, so we stay put until you're able to travel."

Vaughn's eyes flared in anger and helplessness. She wanted to fight, to convince Justine to leave and take Sage with her, to get them out of harm's way, but exhaustion caught up to her. The pen slid out of her hand as her eyes closed.

∽ꙮ৵

Sage brushed her fingers over the back of Vaughn's hand, moved a lock of her hair, and then rearranged the blankets.

Although Vaughn stirred, she did not wake. The doctor finally removed her from the ventilator several hours ago and, after she struggled briefly to get air, her breathing stabilized. The effort sapped what little energy she had, and Sage was happy to see her resting comfortably.

Vaughn looked so much younger when she slept—so much more at peace. Whatever demons haunted her, and Sage suspected there were many, they appeared to be sleeping too.

Vaughn was such a complex woman. Sage wished, yet again, that they'd had more time to get to know each other under different circumstances.

"Who are you really, Vaughn Elliott?"

"I'm exactly who I said I was when we first met," Vaughn answered, her voice hoarse from disuse, her eyes still shut.

"Oh. You're awake."

"Barely."

"How do you feel? Can I get you anything?" Sage knew she sounded nervous, and she was. Had Vaughn felt her fussing? Would she have minded? She realized with a shock that this was the first time they'd been alone together and not in immediate danger since the night of passion they'd shared in her house. It seemed like a lifetime ago.

"I'm fine, thanks."

"Vaughn, I never had a chance... That is to say... I..." Sage threw her hands up in the air. Vaughn was staring at her now, an inscrutable expression in her eyes.

"Sage, it's fine. I'm on my way to a full recovery. This is not on your conscience. I made my own choices every step of the way."

A ball of anger rose from Sage's stomach and settled in her throat. "That's it? What, like maybe you decided to be chivalrous and lay your coat in a puddle so I wouldn't get my shoes wet?"

"Sage—"

"You could've died. Hell, you did die, probably more than once before Justine and the doctor saved you. And for what? For me? Why? Why?"

The anger turned to tears as Sage continued. "I don't even know why any of it happened in the first place. I don't know why I was taken, I don't know why people wanted to kill me. What was the point? And why are they still trying to find me? I'm just a stupid civil servant."

Sage knew she sounded hysterical, but she couldn't stop herself. "Until I met you, I led an incredibly boring life. Next thing I know, I'm having mind-blowing sex with a gorgeous woman, who, by the way, I think I may be in love with, and being kidnapped by restless natives who want me dead."

Sage finally took a deep breath. Her cheeks blushed bright red when she realized what she'd just said. "I-I'm sorry. I don't know where all that came from. I'll just—"

"Sage. Stop. Sit here." Vaughn patted the bed as she gingerly shifted to make room.

With as much dignity as she could muster, Sage sat on the edge of the bed. She was surprised when Vaughn reached for her hand. The look in her eyes was one of...amusement?

"Now you think I'm a complete joke."

Vaughn lifted a finger to Sage's lips. "Not at all. I think you've been through a very traumatic experience, and your reaction is perfectly understandable. I don't know what interest these people have in you either, but together we'll figure it out. In the meantime, we need to keep you safe." She trailed her fingers across Sage's knuckles, and Sage felt her heart rate increase. "As for the rest, you can't think you love me. I'm not the kind of person who deserves the love of a beautiful, innocent woman like you."

Although Vaughn said the words gently, softly, Sage's heart constricted and momentarily robbed her of breath.

"I don't know what happened in your life before, that's true," Sage said. "And I readily admit, I've never seen anyone who can handle a gun the way you can. For a while there, I thought I was in the middle of *The Bourne Ultimatum*."

Vaughn's laughter morphed into a bout of coughing. She winced and swore. Sage propped her up higher in the bed.

"But please, don't tell me I don't know my own heart."

"Fair enough. I don't want to hurt you, Sage. You are a very desirable woman, and I couldn't have helped myself if I'd wanted to."

Sage started to open her mouth, but Vaughn silenced her once again with several fingers over her mouth. "Nor do I regret what happened between us, unless in some way that was responsible for what happened afterward. But it was a mistake."

Sage's heart shattered. "I see."

"No, I don't think you do. Sage, you've seen what I can do. This is the world I live in. It's no place for someone like you. You're so much better than that."

"Better than you, you mean?"

"Yes." Vaughn's hand dropped back to her side.

"Sorry, but I don't see it that way. I don't know anybody else who would track me to the middle of nowhere, intentionally put herself in harm's way, take a bullet for me, or kill so that I might live. You're right—that's not within my normal frame of reference, but then, I'm pretty sure that's true for most of humanity." Sage stood up and paced to the foot of the bed. "Why is it that you can't accept that you're a good person?"

"Because I'm not," Vaughn said simply.

"You're wrong, and somewhere inside, you know that. I don't know what it is you feel so guilty about, but whatever it is, you need to let it go or you'll never be able to live. I can't help how I feel about you, Vaughn, and I won't apologize for it either." Sage stormed out of the room.

Justine stood by as the doctor examined Vaughn. She'd seen Sage run out of the room in tears a few minutes ago. If she hadn't stopped her, Sage would have run right out the front door. As it was, Sage went into the room where a bed had been set up for her and slammed the door. When the doctor was done with Vaughn, Justine would find out what happened.

"Everything's looking good," the doctor said. "If this continues, we should be able to remove the chest tube in a few days."

"Doctor—" Vaughn said.

"I know, I know, you are in a big hurry to be on your way. If we don't take proper care of you now, you'll be in a big hurry for your own funeral. I am not sure you fully appreciate the severity and delicacy of your condition."

Justine watched Vaughn clamp down on her frustration. "I'll give you two more days."

"What you mean is that you will give yourself two more days," the doctor said, completely unaffected and definitely not intimidated. He draped the stethoscope around his neck and left the room.

"I think he's got your number," Justine said when Vaughn growled.

"We're wasting time."

"Getting you healthy is hardly a waste of time, and as long as you're already in a lather, what happened with Sage?"

"What do you mean?"

"She ran out of here crying. If I hadn't stopped her, she would've run out the door and kept going."

"Great." Vaughn pressed her head back into the pillows.

"Well? What was it all about?"

"That's between me and Sage."

"Vaughn, I don't want to pry, and I know whatever that was is between the two of you, but there are a few things you don't know that you should."

"Such as?"

Vaughn's seeming indifference raised Justine's ire. "Let's start with the fact that Sage has spent every night sleeping in one of these chairs, holding your hand. She hasn't left your side except to eat and go to the bathroom. It was all I could do to get her to walk down the hall so the doctor could check her stitches and put her in a proper sling."

Justine walked closer until she was standing directly over Vaughn. "I know you're still hurting over Sara…" She watched the flicker of pain cross her face before Vaughn was able to hide it. "But Sage is not Sara, and you can't push her away because you've got some misguided notion that you're the plague where women are concerned."

Vaughn's cheeks flushed. "Who are you to tell me what I am? I live every day knowing that I got Sara killed. She was so young, so innocent. If I hadn't said yes to Fairhaven when he came to recruit us in college, Sara would still be alive." Vaughn blinked hard as moisture pooled on her lashes. "She never should have become an agent. She was just like Sage—optimistic, lovely, fresh, innocent, and in love with me. I won't corrupt someone else. I can't." Vaughn's voice broke.

Justine put a hand on Vaughn's leg. "I'll say it again—Sage isn't Sara. She isn't about to run off and join the CIA and, for the record, Sara loved being an agent. She wouldn't have chosen any other life, so stop thinking you were all-powerful enough to change the course of her existence. She was an adult just like you, and she made her own decision for her own reasons, not all of which had to do with you, as she told me."

"Is that so?"

"Yes, that's so. You're right about one thing, though—Sage is a lovely woman. So are you, if only you'd get your head out of your ass long enough to realize it. You've punished yourself long enough, Vaughn. It's time to live, before it's too late."

CHAPTER SEVENTEEN

Edgar Fairhaven and Brian Pordras were playing their weekly racquetball game. "They've gone underground," Fairhaven said, his chest heaving, his T-shirt stained with sweat.

"How do you know?" Pordras was also breathing heavily from exertion.

"There's no sign of them having used a car or plane to get out, and my man has checked every hospital and clinic in the country."

"Maybe they're all dead."

"That would be nice but highly improbable. We have to assume they're all alive and in play, and that they've got enough information to figure it out."

The secretary stopped mid-stride and the ball hit him in the gut. "What do you mean, 'figure it out?' As in, implicate you and me?"

"Yes. I think we have to assume that's true. Hence the reason we have to find them."

"Ed, we can't go through with the plan. If we don't, they can't prove anything. There won't be any—"

"Get a grip. This isn't just about things that haven't happened yet." Fairhaven waited for his words to sink in.

"You said they would never... You promised they couldn't..." Pordras sagged against the wall, his head in his hands, the racquet dangling from his wrist by its safety strap.

"Relax. If they had connected all the dots, they wouldn't be underground in some third world country—they already would have come for us."

"That's a comforting thought," Pordras said sarcastically.

"It means time is still on our side. We'll find them before they leave Mauritania, determine what they know and whom they've told, and eliminate them."

"We're running out of time. We need to think about altering the plan."

"If we haven't found them in the next day or two, we'll talk about that."

"You promised me it would be over in forty-eight hours. That was three days ago."

"It will be over soon, Bri. Now play the game." Fairhaven served the ball.

❧❧

Vaughn sat hunched over on the edge of the bed waiting for Justine to come back with Nate. Her chest hurt and her side ached where the chest tube had been removed several hours ago. She was unable to sit up straight or take a deep breath, but none of that mattered to her. Every day that they stayed endangered Nate and the doctor.

"You look much improved," Nate said when he entered the room.

"It's good not to be tied to this bed...that's for sure. It's time to talk about an exit strategy."

Justine shook her head. "Vaughn, you're still not strong enough—"

Vaughn pierced Justine with her eyes. "You and I both know it could be weeks before I'm sound. We don't have that kind of time." She paused to catch her breath. "I think Switzerland is a good option. It's not a destination they'd be expecting, which may help us stay undetected. Also, they're not as stringent with security for private planes as London or Paris would be."

"Agreed," Justine said. "I've got some good contacts in Zurich who could meet us at the airport and arrange a place for us."

"Good. Can they help us doctor the flight plan?"

"What flight plan?" Justine said, smiling.

"Excellent. I'm sure it's not everyday that private jets arrive there from Mauritania. How's our pilot doing?"

"He is well-rested and ready to go," Nate said.

"He understands that the $20,000 ensures his silence?" Vaughn asked.

"I have spoken to him myself," Nate answered. "He is what you would call a mercenary. Since you are paying him, his loyalty is with you. Also, although he does not know the nature of your business and who you are running from, he does not like that they would shoot women."

"Well, that's in our favor," Justine said. "I don't want to ask how he did it, but Sabastien assures me that $10,000 in untraceable bills will be in the cockpit, waiting for the pilot. My friends will have the other $10,000 waiting once we're safely on the ground in Zurich."

"I should call Sabastien," Vaughn said.

"Yes, he's been very worried about you."

"If we can smuggle him in, we could use his help on the ground. I don't suppose you know where he is?"

"I haven't asked, and he hasn't told."

"All right, we'll take care of that later. Nate, when's the best time for us to take off?"

"The plane is fueled and ready to go. The man who is looking for you is expecting something under cover of darkness."

"You sound awfully certain of that. You met with him?"

"This morning. As chief of police here in Mauritania, it is natural that he should seek me out and enlist my help in locating these three very dangerous women who are in my country illegally," Nate said, keeping a straight face.

"Three?" Vaughn asked, her eyes going wide.

"Yes, he showed me pictures. I have to say they were not very flattering."

"Shit. I'm sorry," Vaughn said to Justine. If they'd identified her, Justine's career in the Company likely would be over. "None of this was supposed to happen. You were supposed to be in and out with no one the wiser."

"You and I both know things seldom go as planned." Justine shrugged. "I wasn't having all that much fun anymore. Change is good."

Vaughn addressed Nate, "Did the man introduce himself?"

"He said he was Arthur Sielig from the United States State Department."

"Sielig?" Justine asked. "He's Fairhaven's top henchman."

"That makes sense," Vaughn said. She turned her attention back to Nate. "State Department, huh? That's interesting. What did you tell him?"

"I thanked him for bringing the issue to my attention, assured him that I had neither seen nor heard of a Vaughn Elliott, Justine Coulter, or Sage McNally, but that if I did, I would notify him right away."

"Well done."

"Also, he asked me to have my men stationed at every airport and border crossing, and to distribute your pictures so that we were familiar with what you looked like. He indicated that he thought at least one of you might be injured."

"An instruction I'm sure you followed," Justine said.

"Of course. I distributed your pictures at every border crossing. I haven't gotten to the airports yet because I've been so busy, but I'm sure I'll get to it in the next day or two."

"Yes, I'm sure you will," Vaughn said. "You know the layout. How should we do this?"

"Better to leave in the middle of the day," Nate said. "I could arrange it so that several private planes take off in quick succession. None of them will have filed a flight plan—after all, we third world countries are so backward and lax about things like paperwork." Nate winked.

"Sounds good, but that still leaves the issue of us getting to the plane without detection."

"I think I might need to meet with Mr. Sielig at around that time. You know, update him on what I have done, how I have beefed up security to ensure that you cannot get away."

"Nate, I don't want to put you in jeopardy. Sielig is a very dangerous man," Vaughn said.

"I am not concerned. I will bring in the head of several hospitals to testify that he has never seen any of you. I can make the meeting last for at least an hour or longer. By that time, you will be in the air and safely on your way."

"He'll figure it out, Nate," Justine said. "There's no need to put yourself in danger."

"I made a promise to Jackson. I owe this to him—and I have to admit, I like all of you a great deal. Do not worry about me. I can take care of myself."

"Okay, it's settled then. We leave tomorrow."

"I will make the preparations," Nate said, taking his leave.

"Have you seen Sage?" Vaughn asked Justine when they were alone. "We should meet and try to figure out what started all of this." She hoped her voice sounded casual. She hadn't seen Sage in twenty-four hours and she missed her; she missed holding her hand or just having her nearby, but Justine didn't need to know that.

"No. She's been closed up in her room since your little chat yesterday."

Vaughn frowned but said nothing.

"You know you shouldn't be flying yet. It's too risky."

Vaughn sighed. "I know. But we can't put it off any longer. I can use the oxygen if need be, and we'll take supplies with us."

"I'm not happy."

"I'm sure you're not, but it's a risk we have to take."

"I'll go talk to the pilot," Justine said, conceding that this was an argument she wouldn't win.

❧❧

"Hey," Vaughn said, peeking her head into Sage's room. Sage was lying on the bed with her good arm behind her head. She barely acknowledged Vaughn's presence. "Can I come in?"

"I suppose," Sage said, not moving.

Vaughn sat on the side of the bed, forcing Sage to move over to avoid contact. Sage continued to stare at the ceiling.

"How's your arm?"

"I'll live."

"Glad to hear it," Vaughn said. "I know I was an ass yesterday. I'm sorry."

"S'okay."

"No, it's really not. I should explain some things to you."

"You don't owe me any explanations. We had a night of hot sex. End of story. I get it."

"That's not true, Sage." It was all she could do to avoid the urge to brush her fingers under Sage's T-shirt.

"It doesn't matter."

Vaughn turned Sage's face so that she could look into her eyes. They were swollen and bruised from crying. *You're an idiot, Elliott.* "It matters a great deal to me. I told the truth when I said there were many things about me you don't know. There are some that I can't tell you, not because I don't want to, but because that's the way it has to be."

"Like I said, you don't need to explain to me."

Vaughn kept talking as if Sage hadn't interrupted her. "There was a woman once, my college sweetheart. I loved her very much. In fact, she's the only woman I ever loved." Vaughn swallowed the sudden lump in her throat. "She followed me into law enforcement. Assignments took us in separate directions, and we went long periods without seeing each other. Despite the physical distance, I never stopped caring about her, and I think it was the same for her."

Vaughn was staring at a point on the wall, but she didn't have to look to know that she had Sage's full attention. "Anyway, last year she called me. She was going on a very difficult mission. I begged her not to go, and certainly not alone. I convinced her to let me come along." Vaughn's voice faltered, and she took a moment to compose herself.

"It's okay, Vaughn. You don't have to tell me, really. I can see this is painful for you."

"No. Let me finish. I was supposed to meet her at a certain time, in a certain place, but I had a meeting with superiors that ran long. I got there as soon as I could, but…" Vaughn cleared her throat, which had gone very dry.

Sage turned onto her side and linked their fingers together. Vaughn avoided her searching gaze.

"She died right before my eyes—blown up by a bomb—and there was nothing I could do. I was too late. If I'd just…"

"I'm so sorry. That must've been awful. Watching you get shot and knowing you lived was hard enough. I can't imagine…" Sage's voice trailed off. "Is that where you got the scar over your ribs?"

"Yes. I took some shrapnel in the side, among other injuries." Vaughn smiled sadly. "You remind me a lot of her."

"I'm sorry. I can't help that."

"I know."

"What was her name?"

"Sara."

"She was a very lucky woman."

"No, I was the lucky one. Until last week, I'd never been with anyone—never even looked at another woman. I couldn't."

"And then I came along and threw myself at you."

Vaughn shook her head. "You didn't, Sage. That's the thing. I was attracted to you the second I laid eyes on you. Maybe that's the reason I was so gruff. I didn't want to let you inside. I didn't want to let anyone close, and without even saying a word, you'd already gotten under my skin."

"Was that really so awful?"

"Yes. When I lost Sara, I lost the right to have someone meaningful in my life...don't you see?"

"No, I don't. What I see is an honorable woman who had her lover tragically ripped away from her. I see a woman who's been blaming herself for something that wasn't her fault."

"Sara died because of me."

"You have to know that's not true. You didn't plant the bomb, did you?"

"Of course not."

"Whoever did is the one responsible for Sara's death, Vaughn, not you."

Tears streaked Vaughn's cheeks. "If I had been there when I said I would..."

"She could have waited for you to show up. It wasn't your fault, and blaming yourself is just a convenient excuse for not having to live without her. You can just go on acting as though you died with her, because that eases your guilt."

"What?"

"What would Sara say about you locking your heart away for the rest of your life?"

Vaughn opened her mouth to speak and clicked her jaw shut again. *She would've been pissed as hell.* "That's not the point."

"What is the point, then?"

"I'm not safe to be around. Bad things follow me. If something happened to you, I could never survive it. Don't you see?" Vaughn didn't bother to wipe away the tears.

"If something happens to me, it certainly won't be because you didn't do everything in your power to keep me safe. Let me in, Vaughn. I'm not saying you have to fall in love with me. Just give us a chance. Please?"

Vaughn looked into those earnest eyes filled with hope and pain. "I can't promise you anything, Sage. Honestly, I don't know what I have to offer."

Finally unable to resist any longer, Vaughn gave in and ran her fingers along Sage's cheek. She thought about everything this woman had been through in the past week, how worried she had been for her safety, how much she'd come to enjoy her company and the simple comfort of her touch. She leaned forward and brushed her lips lightly against Sage's. "When we get through this, let's see where we are, okay?"

"Okay," Sage said, her eyes still closed after the kiss. "Thank you."

Without another word, Vaughn rose from the bed and left the room. She was afraid if she stayed any longer, she would fall into Sage and never be able to pull away. There was still much to be done, and she couldn't afford to give her emotions free rein just yet.

⊰⊱

As planned, an airplane fuel truck idled out of sight behind the clinic. Abrim was in the driver's seat. Salam climbed out of the back, where he had been loading supplies and luggage. The inside of the tanker portion of the truck had been converted into a seating and storage area.

Vaughn, Sage, Justine, and Nate stood just inside the back door of the clinic. The pilot walked past them and clambered into the back of the truck.

"I can't thank you enough for all you've done," Vaughn said, shaking Nate's hand. Relentless waves of pain forced her to hunch over. Perspiration dotted her forehead. "We couldn't have made it this far without you."

"You are most welcome. I was happy to be of service. Are you sure you are okay to travel?"

"Yes."

Nate's expression was incredulous, but he did not push the matter. Instead, he said, "Abrim will drive you into a hangar, where you will be able to board the plane away from prying eyes."

"Perfect. Your meeting with Sielig is all set?"

"Yes, and five private flights are scheduled to take off without flight plans today. Two are already underway."

"Excellent. Stay safe, my friend."

"I will be fine. Please do not worry about me. I am well protected."

Justine hopped up into the back and reached down to help Sage, who was having trouble negotiating the step with only one good arm.

When Vaughn moved to follow, Nate stopped her. "Let me help you." He linked his hands together so that she could step into them and boosted her up into the truck, where Justine steadied her. "Good luck to all of you."

∽৯৵

"I am sorry to keep you waiting," Nate said. In fact, he had let Sielig cool his heels outside his office for half an hour, until he was sure the plane was safely away. Now he stood in the doorway in full dress uniform, gesturing for Sielig to enter. "Please, come in."

Once seated, Sielig stared unhappily at Nate from across the desk. "You said you have news for me?"

"Yes. I wanted to update you on our efforts. Flyers have been circulated at every border checkpoint. Every one of my officers has been given a full description of the fugitives, and they are canvassing the airports. We are doing everything possible to assist you in your search. If these women are in our country, we will find them."

"I appreciate your cooperation." As Sielig got up to leave, Nate put up a hand to forestall him.

"I thought, perhaps, since you believed one of the women to be injured, I would bring in the head of our major hospitals to brief you as well."

Sielig appeared as if he would object. It was clear to Nate that he had little patience and less respect for his abilities. That would work to his advantage.

"I'm sure—" A knock on the door forestalled the rest of Sielig's remark.

"Come," Nate called. "Ah, doctor. You're just in time. Dr. Jeantou, may I present Mr. Arthur Sielig from the United States State Department."

"A pleasure, sir. I understand you are looking for several American women, at least one of whom you believe may be suffering from a gunshot wound."

"That is correct." Sielig pulled pictures from his briefcase and laid them on the desk for the doctor to study.

"I assure you, none of these women has been treated at any of my hospitals."

"How can you be so sure?"

"Several reasons. First, my personnel would have had to file a report, so I would have found out that way. Second, if, as you say, there was a gunshot wound involved, I would have been the one to operate. So yes, I am positive that none of these women has been treated in any of my facilities."

"How many hospitals do you oversee?"

"Every major hospital or clinic in this city, and several in outlying areas. In short, Mr. Sielig, if these women were in Mauritania and injured, I would know about it."

Sielig again rose to leave.

"Perhaps," the doctor said, "it would be helpful if you could explain to me what you would have me do if your fugitives do present themselves at one of my facilities."

CHAPTER EIGHTEEN

The house was in the foothills of the Alps and could have belonged to a business tycoon or a Hollywood star. It featured a wraparound deck with built-in benches, an upstairs balcony that overlooked a lake, five bedrooms, each with a private bath and Jacuzzi, a sunken living room, a game room, a gym, a formal dining room, and a kitchen that would rival the best restaurant kitchen in New York.

"I think I like your friends," Sage said to Justine as they toured the house.

"They have their good points," Justine answered with a wink.

Sage lowered her voice to make sure she wouldn't be overheard. "Is Vaughn going to be okay? She looks so frail. I know she doesn't want to be fretted over, but I can't help it."

For the majority of the flight, Vaughn had been doubled over and wearing an oxygen mask. She had spoken little and kept to herself, refusing to look at Sage or engage in conversation. Several times Sage had seen Justine bending over her, taking her vital signs and talking softly. At the moment she was resting in a bedroom down the hall.

"Vaughn had major surgery for a life-threatening injury. Frankly, it's remarkable that she's doing as well as she is. Normally, you would never let a patient with lung trauma get on an airplane. Unfortunately, we didn't have much choice."

"Did the flight do additional damage?" Sage asked, wide-eyed.

"I don't think so, but she'll need some time to recover."

"We're safe here, right? So we could stay until she's better."

"It's not that simple," Justine said. "We know we weren't followed, but we also know that they won't stop trying to find us, and that eventually, they'll succeed."

Sage's stomach did a flip. "They will?"

"We don't know what this situation is really all about. Until we do, we can't determine how to turn the tables on them. If we can't turn the tables, they're always going to be a step ahead of us and we're always going to be looking over our shoulders."

Sage's mouth formed an *O*.

"I'm sorry. I don't mean to scare you, Sage. For now, we're as safe as we can be."

"Okay. I think I'll go check on Vaughn." She felt an overwhelming need for the comfort of Vaughn's solid presence. Even in Vaughn's weakened state, Sage felt a sense of security with her that she didn't feel with anyone else.

She peeked around the door. Vaughn was awake and staring at the ceiling.

"Can I come in?"

"Of course."

"How are you?"

"Ducky."

"Really, Vaughn. You look so pale, and it seemed like you were in so much pain on the flight." Sage didn't wait for an invitation to sit down on the spacious bed next to her.

"I'm okay, Sage. Just tired."

"Can I lie with you for a while?"

"Sure."

Sage kicked off her shoes and stretched out on her right side, leaning her head gently on Vaughn's left shoulder. "Is this okay? Am I hurting you?"

"No, it's fine. But I can't imagine it feels good for your shoulder to be suspended in mid-air like that."

Sage shifted slightly so that her left forearm rested on Vaughn's stomach. "I don't want to jostle you."

"That doesn't hurt." Vaughn wrapped her left arm around Sage's good shoulder so that they were snuggled more tightly together.

Sage let out a contented sigh. It was the most at peace she had felt since the entire ordeal began. Within seconds, she was asleep.

⋘⋙

Justine stood in the doorway smiling. Both Vaughn and Sage were fast asleep, clinging to each other in a way Justine imagined Vaughn would never allow if she were awake. *Good for you, Sage, you're just what the doctor ordered.* Quietly, Justine retreated down the hallway to the living room. The best thing for both women at this point was rest. The flight had taxed Vaughn to her limits, and Justine feared that if she didn't take this time, she would not have the strength to fight whatever battle lay ahead.

That thought brought the current dilemma fully into focus. They didn't have any idea what had prompted this whole ordeal in the first place. They would have to figure it out soon.

⋘⋙

"Five flights took off yesterday without any flight plans." Arthur Sielig was pacing in front of Nate's desk. "Isn't that a bit unusual?"

"Were these commercial flights?"

"No. They were private aircraft."

"Sometimes our air traffic controllers are a bit lax with the paperwork. Most often those are quick domestic flights."

"But you don't know that."

"I am sorry, Mr. Sielig. Air traffic is not within my scope of responsibilities. I can make some inquiries for you, if you like, but it may take several days."

Sielig leaned across the desk until his face was inches from Nate's, but Nate did not retreat. "I don't have days. I want answers, and I want them now." His voice was deadly quiet.

"I understand your desire to find these fugitives, and I assure you we are doing everything we can to cooperate with your government. Now, if you will excuse me, I will get to work on your question. I will call you as soon as I have any information. Good day, Mr. Sielig."

Nate waited until he saw Sielig exit the building and cross the street below. He pulled out his cell phone. "Justine?"

"Yes."

"Nate. I thought you would like to know that I just had a visit from Mr. Sielig. He is most displeased with the speed of investigations here in my country."

"Is that so?"

"He is demanding to know what the destinations were of the five planes that took off yesterday without filing flight plans. I told him that air traffic was not in my jurisdiction, but that I would look into it for him."

"How much time do we have?"

"Perhaps two or three days at most." He heard Justine's sigh through the phone. "You had no difficulty on your end?" Nate asked.

"No. Everything went like clockwork. Thank you, again, for everything you've done. Please don't delay Sielig any further if it puts you in jeopardy."

"Do not worry about me. I will have no trouble stalling him for a few days. My concern rests with any detective work he might undertake on his own. I can keep an eye on him, but I cannot control everyone he might talk to."

"That's okay. We appreciate the heads up."

"You are welcome. I will let you know if I find out anything more. At the very least, I will be able to tell you when he leaves the country."

"Thanks. Be careful, Nate."

"You too. I wish you well."

৵৵

"I'm being stonewalled here," Sielig said.

"What's the roadblock?" Fairhaven asked.

"It's not a what, it's a who, and he's the chief of law enforcement for Mauritania. He's either incredibly incompetent, or he knows things he's not saying."

"Perhaps you might need to be a bit more...persuasive."

"As far as he and everyone else here is concerned, I represent the United States government. Are you sure you're willing to raise this to a level that could arouse attention?"

Fairhaven snapped a pencil in half. This whole situation was spinning out of his control. "Do you believe they are still in Mauritania?"

"No. I think they were on one of those flights that slipped out yesterday."

"By now, they could be anywhere."

"I am tracking down the registrations of those planes and the names and addresses of the pilots. I will have more answers before the day is over."

"You'd better." Fairhaven closed the phone and tapped it thoughtfully against his chin. If they couldn't locate, question, and eliminate Elliott and the others within the next twenty-four hours, they would have to make major adjustments to the plan. He hoped it wouldn't come to that.

ॐ ॐ

"Let's review what we know," Vaughn said. "The Tuareg took Sage, but they did so at the behest of an American of sufficient rank to order the ambassador to have her killed."

"How do you know that?" Sage asked.

"Sabastien intercepted a phone conversation between someone with an American accent and the ambassador," Justine said.

"Based on the fact that Torgensen showed up on the scene so quickly, can we agree that the man behind the voice was likely Fairhaven?" Vaughn asked.

"How can I agree to anything?" Sage asked, her voice shaking with frustration. "I don't even know who any of these people are."

"Torgensen, the hit man who shot Vaughn, was a CIA agent. Ostensibly he was sent by Washington to replace you after you were taken. It was a setup—his true purpose was to keep an eye on Vaughn and to prevent her from rescuing you."

Vaughn watched as Sage physically flinched. She touched her gently on the arm. "Listen, Justine and I can sift through all of this stuff. The only thing you need to think about is if there was anything unusual leading up to your abduction—anything at all out of the ordinary."

"I don't need to be coddled or sheltered, Vaughn. Don't patronize me." Sage stood in front of her defiantly, jaw set, eyes blazing. After an uncomfortable pause, she asked, "Who is Fairhaven?"

Vaughn sighed. Sage could be of use—she had a good mind and strong analytical skills. She also offered a different perspective that might prove important. "Edgar Fairhaven is the second most powerful person in the CIA."

"How do you two know these people?" Sage looked from Vaughn to Justine.

Vaughn exchanged a glance with Justine. Not only was it against regulation to disclose any affiliation with the CIA, but it also would put Sage at risk. *They're already trying to kill her, what more could they do to her, genius.* She nodded to Justine.

"Sage, this is the world we move in," Justine said.

After a moment, comprehension dawned in Sage's eyes. "You're CIA agents?" She looked from one of them to the other. "So, what, you've been lying to me all along? Your assignment with DS was just a cover?" She faced Vaughn.

"No. I don't work for the CIA anymore. My job was real, my assignment was real, and I never lied to you about anything."

"That's part of what's so confusing to us, Sage," Justine said, stepping in. "There was no reason for the Company—the CIA—to have any involvement here."

"But you're CIA, and you're here."

"I'm here because Vaughn called me after you were taken, and I offered to help. I'm not here in any official capacity. In fact, I'm on 'vacation.'"

Sage sat down heavily on the sofa. "Wow. This is seriously convoluted."

"Yes, it is, and that's not all of it, either," Vaughn said. "Fairhaven is a childhood chum of the secretary of state. Do you remember when we first met, you told me my papers didn't come through the usual channels?"

"Yes. They came directly from the secretary."

"Right. Well, I think it's pretty clear my posting wasn't a coincidence. For some reason, Fairhaven wanted me here."

"The question is," Justine broke in, "why? Vaughn and I believe that you were the primary target, although we still don't know why. It doesn't make any sense to want a trained former

CIA agent hanging about. There was too big a chance that Vaughn would come after you."

All three women were silent for a few minutes as they considered the possibilities. Finally, it was Sage who spoke. "Has it occurred to you that perhaps my being taken wasn't pre-meditated?"

"Sage, it was a well-coordinated strike. There's no way that wasn't thought out ahead of time," Vaughn said.

"You're missing my point. Maybe they didn't know they were going to kidnap me until after you had already arrived. That still would have given them several days to plan the kidnapping. Wouldn't that have been enough time?"

"You're a genius." Vaughn kissed her on the top of the head.

"I'm glad you think so." Sage laughed.

"If she's right," Vaughn said to Justine, "then the real question is, what happened in those couple of days after I arrived that set this in motion?"

. "That scenario certainly would narrow the possibilities, although I'm not convinced it's that simple."

"Sage, I really need you to think about those days. Was there anything out of the ordinary? Anything that sticks out in your mind?"

"You mean, apart from…" Sage blushed.

"Yes," Vaughn said too quickly. "Apart from that." Vaughn chanced a quick glance at Justine and noted that she had the decency to pretend she didn't know what they were talking about.

"Let's see," Sage said, thinking out loud. "I followed my usual routine, set up meetings for your visit, sifted through piles of mail…"

"Was there any unusual correspondence, anybody you met that seemed out of place?"

"No."

"Did you see the ambassador during those two days? Have any contact with him?"

"No."

"Did you take any calls from the States?"

"No."

Vaughn shook her head. "This is no good. We're not getting anywhere. We must be coming at this from the wrong angle."

"You and I already discussed and dismissed the possibility that they took Sage as a means to flush you out," Justine said. "You said yourself that if Fairhaven had wanted you, he could've had you any time during the last year."

"Unless he wanted me out of the country when he did it."

"Even so, he didn't need to kidnap Sage to take care of you and you know it. He could've taken you out on the street or in the hotel. You could've contracted a case of dysentery or food poisoning. There are a hundred less complicated ways he could've gotten the job done."

"True, but we can't ignore the fact that my orders came directly from Pordras. What was that about?"

Justine shrugged. "How about if we treat you and Sage as two separate issues for now?"

"Fair enough." Vaughn bent over. Her chest was aching and fatigue clouded her mind.

"I think we ought to call it a night," Sage said. "We could all use some rest."

"We don't have time," Vaughn protested. "Nate said we had forty-eight hours max before we got made."

"Sage is right. Nothing good is going to come of banging our heads against the wall. A good night's sleep will help clarify things."

"I hate that the two of you are ganging up on me, you know that?" Vaughn grumbled but nevertheless headed for the bedroom she'd napped in earlier that day.

✍❦

Sage awakened to the sound of her own scream. She was breathing hard and sweat stained her T-shirt. The nightmare was the same one she'd had every night since being taken. The gun was against her head, the sword in her back, and she was being forced into a pit where she would be buried alive.

She shivered involuntarily. If she went back to sleep, it would start all over again. She bit her lip. "You know what you want. Why bother pretending?" She slipped into a pair of shorts and padded quietly down the stairs.

For several moments, Sage simply watched Vaughn sleep.

"Are you just going to stand in the doorway?"

"You knew I was here?"

"Before you even reached the bottom of the stairs."

"How?"

"Training."

"Oh."

"What's on your mind?"

"I-I was having a nightmare, and I couldn't sleep."

"C'mere," Vaughn said.

"Are you sure?"

"Yes." Vaughn held the covers open while Sage slid between the sheets. "Aren't you going to take your shorts off?"

"Um, I didn't know—"

"Sage, take your shorts off. It's okay. I don't think either one of us is in any shape to get aroused, do you?"

"No, but..." Sage wiggled out of her shorts, noticing for the first time that Vaughn was naked.

"Is there a problem?"

"N-no. Of course not. Do you want me to..."

"If you're more comfortable leaving your shirt on, go ahead. The choice is yours."

Sage removed her good arm from the sleeve, pulled the shirt over her head, then eased it over her bad arm.

"You're not sleeping with the sling on?"

"It's too uncomfortable."

"I don't want to jostle you."

"Then don't," Sage said, cuddling up to Vaughn and laying a soft kiss on her shoulder. A feeling of peace engulfed Sage, and she drifted off.

CHAPTER NINETEEN

I know! I know!" Sage's eyes snapped open.

"What?" Vaughn's voice was rough with sleep.

"There *was* something unusual that happened. But it was so bizarre, so ridiculous, I didn't even realize."

"What are you talking about?"

Sage sat up against the headboard. "You asked me about any unusual correspondence. I don't know why I didn't think of it sooner."

"Think of what?"

"Do you remember when we ran into each other outside the ballroom? I'd been pissed at you and avoided you. You asked me to lunch."

"Yes. What does that have to do with anything?"

"Remember at lunch I told you I'd had an awful morning?"

"Vaguely."

"That was because of my run-in with the head of the mailroom. I told you that at the time."

"Okay."

"Don't you see?"

"Apparently not," Vaughn said dryly.

"The classified mail clerk had just dropped off my mail. I read it, and there was one piece of correspondence that didn't make any sense. So I looked at the envelope. It was addressed to the ambassador, not to me."

"How did it get to you then?"

"It was in the pouch from Washington that had to do with the upcoming congressional visit, so the clerk assumed it should go to me, since I was the control officer."

Now Vaughn sat up. "What did it say, and who was it from?"

Sage closed her eyes and tried to recall. "Something about camels being in place to spit and teaching the shrew a lesson at recess." Sage opened her eyes again. "Like I said, it didn't make any sense."

"Can you remember who the memo was from?"

"I don't think it said. That was one of the strange things about it. It was on plain white paper, not stationery, and there was no letterhead. It was so odd that I looked at the envelope again. On the bottom it said 'Ambassador's eyes only,' but it was smeared."

"What did you do with it when you realized it wasn't for you?"

"I walked it down to Trindle, the head mail clerk." Sage remembered what a jerk the man had been.

"What's that face for?"

"What face?"

"That look, like you just stepped in dog shit."

Sage laughed. "The man was a total idiot. He treated me like I was a moron, and then he called over the poor guy who had mistakenly delivered the piece to me in the first place and ripped him to shreds."

"What happened after that?"

"Nothing. He sealed it back in the envelope and no doubt took it himself to the ambassador."

"He didn't read it?"

"No."

"Did he ask if you had read it?"

"Yes, and I said I had, before I realized that it wasn't meant for me."

"Would the clerk who gave it to you have read it?"

"No, that's not his job."

"So the head clerk knew that you were the only one who read it?"

"Yes."

"And he took it to the ambassador?"

"I can't say that as an absolute fact, but I'm sure that's correct. It was for the ambassador's eyes only, and someone in the mail room screwed up. Trindle would've had to explain what happened."

"That was the day before you were taken," Vaughn mumbled. "Spitting camels and shrews at recess? Are you sure?"

"Positive, and let me tell you, if I never smell a camel or hear one spit again, it'll be too soon."

"What?"

Sage shivered involuntarily. "I said—"

"I know what you said, I just don't understand why you're saying that."

"You try riding a camel blindfolded with your hands tied to the saddle." Sage crossed her wrists in front of her to demonstrate.

"Is that how they got you up north?"

"Yes, we traveled by camel."

"Sage, I need you to remember exactly how the memo was worded."

Sage closed her eyes again. She had always had a gift for recall—it was one of the things that made her good at what she did. "The camels are in place and ready to spit. Your job is to give the shrew an education at recess on the twenty-third. She'll need some fresh air between classes. Confirm receipt and destroy immediately."

Vaughn scrambled out of bed and stood before the windows. The sun was not yet up, and the mountains appeared ominous in the inky darkness. "Remind me," she said, her back to Sage, "what was the majority leader's schedule?"

"First of all, if you want me to concentrate, you ought to put on some clothes." Sage stared appreciatively at Vaughn's shapely backside.

Vaughn turned and rolled her eyes, but threw on a T-shirt and a pair of shorts. "Better?"

"No, but I did ask for it. The majority leader's visit starts with a formal reception, an address to the National Assembly, then there are the trips to the schools up north..." Sage's voice trailed off and her eyes opened wide. "Surely you don't think..."

"Give the shrew an education at recess? That's what you said, right?"

"Yes, on the twenty-third."

"Do you remember what days the majority leader was supposed to be visiting the schools?"

"Not off the top of my head."

"No matter," Vaughn said, going to her duffle. She unzipped it and removed her briefcase. "I ripped this month's page off your blotter."

"You…"

"I was looking for clues, and I thought I might find something useful on it."

Sage got out of bed and went to Vaughn. She put her hand on Vaughn's face. "Have I said thank you yet? If I have, great. If not, I'll say it now. Thank you for caring about me. Thank you for coming after me. Thank you for risking your life and your career for me." She blinked away the tears that formed on her lashes.

"You're welcome," Vaughn said. She leaned down and kissed Sage gently. "I'm sorry it took me so long." Her voice was hoarse with emotion.

"I knew you'd come. Every time I got scared, I reminded myself that you were out there looking for me."

"So you told me. I'm glad you were so sure."

"I'm glad I was right." Sage kissed Vaughn, just because she could, and because the temptation was too great. She avoided looking at the bandage inches below the right shoulder and inches above the breast. She didn't want to think about how close she'd come to never having this opportunity again.

"Anyway," Vaughn said, pulling back and unfolding the blotter page. "Let's take a look." She spread the page out on a table, then recoiled as though she'd been slapped.

"What is it?" Sage asked.

"Trindle," Vaughn said, and pointed to a doodle in the corner of the square of the day before Sage was taken. The disappointment was clear on her face.

"So?"

"Do you have any idea how many times I looked at this page? I never made the connection. I didn't see it."

"Why would you? You couldn't know who he was."

"I had a list of employees. I could've cross-referenced."

"Vaughn, no human being would've known to check that."

"It doesn't matter. The issue now is to get answers."

Sage could see that she was trying to shrug it off, so she let it go. Vaughn's impossible expectations of herself would be a topic for another day. "The school visits are planned for the twenty-second and twenty-third."

"That's it, then. The majority leader is the shrew. They're planning to take out the majority leader on the twenty-third and make it look like it's the act of a band of renegade locals."

"The camels spitting would be Tuareg assassins?"

"Yes." Vaughn's eyes were bright and her voice had lost its sleepy quality.

"Wait a minute. This doesn't make any sense. Who would want to kill the senate majority leader? If the message was meant for the ambassador, that means he's part of the plot, right?"

"So it would seem. Or, at the very least, he knows about it."

Sage sat down on the edge of the bed. "So this is sanctioned by the U.S. government? *Our* government wants to kill the most powerful female elected official in the country?"

"I didn't say that."

"But…" Sage's head hurt.

"Let's get dressed and find Justine. We've got a lot to discuss and not much time to work with."

❦

"Where are you now?" Vaughn was trying hard to be patient, but time was slipping through their fingers.

"An hour closer than I was last time you called me. I'm glad you're feeling better, Elliott," Sabastien said. "You know how I can tell you're feeling better? Because you have no patience."

"I'm glad you think that's a good sign. You're going to have some serious gadgets with you, right?"

"Of course. Elliott, don't worry. I've got it covered."

"Okay. Hurry."

"I'm going as fast as I can."

"You're not being followed, right?"

"Actually, I thought it would be really cool if I led them right to your door," Sabastien said.

"I'm sorry. It's just—well, be careful and watch yourself."

"Your concern is touching. I'll be fine. See you in a bit."

Vaughn terminated the call and sat down gingerly in an oversized chair across from Sage and Justine. "He'll be here soon."

"Good," Justine said. "Here's hoping he can find answers that fill in some of these huge gaps."

Vaughn nodded. "We can start doing some of the research ourselves while we wait." She pointed to the laptop sitting on the coffee table. "We need to know what political enemies the esteemed majority leader has made, particularly of late."

"She's a strong female in a male-dominated field. What enemies hasn't she made?" Sage asked.

"She's got a point," Justine said, as she booted up the laptop.

"True, but we're looking for someone who thinks her sins are egregious enough to warrant death. That ought to narrow the field significantly."

"One can hope," Justine said. "How about if we search the *New York Times* database, for starters? We can see what positions she might've taken that would be especially controversial."

"You should check the *Washington Post* too," Sage offered. "It's the second paper we review here after the *Times*."

"Anything you can think of off the top of your head?" Vaughn asked Sage.

"No. I've been following her since she got elected, because I just think she's a smart politician and such a good leader. She's taken some strong positions, and they've earned her plenty of heat from special interest groups and the Republicans but nothing that's worth killing over."

"What about members of her own party?"

"Someone who got passed over when she was named majority leader?" Justine asked.

"If that's true, I don't know about it," Sage answered.

"Disagreements with the president?"

"She's certainly no rubber-stamp for his policies, but if they have major differences, they're not public. Heck, rumor had it that she was his choice, and that he was twisting arms behind the scenes to get her the post. I can't imagine that he'd want to do her harm." Sage's hand was trembling.

"What is it?" Vaughn asked.

"I can't believe this is happening—that someone wants to kill her for being a great politician."

"We don't know that that's the reason," Justine said. "I'm scrolling through all these articles, and I don't see any major red flags. Just the usual posturing and public policy arguments."

"Why else would the administration want her dead?" Sage asked.

"Maybe it isn't the administration at all," Vaughn answered. "So far, all we know for sure is that Fairhaven has issued the orders. Pordras is at least complicit, and so is the ambassador. Hence the reason they were able to put Torgensen in play. We don't have anything solid to assume it goes higher than that."

"Rogues?" Justine asked. "I have a hard time believing that even a blowhard like Fairhaven could be so bold."

Vaughn raised her eyebrows. "It goes down in a remote area of a third-world country, at the hands of a tribe of nomads known to have warrior-like roots and a history of unrest in the not-too-distant past. It's the perfect setup. Nobody need ever know."

"Except that Sage knew, or at least they thought she did," Justine added.

"Which upset the applecart, big time."

"Because if nobody knew, nobody could point a finger, and they could be as bold as they wanted."

"Exactly. You know they would've sent a cleanup crew," Vaughn said.

"Of course. You can't leave any loose ends."

Sage held up a hand. "First, what is a rogue?"

"Someone acting without higher authority," Vaughn answered.

"Okay. So you're saying this Fairhaven might be acting on his own and taking the secretary of state and the ambassador along for the ride? That's pretty far-fetched, isn't it?"

"That depends on what he has on either or both of them. We already know that Fairhaven and Pordras were boyhood friends, and that Fairhaven managed to bury Pordras's drug issues so deeply that there's virtually no remaining record of it."

"What drug issues and, if they were buried, how do you know about them?" Sage asked.

"Pordras got arrested for drugs when he was in his twenties and Fairhaven made the whole thing disappear," Justine said. "If you dig deeply enough, you can find almost anything that ever existed."

"That's comforting—not. By cleanup crew, I assume you don't mean housekeepers."

Vaughn laughed. "I guess in a sense you could call them that. A cleanup crew is a hit team that takes care of any potential problems. In other words, they would come and kill the Tuareg who carried out the plan so that they could never be tortured into telling."

Sage's jaw hung open. "This stuff happens in real life?" She shook her head in disbelief.

"Unfortunately, it does," Justine said quietly.

Sage jumped up from the sofa, outrage and disgust plainly evident in her expression. "And this is part of what you do? This is the kind of thing our government sanctions?" She was staring directly at Vaughn, disillusionment darkening her pupils.

"Sage—" Justine started.

"It's all right," Vaughn interrupted. "I tried to tell you several times that I was not someone worthy of a woman like you, Sage. You wouldn't listen. Now you know the truth."

Without a word, Sage pivoted and ran from the room. Vaughn closed her eyes to shield her pain from Justine's penetrating gaze.

"Why did you let her think that?"

"Is she so wrong?"

"She is, and you know it. You've never killed anyone who wasn't a direct threat. You've never been part of any cleanup crew that I'm aware of."

Vaughn shook her head. "But I could've been."

"You could, but you wouldn't do that, and we both know it. Why let her believe an untruth?"

"Heaven knows I've killed when it was required. Besides, you saw for yourself—she assumed the worst. I don't want to live with someone constantly wondering whether I'm a good guy or a bad guy. Better to disabuse her of any illusions now."

"Those aren't illusions, Vaughn. Those are outright falsehoods. Maybe you're so afraid to let that woman in your life that it's easier for you to let her think outrageous things about you."

"What's your point?"

"It's cowardly, and you're no coward."

Vaughn simply shrugged. "Sabastien will be here soon. I'm going to lie down."

❧❦

Justine found Sage standing rigidly on the upstairs balcony. She had her good arm folded across her midsection, and her jaw muscles stood out in sharp relief.

"Sage—"

"I don't want to talk about it."

"Maybe not," Justine said. Her temper made her enunciate the *t*.

"But you're going to make me, right?" Sage turned to face her.

"Yep, that's right, and do you know why?"

"No, why?"

They were standing toe-to-toe.

"Because you were way out of line, and Vaughn doesn't deserve your haughty assumptions and sanctimonious judgments. Because Vaughn Elliott is a hero with more commendations for valor and bravery than could fit on her chest."

"But—"

Justine held her hand up when Sage tried to interrupt her. "What did I just say? You listen to me, Sage McNally. That woman has saved more lives than any other agent I know. When she's taken a life, it has always been with cause, and always with remorse. She is a fine, upstanding human being, and I am proud to serve our country alongside her. Save your recriminations for someone who deserves them. Vaughn Elliott isn't that person."

The doorbell rang and Justine retreated inside. "I have to go. That should be Sabastien. We have to focus on the real bad guys." She didn't bother to look over her shoulder to see if Sage was following her. She was too angry to care.

CHAPTER TWENTY

F airhaven and Pordras sipped their drinks in Fairhaven's townhouse overlooking the Potomac. Pordras was poring over a map of West Africa.

"The congressional delegation is traveling to Ghana, Cameroon, and Senegal before they get to Mali. None of those is as ideal as Mali for our plan, but we can figure something out."

"No," Fairhaven said, his voice a steely calm.

" No, what?"

"No, we're not going to do it in any of those places."

"Well, we sure as hell aren't going to do it in downtown Paris."

"Of course not."

"And we agree that the Mali plan is too risky now."

"Uh-huh."

Pordras took Fairhaven by the shoulders. "Ed, you're the one who said we have to do this. You convinced me—"

"Get hold of yourself, Bri. You're turning into a simpering fool."

Pordras lit a cigarette with shaky fingers. "Everything rides on this. Everything. You said so yourself."

"No kidding. Which is why we can no longer consider any of the scheduled stops."

"Why?"

"Elliott knows everything about the existing route—it was part of her DS assignment. Assuming she's debriefed McNally by now, she's figured out what the end game is. She's also smart enough to realize that we would alter the plan. That means she would take steps to secure all the other stops. We need to add a stop to the itinerary."

"How do you propose to do that?" Pordras asked, his voice teetering on hysteria.

"You're the secretary of state, Bri. Surely you can think of a reason why an important representative of the United States government would need to add an additional stop to her trip."

"You're insane. Why would Stowe agree to it?"

"Because the suggestion is going to come from the president, and because it will be a good opportunity for her to beef up her international credentials."

"You want me to go to the president and recommend that Senate Majority Leader Stowe be sent as his emissary to…where?"

Fairhaven picked up a red Sharpie off the table. He used it to make a big "X" through the capital of Mauritania. "There."

"Have you lost your mind? I thought you said Elliott was just there."

"She was. Which is exactly why that's the perfect spot. She'd never expect it. Besides, I've got a score to settle with Mauritania's chief of police. I couldn't do it before because it would've raised too many questions, but if he just happened to be caught in the crossfire…"

"Why do we care about him?" Pordras asked.

"Either he was a complete incompetent, or he intentionally obstructed our search for Elliott and her friends. He needs to pay. That's why."

"Ed, I'm not sure you're thinking all that clearly. We don't care about some peon in a third-world pit. That's just your ego—"

Fairhaven's face turned beet red. He got to within inches of Pordras and poked him in the chest. "If it wasn't for you, we wouldn't have to be doing this at all. Now you have the nerve to stand here and question my professional judgment and years of experience in wet ops?"

"I-It's not that. It's just… I'm not comfortable—"

"You're not comfortable? *You're* not comfortable? I don't give a rat's ass about your comfort." Fairhaven's voice was loud enough to echo off the walls. "It's going down in Mauritania. You figure out what story to sell to the president. I would suggest you start with the fact that Mauritania recently held its first free and fair parliamentary and presidential elections. We should celebrate the country's return to democracy."

Pordras opened and closed his mouth several times, emitting no sound.

"Spit it out, Bri, or is this another ridiculous fear of yours?" Fairhaven stepped back and took another sip of his drink.

"What's to stop Elliott from going directly to Stowe?"

Fairhaven barked out a laugh. "Me."

"You?"

"Yes, me. For one thing, I've got Stowe's phones bugged. For another, Elliott can't get within two miles of Stowe without me knowing it."

"You're running surveillance on the majority leader?"

"Naturally. Do you really think I'd leave anything to chance? She's been under twenty-four hour watch since Elliott left Mauritania. Madeline Stowe is on a plane between stops even as we speak, with the press corps in tow."

"One of those reporters is a plant?"

"Convenient that the *L.A. Times* was in search of someone new to cover the congressional beat." Fairhaven smiled smugly.

"He's not going to actually do it, is he? I mean, that's too close. The Tuareg were good because no one could link them to us."

"You'd be surprised how easy it is to get caught up in the unrest between the White and Black Moor and the Afro-Mauritanians. If Ms. Stowe's visit were to stir up protests, you never know what might happen in a crowd."

"Yeah, you never know," Pordras parroted. "You are still hunting Elliott, though, right?"

"Yes, Bri. My man is tracking her even as we speak."

"Anything?" Vaughn asked Sabastien.

"I'm working on it. It won't happen any faster for you standing over my shoulder, you know."

"Hi," Sage said, coming down the stairs.

"O, la, la, Elliott. Who do we have here?"

Vaughn punched Sabastien in the shoulder. "Sabastien, Sage. Sage, Sabastien." Vaughn made a point of avoiding eye contact with Sage.

"Nice to meet you," Sage said.

"The pleasure is mine, I assure you," Sabastien responded.

"Down, boy," Vaughn said. "Eyes on the screen."

"Vaughn, can I see you outside for a minute?" Sage asked sheepishly.

"We're in the middle of something right now."

"I can spare you," Sabastien said. "In fact, you'd be doing me a favor," he said to Sage. "She's hovering."

Vaughn gestured to Sage to precede her onto the deck. "What?" she asked, after shutting the door behind them.

"I..." Sage bit her lower lip. "I owe you an apology." She stood stiffly, her hair blowing in the breeze. "I—"

Vaughn dove at her and pulled her to the ground as a bullet whizzed in the air overhead. "Inside. Now. Stay on the ground and crawl on your belly. Let's go."

When Sage hesitated, Vaughn whispered harshly in her ear and pulled her by the shirt. "Now, Sage! Keep your head down. Move!"

Vaughn pried the sliding glass doors open with her fingers and shoved Sage through. She followed as another bullet embedded itself in the wood decking near her hand.

"Time's up," Vaughn said to Justine, who was just coming into the room from the mini-kitchen. "Let's go."

"Go where?" Sage asked, scrabbling to her feet.

"Get away from the windows. I want you and Sabastien in an interior upstairs bathroom, right now."

Justine already was in motion, grabbing several weapons and two Kevlar vests from the closet where she'd stored them. She shoved one pistol into Sabastien's hand. "Do you know how to use this?"

"I'll figure it out," he said. His voice was shaking.

"Take your laptop with you," Justine said. "Stay away from any windows or exits. Don't get curious, either one of you. Give us three hours. If neither one of us comes to get you by then, stay down and get to the car. There's a farm down the road. The owner is a friend of mine named George. Tell him you're with me. He'll take it from there."

"Vaughn—"

"Sage, this is no time to talk. Just get up those stairs. Now." Vaughn kept Sage in her peripheral vision long enough to be sure that she did, indeed, go upstairs with Sabastien.

Vaughn and Justine finished affixing the long-range sights.

"How did you know?"

"Laser sight. Her forehead was painted."

"Jesus," Justine said.

"Good thing he was going for her first, although I can't for the life of me figure out why he would've. That stupidity is going to cost him his life."

"Single shooter?"

"Yes. Otherwise I'd be dead by now."

"How far?"

"At least two hundred yards. Although now that we know he's out there, there's no telling where he is."

"Unlikely that he would run."

"That's for sure," Vaughn agreed. "And I seriously doubt he'd try a direct assault on the house. He knows there are at least two trained agents in here. I don't see him risking a shootout at close range."

"True."

"Okay," Vaughn said. By silent agreement they'd made their way to the garage. "You want clockwise and I'll take counterclockwise?"

Justine nodded. "You sure you're up to this?"

"Do I have a choice?"

"You could protect them while I hunt."

"In a pig's eye."

"I figured you'd say that. Okay, on three." Justine opened the door and they both crouched behind the car. "Nothing," she whispered, moving around the car to the left.

"Nothing," Vaughn agreed, finishing a circle to the right. "Okay. What do you say we get him to give away his position?"

"I was thinking the same thing."

They looked around the garage until Vaughn spotted an old tractor tire. "How's your aim?"

"Pretty good," Justine said.

"Excellent. I don't think I can put enough on it." She rolled the tire toward Justine. "Last known position was thirty degrees to your left."

"In that case, I think I should assume that he's moved and roll it in the direction of his last position. Ready?" She opened the side door to the garage a crack.

Vaughn checked the magazine of the Sig, which she stuck in her waistband. Then she made sure that there was a round in the chamber of her rifle. "High-low?"

"You take low. I get high so I can roll the tire clear."

"On three."

At the count of three, Justine shoved the door wide and rolled the tire to her left. The rubber blew into pieces. Vaughn fired five shots in rapid succession from a position below and just to the side of Justine. Based on the trajectory and speed of the bullet that had shredded the tire, she aimed at a spot fifty yards away to the right. "Go, go, go!"

Justine sprinted to the left. Vaughn covered her with a series of shots. Then she ran back through the house and out the kitchen door at the other side of the house. They would converge on the shooter from both sides.

Vaughn spotted the glint of steel as the sun cleared a cloud. The shooter was concealed behind a large rock about fifty yards from the upstairs balcony and down a grassy incline. Through the rifle scope, she could see that he was aiming at Justine, who was circling around to flank him from the other direction.

The shot wasn't as clean as Vaughn would've liked, but she couldn't afford to wait for a better opportunity. She wiped the sweat from her eyes with her forearm and braced her elbows on the ground. The exertion of sprinting had left her wheezing and struggling for air. She ignored the searing pain that shot through her chest, sighted the target, and squeezed the trigger evenly.

The first shot hit him in the side of the neck. Through the scope Vaughn watched blood explode from his carotid artery. As he twisted, she fired a second time, hitting him directly between the eyes. His body twitched several times before becoming completely still. He was staring blindly up at the sky.

Vaughn released the rifle and collapsed, the coolness of the grass soothing her heated cheek. Her efforts to suck air into her lungs were only moderately successful.

∽৯৹⌒

Justine cautiously made her way from her position to where the shooter lay dead and confiscated his weapon. A quick check of the area satisfied her that the man had no backup. She looked around for Vaughn, who hadn't showed herself yet.

"Vaughn?" When she got no answer, dread settled in the pit of her stomach. "Shit." She hadn't seen a flash from the shooter's rifle. Had he fired a shot? Was Vaughn hit? "Vaughn?" she called, a sense of urgency making her voice louder. She thought she might've heard a weak reply, but she couldn't be sure.

Her steps took her to a grassy knoll at the side of the house. Vaughn was lying face down, her rifle on the ground at her side. "Vaughn!"

Justine dropped the weapons and knelt next to her.

"P-present," Vaughn whispered. Justine could see that she was struggling for air.

"Are you hit?"

"No. Just can't seem to c-catch my breath."

"It's okay. C'mon, let's get you sitting up." Justine helped Vaughn roll over and sit up. She moved behind Vaughn to offer support. "Lean against me…That's it. Relax. Easy breaths. Nothing too deep." She felt Vaughn begin to relax and the wheezing ease.

"All clear?" Vaughn asked.

"Yep. You got him."

"Sielig?"

"What's left of him."

"His plan sucked."

"He wasn't a field agent."

"Now we know why."

"Don't you think that strengthens the case for Fairhaven being rogue? If he wasn't, he would've sent a swarm of the best field agents available. Instead, he sent his deputy."

"A guy with no field experience," Vaughn paused for a breath, "but whom the boss could trust with the assignment."

"Exactly." Justine shifted so that she could see Vaughn's face. Some of her color had returned. "Think you can stand?"

"Yeah. We can't stay here. We need to check on Sage and Sabastien."

"We also need to dispose of Sielig."

"Can your friends take care of that?" Vaughn asked.

"Yes."

"Good. It isn't safe here. We've got to move."

"Not until you rest for a while."

"There'll be time for that later. If Sielig made us, he probably relayed our location."

"Maybe so, but if we're right, Fairhaven can't dispatch just anybody. It will take time for him to get a backup crew here," Justine said.

"He's lost Torgensen, now he's lost Sielig. What if he's getting desperate enough to designate us as rogues? Then he can make it a matter of national security to take us out."

"We're making a lot of assumptions here."

"Did you pick up Sielig's cell phone? Did he have one on him? That might prove interesting."

"I'll go check. Wait here."

Justine found the phone in one of Sielig's inside pockets. She grabbed it and returned to where Vaughn was slowly standing up. "Got it."

"Another sign that he had no idea what he was doing. No hit man would ever carry anything that could identify him, and especially not a phone that could give us so much information."

Justine noted that Vaughn's chest still was heaving and she was laboring to breathe. "Nice and slow, okay? There's no rush."

❧

Sabastien's face was white as a ghost.

"Are you okay?" Sage whispered.

Sabastien blotted at the perspiration on his upper lip. "Oui. Don't get me wrong, being locked in a bathroom with a beautiful woman is certainly on my top five list of fantasies, especially when there is a hot tub involved, but…"

"You should try being tethered to a camel while blindfolded."

"Ah, yes. I am so sorry. I know you have been through a terrible ordeal. I should be…how do you Americans say…tougher."

"That's all right," Sage said, touching him on the arm. "I'm scared out of my mind too."

"I'm glad it is not only me."

They both heard the shots and huddled together on the floor.

"Oh, my God," Sage said. "Please let them be okay."

Sabastien wrapped his arm around her. "I'm sure they're fine. They are both trained for these types of situations, and they are very good at what they do."

"Vaughn just saved my life—for the third time. What if I never get a chance to apologize…"

"Shh, it will be okay." Sabastien patted her on the back. "Why would you need to apologize for her saving your life?"

"Oh. Um, I didn't mean that I should apologize for that. It's just…" Sage blushed. "I behaved really badly earlier today before you arrived. I'm afraid I was a complete jerk."

"I cannot imagine that being the case, but even so, you will have plenty of time to apologize. I'm sure Elliott and Justine will be back in no time, having dispatched the bad guy with no problem."

They both were quiet for several moments, and Sage strained to hear anything that might be going on outside. Since there were skylights but no windows in the bathroom, she couldn't see anything, even if she had wanted to.

"What are you doing?" she asked, when she noticed Sabastien playing with his laptop.

"What? Oh." He smiled shyly. "When I get nervous, it helps me to do something useful. I am tracking the action outside via satellite."

"You can do that?"

"Bien sûr. I can do almost anything with a computer."

"What do you see?" Sage moved so that she could see the screen.

"See these orange blobs?" Sabastien pointed to two areas on the screen.

"Yes."

"Those are people. These two are together, at least I think it's two, and the other one is a distance away."

"Can you tell who's who?"

"No, but…"

"What is it?"

"One of the two is moving back toward the third."

"Why?"

"That I cannot tell. Merde!"

"What?" Sage asked, alarmed.

"I lost the feed."

"Can you get it back?"

"I'm trying."

"Hurry."

"I can only go as fast as the machine will let me."

For several minutes, the only sound was that of Sabastien wildly clicking keys on his keyboard.

A knock on the door made them both jump. "Sage, Sabastien? It's Justine. Open the door. It's okay."

Sage jumped up and unlocked the door to find a somewhat disheveled Justine on the other side.

"Looks like you guys are having a party," Justine said.

"Yes, a blast, as you would say," Sabastien said, as he rose from the floor. "Where is Elliott?"

Sage held her breath. It was the first question she'd wanted to ask, and yet she was too afraid of the answer.

"She's downstairs. Come on. It's all clear." Justine motioned for them to follow her downstairs.

The first thing Sage noticed was Vaughn, hunched over in a chair. She looked very pale and lines of pain were evident on her face. She went directly to her.

"Are you okay?" Sage reached out her hand as if to touch Vaughn's face, but she stopped short.

"We need to get going," Vaughn said, without looking at Sage. "We don't know if there are more men on the way." She stood up and addressed the room in general. "Pack your things and be back here in ten minutes."

"Vaughn—" Sage began.

Vaughn made a point of looking at her watch. "Nine minutes and forty-five seconds." She walked toward the bedroom.

Sage turned on her heel and headed for the stairs. She supposed she deserved the cold shoulder Vaughn was giving her, but it stung nonetheless.

CHAPTER TWENTY-ONE

Brian Pordras fidgeted nervously with a paperclip. "I should've stayed in the private sector," he muttered to himself. "None of this would've happened if I'd just kept my head down and stayed where I was." The paperclip snapped in half.

"Sir? You have a call on your private line. Do you want me to pick it up?"

Pordras jumped at the sound of his executive assistant's voice through the intercom. He'd been so preoccupied he hadn't even heard the phone ring. He depressed the intercom button. "No, I've got it." He cleared his throat and depressed the blinking button. "Pordras."

"Picnic in the park. Half an hour."

"Right." Pordras swallowed hard. He hadn't been scheduled to meet with Ed until that night. A middle-of-the-day rendezvous couldn't mean anything good. Ed normally would never take a chance like that. Pordras grabbed his coat and headed out the door.

Rock Creek Park was quiet at this time of day. It was too early for most workers to be on lunch break and too late for early morning joggers.

When Pordras spotted him, Fairhaven was feeding the ducks in the pond.

"You're late."

"I had to take my own car. Somehow, I didn't think this would be perceived as an appropriate use of my driver and official vehicle."

"See, Bri," Fairhaven patted him on the cheek, "you have learned something from me over the years."

Fairhaven's patronizing tone rankled, but Pordras knew better than to protest. The last thing he needed to hear was another lecture about how his inadequacies and recklessness had created this situation in the first place.

"What was so urgent?"

"I've procured the necessary personnel for the job. They'll be in place within twenty-four hours."

"Are they locals?"

"No, but they'll blend in."

"Do I want to know where you found them?"

"Probably not." Fairhaven threw some bread crusts into the water. "Your conversation with the president went well?"

"Yes. I was present when he called the majority leader and requested her to make an additional stop."

"I take it she accepted."

"Of course. I was instructed to prepare a brief for her. My staff is working on it right now."

"Good. See, Bri? Everything is going to be just fine."

"Yeah? What about Elliott? Has your man checked in?"

"He relayed her presumed location and went hunting."

"How long ago was that?"

"It's not your concern." Fairhaven thrust a plastic bag full of bread crusts into Pordras's hand. "Try to fit in a little better, will you?"

"We're two executives in suits standing in front of a duck pond at mid-morning. You think we don't look odd just on the face of it?" Pordras threw some crusts. "I want to know if you've heard from you're man or not. Is the job done?"

"He hasn't checked in yet."

"When was he supposed to do that?"

Fairhaven tossed more bread but didn't answer.

"Ed?"

"Four hours ago," Fairhaven mumbled.

"Fo… Did you try to call him?" Alarm pitched Pordras's voice higher than normal.

"Of course I didn't try to call him," Fairhaven snapped. "If he hasn't checked in within twelve hours of the appointed time, I have to assume he's been compromised."

"Great. How many men are we going to lose chasing this woman?"

"We? *We?*" A vein bulged in Fairhaven's forehead. He inhaled deeply, visibly restraining his temper. "I've declared Elliott and Coulter to be rogue. Every agent in the Company has been instructed to shoot them dead on sight. There isn't any place they can hide now."

"You..." Pordras's head was spinning. "Elliott is DS. How do you have the authority—"

"She deserted her position and, in so doing, endangered the lives of members of Congress. Coulter is AWOL and believed to be traveling with her. We believe they are a threat to the majority leader of the United States."

Pordras took a moment to synthesize this information. "So, if either Elliott or Coulter is spotted anywhere near the majority leader, they'll be killed by your agents."

"Exactly."

"Brilliant."

"Don't sound so surprised. I suggest that, when you go back to your office, you fire Elliott and send a bulletin to every embassy and DS declaring her to be a direct threat to the government of the United States and its elected and appointed representatives. You might mention that she's considered to be armed and dangerous."

"Okay. Anything else? I'd better get back."

"No. That's it for now."

Pordras turned to go but looked back over his shoulder. "Do you think your man is dead?"

"I think he's normally a very punctual kind of guy." Fairhaven walked off in the opposite direction, but not before Pordras noted the expression of concern on his face.

Vaughn, Justine, Sage, and Sabastien sat in the converted barn of a farmhouse outside of Brussels, Belgium. The place was humming with computer equipment of all shapes and sizes. There were cords and wires everywhere.

"What do you think?" Sabastien asked.

"I think Bill Gates would be envious," Vaughn said. "How long have you had this place?"

"A couple of years. My father left me the property via a dummy corporation, so it can't be traced back to me."

"Aren't you just a chip off the old block," Vaughn said.

"Hey, hey. There's no call for sarcasm here. After all, I'm saving your ass at the moment."

"So noted. This is where you went when I told you to get out?"

"Yes. I figured sooner or later I would need a backup plan. In here, I've replicated everything I had in Paris. Shall I show you?"

"Actually," Justine broke in, "Vaughn needs to lie down somewhere for a while." When Vaughn started to protest, Justine talked over her. "You promised me that once we got someplace safe you would rest. Sabastien and I will work on getting the intel we need."

"We don't have time—"

"What we don't have time for is for your body to break down when we decide on our next move. It's the middle of the night, you haven't had any sleep, and most people with your injuries would still be in bed recuperating. Go lie down. Now!" Justine ordered.

"Use the bedroom on the first floor in the corner of the main house—it has its own bathroom and tub." Sabastien said. "I can set the alarm from here after you're in and I've got cameras set up. You'll be perfectly safe in there. But do me a favor, keep your clothes on until you get into the bathroom, which, sadly, has no camera coverage. There are some things I shouldn't see."

"Turn the camera off in the bedroom, you perv," Vaughn growled.

"Right. Off. Got it." Sabastien nodded vigorously. "At least I told you it was there," he called after Vaughn as she exited the barn.

Sage started to follow her, but Justine grabbed her by the good arm. "No. Let her go."

"But—"

"Sage, now is not the time."

"When will be the time? Tell me that? We're constantly in danger and on the move..." Her voice was shaking.

Despite the fact that she was still angry at her, Justine pulled Sage into a hug. "It's going to be okay."

"Sure it is. Strangers have tried to kill me three times, Vaughn nearly died protecting me twice, someone is trying to assassinate the senate majority leader, and we're hiding in some high-tech barn and eating bonbons."

"You brought chocolate?" Sabastien asked.

"Very funny."

"Let's get to work," Justine said. "First, let's find out what our status is." She turned to Sabastien. "Can you tap into the Company's database of bulletins released in the past forty-eight hours?"

"Can birds fly? Do pretty women turn me on? Is the sky—"

"We get the idea. Just get on with it."

"Okay. Here we go…"

❦

Once she'd closed the door to the bedroom, Vaughn grimaced in pain and put her hand to her chest. When she was able to catch her breath, she removed her shirt and checked the bandage, something she hadn't allowed Justine to do in the field. The dressing was dry. *Thank God for small favors.*

Vaughn stripped the rest of the way and ran a bath. She hoped the steam would help her breathing, in addition to relaxing her aching muscles. She hadn't had to run far, but Justine had been right—stretching and diving had done nothing for her recuperation. It frightened her that she might not be able to do her job effectively, and someone else could die as a result.

The water was soothingly hot, and she gratefully lowered herself into it. Since the bandage was waterproof, she didn't have to worry about getting it wet. When she was settled, she closed her eyes. Images flitted behind her lids—Torgensen twisting in mid-air, Sielig hemorrhaging blood from the wound in his neck, his gun still trained on Justine and, as always, Sara, her face shredded, her lifeless body spasming before going slack in Vaughn's arms.

She was a killer. It was what she did. There was no place in her life for a woman like Sage with her moral compass set firmly on north. It was just as well that they were interrupted by Sielig when they were. From this moment forward, she would do everything in her power to ensure that she was never alone with Sage. It was best for both of them. "What the hell were you thinking to get involved with her in the first place? How else did you think it would go down? You saw how she looked at you—like you were a monster."

Pain of a different sort pierced Vaughn's chest. She hadn't wanted to care, hadn't meant to want, didn't want to feel the sharp stab of heartache, loneliness, and disappointment. A single tear streaked her cheek and she didn't bother to wipe it away. Instead, she vowed that it would be the last she would cry until all of this was over. Then, if she survived, she'd go somewhere quiet and remote and get back her emotional bearings.

When she returned to the barn two hours later, having napped after the bath, Sabastien and Justine were staring at multiple computer consoles. Sage was dozing on a couch.

"What've you got?" Vaughn asked.

"Your hunch was right. We've been declared rogues. Worldwide bulletin to all field agents to kill us on sight without asking any questions."

"All of us?"

"No, just you and me," Justine said.

"Well, bucko, at least they left you out." Vaughn clapped Sabastien on the back.

"I'm thrilled. Of course, they're probably still hunting me from before…"

"Probably," Vaughn agreed amiably. "How'd they handle me? After all, I'm not Company property anymore."

Justine was the one who answered. "Seems you deserted your post, thereby endangering the lives of the members of the visiting delegation. The kill order says you are a threat to the senate majority leader and that I'm believed to be traveling with you."

"Oh, and you've been fired from the State Department," Sabastien added. "Hope you weren't too attached to the job."

Vaughn pressed her thumb and forefinger to the bridge of her nose to stave off the onset of a headache. "What about Sage?"

"Not a word about her. I guess their only interest in her was in what she knew. Since they've assumed she's already told you, they're apparently not hunting her anymore."

"Wrong, Sabastien. They can't possibly peg her as a threat to national security, and they can't publicly justify shooting her. But please don't make the mistake of assuming that if Fairhaven gets the chance he won't eliminate her. Since the Tuareg who took her can't talk, Fairhaven can't know what she might've seen and how much of the plot she might've figured out. She's a witness—a loose end—and you can be sure they don't intend to leave any of those."

"You have to admit," Justine said, "he's done a good job of covering his bases. Now, he can legitimately have every available agent looking for us, and he's ensured that we can't get within a mile of the majority leader to protect her."

"We'll find a way," Vaughn said.

"I wouldn't suggest calling her," Sabastien said. "If it were me, I'd have cloned or bugged her phones."

"We'll have to find some other way to get in touch with her," Justine said.

"Actually, I'm not sure we want to get in touch with her at all," Vaughn said.

"Are you suggesting that we shouldn't warn her that she's in danger?"

"I think there are bunches of things we should discuss before we make a determination what course of action we should take." Vaughn leaned her back against the wall to keep from falling over. Although she badly needed more rest, she would never let that show. "For instance, is the plan still in play?"

"If Fairhaven is smart, he'll realize there's too much heat, and he'll put the plan on the shelf," Justine said.

"I disagree." Vaughn shook her head. "He's got too much invested. He still needs to take us out because we know that, at the very least, there was a real plan. He can't leave us alive to testify to that fact, and if he's going to take us out anyway, he might as well go ahead with the plan."

Justine picked up her line of thinking. "The majority leader could be caught in the crossfire and killed by a 'stray' shot if an agent was shooting at us to protect her."

"That's one possibility," Vaughn agreed. "It could also be that Fairhaven uses locals to kill her and makes it look like we hired them."

"After all," Justine pointed out, "using indigenous peoples was his original plan."

"Let's not forget that it cuts down on the paperwork and internal investigations too."

"Okay, so we assume that the plan is still in the works. Where does it take place?" Sabastien asked, never taking his eyes off the bank of computer screens in front of him.

"He wouldn't dare do it in Mali now, would he?" Sage asked, sitting up and rubbing her eyes.

"I don't think so," Vaughn said. She examined a non-existent cuticle rather than look at Sage in her sleep-tousled state.

"I don't think so either," Sabastien said. "Check this out." He rolled his chair back and pointed at one of the screens.

"What is it?" Vaughn asked, trying to make sense of the words on the screen.

"What does it look like? This, Elliott, is Senate Majority Leader Madeline Stowe's personal electronic calendar."

"How did you…?"

"Never mind how, Justine, my sweet. Just concede that I am a genius."

"Okay, genius," Vaughn said, using the mouse to scroll through the days, "what did you find?"

"The calendar was updated this morning. It seems an additional stop has been added to the congressional tour."

"Isn't that handy. Where and when?"

Sabastien nudged Vaughn and Justine aside. "See here? Stowe already visited Cameroon and Ghana and is on her way to Senegal."

Vaughn watched over Sabastien's shoulder as he scrolled through the calendar. "You won't believe this," she said, looking back at Justine. "Guess what the added stop is?"

"What?"

"Mauritania."

"You're kidding, right?"

"Absolutely serious."

"He's lost his mind," Justine said.

"I don't think so." Vaughn turned and sat on the edge of the table. "It conveniently shares borders with Senegal and Mali, it moves the timetable for the hit up by a few days, and he knows we've already been there and left—"

"When is the delegation scheduled to be there?" Justine asked.

"I don't think the delegation is going at all," Sabastien said. "The notation on the calendar says the delegation will stay in Senegal. The majority leader will take a solo day trip to Mauritania and rejoin the group for their scheduled arrival in Mali."

"When?" Vaughn asked. She didn't like the sound of that at all. Isolating the majority leader would make her an easy target and limit the possibility of collateral damage. *Ideal conditions for a hit.*

"Day after tomorrow."

"Good," Vaughn said. "For a second there, I thought this was going to be difficult." She rolled her eyes. "Justine, do you have a way to contact Nate?"

Justine nodded and pulled out her cell phone. She highlighted his number on her call log and handed it to Vaughn as the call connected.

"Nate? Hey, it's Vaughn."

"You sound much stronger than you did a few days ago. I am glad."

"Thanks. I don't suppose you've gotten wind of a surprise visit by United States Senate Majority Leader Stowe, have you?"

"As fate would have it, I was just informed. Why?"

"She's the target. Can you tell me what you know about the itinerary?"

"She is to meet with the president and prime minister day after tomorrow. Following the meeting, she will be given a tour of several places of historical significance to Mauritanians. Then she will be on a plane to Mali."

"Will the tour involve any walking outdoors?" Vaughn asked. In her gut, she knew the answer, but she needed confirmation.

"Yes. In fact, there will be an outdoor procession."

"Any likelihood of protests?"

Nate's laugh was rich. "This is Mauritania. Of course there will be protests."

"That's it, then," Vaughn said. "They're going to use the chaos of a demonstration to mask the hit."

"I will do my best to ensure that such a thing does not happen on my watch."

"I know you will. Do you keep a list of known agitators? Anyone you can think of who would be happy to see a high-ranking American official dead?"

"The list is long, Vaughn."

"I don't suppose there's any chance you could round them up quietly between now and day after tomorrow?"

"If I do, we will tip our hand and they will send surrogates. Perhaps of more use to you would be for me to use some of my back channels to find out who would've accepted such an assignment."

"Yes, please." Vaughn hesitated. "Nate, I don't want to endanger you any further, but I need to find a way to have a moment alone with the senate majority leader before the procession. It can't be public. A restroom following the presidential meeting would be ideal."

"A restroom?"

"Yes. Agents of my government have been ordered to kill me on sight. I can't be seen anywhere in the area. So I would need to be in the restroom at least three hours before the majority leader arrives in the building."

"I can arrange it."

"The only other issue is how to get me into your fair city without being made."

"I can handle things at the airport on my end, but you know I will not be the only person watching flights."

"Yes, I'm sure I'll be expected." Vaughn needed to know one more piece of information. "Is anyone else traveling with Ms. Stowe, and have they attached any U.S. security to you for the visit?"

"I've been told there will be one, what you would call, pool reporter traveling with the majority leader, and the regional security officer and assistant regional security officer from your embassy will be assisting with the protective detail."

"Do you know the security officers?"

"Yes, they've been here for several years."

"Okay. Do you have a name for the pool reporter?"

"I only know that he is from the *Los Angeles Times.* A newspaper, I think, yes?"

"Yes. Okay, I'll check into him on my end. If I were to arrive tomorrow, could you keep me out of sight? I'll be traveling under the name Lucinda Barrett, a French philanthropist looking to help the Mauritanians build a new hospital in Nouakchott."

"I will have someone meet you. I do not think it wise to go myself, in case I am also being watched. I will send someone I trust with my life—my wife."

"I'll call you back when I have flight times."

"No need. I have access to that information. I assume you will not look like yourself, but she will have enough of a description to find you."

"Thank you, my friend. See you tomorrow." Vaughn closed the phone. It was only then that she noticed the three unhappy faces in the room.

CHAPTER TWENTY-TWO

"What?" Vaughn asked.

"There's no way in hell you're going by yourself," Justine said. She stood with her hands on her hips. Fire smoldered in her eyes.

"Of course I am, don't be ridiculous. They're expecting two or three of us. It will be a lot easier for me to slip in unnoticed, take care of this, and get back out."

"Just what, exactly, does 'take care of this' entail?" Sage asked.

"I'm going to talk to the majority leader, warn her about the plot, find out why she's being targeted, stop the hit, and get out."

"Oh, is that all?" Anger propelled Sage to her feet. "Are we supposed to sit here and knit sweaters in the meantime?"

"No," Vaughn fired back. "You're going back to the States to get your shoulder properly cared for, get your stitches out, and get the hell out of the line of fire."

"Vaughn," Justine began.

Vaughn whirled to face her. "This is not negotiable. I need you to make sure Sage gets tucked away somewhere safe until this is all over." She held up her hand to stave off Justine's objection. "I'm also going to need you in place to keep an eye on the principals so that they can't run before we wrap this up."

Justine opened her mouth to speak and closed it, her lips forming a thin line of displeasure.

"Sabastien." Vaughn redirected her attention. "You have been working while I was on the phone, right?"

"I'm on it. I've booked a ticket for Lucinda. I also booked a flight under your real names. The three of you supposedly are leaving Zurich ten minutes from now for New York."

"What happens when we don't get on that plane?"

"I'll rig the passenger manifest so it looks like you did." Sabastien worked the mouse for one PC with one hand, and a second mouse for a second PC with his other. "I'll have Lucinda's passport ready within the hour. I'll also create new identities for Sage and Justine."

"Thanks."

Sabastien shrugged. "I like having you owe me."

"Does anybody care what I want?" Sage took a step forward.

"No." Vaughn and Justine answered at the same time.

"Sage," Justine said, "you're a key witness in the middle of a federal investigation. Vaughn and I have an obligation to keep you out of harm's way and under wraps until we've seen this through to a successful conclusion."

"A minute ago you were spitting nails at Vaughn for excluding us."

"Correction—for excluding me, not you. But I realize that Vaughn is right. This isn't just about keeping the majority leader alive. These men already have committed federal crimes, and they must be held accountable. As soon as they figure out that the plot failed, they'll cover their tracks and disappear."

"Where do you want to go?" Sabastien asked Justine.

"Denver, Colorado."

"Denver?" Sage asked.

"I've got a great orthopedic surgeon there and a hideaway in the mountains where you can recuperate afterward. You'll be protected round the clock."

"You mean while you're in Washington waiting for a call from Vaughn," Sage said, clearly unhappy with the arrangement.

"I'll fly with you to Denver and get you settled in," Justine said.

"Then fly right back out."

"Yes. It's the only way."

"It's inefficient. You should go directly to D.C."

"Sage is right," Vaughn broke in. "We're going to need you in position with plenty of time to spare."

Justine pursed her lips. "I've already got somebody on the ground there. My brother is FBI. I'm sure he and his partner would keep an eye on our boys if I explained things. All I need to do is make a phone call."

When Vaughn raised an eyebrow, Justine said, "Paul is a member of the fibbie's Public Corruption Task Force."

"I'm glad for the fact that you've got very handy allies, but I still want you directing things personally," Vaughn said.

"Fine." Justine touched Sabastien on the sleeve. "But take us in via Baltimore, and give us an out-of-the-way plane change with another ID swap. I don't want to take any chances. That's too close to Fairhaven's den."

"No problem," Sabastien said.

"What about you?" Sage addressed Sabastien.

"Moi? This is my home. I'm safe here. Besides, you will still need me. I can help get Vaughn out, cause all manner of mayhem, intercept communications..."

"I get the idea," Sage said.

"I suggest we all get ready." Vaughn itched to get moving.

"Yes, Elliott," Sabastien agreed. "Your plane leaves in less than four hours and it will take a half hour to get you to the airport."

"I'll need a stop at a department store and a pharmacy on the way."

"No need. I've got all sorts of hair dyes, wigs, and wardrobes here."

"You have women's clothes and wigs in your closet?" Vaughn asked incredulously.

"My father had many mistresses," Sabastien answered, nonplussed. "At least one of them must have been your size."

Sage paced back and forth in one of the spare bedrooms of the main house. She hadn't had any opportunity to talk to Vaughn alone since those frantic moments on the balcony in Zurich. She hadn't even been able to get Vaughn to look at her. Now it was entirely possible that they would never see each other again. *No, I have to tell her.*

She found Vaughn in the main bedroom, half-naked and fresh from the shower. Sage swallowed hard, clamping down on the surge of desire that swamped her senses. *You are so beautiful.*

She imagined the hunger must have shown in her eyes, because Vaughn quickly turned away and put on a robe.

"I'm sorry," Sage started, "I didn't know..."

"If you had knocked, you might've known," Vaughn said.

Don't be angry with me. "I-I didn't know if you'd want to see me."

In fact, Vaughn was not looking at her. Instead, she busied herself around the room, laying clothes out on the bed.

"So you charged right in because you thought I might've said no?"

Vaughn's tone of voice was cold and hard, and Sage was reminded of their first couple of meetings.

"There are things I want to say."

"What makes you think I want to hear them?"

"Vaughn, please. Don't do this. I may never get to see you again, never get the chance to tell you I'm sorry for making judgments I had no business making. Never get the chance..." Sage paused to collect herself. She lifted her head up high and jutted her chin out. "I might never get the chance to say thank you again. You saved my life three times. You came after me when you could've just stayed at your post and done your job. You took a bullet because of me, and you comforted me when I was terrified. I don't know how I could ever repay you..."

"You already thanked me, and I don't want anything from you, Sage. What I did I would've done for anyone." Vaughn was facing the bed, her back to Sage.

Sage tried not to let the words hurt—tried to tell herself that Vaughn didn't really mean them. She wanted to believe that the reason Vaughn wouldn't look at her was because her eyes would betray her true feelings. She wanted to know that Vaughn still wanted her, and that, after this was all over, they might have a chance together, but she knew the timing was wrong for such a discussion.

Instead, she asked, "Are you going to be all right?"

"I'm fine. Please don't worry about me. This is what I do. This is who I am."

"What I said about the cleanup crew stuff—"

"I don't want to talk about it, Sage. Now, if you'll excuse me, I have a lot of work to do and not much time to do it in."

"That's it, then? You won't let me apologize properly?" Sage spoke in a rush, unable to hold herself back and afraid that at any moment Vaughn would kick her out of the room. "You don't want to know that I love you, that I ache to make things right? That I'm frantic because I don't know how to reach you emotionally?"

Vaughn's hands hesitated momentarily as she searched for another outfit in the closet. It wasn't much, but Sage saw it. It gave her hope.

"Justine will take good care of you. You're as safe with her as you would be with me. I know it's going to be hard for you to be alone for a while, but that will fade in time. You should see a psychologist for post-traumatic stress disorder when this is over." Vaughn put the outfit on the bed without turning around to face Sage.

"If it's any consolation," she continued, "the bad guys are far more interested in me right now than they are in you. I pose a bigger threat. I don't think anyone will be actively looking for you, but we need to take precautions. Listen to Justine, and do everything she tells you to do. Don't question her. She's very good at what she does."

Finally, Vaughn turned to face her. "Justine is a healer. She only kills in self-defense. She's never been part of any cleanup crew, and she's a fine, upright person. You're in the best possible hands."

Sage nodded. Tears were streaming down her face, and she covered her mouth loosely with a trembling hand. "I was in good hands with you." She grabbed a tissue from the dresser. "Will I ever see you again?"

Vaughn ignored the question. "I've got work to do, Sage. Stay safe and find your joy. You're a beautiful woman with your whole life in front of you. I hope you find everything you're looking for."

Sage wanted to move forward—to throw herself into Vaughn's arms and be held. Before she could do anything, Vaughn walked into the bathroom and closed the door. Sage thought she heard a muffled cry of anguish through the wooden barrier, but it might've been wishful thinking. She turned slowly and went back to the spare bedroom, where she threw herself on the bed and cried in earnest.

⋘⋙

The announcement from the flight crew that they would soon be landing jarred Vaughn awake. She'd been traveling twenty-four hours straight, and despite having taken several short naps, she was beyond exhaustion. Normally, that would've been a bad thing, but in this case it helped with the image she was seeking to project. Anyone looking at her would see a dowdy older woman with gray hair, wrinkles, a bulging belly, sagging breasts, and failing eyesight. When she emerged from the bedroom at Sabastien's house, not even Justine recognized her.

Vaughn checked her watch and thought about Sage and Justine. By now they should've reached their destination and gotten settled in. She and Justine agreed that they would make contact only when absolutely necessary. She hoped they were sleeping peacefully and that their trip had been uneventful.

Vaughn wanted to know that Sage was okay, that she was safe, and that...*Shit. Stop it. You can't do this now. It's all about focus. Stay focused. Eyes on the prize.* She fumbled with her seatbelt the way old people do when their hands aren't as dexterous as they once were. The liver spots she'd created on the backs of her hands with the magic of makeup helped to reinforce her disguise.

She made sure to exit the plane in the middle of a pack of passengers and moved slowly, taking halting steps. Her face was a mask of confusion as she looked around for the party that was supposed to meet her at the gate.

"Madame Barrett?"

"Oui, c'est moi." Vaughn's voice was thin and reedy, as befitted her age.

"On behalf of the citizens of Mauritania, I want to thank you for your generosity. This hospital will be a godsend. Come this way, please."

"Yes, yes of course." Vaughn allowed Nate's wife to take her by the elbow and lead her to the baggage claim area.

When they were alone in the car, Vaughn said, "I can't tell you how grateful I am to you and Nate for all your assistance."

"I am just glad I was able to figure out who you were. Nate said you might be dressed somewhat differently, but I never expected such a drastic change from the way he described you."

"How did you know which one was me?"

"Your eyes. They were far too alert for someone as elderly as you appeared to be."

"Then I'm fortunate that no one else was paying as close attention as you."

"The airport exits were being watched, and I noticed several new employees at ticket counters and in baggage claim. Also, there was someone at the gate."

"I saw that one," Vaughn said. She regarded Nate's wife critically. She was young—no older than twenty-five—and very pretty. Obviously, she had other attributes, as well. "You're very perceptive."

"I am the wife of the most important law enforcement official in this country. I have to be observant. Here, we cannot afford to take our safety for granted. If there were a coup, we would be among the first the opposition would seek to capture."

"I see. I'm sorry you have to be so vigilant."

"It is something I accepted when I married my husband."

Nate's wife turned into an alley. Vaughn thought she recognized where they were. Before she could ask, Nate emerged from the back of the building.

"Madame Barrett, it is such a pleasure to see you."

"And you, Nate."

"Please, come in. I thought you would appreciate some familiar surroundings."

"Yes, thank you. That was very thoughtful of you."

Once they were inside the clinic, Nate said. "You are safe in here. We are alone and will be for the length of your stay. I thought you might prefer to be able to be yourself, so I sent the staff home."

"Thank you, my friend."

"Your trip was without incident?"

"Mercifully, yes. How are things here?"

"Everything is in place. But there are some developments that might interest you."

Vaughn nodded. "Let me get changed and we can talk."

∽ঔ৯৯

Sage awoke to the sound of her own scream. Sweat drenched her T-shirt and the sheets.

"Sage? Sage, are you all right?" Justine called through the door.

"I'm fine. It was just a nightmare. Sorry."

"Do you need anything?"

"No, thank you. I'm going to go back to sleep."

"Okay. If you change your mind, I'm right down the hall."

"Thank you." Sage threw off the covers and sat up against the headboard. She drew her knees up and rested her chin on them. She wondered how long it would be before she could sleep through an entire night without waking in terror.

The only true rest she'd gotten was when she had slept in Vaughn's arms. She sighed. Vaughn would be on the other side of the world by now, and the chances of ever seeing her again seemed too remote to consider.

Sage tried to imagine what Vaughn might be doing. Had she arrived safely? Was she sleeping? Had the trip been too taxing for her lung? *This is crazy. She's not sitting around worrying about you. Go to sleep.* Sage scooted back down and pulled the covers up to her neck. Although she closed her eyes, sleep was a long time coming.

∽ঔ৯৯

Fairhaven and Pordras shared a bottle of port in the living room of Fairhaven's townhouse.

"The majority leader will meet with the president and prime minister at the presidential palace five hours from now." Fairhaven paused to sip his drink. "Following the meeting, there will be a procession down one of Nouakchott's main streets. The route will lead to several historic sites. Unfortunately for the majority leader, she'll never arrive at her destination."

"Any sign of trouble?"

Fairhaven debated whether to tell his friend that Elliott and company supposedly had been on a plane to New York that had landed several hours ago. He'd had the plane searched, but there'd been no sign of any of them. He seriously doubted they'd ever been on the flight.

"No sign of trouble. My men have been staking out the airport, the police headquarters, the police chief's house, and the palace. Neither Elliott nor Coulter are anywhere to be found."

"Any word from your man? Maybe he took them out?"

"We have to assume he was lost," Fairhaven said.

"But maybe he killed them before dying of his injuries?"

"Possibly, but we have to go on the assumption that they are both still in play, and that they know what the plan is."

"You're sure this will work?"

Rather than answer directly, Fairhaven said, "Drink up, Bri. You should go home and get a good night's sleep. Tomorrow's going to be a big day."

✧✧

"Hello?" Justine answered her cell phone and fumbled for the light in the bedroom of her sister-in-law's weekend retreat twenty miles outside of Washington, D.C.

"Pordras is leaving Fairhaven's townhouse."

"Okay. You're going to stay with Fairhaven?"

"Yep. I've got someone tailing Pordras. He'll stay with Pordras wherever he lands next."

"Good. I can't tell you what your help means to me," Justine told her brother. They'd been nearly inseparable as kids. She was eighteen months older, and when she'd gone into law enforcement, he had followed in her footsteps, entering the FBI academy at Quantico, Virginia.

"Hey, if these two are dirty, we're going to take them down like a ton of bricks."

"You're keeping this quiet, right, Paul?"

"Yes, sis. Nothing's going to go bad. I promise you."

"I know. It's just—"

"I get it. I get it, all right? Go back to sleep. I've got your ass covered out here."

"Thanks, Pee Wee."

"Call me that again and I might change my mind. G'night, sis."

Justine closed the phone and turned off the light. Paul and his partner would take care of the surveillance so that she wouldn't have to risk being made, and she could stay with Sage. Although the plan made ultimate sense, she resisted vociferously when Paul suggested it. The thing that made her agree in the end was the look of relief on Sage's face when Justine said she'd be the one to stay with her.

Poor kid. Vaughn hadn't even looked at Sage when she left the farmhouse in Brussels. A blind person could've seen the pain in Sage's features. She didn't utter more than two words at a time from that moment until they arrived in the States. She went to her assigned bedroom as soon as she could and hadn't come out since.

Justine closed her eyes. She wondered if Vaughn was in any better shape than Sage was. She doubted it.

⤜⤐

"I have feelers out all over town," Nate said. "It seems some of the usual suspects were approached, but all of them turned down the assignment."

"You believe them?" Vaughn asked. They were sitting in the kitchen of the clinic, eating a small meal. She couldn't remember the last time she'd eaten.

"Yes. Our interview techniques can be very…persuasive."

"I had my guy run a check on that pool reporter after our phone conversation. He's definitely a plant."

"So you think he is the one who will carry out the assignment?" Nate asked.

"I doubt it. It's too obvious and too easily traced. My guess is that his job is surveillance. Unless, of course, he catches sight of me, in which case he has orders to shoot to kill."

"What is the alternative scenario for the assassination?"

Vaughn drummed her fingers on the table as she contemplated the possibilities. "I tend to think Fairhaven was trying to replicate the setup he had in Mali. He wants it to take place in the middle of a crowd. If the locals said no, he most likely would plant a couple of mechanics in the crowd who look like locals."

"I am sorry. Mechanics?"

"Assassins."

"Ah. Yes, that might work."

"In which case, they could be anybody."

"True. As much as I would like to tell you I could pick out any individual in a crowd as not being Mauritanian, I cannot."

"Given that, I don't think we can risk letting the majority leader go through with the procession." Vaughn considered and discarded ten options in her mind before she next spoke. "Is there a way you can get the majority leader and me out of the palace, on a plane, and safely off to Brussels without creating a national incident?" Vaughn suspected Stowe might want to continue on to her stop in Mali, but, with Dumont still sitting as ambassador, Vaughn wouldn't let her risk it.

Nate whistled tunelessly. "What you ask will not be easy, but I think I can make it happen."

"How?" Vaughn sat forward in her chair.

"The president and prime minister trust me on matters of security. I could go to them once you are safely in place. I will tell them that there has been a credible threat to our esteemed visitor, and that it is my best judgment that we should get her out of the country immediately following her meeting with them."

"What about the pool reporter?"

"I will have him detained as he waits outside the president's office. He will not be a factor." Nate continued, "We can take you both out through the president's exit underneath the palace. You'll be in the president's bullet-proof car, escorted by a platoon of my own hand-picked men."

Vaughn nodded. "Okay. I don't think it's necessary for your leaders to know all the details of the plot."

"I understand the delicacy of the politics. But I will have to tell them enough to convince them that the threat is real."

"Bring in one of your original local suspects," Vaughn said. "Have him explain how he was approached and what he was asked to do."

"I am not sure they will want to talk."

"Explain that if they don't, they'll rot in jail."

Nate chuckled. "Yes, that might work. In fact, I will bring in several just to make sure the president understands the seriousness of the situation."

Vaughn looked at her watch. "We should get going."

"Yes, it is time."

"You have janitors in the palace? People who clean the restrooms?"

"Of course."

"I will need to look like one of them so that my being in the bathroom for so long does not look suspicious."

"You will not need to do that. The bathroom will be locked until the majority leader is ready to use it—a routine security precaution, of course."

"I will still need to get into the building, so I'll wear a disguise on the way in and change back once you've locked me in."

"Okay."

"Who will have access to the floor?"

"I will have two of my best men posted outside the door and another plainclothesman patrolling the hallway."

"Very good." Vaughn rose from her chair. "Let's get on with it, shall we?"

"Indeed, we shall."

CHAPTER TWENTY-THREE

Vaughn wheeled a cart full of cleaning supplies slowly down the corridor. She was wearing a set of coveralls with rags in the pockets. The disguise was only a precaution. Nate had assured her there wasn't another person on the floor. He would put the guards in place after she was already inside. Even they would know nothing of her presence or her purpose until the majority leader was safely inside the bathroom.

When she was halfway down the hall, Nate rejoined her. He personally had made a sweep of the floors directly above and below. "Everything is ready," he said. "Do you have all the…cleaning supplies…you need?"

"Yes, thanks." Vaughn patted the plastic garbage bag attached to the cart. It contained a small duffle, an M-16 rifle, and two Kevlar vests. Hidden inside her duster were a Glock-40, ammunition, and her cell phone.

"I had the lock for the restroom changed while we were on the way over here. There are three keys, and it can be unlocked from either side. You will have one key, I will have one, and my roving plainclothes officer will have the other."

"You'll accompany the majority leader as she leaves the president's office and heads down here?" Vaughn asked.

"Yes. I will be with my officers every step of the way until you are in the air." Nate stopped walking. "Here we are."

Vaughn checked the corridor in both directions out of habit. There were no windows and only one staircase. "The staircase will be covered?"

"Yes. From below and above."

"Well, this is it, then."

"Here is your key. Everything will be fine. Two of my men are out rounding up some of the usual suspects right now."

"I'll see you in a little while," Vaughn said and pushed the cart ahead of her into the bathroom. Once inside, she locked the door and checked every stall. There were no exterior windows, a fact that would make her job easier.

When she was satisfied that everything was as secure as it could be, she pulled out her cell phone.

"Oui?"

"Sabastien?"

"Bonjour, Elliott. Are you enjoying your vacation?"

"So far it's been very scenic. Everybody else get off all right?"

"Yes."

"Okay. Any interesting phone chatter?" Vaughn had asked Sabastien to monitor Pordras's phone, knowing Fairhaven would've taken precautions with his own, just as she had.

"No. Although you might be interested to know that Pordras has been moving quite a bit of money offshore in the past couple of days."

"Can you prove it?"

"Of course. I've got account numbers, dates, amounts…the works, as you would say."

"Good. Send that to Justine, please."

"On it. Anything else I can do for you?"

"How secure is our connection?"

"Ironclad."

"You're sure?"

"Elliott, who do you think you're talking to? I'm positive."

"And the same would be true of a call from you to Justine?"

"Yes."

"Good. I want you to call her." Sabastien's reassurances not withstanding, Vaughn decided to err on the side of caution. "Tell her this will go down in the next two hours, and depending on the information I get from our guest, I may need her to do more than just tell her fib. Her fib might need to make a couple of house calls with friends in tow."

"Was I supposed to understand that?" Sabastien asked.

"Justine will get it. Please make sure you repeat it exactly as I told it to you." Vaughn waited. "Do you need me to say it again?"

"Do I look stupid? No, Elliott, you don't need to repeat yourself like I'm some feeble-minded simpleton who just fell off the potato truck."

"It's turnip."

"What?"

"If you're going to use American expressions, at least get them right. The expression is 'just fell of the turnip truck.'"

"Oh."

"Later, Sabastien. Wish me luck."

"Bonne chance, Elliott."

Vaughn closed the phone and sat down on the floor to wait. She would stay in the coveralls for a while longer until she was satisfied that the guards were in place. A check of her watch told her it would be another hour before she could expect the majority leader.

⤜⤛

"Report," Fairhaven said to his plant at the *Los Angeles Times*. Although it was the middle of the night, he was wide awake.

"I am in the car behind the majority leader. We are pulling up to the presidential palace now. No sign of any trouble."

"Elliott? Coulter?"

"As I said, everything is clear and on schedule. Majority Leader Stowe doesn't suspect anything and is looking forward to her visit. A crowd of protestors was just beginning to form when we rounded the last corner. I assume some of those are yours."

"Yes, they checked in several minutes ago. They are in place and ready."

"Okay. I have to go. Don't worry. Everything is going like clockwork."

"You know what to do in case…"

"Yes, yes. As I said, everything is under control."

"All right. Call me as soon as it is done." Fairhaven disconnected the call. He had an itch between his shoulder blades that usually signaled trouble. *Relax. You've created a good plan, the players are skilled and in position, there's no sign of Elliott…*

That was it. That was what bothered him. Where the hell was Elliott? He was sure she had left Zurich, but he was equally certain that the New York trip had been a red herring. So where was she really? She could be anywhere, although there'd been no activity in any of her bank accounts or on her credit cards.

She had to be eating, sleeping, and was likely on the move. If she had cash, where was she getting it? He thought of Brian's remark—that perhaps she'd been mortally wounded by Sielig. It was obvious that either she, McNally, or Coulter had been wounded in Mali. He doubted that Elliott was dead, but if it had been her blood in the car and Sielig had hit her a second time, she might be keeping a low profile because she was too badly hurt to do otherwise. Coulter could've pulled off the misdirection regarding the flight to the States just to keep him worried. He certainly hoped that was the case, although he wasn't deluded enough to believe that.

Assuming she was alive, Fairhaven had no doubt that Elliott had connected the dots enough to know the target, but it was unlikely that she understood why. He intended to keep it that way. After Stowe was disposed of, if Elliott was still in the mix, he would see to it personally that she was terminated, even if he had to do it himself.

❧❧

Justine answered the cell phone on the third ring. "Mmm-hmm?"

"Bonjour, Justine. C'est Sabastien. It sounds as though I've disturbed your sleep."

"S'okay. You're not the first, and you won't be the last. What's going on?"

"Elliott asked me to let you know that Pordras has been moving significant sums of money into an offshore account in the last few days."

"Is Vaughn okay?" For the second time that night, she fumbled for the light switch and sat up in bed.

"Yes. She is in place."

"Good. E-mail me what you have on Pordras."

"It's already done. I also have another message from Elliott for you, although it makes no sense to me."

"Let's hear it."

"She wants you to know that this will go down in the next two hours and depending on the information she gets from her guest, she may need you to do more than just tell your fib. Your fib might need to make a couple of house calls with friends in tow. Does that make any sense to you?"

Justine blinked several times. "Yes, it makes perfect sense."

"Care to explain?"

"No."

"I was afraid you would say that."

"Okay. Everything still secure on your end?" Justine asked.

"Yes. By the way, I forgot to tell Elliott, it seems your flight to New York created quite a stir. Your names were flagged before you'd crossed the ocean. Fairhaven must have it set up so that as soon as you are in the system he is notified. Airport officials were ordered to keep the plane sealed until there were agents in place to search it once it landed."

"Good to know. Fairhaven's probably tearing his hair out by now trying to figure out where we actually are."

"Maybe you should play with him one more time, since he knows now that you are not in New York," Sabastien said.

"You want to put us on another flight?"

"Perhaps you should be booked from Paris to Mali?"

"That might be fun. When would we take off?"

"Half an hour from now, arriving in Mali tomorrow morning."

"When the delegation arrives," Justine said. "Yes, I think that would be most helpful. Do it. Anything that keeps Fairhaven off balance at this point is a bonus."

"Consider it done," Sabastien said. "I expect Fairhaven will get word within the hour, if that matters to you."

"It does. Thanks, Sabastien. Stay safe."

"I should say the same to you. Say hello to the beautiful Sage for me."

"Bye." As soon as she ended the call, Justine punched in another number.

"Yeah?"

"Hey, Pee Wee."

"What did I tell you about calling me that?"

"Um, that you love it?"

"Is there something you wanted in the middle of the night, or did you call to harass me and make sure I'm awake?"

"I just got news. You may need some heavy duty backup in the next hour or two. Looks like we'll have our package in hand by then. Depending on the information, immediate custody might be appropriate. That would be FBI jurisdiction."

"I'll take care of it."

"Paul, you're going to want to get them before they leave their houses."

"I'm not exactly new at this, sis. I've got it covered. Fairhaven still hasn't gone to sleep. He's been pacing in front of the window for so long he's making me dizzy. I'll wait to hear from you. Now go back to bed. God knows you need your beauty rest."

"That was uncalled for."

"I'm your little brother. What did you expect?"

Justine ended the call. She thought about Vaughn, who probably was sitting in a ladies' room somewhere in the presidential palace at that moment, waiting for the majority leader.

If Madeline Stowe could provide a motive for the plot, the FBI would have grounds to make the arrests. If, on top of that, Vaughn could somehow tie the mechanics directly to Fairhaven and Pordras, that would make the case even stronger.

Vaughn heard the commotion in the hallway. She was dressed in her own street clothes and standing in a corner behind the door. It would be impossible to see her unless someone stepped all the way inside. Her hand was on the Glock concealed in the duster.

The sharp clicking of high-heeled shoes on the marble floor in the corridor was unmistakable. The strides were quick and purposeful.

"Madame, perhaps you would like to freshen up?" Vaughn heard Nate's voice directly outside the door.

"That won't be necessary, I—" The majority leader's tone was brusque.

"I assure you, you'll feel better afterward. Please?"

Vaughn watched as the deadbolt was unlatched from the outside. She tightened her grip on the pistol. Like any good agent, she would not trust the situation until it was completely within her control.

"One moment, Madam," Nate said. "Let me ensure that the area is secure." He spoke the last four words loudly. Vaughn understood that they were meant for her. Still, she did not let down her guard.

Nate stepped inside and held his hands out in front of him where Vaughn could see them. He peeked around the door. "I see everything is the way I left it." He smiled at her.

"Is everything okay?" Vaughn asked, her voice pitched low so that only Nate could hear her.

Nate matched her tone. "Yes. The car is ready, as is the plane. The president and prime minister were persuaded once they were presented with evidence."

"The reporter?"

"At the moment, he is enjoying the hospitality of our local jail."

"You took his phone?"

"He was strip searched. I must say, he had some interesting implements for a journalist."

"I bet. How is our guest?"

"Annoyed. She's not happy with the inconvenience."

"In that case, I suggest you let her in so that I can explain."

Nate nodded and stepped outside. "Madam, everything is secure."

The majority leader strode into the bathroom and tossed her purse onto the sink. When she looked up into the mirror and saw Vaughn standing there, her eyes registered shock followed by something indefinable.

Stowe was every bit as imposing in the flesh as she appeared on television, although she was younger and smaller than Vaughn expected. Her hair was drawn back in a severe chignon, her suit was classically tailored, and her heels were practical, rather than showy. "Madam Majority Leader. Please don't be alarmed."

"Agent Elliott." Madeline Stowe turned from the mirror. "Your picture doesn't do you justice. You're much better looking in person."

"I'm sorry?"

The majority leader stepped forward and extended her hand. "It's a pleasure to meet you."

Vaughn's mind raced as she shook hands automatically. "You know who I am?"

"Oh, yes. Your file has been on my desk for many months."

Of all the scenarios Vaughn had played out in her head in the three hours she'd spent in the bathroom, this wasn't one of them. "I'm afraid to ask why?"

"You shouldn't be."

Vaughn tried to regain her professional equilibrium. "Madam Majority Leader, I don't know what you were told by the president and prime minister upstairs—"

"Not much, except that there has been a drastic change in my itinerary due to an unspecified threat."

Vaughn suspected Stowe was a woman who would appreciate directness and efficiency. "I assume you know Secretary of State Pordras. Are you familiar with Edgar Fairhaven?"

The majority leader's eyes narrowed. "His file has been on my desk for months too." The words were said with extreme distaste.

"There is a very real, very specific plan in play to assassinate you here in Nouakchott—as soon as you step outside the front door."

"And you believe Fairhaven and Pordras are at the end of the food chain?"

"Yes, ma'am. I have quite a bit of proof."

"You don't need to convince me. I'm not the least bit surprised."

Vaughn raised her eyebrow. This was not going at all the way she had expected. "Madam Majority Leader, why would Fairhaven and Pordras want you dead?" It was the question that had plagued Vaughn since she and Sage figured out the target.

The majority leader sighed and leaned against the counter. "How much time do you have?"

"We have an entire plane ride to Brussels and then to the States. But first, I need to know enough so that we can pick up Fairhaven and Pordras."

"I don't know if you're aware of it, Agent Elliott, but I began my career as a prosecutor."

Vaughn nodded. "I had heard that."

"What you probably didn't know was that one of my first cases was against a young punk named Brian Pordras."

Light dawned in Vaughn's eyes. "The drug case that Fairhaven had swept under the rug."

"Yes. It was one of my first lessons in politics. Back then, I was young and naïve, and I thought justice prevailed." Stowe pursed her lips. "Anyway, fast forward to last year. A lovely young girl named Jennifer was an intern in my office. She and several other interns attended a party given by Brian Pordras's much younger, and very secret girlfriend. Apparently, heroin was the main course. The quality of the drugs evidently was quite pure. While under the influence, Pordras bragged that this was the finest strain of heroin produced anywhere in the world—shipped directly from Afghanistan.

"Unfortunately, Jennifer ingested a bit too much and overdosed. She died on the way to the hospital." Stowe shuddered. "She was twenty-two years old, bright, and had her whole life in front of her. It was the first time she'd ever done drugs." Tears glistened in Stowe's eyes when she looked at Vaughn.

"So you began looking into the details."

Stowe shrugged. "Once a prosecutor, always a prosecutor. It took me a while to unearth Pordras's name. As you might imagine, all of the kids who were there were afraid to talk. After all, he's the secretary of state, and they were doing illegal drugs."

"Makes sense."

"Given what I already knew about Pordras but couldn't say publicly, I wasn't going to be satisfied to see him charged only with supplying the drugs—I wanted him for Jennifer's murder." Stowe's eyes turned hard as coal. "Unfortunately, I couldn't prove beyond a shadow of a doubt that he was the one who'd supplied the heroin. He was pretty clever about distancing himself from the product."

Vaughn's respect for this woman was growing by the minute.

Stowe looked at Vaughn as though assessing whether or not the agent was trustworthy. Apparently satisfied, Stowe continued. "Here's something that isn't on my resume." She took a deep breath. "I had a younger brother. The official story is that he was killed in combat in Vietnam. The truth is that he died of a drug overdose—the same heroin that was smuggled from Vietnam into the States via the bodies of American soldiers."

The majority leader's voice shook with emotion. Vaughn put a sympathetic hand on her arm.

"So, when you heard the boast about the drugs being from Afghanistan, you figured the same thing was happening all over again."

Stowe nodded. "I couldn't bear to see another generation of promising kids ruined like my brother." This time the tears did begin to fall. Vaughn handed her a tissue.

"Thank you." Stowe dabbed at her eyes. "Anyway, I started looking into who had access to the bodies coming back from Afghanistan. I wasn't getting too far, until I saw the report of an explosion at Andrews Air Force Base in which a young woman mechanic was killed."

"Sara." Vaughn whispered the name, the pain as fresh and real as if she were still holding her mangled body.

"Yes." The majority leader was looking at Vaughn with great kindness. "I'm sorry. I know she was very special to you."

Vaughn's head snapped up.

"I'm the senate majority leader. I have access to almost any piece of information I desire, even if it's classified." Stowe continued, "When I got the victim's name and heard that a second woman had been injured in the blast, I began digging deeper and demanded to be briefed by the FBI. They referred me to the then-director of the CIA, who handed me a report written by none other than Edgar Fairhaven."

"You didn't believe the president's explanation of terrorism on American soil?"

"No. As soon as I saw Fairhaven's name in such proximity to Pordras's, the hair on the back of my neck began to stand up."

"I'm sure."

"I asked for, and was provided with, your dossier…and Sara's. At first, when I realized that Fairhaven was the one who recruited you both out of college, I wondered if you weren't part of the plot and he was going to sweep this one under the rug too."

"Well, the bastard accomplished that," Vaughn murmured.

"Not exactly. Fairhaven stuck you on desk duty, and that didn't fit with my theory that he would reward you or promote you to keep you quiet."

"No. He wanted me buried. I knew someone in the Company was responsible for bringing in the drugs and for Sara's death, but I had no idea who. Fairhaven assumed correctly that I wouldn't let the matter drop until I found Sara's killers. He wanted me where he could keep an eye on me."

This time it was Stowe's turn to nod. "The whole thing stunk. But again, I didn't have any proof. So I kept tabs on you, figuring you might be the key to cracking open this case."

"I don't know whether or not I should be flattered," Vaughn said.

"Fairhaven had you transferred to DS, under Pordras's control, and my Spidey sense was tingling."

Vaughn laughed in spite of the seriousness of the situation. The cartoon reference was completely at odds with the woman who made it.

"Then when he assigned you to my trip, I knew something was afoot. It was just one too many coincidences."

"Did Fairhaven and Pordras know you were looking into all this?"

"I'm sure they did. After all, the fact that Jennifer worked in my office was splashed all over the newspapers. Add to that the fact that I requested information from the FBI and CIA on the Andrews Air Force Base explosion, and you can draw your own conclusions."

"No doubt that made Fairhaven and Pordras very nervous."

"Agent Elliott, I don't know if you have any idea how much money we're talking about here, but the little heroin scam they're masterminding brings in millions of dollars a year."

"Enough money to kill for," Vaughn said.

"You bet your salary. I do have to admire their audacity and ingenuity, though. Killing the majority leader on foreign soil is a stroke of genius. If you hadn't figured it out…"

"You didn't need me to figure it out, Madam Majority Leader. You already knew."

"I suspected. That's different."

"So you willingly left yourself vulnerable?"

The majority leader shook her head. "I left all of my investigative notes and proof in the hands of the Director of the FBI before I left Washington. If anything had happened to me, he would've had enough probable cause to bring in Pordras and Fairhaven."

"But you would've been dead."

"I had faith in you, Agent Elliott. Great faith. Now I know that it was well placed."

Vaughn blushed.

"What do you say?" Stowe asked. She checked her reflection in the mirror. "Shall we put those bastards in their place?"

Vaughn laughed and shook the majority leader's outstretched hand. "Nothing would give me greater pleasure. I've got an agent on the ground in D.C., and FBI officers waiting outside Fairhaven's townhouse and Pordras's house. They've been in place all night."

"I suspect their jobs might be made easier with an arrest warrant from the U.S. Attorney. God knows we've got more than enough probable cause to hold them on any number of federal charges right now. Do you have a cell phone I can borrow? I suspect mine might have been compromised." She winked.

"Yes, ma'am."

Stowe took the phone and dialed a number from memory. "Jordan? This is Majority Leader Stowe."

CHAPTER TWENTY-FOUR

Edgar Fairhaven hung up the phone and swung his feet over the edge of the bed. He'd been asleep for less than fifteen minutes when the shrill ring jarred him awake. His first thought was that it would be news from Mauritania, but it wasn't. Instead, it was a new alert from the Federal Aviation Administration. It seemed that Elliott, Coulter, and McNally had boarded a plane from Paris to Mali. It was due to arrive at approximately the same time as the congressional delegation the next morning.

Fairhaven stood up and raked a hand irritably through his hair. Although the information seemed credible, so did the last report that had the trio arriving in New York. Still, it made more sense to him that Elliott would return to Mali, since that was where the hit was originally scheduled to take place. She must not have sussed out the unscheduled stop in Mauritania. If she had, there was no reason for her to be traveling to Mali.

"Screw you for jerking my chain, Elliott," Fairhaven screamed out loud. It was the middle of the night, he was exhausted, and he was tired of cat and mouse games. His hands shook with rage. He snapped up a book from the bedside table and hurled it across the room. The novel landed with a loud thud against the wall, but it did nothing to stem Fairhaven's rising anger. "And screw you too, Bri. I swear to God this is the last mess I'm going to clean up for you. What the fuck were you thinking, sampling the product? Then you come crawling to me when the girl dies. You fucking idiot! We were on easy street."

Fairhaven threw on a robe, belted it, and stomped barefoot into the kitchen to start the coffeemaker. Maybe the caffeine would improve his mood and help him think more clearly.

He poured the water, started the brew cycle, and paused. Brian's stupidity and lack of willpower weren't the issue at the moment. It was Elliott who was giving him fits. If she and McFarland hadn't interfered with the smuggling operation at Andrews, none of this would've been necessary. Then that meddling bitch Stowe would've had to let the matter of that girl's death go, since she couldn't prove anything.

Fairhaven's temper simmered just below boiling. He stalked into his office and unearthed the leather-bound journal that was buried under mounds of paperwork on his desk. Lately, for reasons he couldn't fully explain, he'd taken to reviewing details of the whole fiasco, as if doing so would change the outcome or bring the matter to a quicker conclusion.

He picked out selected passages at random and read aloud. "Fixed Brian's mess again. No one will come forward and publicly identify him as being at the party."

Fairhaven's eyes traveled farther down the page. "Stowe asking too many questions. Luckily, I've eliminated any way to tie Brian directly to the drugs. Case dead in the water."

Fairhaven turned several pages. "McFarland sniffing around the Andrews operation. Hope she lets it go."

His eyes skimmed over the next entry—perhaps the most damning of all. "McFarland went to the hangar to get proof. Enlisted Sturges to terminate her. Elliott showed up—unexpected complication. Too risky to move on her. Will have to bide time."

Fairhaven flipped to one of his most recent entries. "Stowe not buying president's explanation of explosion as act of terrorism. She's digging hard and too close to home—looks like she may be ready to point fingers. Time to take action."

He smiled as he read the last entry. "Stowe taking a trip abroad. Perfect opportunity to kill two birds with one stone—wipe her out in sectarian violence and take out Elliott at the same time with a 'stray' shot. Brilliant."

He closed the book and felt the weight of it in his hands. The moment of triumph was at hand. Still, it was foolish to keep written records, and he acknowledged to himself that it had been an extravagance of ego he couldn't afford. With a sigh of regret, he tore the pages from the binding and fed them to his shredder before returning to the kitchen.

As Fairhaven poured his first cup of coffee, there was a knock on the front door. He checked the kitchen clock—4:45 a.m. His cheeks flushed an angry shade of red as his moment of calm evaporated. "Bri, if that's you, I'm going to kill you," he called as he walked to the door. "I told you I'd ca—" He stopped talking abruptly when he yanked the door open to find five FBI agents standing outside his door, guns drawn.

"Edgar Fairhaven, you're under arrest for conspiracy to commit the murders of Senate Majority Leader Madeline Stowe, Vaughn Elliott, Justine Coulter, and Sage McNally, kidnapping, the murder of Sara McFarland, money laundering, and drug smuggling. You have the right to remain silent..."

Brian Pordras hurried to answer the knock on the door. "I'm coming, Ed. Is it don—"

"Brian Pordras, you're under arrest..."

Ambassador Raymond Dumont was putting the final touches on the plans for the visit of the congressional delegation the following day. He'd heard nothing further from Washington and wondered if there was anything he was supposed to be doing.

He answered the knock on the door, still preoccupied with that thought. "Yes?"

"Raymond Dumont, we are with the FBI. You are under arrest for conspiracy to commit the murders of Sage McNally and Senate Majority Leader Madeline Stowe, and conspiracy to kidnap Sage McNally..."

Vaughn watched the majority leader's face as she spoke for the third time in the past two hours to U.S. Attorney General Jordan Miles and FBI Director Carlton Riggs.

"Right... Good... Very well... Okay...Thank you, gentlemen. That's excellent work. No, Agent Elliott and I are on our way home now. We're waiting to take off... I'll tell her. I'm sure she'll be glad to hear that. I'll call you when we get back to the States... Right. Bye."

The majority leader closed the phone and handed it back to Vaughn.

"Everything okay?" Vaughn asked.

"Better than that. Carlton tells me they've picked up Fairhaven, Pordras, and Ambassador Dumont."

"That's great."

"There's more. Did you know there was an order outstanding to kill you and agent Coulter on sight?"

Vaughn nodded ruefully. "Yes, I did."

"That's been lifted. Also, I've been assured that you may return to the CIA as soon as you choose. I promise you, you'll be behind a desk only if you want to be."

Vaughn nodded again. The news should have made her happy. Being an agent was what she knew. It was who she was. And yet... The majority leader was staring at her intently, but Vaughn couldn't bring herself to do more than say thank you.

After a minute, she flipped open the phone and dialed.

"Hello?"

"Justine, it's Vaughn."

"They've picked up Fairhaven and Pordras," Justine said.

"Dumont too," Vaughn told her. "Are you and Sage okay?"

"We're fine, except that I'm pissed at my brother. Apparently, his unit got a major tip and some really credible information earlier this week implicating Fairhaven and Pordras for smuggling drugs into the U.S. via Andrews, and for Sara's death."

"Let me guess, your brother didn't tell you anything about it when you asked him to do a stakeout on our boys."

"Yeah. The rat."

Vaughn was enjoying Justine's righteous indignation. "Imagine the nerve of him, sticking to proper protocol and keeping mum about an ongoing investigation."

"I'm his sister, for heaven's sake, and it's not like I don't know how to keep secrets."

"Ought to be fun at your family's next Christmas." Vaughn laughed.

Justine grumbled and changed the topic. "Where are you now?"

"The majority leader and I are just getting ready to take off."

"How was the trip to the airport?"

"No problems. We got a ride in the Mauritanian president's bullet-proof car. Nate personally escorted us onto the plane and hand-picked the flight crew. I've been allowed to keep my weapons as a precaution until we get to Brussels."

"Are you coming on to D.C. with the majority leader?"

"Yeah, I want to make sure she gets home all right."

"You might want to know that Sage has been very quiet. She had a nightmare in the middle of the night. She woke up screaming, but she wouldn't let me in the room. Vaughn—"

Vaughn's heart constricted as she saw an image of Sage in her mind's eye, frightened as she had been when Vaughn had rescued her. *No, I can't...* "Don't, Justine. I've got to go. I'll call you when we land. Bye." Vaughn closed the phone before Justine could say anything more.

"Everything all right, Agent Elliott?" the majority leader asked.

"Fine, thanks, ma'am."

"Uh-huh."

Further conversation was stalled by the ringing of the phone.

Vaughn answered the call, glad of the diversion. It came from an unregistered phone number. "Hello?"

"I'm looking for Majority Leader Stowe." The voice was commanding, authoritative, and Vaughn knew immediately to whom it belonged. "Yes, sir, Mr. President, sir." She handed the phone to the majority leader.

"Sir?... Yes, sir, I'm perfectly safe now... Yes, sir, Agent Elliott is taking excellent care of me... That's not necessary, sir... If you insist... Yes, sir. That was her you were talking to... Yes, sir. Hold on, please." The majority leader handed the phone back to Vaughn. "The president would like a word."

"Yes, sir?"

"Agent Elliott, I want you to know how much I appreciate your hard work and valor on this case."

"Thank you, sir, but I had help—"

"I've heard. I'm sending Air Force One to pick up Majority Leader Stowe and you in Brussels. I'd like to see you in my office as soon as you get back."

"Yes, sir."

"Pleasant journey."

"Thank you, sir."

"Goodbye, Agent Elliott."

Vaughn closed her eyes and blew out an explosive breath.

"Look at it this way," the majority leader said, "we'll be riding home in style."

≪·≫

Vaughn shifted from foot to foot, trying not to appear as awed as she felt to be standing in the Oval Office. The majority leader's driver had dropped her at home so that she could shower and change for the meeting with the president.

Then the driver returned for her, and she and the majority leader rode together to the White House.

"I take it you've never been in here?" the majority leader asked.

"No, ma'am."

"It's the ultimate home court advantage."

"It is very impressive and somewhat intimidating."

"Why, Agent Elliott, I didn't think anything intimidated you."

"There goes my reputation."

"On the contrary, your secret is safe with me." The majority leader winked.

A door opened and Vaughn turned, expecting to see the president. Instead, it was Sage and Justine who were ushered into the room. Vaughn managed to hide her surprise, but she couldn't deny the ripple of desire mixed with relief at seeing Sage safe and smiling at her bashfully.

"Vaughn—"

Before Sage could finish her thought or take another step forward, Vaughn broke in. If Sage touched her now, if she hugged her close, she would never be able to walk away. She had to be able to do that—for Sage's sake. "Senate Majority Leader Stowe, I'd like you to meet Dr. Sage McNally and Agent Justine Coulter."

"It's a great pleasure to meet both of you," the majority leader said, clasping each of them by the hand. "I understand you all have had quite an adventure in the past couple of weeks."

"Yes, ma'am," Sage said, unconsciously touching her sling.

"I owe both of you a great debt of gratitude. Especially you, Dr. McNally. Vaughn tells me that your sharp memory was instrumental in figuring out what was afoot."

"Ma'am, it was Vaughn who—"

A door opened opposite the one Sage and Justine had come through, and the president of the United States strode into the room. "Ladies, I'm so sorry to have kept you waiting." He walked directly to the majority leader and enveloped her in a hug. "Madeline, are you all right?"

"I'm fine, Mr. President, thanks to these remarkable women."

The president stepped back and surveyed the group. "Agent Elliott?"

"Yes, sir." Vaughn stood at attention.

"You showed tremendous intelligence, initiative, and courage. I understand you were wounded in the line of duty. Despite your injuries, you prevented others from being harmed, eliminated several threats to national security and, at the potential cost of your own life, protected the life of Majority Leader Stowe."

Vaughn didn't know what to say, so she remained silent. She thought of Jackson—the one man whose life she hadn't been able to save. *I wish you were here, my friend.* She never would be able to disclose his role in Sage's rescue without raising too many diplomatic issues. But Vaughn would always remember. The president's voice brought her back to the present.

"Along with my personal thanks, I offer you the thanks of a grateful nation. I hope this will bring to a close a very ugly chapter in the history of this administration." The president handed Vaughn a velvet box with the President's Award for Distinguished Federal Civilian Service inside. "This is the highest honor a president can bestow upon a government employee. I think you should take some time to recuperate from your injuries. Then I hope you'll consider staying here in Washington and working more closely with me."

"Thank you, sir. But—"

The president held up his hand. "Please don't answer me right now. I want you to take all the time you need and think about it." He turned to Justine. "Agent Coulter."

"Yes, sir."

"I understand you've been on vacation for the past two weeks." The president's eyes were twinkling.

Justine's face registered surprise. "Yes, sir."

"I've heard of folks who are thrill seekers when they take time off, but I think your idea of rest and relaxation tops anything I've ever encountered." The president smiled at her. "I suggest you take a real vacation this time. On me."

"Yes, Mr. President. This time, sir, I think I'll opt for something a little more low-key."

The president laughed. "Yes, I would recommend that." He handed Justine another velvet box. "Please accept this Award for Distinguished Federal Civilian Service as a token of the nation's gratitude for your valor." The president shifted his gaze to Sage. "Dr. McNally."

"Yes, sir."

Vaughn looked at Sage's face, alight with wonder and admiration as she regarded the president. She was wearing a tailored suit and a hint of makeup and, to Vaughn's eyes, had never looked more beautiful. Vaughn's heart tripped painfully. There was no point wishing for what wouldn't—and shouldn't— be. She worked hard to keep her face neutral, especially when she caught the majority leader staring at her speculatively.

"Dr. McNally, I understand you've had a particularly difficult time." The president looked at Sage kindly. "How is your shoulder?"

"I'll be fine, sir."

"From what I hear, you may require surgery. All of your medical costs will be paid by the government, along with any psychological treatment you might require. We have excellent counselors available who specialize in post-traumatic stress syndrome. I can't tell you how sorry I am for your ordeal."

"It wasn't your fault, sir."

280

"Nonetheless, I want you to know how much I admire your poise under extreme duress and your problem-solving skills." The president handed Sage the last velvet box on his desk. "Please accept this with the thanks of a grateful nation, and with my personal thanks for service above and beyond the call of duty."

"Thank you, sir." Sage's voice was full of awe.

"Once you are fit again, I'd like you to come to work here with my African task force. I understand you've got extraordinary insight into the West African peoples, and I expect you would have much to contribute to the shaping of our policies in that part of the world."

"Thank you, Mr. President. Sir, if I might be so bold as to ask, how is it you know so much of what happened?"

The president smiled enigmatically. "I'm the president, my dear. It's my job to know. Oh, and your friend Sabastien says hello. I'm putting him to work in our counter-terrorism unit. He certainly has a penchant for being able to get around any electronic security obstacles."

Vaughn laughed. She, too, had been wondering at the president's familiarity with the specifics of their exploits. Now she understood. Leave it to Sabastien to send an e-mail report directly to the president.

The three women emerged from the West Wing a short time later, while the majority leader stayed to brief the president. Vaughn looked up at the clear blue sky and took in a deep breath. Today was a great day for the good guys.

"I'm going to get going," Justine said. Vaughn thought the ploy less than subtle. "Sage, you're going to keep in touch, right?" Justine gave her a hug.

"I promise."

"And you're going to see the orthopedic surgeon I recommended?"

"Yes, yes."

"Vaughn," Justine faced her. "You need at least a week of bed rest, and don't argue with me."

"I wouldn't dream of it," Vaughn said. She pulled Justine into a hug. "Thank you for everything. I couldn't have done it without you."

"I've got to say, you sure know how to show a girl a good time." Justine backed away from the hug and waved as she walked away.

"Vaughn—"

"Sage, don't." Vaughn struggled to keep her voice from breaking. If she gave an inch now, she'd sweep Sage into her arms and carry her home. Sage just needed time—that was all. She would get over this crush and find someone more suitable. Still, the look of hurt on Sage's face was nearly Vaughn's undoing.

"You look tired. Are you okay?" Sage asked. She lowered her eyes and stared at her feet.

Vaughn's heart cracked a little more. "I'm fine, thanks. Nothing a little sleep won't cure."

"Right." When Sage looked up, tears shimmered on her lashes. "I know you don't want to hear it, but I need you to know meeting you was the best thing that ever happened to me."

Vaughn's eyebrow disappeared into her hair line. "Sage, since you met me, you've been kidnapped, beaten, shot at, seen people killed…"

"I know all that. But I've also been more alive than I've ever been, and I understand now what it feels like to be in love."

No, Sage. You can't be in love with me. "The president is offering you a fantastic opportunity," Vaughn said, abruptly changing the subject.

"Yes, he is."

"You'll take it, right?"

Sage sighed. "Yes, Vaughn, I'll take it." Sage's voice cracked and tears rolled down her cheeks. She looked miserable, and all Vaughn wanted to do was take her in her arms. Instead, she put her hands in her pockets.

Finally, Sage broke the silence. "What about you? Are you going to take the president up on his offer?"

"I don't know yet." Vaughn shifted uncomfortably. It was so hard not to reach out—not to give Sage something—not to offer words of reassurance and comfort.

"Oh."

"I've got to go." Vaughn suddenly felt an irrepressible urge to bolt. If she stayed any longer, she might… "Take care of yourself, Sage."

"You, too, Vaughn." Sage started to walk away. Her head was bent and her shoulders sagged. When she'd gone several feet, she turned around one last time. "I love you." She glanced longingly at Vaughn one more time, then hurried down the sidewalk.

When Vaughn was sure Sage was out of earshot, she said, "I love you too, Sage." She balled her hands into fists in her pockets and walked in the opposite direction.

It took everything she had not to turn around and go after Sage. In a few months, or a year, this would all be behind them. It didn't matter what Vaughn wanted—Sage was about to embark on a new and exciting chapter in her life, and Vaughn would content herself with watching from afar, just to make sure Sage was all right.

In the meantime, Vaughn would find some out-of-the-way place to rest, recuperate, and figure out what to do next. Perhaps she could even convince herself that the last two weeks had never happened. Perhaps…

EPILOGUE

Vaughn squinted in the bright sunlight, quickly donned her shades, and headed to the taxi stand at Dulles International Airport. She had missed her connection and was more than two hours late. The jury was scheduled to begin deliberations earlier that morning in the trial of Edgar Fairhaven.

Both Senate Majority Leader Stowe and the assistant United States attorney prosecuting the case assured Vaughn that the verdict was little more than a formality. She hoped she wasn't too late. Former Secretary of State Brian Pordras and former Ambassador to Mali Raymond Dumont had testified for the prosecution in exchange for reduced sentences. The detailed information they supplied implicated Fairhaven as the mastermind behind the drug-smuggling operation, Sara's murder, Sage's kidnapping and attempted murder, and the attempted murders of Vaughn, Justine, and Senate Majority Leader Stowe.

Vaughn settled herself in the backseat of the taxi. "Federal Courthouse, please." As the cab weaved in and out of Washington, D.C. traffic, Vaughn reviewed the events of the trial.

The majority leader's comprehensive, succinct testimony added to the weight of the prosecution's case. Vaughn's heart-wrenching account of Sara's death and Sage's rescue resonated with the jury and made the crimes seem all the more personal and heinous. Justine's description of Vaughn's injuries and the desperate race to save her life solidified the case for the conspiracy to commit murder, and Sage's harrowing recitation of her time in captivity virtually slammed the door on any chance Fairhaven had for freedom in his lifetime.

Vaughn frowned. She had argued privately with the prosecutor that there was more than enough evidence to convict Fairhaven without Sage's testimony. She would've done anything to spare her from having to relive her trauma.

When she lost the argument, Vaughn considered showing up in the courtroom to offer what moral and emotional support she could. In the end, she stayed away and relied on Justine's accounts of how Sage was faring.

"We're here," the cabbie said.

Vaughn paid him, grabbed her bag, and got out. She checked her watch. If she was lucky, the jury might still be out. She hustled into the building only to find a large crowd milling around outside the courtroom.

From a distance, she caught a glimpse of Sage. Even after so long spent apart, Vaughn's heart still skipped a beat at the sight. Over the course of the eight months of soul-searching, she finally had come to accept that she was in love with Sage. She just wasn't sure she was ready to do anything about it.

Sage looked beautiful. She wore an expensive, sharply cut suit that accented her trim figure. Her hair was lighter than Vaughn remembered, and her cheeks had a healthy glow.

Sage must have sensed her presence, because at that moment, she turned and their eyes met through the throng of people.

"Ladies and gentlemen, if you'd take your seats, the jury is coming back."

❧❧

Sage felt Vaughn's presence before she saw her. When their eyes met, Sage's palms dampened and her mouth went dry. *Good Lord.* Vaughn looked like a bronzed goddess. Her intelligent, expressive eyes stood out boldly against deeply tanned skin. She wore a fitted pantsuit and a crisp, white blouse. And, most remarkably, she looked rested and relaxed in a way Sage had never seen before.

Vaughn didn't take the president up on his offer and, after that day at the White House, she just seemed to disappear. Despite her best efforts, Sage was unable to find out where she was. Finally, in desperation, Sage turned to Justine for information.

Justine would say only that Vaughn decided to take some time off and was living somewhere in the Caribbean. Sage hoped to see her when she was in D.C. to testify, but Vaughn managed to slip into and out of town in a single day, and Sage was bogged down in an international conference.

The bailiff summoned the crowd back into the courtroom just as Sage started to move in Vaughn's direction. By the time Sage made it inside, she had lost sight of Vaughn.

ﾐ☜☞

Vaughn wasn't the least bit surprised to find Justine at her side as she took a seat.

"Hi, stranger."

"Hi," Vaughn said.

"Long time no see. I thought you'd be here before this."

"Believe me, I meant to be. Damn airlines."

"Well, if you weren't coming from the middle of nowhere…"

"You're not going to start that again, are you?"

"Nope," Justine answered. "Did you see Sage? She looks fantastic, doesn't she?"

Vaughn's pulse quickened merely at the sound of her name. "Yes, she does. Her shoulder is all healed?"

"Yep. The surgeon did a wonderful job. She has full functionality."

"That's great." Vaughn let silence fill the air.

"She asks about you all the time, you know."

"Justine—"

"Don't 'Justine' me."

Vaughn sighed heavily. "How's she doing with the nightmares and stuff?"

"She doesn't talk about it much, but every time I see her, she looks a little more comfortable in her own skin."

"You see her often?" Vaughn asked, glancing sideways.

"Jealous?" Justine laughed. "We get together for lunch once a week."

"That's nice."

"You should talk to her, Vaughn."

"Don't—" Even now, Vaughn wasn't sure she could or should act on her feelings.

At that moment, the jurors filed in and took their places. The courtroom went very quiet.

"The defendant will rise," the judge intoned.

Vaughn watched as Fairhaven rose to his feet. His hair was grayer than it had been, and his face was gaunt.

"Have you reached a verdict?" the judge asked the jury foreman.

"We have, your Honor. On the count of kidnapping in the first degree, we find the defendant…guilty."

Vaughn sought Sage's face in the crowd. She made eye contact and smiled reassuringly.

"On the three counts of conspiracy to commit murder, we find the defendant…guilty."

The crowd began to buzz.

"Order!" The judge gaveled the court to order.

"On the count of second degree murder, we find the defendant…guilty."

"That one's for you, Sara," Vaughn murmured. Tears formed in her eyes. Justine squeezed her hand.

"On the count of money laundering, we find the defendant…guilty."

"On the count of drug smuggling, we find the defendant…guilty."

"I accept your finding," the judge said, "and I thank you for your service. The jury is dismissed. Sentencing is set for ninety days from today. Court is adjourned."

Newspaper reporters rushed out the door to file their stories. Television reporters retreated to various corners of the courtroom to do their stand-ups.

Vaughn and Justine hugged.

"He got what he deserved," Justine said.

"It won't bring Sara back," Vaughn said around the lump in her throat. She hadn't thought the moment would be so emotional.

"You fought for her, Vaughn. Somewhere up there, she knows that."

Vaughn nodded.

"She'd also want you to move on. You know that too."

Vaughn stiffened, but Justine held her close when she would have pulled away. It was true that she loved Sage, but she wasn't sure she was ready to let go of Sara's memory and what Sara had meant to her.

"You can't keep running away. Sage loves you. And don't tell me you don't feel the same way, Vaughn Elliott. I saw that look in your eyes."

She hadn't thought herself to be so transparent. "You don't know what you're talking about."

Justine released Vaughn and shoved her forward and to the left. "Go talk to her. You at least owe her that."

Sage stood some fifteen feet away. The misery in her eyes touched Vaughn's soul, and something inside her shifted.

"Hi," Vaughn said when she was close enough to be heard.

"Hi."

"It's over."

"Yes, it is." Sage wasn't looking at her.

"You look marvelous. Justine tells me your shoulder is completely healed."

"Yeah, the doc did a great job."

"I'll believe that when I get a demonstration."

Sage's head snapped up. Her eyes showed confusion.

"Can I have a hug?" Vaughn asked. She opened her arms and pulled Sage close when she stepped into the embrace.

Vaughn inhaled the fresh scent of Sage's hair and the sweet fragrance of her perfume. She closed her eyes and savored the moment. Sage fit so perfectly in her arms. Vaughn's resistance crumbled and she surrendered. *I love you, Sara. I always will. But it's time to get on with my life.*

"So," Vaughn said, pulling back just far enough to see Sage's face. "I hear you make a mean chicken cordon bleu."

THE END

Other Books in Print by Lynn Ames

Eyes on the Stars
ISBN: 978-1-936429-00-4

Jessie Keaton and Claudia Sherwood were as different as night and day. But when their nation needed experienced female pilots, their reactions were identical: heed the call. In early 1943, the two women joined the Women Airforce Service Pilots—WASP—and reported to Avenger Field in Sweetwater, Texas, where they promptly fell head-over-heels in love.

The life of a WASP was often perilous by definition. Being two women in love added another layer of complication entirely, leading to ostracism and worse. Like many others, Jessie and Claudia hid their relationship, going on dates with men to avert suspicion. The ruse worked well until one seemingly innocent afternoon ruined everything.

Two lives tragically altered. Two hearts ripped apart. And a second chance more than fifty years in the making.

From the airfields of World War II, to the East Room of the Obama White House, follow the lives of two extraordinary women whose love transcends time and place.

Outsiders
ISBN: 978-0-979-92545-0

What happens when you take five beloved, powerhouse authors, each with a unique voice and style, give them one word to work with, and put them between the sheets together, no holds barred?

Magic!!

Brisk Press presents Lynn Ames, Georgia Beers, JD Glass, Susan X. Meagher and Susan Smith, all together under the same cover with the aim to satisfy your every literary taste. This incredible combination offers something for everyone—a smorgasbord of fiction unlike anything you'll find anywhere else.

A Native American raised on the Reservation ventures outside the comfort and familiarity of her own world to help a lost soul embrace the gifts that set her apart. * A reluctantly wealthy woman uses all of her resources anonymously to help those who cannot help themselves. * Three individuals, three aspects of the self, combine to create balance and harmony at last for a popular trio of characters. * Two nomadic women from very different walks of life discover common ground—and a lot more—during a blackout in New York City. * A traditional, old school butch must confront her community and her own belief system when she falls for a much younger transman.

Five authors—five novellas. Outsiders—one remarkable book.

Heartsong
ISBN: 978-0-9840521-3-4
After three years spent mourning the death of her partner in a tragic climbing accident, Danica Warren has re-emerged in the public eye. With a best-selling memoir, a blockbuster movie about her heroic efforts to save three other climbers, and a successful career on the motivational speaking circuit, Danica has convinced herself that her life can be full without love.

When Chase Crosley walks into Danica's field of vision everything changes. Danica is suddenly faced with questions she's never pondered.

Is there really one love that transcends all concepts of space and time? One great love that joins two hearts so that they beat as one? One moment of recognition when twin flames join and burn together?

Will Danica and Chase be able to overcome the barriers standing between them and find forever? And can that love be sustained, even in the face of cruel circumstances and fate?

One ~ Love, (formerly *The Flip Side of Desire*)
ISBN: 978-0-9840521-2-7
Trystan Lightfoot allowed herself to love once in her life; the experience broke her heart and strengthened her resolve never to fall in love again. At forty, however, she still longs for the comfort of a woman's arms. She finds temporary solace in meaningless, albeit adventuresome encounters, burying her pain and her emotions deep inside where no one can reach. No one, that is, until she meets C.J. Winslow.

C.J. Winslow is the model-pretty-but-aging professional tennis star the Women's Tennis Federation is counting on to dispel the image that all great female tennis players are lesbians. And her lesbianism isn't the only secret she's hiding. A traumatic event from her childhood is taking its toll both on and off the court.

Together Trystan and C.J. must find a way beyond their pasts to discover lasting love.

The Kate and Jay Trilogy

The Price of Fame
ISBN: 978-0-9840521-4-1

When local television news anchor Katherine Kyle is thrust into the national spotlight, it sets in motion a chain of events that will change her life forever. Jamison "Jay" Parker is an intensely career-driven Time magazine reporter. The first time she saw Kate, she fell in love. The last time she saw her, Kate was rescuing her. That was five years ago , and she never expected to see her again. Then circumstances and an assignment bring them back together.

Kate and Jay's lives intertwine, leading them on a journey to love and happiness, until fate and fame threaten to tear them apart. What is the price of fame? For Kate, the cost just might be everything. For Jay, it could be the other half of her soul.

The Cost of Commitment
ISBN: 978-0-9840521-5-8

Kate and Jay want nothing more than to focus on their love. But as Kate settles into a new profession, she and Jay are caught in the middle of a deadly scheme and find themselves pawns in a larger game in which the stakes are nothing less than control of the country.

In her novel of corruption, greed, romance, and danger, Lynn Ames takes us on an unforgettable journey of harrowing conspiracy—and establishes herself as a mistress of suspense.

The Cost of Commitment—it could be everything...

The Value of Valor

ISBN: 978-0-9840521-6-5

Katherine Kyle is the press secretary to the president of the United States. Her lover, Jamison Parker, is a respected writer for Time magazine. Separated by unthinkable tragedy, the two must struggle to survive against impossible odds...

A powerful, shadowy organization wants to advance its own global agenda. To succeed, the president must be eliminated. Only one person knows the truth and can put a stop to the scheme.

It will take every ounce of courage and strength Kate possesses to stay alive long enough to expose the plot. Meanwhile, Jay must cheat death and race across continents to be by her lover's side...

This hair-raising thriller will grip you from the start and won't let you go until the ride is over.

The Value of Valor—it's priceless.

All Lynn Ames books are available through lynnames.com, from your favorite local bookstore, or through other online venues.

About the Author

An award-winning former broadcast journalist, former press secretary to the New York state senate minority leader, former public information officer for the nation's third largest prison system, and former editor of a national art magazine, Lynn Ames is a nationally recognized speaker and CEO of a public relations firm with a particular expertise in image, crisis communications planning, and crisis management.

Ms. Ames's other works include *The Price of Fame* (Book One in the Kate & Jay trilogy), *The Cost of Commitment* (Book Two in the Kate & Jay trilogy), *The Value of Valor* (winner of the 2007 Arizona Book Award and Book Three in the Kate & Jay trilogy), *One ~ Love* (formerly published as *The Flip Side of Desire*), *Heartsong*, *Eyes on the Stars*, and *Outsiders* (winner of a 2010 Golden Crown Literary award).

More about the author, including contact information, news about sequels and other original upcoming works, pictures of locations mentioned in this novel, links to resources related to issues raised in this book, author interviews, and purchasing assistance can be found at www.lynnames.com.

You can purchase other Phoenix Rising Press books online at www.phoenixrisingpress.com or at your local bookstore.

Published by
Phoenix Rising Press
Phoenix, AZ

Visit us on the Web: **www.phoenixrisingpress.com**

CPSIA information can be obtained at www.ICGtesting.com
Printed in the USA
LVOW12s1616120614

389807LV00016B/902/P